PIGGY

By Jill Keiderling

To Leslie, who supported me throughout this book as a friend, cheerleader, sounding board, and a tireless editor.

To Sean, for his support in my little project.

Chapter 1

It's a cloudy, somewhat misty day, and I'm cold as usual. I wish Dan didn't sell my coat. He'll sell anything that's not bolted down. He didn't even ask me. There was just a buck to be made and he took it.

Clutching my arms in an attempt to hold my body heat in, I scan the expansive dump that is my home. About the size of a baseball field, Dan's junkyard is a field of loose, uneven dirt with a smattering of junk on top. 'Treasures', he calls them. Situated between two small towns in the middle of Wisconsin, the property sits a half mile from the highway and a quarter mile from where the paved road begins. Near the highway on ramp, there's a gas station with a small grocery store attached. There are no other buildings for over five miles in either direction.

Dan's property borders several acres of undeveloped land which is covered with low brush. Sometimes, if we get enough rain, wildflowers will grow during the summer. I like to run through the field when that happens and breathe in the sweet scent that is rarely associated with where I live. A rusty wire fence separates the junkyard from the vacant property with a *For Sale* sign bolted on the gate where the gravel road ends. But no one has ever come by to even walk on the land.

"Piggy, you gonna sit there all day?"

I look up, expecting a blow to my head.

"Start organizing the merchandise. You never know when people will come."

I ease myself out of the ripped and broken brown upholstered chair, knowing that if I don't get up just right, I'll be stabbed by an errant coil. I walk to the pile of crap to my right. I start picking things up and placing them in slightly different piles to at least give the appearance of complying with Dan's order. I'm not really sure what the 'retail' strategy is to move junk.

It used to be every Friday and Monday; Dan would take the van and drive to one of the towns. He would retrieve stuff from the back alleys of neighborhoods, leaving me to stay and stand guard. Now, he

Piggy

only does his circuit on Mondays. Replacing his Friday trip, Dan has a truck come twice a week to buy its load, sight unseen. Normally, the truck dumps its stuff and Dan weeds through it, but today, Dan has assigned me the privilege of organizing the delivery. 'Retail management' he called it. Earlier, I had asked the truck driver to spread his load across 25 yards to make the sifting easier. I examine the long pile of debris and devise a plan.

I notice an anomaly to my far left, a relatively empty patch of ground. I drag the two bald tires to the area and lay them on their sides. Placing a steering wheel next to them, I decide this will be the automotive section. I walk back toward Dan to get the wagon before starting my forage for more auto parts.

"What are you doing, idiot?"

"I'm going to put stuff into groups. You know, so they'll sell better."

"Retail queen to the rescue," he snorts as he takes a long draw on his beer.

There are five empty beer cans next to his chair, but I don't dare pick them up. He stopped trusting me to bring back the recycling cash a long time ago. Now he walks beside me, as I carry the dripping cans to the grocery store, and pockets the cash.

Continuing my search, I find more auto related items and a few other things that may have been part of a car once and start loading. The ground is hardening up since the last rain was three weeks ago. It's early October so we have six to eight weeks before we have to pack up everything. Dan's sign on the highway does well enough to bring people, but no one comes once it snows. Besides, it's too hard to keep the stuff visible. The best thing to do is to sell as much as we can before it snows. After that, we pile the remaining junk in the middle, cover it with a tarp, and hope it's there when we come back in the spring. Dan hasn't said where we'll go this winter. Hopefully, it's someplace warm. Last year, we went to Texas, but the year before that, Dan drove us to Minnesota. He had gotten a temporary job removing snow from corporate office parks. The pay seemed pretty good at first, although Dan drank most of it away. He got fired six weeks into the job and then we bounced around Minnesota for two months. That was the coldest winter I'd ever spent.

"Aw!" I shout as the sharp edge of a hubcap rakes across my middle finger. Squeezing my finger, blood trickles out, but not enough to worry about. I suck on it and get the taste of blood mixed with dirt in my mouth. Going back to my task, I fill the wagon with another load and head back to the bald tires. After several more loads, I complete the automotive department. I look up at the sun. I can't see much of it through the thick grey clouds. I'm not cold anymore although I know that soon, I will be. I start my hunt again, this time for furniture. Walking to the long pile of junk, I've barely made a dent in today's delivery.

Warren strolls along the dirt path that cuts through the junkyard. Returning from the grocery store, he bends his knees a bit more than necessary with each step as if he's stifling himself from skipping. The twelve pack clutched to his side is hidden behind his thick arms. He's tall and lanky, but his arms are big and strain the fabric of his shirt. Warren's as black as tar, so black his eyes float on his face. At night, they seem to dance in the air around the fire. I usually get into the van early so I don't have to look at them. He wears a plaid flannel shirt under a bulky blue sweatshirt and dark blue jeans. His jeans hover above his ankles making his feet look even bigger than they are. I always laugh at how far out his feet stick out when he stands sideways. He says he's a size 16 shoe. Then he jokes, 'you know what they say, big feet, big…' and then he and Dan laugh.

I look down as he passes so that I don't make eye contact. He still whistles at me.

"Looking good, Piggy, looks like you're gonna organize this whole place."

Much as I try not to, a smile cracks on my face.

Warren laughs a little and then starts whistling a tune. I return to my task and over the next few hours, I finally make a noticeable dent in the pile.

For now, Dan and Warren's voices are laughing and happy, but later, the voices will turn angry and loud. It's the same cycle every day. Warren has been hanging around for a month and I can't decide if life is any better. He keeps Dan entertained; although I'm not sure the inevitable loud voices are a worthy trade.

Piggy

Returning the wagon, Dan looks up at me.

"What are you doing?"

"I'm hungry. Can I have some money for the store?"

"Shit. Take, take, take, that's all you do."

I stare at him until he reaches into his pocket and pulls out a five dollar bill. Reaching for it, he pulls it away from my grasp. "Please," I say.

"That's more like it," he says as he lets me have it. "And fill up the water bottles while you're there."

I lean inside the rusted out dark blue van and grab the two plastic bottles we use for water. Clutching them under my arm, I start walking to the store.

"You still gotta finish organizing all this stuff today!" Dan shouts.

I make my way through the junkyard, avoiding piles and the frequent divots that pepper the field. As I approach the gas station, there are no cars at the pumps. If I didn't know better, I'd say the place was deserted. Someone once told me, this used to be a Texaco, but now the faded sign says "Tex's Gas."

What had been white paint is peeling off the front of the small wooden structure. Inside, there are six rows of snack foods, a row of refrigerated cases mostly filled with beer along the back wall, and a register up front near the door. Behind the register are all the bottles of whiskey and vodka and of course, the cigarettes.

Passing the two gas pumps, I enter the door and see Kathy behind the counter smoking a cigarette. An older slender woman, she has a red tattered cardigan sweater on over her pale yellow T-shirt. Her right wrist is covered with a velcro cast, which makes lighting her cigarettes difficult. She says she hurt it using the cash register and is angling to get the owner to pay for her medical treatments. I think she just wants a cash payout because I've seen her take it off to do her hair.

I slap my five dollars on the counter. "Two hot dogs and a Coke please."

"Big spender. How'd you get that much out of him?"

"I think it was the beer. Plus I don't think he had any ones on him."

Nodding, she hands me a cup for the fountain and turns to get the dogs. As long as I pay for the soda, Kathy usually lets me have as many free refills as I want. First I fill the cup with ice, letting errant cubes brush against my hand. Hitting the Coke tap, I reach for a straw while the cup fills. My mouth waters but I know I have to stir it to ensure its icy cold; that's when it's the best. Sucking the cup dry, I refill and turn my attention to Kathy. She's placing mustard and relish packets on the counter next to my dogs. After assembling my feast, I inhale the first one and barely come up for air. Almost choking, I reach for my soda and take a long drink to wash down the bun.

"Jeez, I'm gonna puke just watching you eat that so fast. Slow down." Kathy shakes her head and looks out the window as she takes a long drag off her cigarette. I steal a look at her; I don't like to look at people when they're looking at me. Kathy's face is a dark tan, but it isn't natural. There's a distinct line where her tan switches to a stark white neck that also matches her arms and hands. Her cheeks have a swipe of peach across them, but it's her eyes that fascinate me. Four colors illuminate her eyelids -- white on top, then brown, then darker brown in the crease, offset by bright blue lids. A solid line of black eyeliner encircles her eyes and seamlessly extends into jet black eyelashes which are twice as thick as mine. Once she let me try her makeup, but only the lipstick which was bright pink. It stained my lips and wouldn't come off for over a day; no matter how much I rubbed at it. Dan had a good laugh at that; he called me 'Piggy the Clown.'

"Is this the first thing you've had today?"

Nodding, I start on my second dog. Slower this time, I actually chew. Kathy places my change on the counter, two dollar bills and some coins. I'm still hungry but decide it's best to save the money for a day when Dan isn't forthcoming with cash.

Wiping my mouth with the back of my hand, I grab the bills leaving the change for a moment. As I kick off my shoe and kneel

Piggy

down, I notice a sign, 'Snack Chip Special.' Pulling off my sock, I pull out a few bills and quickly fold my new ones into them. Stuffing the small wad in my pocket, I gather all the change in my sock and place it on the counter.

"Doesn't that hurt your feet? Walking around with change and stuff in your sock?"

"Sometimes. Do I have enough for another bill?"

"I ain't counting your smelly change."

I sort the coins on the counter. Sliding four quarters toward Kathy, I ask "How much for the snack chips?"

"Forty-five cents plus tax."

"Okay, give me a minute."

Walking back outside, I turn to the garbage can. I push the front slot open but it's too dark to see anything. Pulling off the lid, a rotten stench invades my nostrils. I taste the hot dogs in the back of my throat and swallow hard. The garbage can is jammed with partially eaten food, coffee cups, candy wrappers, and empty motor oil bottles. Grabbing a bottle, I use it to pick through the trash. After a few swipes, I find what I'm looking for – a full size empty bag of chips. It's splashed with coffee and something that looks like dried mustard, but it isn't ripped and you can clearly see the price tag in the corner -- exactly what I need. Liberating the bag from the trash can, I walk over to the faucet that's a few feet away. I bend down and wash the foil bag off. Peeking through the opening, it's cleaner on the inside than out. I shake it out and go back inside.

"What are you doing?"

"I wanted this bag," I say. Scanning the chip aisle, I snatch a snack size of my matching chips and place them on the counter. "I'll take these too."

Kathy picks up the change and gives me back a clean dollar bill and eight cents. I open the snack bag and empty the contents into the bag from the trash.

Piggy

"Shit, you really think that's going to fool him?"

"It's worth a try," I smile. "Hey, can I get a five?" I pull out the bills from my pocket and count out five one dollar bills and place them on the counter.

"What makes you think Dan isn't going to find your stash again?"

"I'm hiding it better now."

"How much do you have saved now?"

"Seventeen dollars."

"You want me to keep it for you?"

I think about it for a moment, and then shake my head. "No thanks, I feel better to have it with me."

"What are you up to today?"

"The truck came this morning, so I've been sorting through it all. Dan has given me the job of retail manager," I proudly say.

"Congratulations. You want a sucker to celebrate?"

She takes one of the penny suckers out of the plastic container in front of the register. The kind of sucker you get when you donate your spare change to some cause.

I shove it in my mouth.

"What's on your hand?"

I shrug. "Dried blood."

"Come around the counter and wash your hands. There are some Band-Aids underneath the sink."

"Can I fill up my water bottles too?"

"Sure."

I walk behind the counter to the small sink. The soap stings as I realize my cut is deeper than I had thought. Kathy walks up behind me.

"Yuck. What did you cut it on?"

"I dunno. Something metal." Under the cool water, my finger oozes out a little blood.

Opening the cabinet, she gets out the first aid kit and places it next to the sink. Turning, she walks back to the register and lights another cigarette. I wrangle out a Band-Aid, trying not to get blood on the kit.

Cleaned and bandaged, I refill my soda for the third time. This time, I take out all the ice to get maximum liquid. Next, I neatly fold the bills and place them inside my sock and pull it on. "I should be getting back," I say tying my shoe. Holding the two bottles against my stomach, I grab the chip bag and my soda.

As I exit the door, Kathy shouts, "Put that garbage lid back on!"

Setting down my stuff, I place the lid back on as a brown pickup pulls into the station. A portly man jumps out wearing a Chicago Cubs hat. I quickly grab my stuff and hurry my pace.

The first time I met Dan, he had a Chicago Cubs hat on. I was, maybe five. Mom had driven to a laundromat and told me to stay in the car. I watched Mom talk to some guy wearing a torn windbreaker over a plaid shirt. He had a scruffy short brown beard and looked like one of those homeless people Mom and I would pass in the car. Mom's back was to the window so I could only see him. He didn't talk much, just sat there, nodding from time to time. Mom shook her head and then gave him something from her purse. He stood up and started shouting at her. She quickly turned and ran out of the place.

"Who was he, Mommy?" I asked as she got into the car.

"He's my older brother," she started to say, but was interrupted by Dan knocking on the car window. Mom locked the doors and started the car.

"Open up!" he shouted as his knocking turned into banging.

Mom opened the window a crack.

"You gotta give me more than that!"

"I told you there wasn't much. Your share was four hundred; the other hundred is from me."

"Bullshit. She had more than that."

"The house wasn't paid for and dad's medical bills nearly wiped her out. I sold everything I could. That's it."

"You're holding out on me."

"Dan, please, not now. There's no more."

Dan looked across to the passenger seat and saw me. His light blue eyes pierced through me. His mouth softened and somewhat smiled showing off yellowy teeth.

"Is this her?"

"Yes," she replied. Turning to me, "Heather, this is your Uncle Dan. Say hello."

"She looks like you did when you were little."

"That's what kids are. Little mini yous." Mom reached over and took my hand as the tension subsided.

"Listen, I'm sorry, there isn't anymore. I wouldn't cheat you."

"Yeah, just money is real tight now. Can you spot me something?"

Piggy

"I gave you what I had. I'm on my own; money's tight for me too."

"Please."

"Are you even working now?"

"Ah, shit. You're just like Mom was! Yes, I'm working!" He said as his voice rose. "It's hard out there. I've got lots of business deals going on, but you gotta spend money to make money."

"Sorry, I don't want to argue. I was just asking."

"You, in your fancy car with your bank job. You've got money, but you won't help out your only brother."

"I have helped you out Dan. Several times. You could just say thank you for the extra hundred."

"Shit, a hundred won't get me through the week. I've got a few deals that could make thousands; hundreds of thousands. I could pay you back double."

"No, I'm done with your 'deals'. Maybe you should get a real job."

"Real job?! You mean like your job? That's for small minded idiots!"

Mom started to roll up the window, but Dan shoved his fingers through.

"Come on, help me out."

"Sorry, not again," Mom said pulling away.

"Bitch! You stuck up bitch!"

The car picked up more speed and Dan withdrew his hands and continued to shout at us. "Go on then, don't help me. When I make it big, don't you ever come and ask me for anything!"

We drove in silence a while. "I'm sorry about that Heather. I'm sorry you had to see that. Your uncle isn't a horrible person; he just needs to get his shit together." She quickly turned her head to me, "Sorry. I mean, he needs to clean himself up."

She turned back to the road and paused. "Don't say all the words mommy says."

Chapter 2

As I cut through the junkyard, Dan and Warren are sitting under their makeshift tent. It's a deep blue tarp that lies lengthwise on the van's roof with several rocks weighing it down. The tarp stretches out over two long sticks, essentially covering the area next to the van like a tent. I reach into the bag and take out a potato chip.

"You took long enough. You still gotta organize the delivery."

"I know, I'm gonna. I wasn't gone long," I say popping the chip in my mouth.

"Where's my change?"

"There isn't any."

"You used the whole five dollars? On what?"

"On lunch. You didn't say to bring you anything back."

"Guess that teaches you," Warren says as he stands up and walks to the hole in the ground they dug to pee in. Our bathroom situation is a bit rustic. I basically sit on a log at the edge of the property line during daylight. At night, when it's really dark, I'll squat next to the hole. Otherwise, I hold it and use the gas station bathroom.

"Gimme those chips. Shit, well your lunch was your dinner. I'm not made of money."

I hand him the bag and take a long drink out of my Coke, before handing that over as well.

"You didn't leave me any," he says looking in the bag. "You really are a pig, Piggy," Dan chuckles. "Go on, finish up."

"Rain's coming in," Warren says looking up at the dark grey sky.

I lean down to take the wagon's handle and feel a drop on my hand. I look at Dan but he sees it too.

Piggy

"Don't just stand there, get the tarps!"

Summoned into action, we frantically dash around the yard covering piles of stuff with tarps. If we don't have rocks to weigh down the edges of the tarp, we use the junk itself. The rain is coming down pretty hard when we're done as we jog back to the van tent for shelter. My green flannel shirt and jeans are no match for the cold. My teeth are chattering as I feel my money slide in my soaking wet sock. I grab a blanket and cover up.

"Shit!" Dan has opened another beer as he surveys the land for any unprotected merchandise. "No one will come after work now."

"Nope," Warren says.

"Why does this always happen on delivery day?" Dan says pacing around the small tented area. His gaze lands on me.

"Gimme the money!"

"I told you there wasn't any change."

"Bullshit, you're always holding out; squirreling away the pennies. Give it to me!" Dan grabs my shoulders and shakes me back and forth.

"There isn't any. I got the hot dog special, the chips, and some penny candy." He stops shaking me to grab at my pockets. I reach into my right pocket and pull out a few pennies. He slaps my hand hard and the coins fly.

"That's all that was left; I told you." Shoving me to the ground, Dan raises his hand.

"Hey, we still got a little money," Warren intervenes. "We can get some hot dogs tonight and still have enough for a twelve pack tomorrow."

Dan turns and looks at him. "People will come and buy something tomorrow. I can feel it," Warren continues. Dan takes a step toward his chair, grabs his beer, and drains it. He sits back down and reaches for another. Warren motions me to get into the van and I comply.

Piggy

Dan and Warren stare at the yard and watch the rain for the next two hours. At some point, even they get cold and start a fire before dusk. When the rain stops, it's too dark for any more organizing; and besides, I want to lay low and let Dan's anger pass. Eventually, Dan gets up and motions to Warren. They start walking to the store without as much as a backward glance to me. I know they're going to get food but I don't dare tag along as Dan's anger will surely erupt again.

Darkness settles in and I move out to the fire to stay warm. When I hear the murmur of voices, I jump back in the van. Remembering my money is still in my sock; I quickly kick off my shoe and retrieve the bills. After losing my stash to Dan before, I don't want to take any chances. Reaching my hand down the front of my pants, I put the bills into my underwear. He's never come close to touching me there. I roll to my side and fake sleep as a light shines on me. It's Dan. Soon they are whistling and laughing with the occasional clink of a bottle in the background. I guess they couldn't wait for the twelve pack. They get louder before they get quieter. Eventually I fall asleep, curled up on my side with my hand between my knees.

The next morning, I awaken to voices. Dan's talking to someone outside but it doesn't sound like Warren. I peek out the window but the glass is dirty and the tarp tent is in my way. I ease myself out of the van, careful to not make much noise opening the door. There's a tow truck parked on the gravel road and a stocky guy wearing a knit cap is talking to Dan near my automotive section. I make my way to my log and relieve myself. I look around to ensure no one is watching and then I shift my stash back to my sock, before heading back. Grabbing my tattered toothbrush, I find one of the water bottles half full and rinse out my mouth and brush my teeth without any paste. I get rid of most of the morning goo that engulfs my teeth.

The tow truck driver is taking a tire with him. As I see him pull out, Dan is waving goodbye to him. Warren comes up from behind Dan and nudges him, when the truck pulls onto the paved road.

"Whoo hooo!" Dan screams. Warren slaps Dan on the back.

"How much you'd get?"

"Eighty bucks for that old tire and hubcap."

"You're kidding? Looked worthless to me."

"It was, but he said it matched his car. I told him I got the tire yesterday."

"You want me to go get some beer?"

"Nah, not yet. I want to get a real breakfast."

"Denny's?"

"Now you're talking," Dan says giving Warren the thumbs up with his fist. "Piggy, we're going out, get your stuff out."

"Can I come?"

"No, I need you to stay here and watch the stuff. Plus someone may come and buy something else."

"Nobody comes in the morning."

"Well, now, someone just did, didn't they?"

"Please, I'm starving and I need to wash up." I give him my best pleading look.

"Everything's still covered in tarps. It'll probably be okay," Warren says.

Dan looks around the junkyard, then back at me. "Fine, but you're coming back and putting all the tarps away and finishing going through the delivery when we get back."

He takes a step toward me and points his finger. "I don't want to see you taking any breaks or asking for lunch, neither."

"I won't. I promise. Can I go?"

"Help us take down the tent."

Piggy

I climb onto the rusted out bumper and balance myself as I hand rocks to Warren. Dan is putting the sticks into the van along with anything else of value. I'm not sure why he bothers; no one comes by this early. The tow truck was a fluke. The main selling times are Friday afternoon through Sunday, with only an occasional mid-week evening visitor. Jumping off the bumper, I dust off my jeans and hear the door shut. The van rolls away.

"Hey!" Running as fast as I can, I catch up to the side and hit it once with my fist before tripping on something and going down.

The van stops and I raise my head to see Warren's face, laughing, in the side mirror. I get up and run to the side door and get in. Dan's laughing with Warren.

"Works every time," Dan says.

So that we can sleep in the van and provide maximum space for Dan's junk runs, there are no seats in the back; only a pile of blankets stretched out to soften the metal corrugated floor. I sit with my back to the cold side wall and look at Warren's profile. His nose is flat and wide and his full lips stick out from his face. He's never been mean to me, but he also hasn't necessarily been kind. Usually at night around the fire, he stares at me but never says a word. This morning is no different; we sit in silence for the fifteen minute drive up the highway. Denny's is crowded when we arrive; we've hit the morning rush. We're seated in a center booth and are immediately poured coffee.

"Three Grand Slams with sausage and white toast," Dan says.

"You want them cooked hard or runny?" the waitress asks.

"Runny, for me," Warren replies.

"Me too, please," I say.

"Two runny, and one hard," Dan responds.

"Can we get extra jam and butter packets?" I ask. Denny's is a once a month trip so I know to stock up.

The waitress nods and leaves. "I'm going to the bathroom," I say.

Grabbing some napkins, I head to the door that says 'Women'. Once in the tiled room, I turn on the hot water full blast and roll up my sleeves. I wash my arms as high as I can get and my face too; taking extra rinses because I like the feel of the warm water. After drying off, I take the napkins, wet them, and unbutton my shirt. I face the corner of the room so no one can see and wipe off my stomach, neck, and armpits. I feel better already.

Wetting the second napkin, I take it into the stall with me. After peeing, I wipe all that I can. Once a week, Dan and I go to a church that has showers. He's not religious or anything, but he talks a good game when there's hot water to be had. Between visits, I feel dirty, especially today since it rained yesterday.

I return to the table as the waitress has come with our food. You would think we were animals. We don't talk. We don't look at each other or look up for that matter. Heck, we don't even allow our faces to venture more than a few inches away from our plates. I eat as fast as I can, but Dan is still faster. He successfully grabs one of my sausages. Before I can protest, he's chewing. Wiping up the yolks with my toast, the plate is nearly completely white. If you didn't look close, you'd think it was clean. Dan lights up a cigarette and leans back.

"That hit the spot," Warren comments.

"Yeah, they do eggs good here," Dan says as the waitress returns to fill our cups.

"Boy, you guys were hungry. I just put those down," she says. "Want anything else?"

"The extra jam and butter packets, please," I say. "And more cream too."

She reaches into her pocket and pulls out a handful of jam packets and lays them on the table. Laying the check down next to Dan, he immediately looks away. We finish our second cup by the time she returns with the extra creamers and butter. As she refills us one more time, Dan pulls out a twenty and lays it down. I savor my last

Piggy

cup of coffee because I'm warm for the first time today. When the waitress returns, Dan picks up all the change and gets up. Warren and I dutifully follow him out.

"Thank ya, Dan, thank you kindly," Warren says as we exit the place. "I'm gonna have a fine nap when we get back."

Warren whistles a tune as we drive back. Exiting the highway, Dan stops at the gas station to get beer before driving the last half mile back to the junkyard. My hands are on the metal floor on either side of me to keep me from falling over when we hit the gravel road and then the yard itself. Coming to a stop, I'm the first to jump out. I start to unfold the tent tarp when Dan walks up to me.

"We'll do that. You start with the other tarps."

I do as he says. Walking from one pile to another and removing the tarps, folding them, and placing them in a neat stack. Returning to the van, Dan and Warren have re-assembled the makeshift tent and are laid out in their chairs under it. Dan is snoring loudly, but Warren is in a peaceful quiet slumber. I stow the tarps and then pick up the wagon and carry it to the delivery pile so that I don't wake them up.

I had finished the automotive and furniture section yesterday; all the big items. Plus, I took several loads of real junk -- the stuff that never sells -- over to the back of the yard near the fence. I scan through the delivery pile and select my next category of junk -- housewares. There's a rusty electric can opener with a broken cord and a bag of pots and pans. I place them both in the wagon and continue my search. I see a taped up box of dinner plates, but as I pick it up, the bottom of the box opens and out comes a waffle maker. Reaching down to retrieve it, my gaze falls on a doll half buried in the dirt. She's white with blonde hair, blue eyes, and a smudged face. Her dress is now a dark brown, but I can still see the red polka dots. I pick it up and hear a familiar cooing sound. Tears stream down my face. The dress is different, but the face and noise are the same. I scrub the dirt off, spitting when necessary.

I can see the Christmas tree full of ornaments and the kind of tinsel that looks like icicles. There's an angel on top but I can only see it when Mom holds me up. I feel warm and remember how Mom would turn the heat up at night so that it was cozy. I'm in my pink flannel pajamas with the feet attached, holding Betty. Betty, the blonde, blue eyed doll Mom gave me, was the prettiest thing I'd ever had. She protected me at night. She knew all my secrets, not that I had many back then. I try hard to remember, almost like I'm straining my mind, but I can't picture Mom. I haven't been able to for years.

    I hug new Betty against my face and inhale deeply. The familiar strawberry scent is gone. Closing my eyes, I remember the first day when Dan came to live with me.

Chapter 3

I was the last to be picked up from day care. Mrs. Simpson was complaining about the lack of respect parents had for her time. I watched as she sat at her desk near the front door and shuffled papers while occasionally looking up at Ms. Walters to make her point. She was wearing a bright pink and blue printed dress with a beige cardigan that could barely close due to her enormous, pointy breasts. Throughout the day, she would constantly pull on one side of her cardigan, then the other, in a futile attempt to make the two sides meet. She was a big lady with wide hips and fat ankles, but a pleasant round face. Her reading glasses were resting on her chest, hanging from the chain she kept them on.

"Maybe we could charge a fine when they're late," Ms. Walters offered.

"I can't afford to lose anyone now," she retorted before transferring her attention to some papers. Ms. Walters shook her head and walked back to the group of tables and continued putting art supplies away.

I sat by the window in my coat waiting for Mom. What had been a sunny playful room with multi-colored bookcases and toys strewn throughout the floor was now dark. All the toys were back on their shelves and only the front room light was on, illuminating the art area and Mrs. Simpson's desk. I could feel the cold air coming through the window. I was glad I had gotten my blue plaid pea coat from the coat rack area.

The dark sky was pierced by flashing red and blue lights, as a car pulled up and two men got out. They entered the building and immediately encountered Mrs. Simpson. Ms. Walters walked over and the four of them talked for a while before Mrs. Simpson gasped and put her hand on her mouth. Suddenly, they turned to me. Ms. Walters had tears in her eyes as she quickly retreated to the bathroom.

Mrs. Simpson slowly walked in my direction as I stood up to face her. She put her hand on my shoulder when she reached me. Then she pulled out a second chair next to mine. "Sit down, dear," she said as she eased herself into the other chair. The child-size chair should have been outmatched by her wide hips, but she seemed to manage. The two men had crossed the room and were now standing in front of us.

Piggy

"Hello Heather, I'm Lieutenant Peters."

I looked up. He had a brown and white bushy mustache and clear blue eyes. His chest was broad but he was slim. He knelt down in front of me and patted my shoulder. The other guy, Dan, stood uncomfortably by him. I recognized him immediately when he got out of the car. While I stared at him, he never looked at me.

I could smell the coffee on Lieutenant Peters' breath as he spoke. He talked for a long time, but I only half listened. Instead, I stared at Dan's shoes. They were caked with mud on the bottom which matched the worn brown leather on top. Dan kept shifting his weight from one leg to the other in what I assumed was an attempt to get comfortable. His right shoe didn't have any laces and his left one had a hole in the big toe; I could see his blue sock peeking through. I wondered if he knew his shoe had a hole in it. Was his toe cold? Why didn't he get a new pair of shoes?

"Do you understand what I've told you, Heather," Lieutenant Peters said.

"Can I see her?"

"No, honey, that's not a good idea," Mrs. Simpson interrupted. "She's in a better place now. She's with the Lord," she whispered.

Mom wasn't coming to get me. She would never come again. Lieutenant Peters said she went to Heaven and that I'd see her again someday. I didn't really understand, but they seemed certain of it. Finally Dan faced me and spoke.

"You're gonna live with me now, baby girl."

Lieutenant Peters shot a look at Dan and then got up.

"Would you like that, Heather?" he asked. "This is your Uncle Dan, do you remember him?"

Dan reached down and took my hand and held it. It was the first time he touched me.

"We're gonna be fine. She remembers me. I'm her favorite uncle," Dan declared as he smiled at Mrs. Simpson.

Piggy

Fifteen minutes later, Lieutenant Peters pulled into our driveway. Leaving the headlights on, he and Dan got out. Dan opened my door. "Come on, Heather honey. We're home."

What does he mean, 'we'? I thought. I ran to the front door and tried the handle. Locked. I rang the doorbell repeatedly as Dan and Lieutenant Peters approached from behind. Lieutenant Peters handed Dan Mom's keys. I recognized them because of the yellow butterfly keychain. Jingling the keys, Dan nudged me aside to unlock the door. Once inside, I ran to every room in the house, looking, but finding nothing. I returned to the living room where Dan and Lieutenant Peters were talking.

Our one-story house had five rooms with the front door opening directly into the living room. Light beige Berber carpet showcased a royal blue overstuffed couch and chair that sat in the center of the room across from a large window overlooking the front lawn. The far wall, opposite the picture window, had floor to ceiling bookshelves filled with books, photos, and Mom's butterfly collection. Since she was a little girl, Mom liked butterflies. She thought they were the most beautiful creatures with their colorful intricately patterned wings. She had had ten different colored ceramic butterflies before she added Grandma's two to her collection. They were proudly displayed on the bookcase's center shelf, low enough so I could reach them. A rocking chair sat off to the side next to the remaining wall partially covered by a large TV and VCR player. Above the TV were a few framed pictures of flowers that Mom had hung a few months ago.

To the left of the front door, was a double wide entrance into a modest sized kitchen. The floors were a checkerboard black and white with white cabinets and pale yellow walls. At the back of the kitchen, there was a closet that hid the washer and dryer and a small table where Mom and I ate. Walking through the living room past the archway to the hall, there were two bedrooms with a bathroom sandwiched in between. Mom's was the first room to the left and mine was to the right at the end of the hall. With the exception of the kitchen and my bedroom, all the walls in the house were white. Mom had painted my room a pastel pink a few years ago.

I paused at the living room entrance after my failed search mission. Remembering Betty, I rushed back to my room and retrieved her from my bed. I held her tight and took a deep breath. She smelled like strawberries. I returned to the living room to see Lieutenant Peters' hand on the door knob. Seeing me, he walked to me and bent down.

"Goodbye, Heather. I'm real sorry about your mom." He gave me a little hug and stood up. "If you ever need anything, your uncle has my card."

I nodded. Then remembering the manners Mom taught me, I said, "Thank you."

The door shut and the sound of his police car pulling out of the driveway filled the air before the vacuum of silence set in. I looked at Dan for a while as his eyes scanned the living room. Finally I asked, "Where are we going now?"

"What do you mean?"

"You said I was going to live with you now."

"I'm gonna live here with you. I don't want to disrupt your routine. Besides, your mom has a real nice place here."

Dan turned his attention to the kitchen and opened the refrigerator. I stood there in the living room, not certain what to do.

"Does your mom have any beer?"

The refrigerator door closed and I heard cupboards being opened and closed.

"Hey, kid, any alcohol in this place?"

"I don't know," I stammered, "What does it look like?"

Shaking his head, Dan grunted. "Shit, Sis was always a goody two shoes," he murmured.

"I'm hungry," I said walking to the kitchen.

"What do you normally eat?"

I stared at him blankly for a long time.

"Hey, I can't read your mind and I ain't waiting on you hand and foot. If you're hungry, find something to eat," he said before beginning his tour through the house.

Entering the kitchen, I pulled at the refrigerator door, but the door often sticks making it difficult for me to open. For some reason, today, I didn't have the strength to pry it open. I opened the pantry closet where Mom stored extra food and saw a box of Cheerios on the top shelf. At first, I tried to pull myself up on the lower shelves but there wasn't anything for me to grab a hold. Then I dragged a chair from the kitchen table but it didn't fit through the door so I positioned it in the doorway and climbed up. Standing, I could barely touch the shelf when I leaned in. Swiping at the box a few times, I succeeded in pushing it back farther.

"What are you doing, kid?" Dan bellowed behind me.

"I can't reach it," I whined.

"You're gonna hurt yourself doing stuff like this." He picked me up and pulled me over the back of the chair and set me down. Sliding the chair out of the way, he grabbed the box of Cheerios and took it down. Then his gaze fell on something. He whistled.

"Now that's what I'm talking about," he said gleefully.

Behind the cereal, way in the back of the shelf was a brown bottle with a red bow on it.

"Can I have the Cheerios?" I choked out.

"Huh? Oh, yeah, here take 'em and go to your room," he said without looking at me. "And quit crying, I hate it when people cry," he barked as I walked away.

Retreating to my room, I shut the door and leaned against it. I surveyed the pink festival that was my bedroom. Pastel pink walls surrounded me with only a thick ivory crown molding around the top of the wall to break the color. I had lobbied for a pink ceiling but Mom refused. Across the door was my one window framed in bright pink curtains with white lace trim. My closet with its sliding doors painted a deeper pink than my walls was to my left. Shoved in the corner was my twin sized bed covered with a pink bedspread with little flecks of tan and blue. Across from the bed was a white corner desk with a mirror on one of the facing walls and next to that was a white bookshelf with the edges of the shelves painted the same deep pink that matched the closet door. The bookshelf was filled with over thirty stuffed animals; my favorite was the elephant. Ellie, I called her. Although Larry the Lion was softer.

Clutching Betty close to me, I crawled onto to the bed and stared at the wall. It didn't seem real that Mom was gone. I tried to recall what we had done this morning but I couldn't remember what Mom was even wearing today. I couldn't remember if I had told her I loved her when she dropped me off at school. Tears welled up in my eyes, as I laid back on the pillows and cried into Betty's dress.

I must have dozed because I was jarred by the phone ringing. It rang several times, before stopping. The growling in my stomach became my next concern. I sat up and pried open the box of cereal. The faint sound of the TV came through my door, but I didn't want to go out and see Dan. I wanted to stay in my room with Betty until Mom came back.

The next morning, I woke up in the same dress. Rolling off the side of the bed, I grabbed Betty and the box of Cheerios and entered the hallway. There was light coming through the windows, yet no sound. Mom was always up before sunrise so I was unaccustomed to the silence. I walked to the kitchen passing the living room on the way. Reaching the doorway, the kitchen was empty. Loud breathing sounds erupted behind me. Startled, I spun around to find nothing there. I walked a few steps to the back of the couch and peered over. There was Dan, stretched out on the couch. The brown bottle still had the red bow on it but now, it was on its side on the floor. A full ashtray and a pack of cigarettes were on the table. I must have squeezed Betty because she made a cooing sound which resulted in Dan jerking awake.

"Hey, don't wake me up," he said.

I watched him; yawning and scratching his eyes and head. He finally looked at me. "Did you just get up?"

I nodded.

Piggy

"You slept for a long time. I checked in on you but you were sound asleep," he said, remaining on the couch and breathing heavily.

"Let's hope your mom has some coffee," he said sitting up and immediately reached for a pack of cigarettes. Pulling a lighter from his pocket, he sucked in a long drag. At first, he looked peaceful as he exhaled, but then he started coughing and hacking. Wiping his hands on his jeans, he got up. I followed him into the kitchen still holding Betty and the Cheerios. He searched the counters and spun around.

"Where's the coffee pot?"

"Mom drinks tea," I said.

"Figures." Looking down, he saw the Cheerios. "You want some breakfast?"

I nodded.

He took the box and put it on the kitchen table then jerked the refrigerator door open to get the milk. He eventually found a bowl and a spoon and motioned for me to sit down. I climbed onto the chair and started eating the bowl he had poured for me.

"You doing alright Heather?" he asked.

I continued to chew not looking up. A knock at the door interrupted us.

"Your mom expecting anyone?" he asked.

I shrugged and continued to devour my breakfast.

Chapter 4

The front door opened and female voices invaded the house. A parade of three women carrying trays, foil wrapped pans, and a few grocery bags marched into the kitchen. Freezing in their stride, their eyes fell on me. Ms. Parks, my friend Susan's mom, was there, along with Mrs. Jones from next door. Ms. Parks had on her tan and red uniform with dark nylons and white tennis shoes. Her blonde hair was pulled back into a ponytail so that you could see her dangling earrings gently bouncing against her neck. Below her right knee was a small snag that had been lacquered with nail polish to stop the rip from getting bigger. One time when I was playing dolls at Susan's house, I watched her paint nail polish on her leg. She told me that's what you do when you have a run.

Ms. Parks walked to me and set down a tray. "You doing okay?" she asked.

Sitting down, she stretched her hands out to me and I noticed one of her long red nails was broken. A whiff of jasmine mixed with Aqua Net filled my nostrils as I focused on the name tag proudly displayed on her lapel; 'Barbara' it read.

Susan was in my first grade class and we rode to school together. Sometimes Ms. Parks would take us; other times, Mom would. In the afternoons, we went to different places, but sometimes we were allowed to play together after dinner. On the weekends, we were inseparable. Ms. Parks lived across the street, two houses down. Her house was smaller than ours and not as nice. They didn't have a VCR player and their carpeting was covered with stains.

I looked up at her; not really sure what to say. Last year, when Grandma had died, Mom explained to me that she wasn't going to be around anymore. That when you got old, you went to Heaven. She said that Grandma would be looking down on me and that I shouldn't worry about her. Lieutenant Peters said some of the same things about Mom yesterday. I knew it meant I wouldn't see her again, but I didn't understand why Mom didn't tell me that herself.

Rubbing my shoulder, Ms. Parks sat there with me in silence, as I finished my cereal.

"Is Susan here?" I asked.

"Oh, I took her to school this morning. Maybe the two of you can play later."

"Do I have to go to school?"

"Not today. Not for the rest of the week. Don't worry, your teacher will understand."

She cupped my hands in hers and we sat quietly for a few moments. I examined her broken nail and followed the jagged edge that showed a hint of white under the red polish. Looking up at her, tears streaming down my face, I asked, "Why did she leave without saying goodbye?"

"Oh, honey. I miss her too. I don't know why. I don't know why it happened. It's just the way it is."

I pulled my hands back and took Betty into my arms and rocked with her back and forth.

"You want to color?" Ms. Parks opened up her bag and pulled out a few books and a torn half full box of crayons. Leaving me at the table, she went to the refrigerator and filled it with all the trays that the women had brought. I turned my head to look for Mrs. Jones and spotted her in the living room with Dan. She was facing me, sitting next to the third lady; both were facing Dan who was seated on the couch.

Mrs. Jones was a heavy set older woman who lived next door. She wore the same thing every day -- a bright yellow button-up-the-front skirt, a turquoise blue crew neck sweater, a purple cardigan that always had tissues stuffed up the sleeves, knee-high athletic socks with red stripes at the top, and red rubber-soled tennis shoes. The only thing she changed every day was the color of her lipstick. Today, it was hot pink. Mom would always laugh when she saw her. She called her the little old *rainbow* lady.

Mrs. Jones slaved over her garden and flowers. She would be outside at all hours of the day and night. Once when we got home late, Mrs. Jones was outside lying on her stomach near her flower bed with a flashlight on her head and a magnifying glass in her hand. She said she was hunting snails and that they only came out at night. Other times, we would hear her mowing her grass at 11 P.M. or see her trimming her flowers with pinking shears because she didn't like to cut the stalks in a straight line.

When they were both outside, they would talk and discuss each other's flowers or lawns. Actually, Mrs. Jones talked and Mom listened. Mrs. Jones would give Mom all sorts of advice on what to do to make her flowers better. As much as they talked, I don't remember Mrs. Jones ever coming into the house, not like Ms. Parks. Mom had Ms. Parks and Susan over for dinner once a week. Mom said she was helping Ms. Parks out, given she was so young and was having a hard time.

"How can we help you with the arrangements?" the third lady asked.

"Arrangements?" Dan replied.

"The funeral."

"Huh?"

"We never knew her to be religious," she said while motioning to Mrs. Jones. "Do you know if she was a member of any church?" Suddenly I recognized her. She lived in the neighborhood and several times a year she would come around selling stuff. Wrapping paper, Tupperware, Avon cosmetics, you name it this woman tried to sell it. At first, Mom invited her in for tea. After that, Mom would be polite, but never step away from the door crack.

"Ah, no we weren't religious. We never went to church as kids."

"Yes, but do you know if she had any preference?"

"Nah, she was like me."

"There's a funeral home a few miles from here and I think they'll do the service right there. A non-denominational service."

"I don't know. Jane was like me. She wouldn't want any service."

"Sometimes the service isn't for the person as much as for her loved ones."

"It's just me and Heather and we don't need a service."

"I'm sure there are friends from her work who would want to pay respects. And certainly, a child needs to have closure."

"I don't want to do any type of service," Dan snapped.

"Heather should be given the chance to say goodbye."

"She's fine, she doesn't need to."

"She's young; this is a turning point in her life. It will be a day she'll always remember."

"Yeah, I don't think we need it."

"This could really damage her," the lady said as her voice cracked. She looked down and took a deep breath. "Listen, I lost my mother when I was young, not as young as Heather, but that moment, those few days… I relive those all the time."

"I said no."

"Okay, honey. Why don't we do this," Mrs. Jones interrupted as she picked up the empty bottle with the red bow on it and set it upright on the coffee table in front of Dan. "Let's have a wake here and invite everyone over and that will be all. A few hours and we'll do it all."

Dan reached for his cigarettes.

"Come on, Danny boy, it'll be swell. You'll get to meet her friends, Heather will have an event, and you'll get a good meal out of it."

"I don't know, sounds like a lot of trouble."

"I promise you, we'll take care of it all."

Dan looked out the window and took a long drag.

"Why I'll bet you even get some donations to help you out, given the situation," Mrs. Jones added. The old rainbow lady, who seemed more concerned with her flowers than anything else, suddenly had a focused look in her eye; as if she wasn't as crazy as Mom thought.

Dan immediately turned, "Well, okay then, if you can arrange it all."

"How does Saturday from noon to three sound?" Mrs. Jones said.

"That's tomorrow?"

"No, that's the day after tomorrow, Dan," Mrs. Jones said with a little smile.

"I put everything away," Ms. Parks said entering the living room.

"I think our work here is done," Mrs. Jones said. "Ladies, let's go next door to discuss the details," she said as she got up.

"Are we leaving now?" Ms. Parks said as she turned to me.

"Yeah, you ladies need to get going now," Dan said seeing his opportunity to get rid of them.

"Heather, I'm so sorry this happened, but it's going to be okay. You know, you can come over to my house anytime you want. You're always welcome. I want you to know that," Ms. Parks said. Giving me a big hug, she whispered in my ear, "Anytime you want, you call me."

"Thanks for stopping by," Dan said as he opened the door wide.

Mrs. Jones walked up to me and put her hand on the top of my head. "Heather, it may not seem like it, but everything is going to be fine. This could actually be a good thing for you."

The Avon lady shot her a look of shock.

Piggy

"Ahh, I know it's not a good thing that's happened, but everything happens for a reason. That's what I meant. Maybe it isn't clear right now, maybe it won't be clear any time soon, but trust me, there's a reason and you'll get through this," Mrs. Jones said confidently patting me on the head.

The Avon lady's expression didn't change with this postscript. Kneeling down to give me a little hug, she said, "I'm very sorry for your loss Heather. I'll pray for you and your mom. I know she's looking down on you right now."

"Thanks," I acknowledged.

"I remember when my Harold died; I thought it was the worst thing ever. But I got stronger from that. It took a few years, but," Mrs. Jones stopped mid-sentence distracted by Ms. Parks who had put her hand on Mrs. Jones' arm.

"I'll see you soon, Heather. And you and Susan can play."

As they exited through the open door, Mrs. Jones looked straight into Dan's eyes. "Make sure you're up by 10 A.M., we're going to have to come over early to clean this place up."

Before Dan could muster a protest, Mrs. Jones was several steps into our driveway.

As quickly as they marched into the house, they were gone. Shutting the door, Dan sighed, "Jesus H Christ! They sure had sticks up their butts."

"Can I watch TV?"

"Sure, but keep the volume low, I've got a headache."

I walked around him into the living room. Grabbing a pillow from the rocking chair, I sat down in front of the TV and immediately turned to my favorite channel.

"I'm gonna take a nap in back. You okay?" he asked.

I nodded and continued my trance-like stare at the TV.

Before I knew it, it was dark outside again. I had fallen asleep on the floor. I laid there for a few moments, looking at the street lights through the front window. Dan banged something in the kitchen and I decided to investigate. He looked up as I entered.

"How does chicken noodle casserole sound?"

"Okay."

He opened the stove and shoved a foil covered pan in.

"I need to run an errand, you gonna be alright here by yourself?"

Without pausing for an answer, he brushed by me on his way out the front door. "Watch some TV, I'll be back in a no time," he repeated.

The garage door began to open, but before I could make it to the window to spy on him, the door slammed shut.

"Shit!" Dan yelled loud enough that I could clearly hear him through the door.

Entering the house, Dan snarled, "Where's your mom's car?"

I pulled Betty to the middle of my chest and squeezed.

"She's got keys here, where's the car?" Suddenly, his face dropped and his anger disappeared. "Right, she was driving," he murmured.

"Ah, sorry, Heather," he said picking up the phone. Hitting the buttons multiple times, he placed the handset down. Bending down, he plugged the cord back into the wall and picked up the handset again. Turning his back to me, he talked into the phone.

"Jay, hey, its Dan. Wanna party?"

"Yeah, I'm out in the 'burbs with no ride."

"My sister's place."

"No, no, it's cool, pick up a case of beer and a bottle on your way over."

Hanging up, he turned around quickly and nearly stepped into me. "Kid, you are like my shadow."

"Can I have something to drink?"

"I told you I'm not waiting on you hand and foot. Get it yourself."

"The fridge door sticks and I can't always get it open."

"Oh, yeah," he turned to look at the fridge, "that door does seem to stick."

Picking up the phone, he dialed again.

"Hey Jay, can you pick up some Coke too?"

"Thanks."

"No not rum & cokes. Just regular Coke."

"For the kid."

He hung up and went to the refrigerator and opened the door. Examining the top of the door, he spun around and opened drawers. Finding a screwdriver, he unscrewed something at the top of the door and removed a small metal part. Shutting the door, he reopened it and then looked at me, "I fixed it, just make sure you close it real good because I took off the magnetic clip from the top."

Bending his head into the open door, he took out the carton of milk and got a *glass* glass from the cupboard. He poured some milk and handed it to me. After a long drink, I leaned my head back only to be surprised at the glass slipping out of my hand and shattering on the floor.

"Shit! You said you wanted a drink and now you've made a mess!"

"I.. I... I didn't mean to," I stuttered.

"Go to your room!"

As I turned to leave, Dan slapped my backside and I erupted into a fresh new kind of tears.

Back in the solitude of my room, I looked for Betty. I must have left her in the living room. Not wanting to go back and see Dan, I retrieved Ellie and Larry, my stuffed elephant and lion off my bookshelf and jumped onto my bed. Lying down on my side, I curled my body up and squeezed Ellie tightly under my arm.

A loud engine thundered in the distance, the sound getting closer and closer. I jumped off the bed and looked out my window, straining to see the sliver of road that was visible from my window. Nothing. I quietly opened my door and peered out. I heard the front door open and the engine sound exploded. I walked to the end of the hallway and peeked around the corner. Dan was outside as the sound revved repeatedly in our driveway. I took a few steps into the living room to get a better look. The sound shut off nearly as fast as I heard it and the aroma of gas engulfed me. Walking to the door, I could make out Dan's voice, but I couldn't see anything because it was too dark. As I reached the door jam and leaned my head out, Dan came into view. I hopped back and out of the way of the door, as a tall man with jet black hair followed Dan inside, carrying a shopping bag.

"Hey, Jay, this is my niece, Heather."

Jay entered the doorway and the light hit him. His straight black hair was long but pulled back into a ponytail. He had a beard, but only around his mouth. Dressed in all black, there was only a red stripe on his leather jacket sleeve to break up the monotone outfit.

"Hello, little girl," he said.

I stared at him as he passed. About a foot taller than Dan, he was much stockier with a broad chest and arms. Dan was loading stuff into the fridge as the crack of a bottle cap rung out.

Piggy

"Thank you, sir, thank you very much," Dan said as he entered the doorframe between the kitchen and living room and handed a beer to Jay. Taking a long drink, he swallowed and then burped. "You have no idea how much I needed this."

"Don't we all," Jay said taking a long drink.

"I thought you were in your room," Dan said as he twisted his head and looked directly at me.

Stepping back, "I forgot Betty." I turned and reclaimed her from the living room floor.

"Okay then, go on."

"What about dinner?"

"Right," Dan said.

"Did you cook for me, dear?" Jay cooed. "Did ya, honeybunch?"

Dan laughed. "Why, yes I did, sweetie pie," he said while shaking his hips as they both busted out laughing.

"No, man, these neighbor bitches came over and filled the fridge."

"Cool. Hey, sorry about your sister."

"Yeah, we weren't close."

"So what are you gonna do? You gonna play house?"

"Let's talk about it later. After dinner," Dan answered as his head nodded in my direction.

I entered the kitchen and smelled chicken and cheese. Checking the floor, Dan had cleaned up the milk.

"How do you know when it's done?" Dan asked.

"Shit if I know."

Dan opened the oven and a puff of steam came out. He then reached into the oven only to pull back his hand quickly and curse.

"I don't know how to cook either, but a stove is hot, man," Jay snorted.

Jay looked around and grabbed a towel. Covering his hand with the towel he pulled out the rack. Peeling back the corner of the foil, more steam emerged. "I think it's done."

Plates and forks were found, along with a big spoon. It didn't look good on the plate, but once it cooled, it sure tasted good. Both Jay and Dan had second and third helpings, in addition to second, third, and fourth beers.

Slapping his top pocket, Jay glanced around. "Gotta a smoke?"

Dan pulled out a pack and lit them both up. "What normally happens, Heather? Do you clean up the kitchen?" Dan asked.

"Sometimes I help Mom dry. There's a stepstool that I use."

"What about the dishwasher?"

"We don't have one."

"Shit," Dan said as he turned around and scanned the kitchen.

Dan got up and walked to the fridge. Fetching two more beers, "Where's the stepstool?"

"Mom keeps it under the sink."

Finding it, he positioned it up in front of the sink. "Why don't you wash up?"

Placing Betty on my chair, I walked to the sink. Dan cleared the table and deposited the dirty dishes and casserole pan on the counter. I washed the plates like I've seen Mom do, although I'm not sure how clean I actually got them.

"You did good, Heather. That's gonna be your chore from now on."

"I didn't get everything off."

"Pans are hard; next time scrub harder. You'll get it. Now off to bed."

I retrieved Betty and headed off to bed, alone. Mom always followed me, told me to wash up, brush my teeth, and put on my pink footie pajamas. It had only been a day, but I was certain Dan wouldn't be doing this for me. I got ready as best I could without supervision when a loud crack followed by laughter surprised me. I quietly opened my door and went down the hall. Sitting at the edge of the hallway entrance, I could hear them in the living room.

"So you gonna play house with a kid now?"

"I kind of have to, at least until I know where all the money falls out. I'm sure as hell not the person to raise a kid, but I'm all she's got."

"What about your parents?"

"Both dead. My mom died last year. She was sixty-two. Bitch held out and left me nothing."

"Did you expect her to?"

"Okay, okay, I'm a fuck-up. Who would have thought I'd be the one to survive? But she's still my mom; she should have left me more than five hundred bucks."

"That was all?"

"My dad passed away two years ago; he was sick for a long time. My sister said his medical bills had drained them, but I always thought there was more." Dan paused. "At the time, I thought Jane was holding out on me, but I guess in the end, I won it all."

"What about the kid's father?"

"Dead. Jane never married him, so it wasn't like he was in the picture anyway. I'm not sure he even knew about Heather. Heck, I only met Heather a few months after my mom died."

There is a long silence.

"You know what?" Dan said. "Heather's parents both died in car wrecks. What are the chances of that?"

"Shit, this kid's been totally fucked."

"Yep."

"So, how much did your sister have?" Jay asked.

"I don't know yet, I gotta call her bank. But I know she owns this place, because I found a mortgage bill."

"You gotta to pay the mortgage?"

"I called the 800 number and they told me if I mailed them a copy of the death certificate, they'd give me a sixty day reprieve since she died."

I tried to muffle my sob but Dan heard me.

"Heather, you better be in bed with the lights out!"

I rushed down the hall as the living room floor board creaked. Jumping onto the bed, on top the bedspread, I assumed the fake sleep position that I would sometimes use with Mom. Squeezing my eyelids shut, the door opened. I tried to control my breathing for what seemed like an eternity. Finally Dan spoke.

"You're fa fa fa… fa—king," he sang.

I didn't move.

"You know how I know you're faking?"

I held firm.

"You didn't turn the lights off."

I opened my eyes and looked at him.

"Get into bed, under the covers, and go to sleep." I crawled to the top of the bed and slid between the sheets.

"You ain't gonna con me. I've done it all. Next time do what I say. Now go to sleep."

The door slammed.

Chapter 5

I woke to silence. The morning sun streamed through my window creating dancing shadows as the rays peeked through the lace trimmed curtains. I stuck my head into the hallway. Nothing. Not a sound. With Betty in tow, I tiptoed the few feet to the bathroom and quickly shut the door behind me. I brushed my teeth, washed my face, and combed my hair, just like Mom would usually tell me to do each morning. Exiting the bathroom, I stumbled on my pajama feet. They were too long for me and sometimes my feet slipped out of the foot part and into the leg part. I pulled them up and continued my quiet walk to the living room.

A loud snore pierced the silence from the living room and I retreated back to the bathroom door. Dan was in there. Last night, I had tried to stay awake and listen to Dan and Jay from my bedroom, but I didn't get very far; their voices were too low and I could only make out the occasional word. I began my walk again toward the living room clutching Betty tight to my side.

Dan was on the couch again and Jay was sprawled out on the floor by the TV. Dan was the one snoring; stretched out across the length of the blue couch. The back cushions were scattered on the floor with Jay was using one as a pillow. His leather jacket was draped over his chest for warmth.

Littered with beer bottles, a bottle of whiskey, empty cigarette packs, and two full ashtrays, the coffee table was the fullest I'd ever seen. There were a few bags of chips discarded on the floor and it smelled like the outside of the soup kitchen that Mom occasionally volunteered at and had taken me to before.

Entering the kitchen, I grabbed a banana lying on the counter which Ms. Parks and Mrs. Jones had brought yesterday. I surveyed the kitchen, overwhelmed by the emptiness without Mom. Straining to think of times I've been alone like this, I felt tears coming. It was so quiet, I could hear the clock ticking. I returned to my room, walking quietly so as not to wake them.

Gently shutting my door, my attention turned to my stuffed animals. Hugging and kissing each one as I took them down and greeted them. I lined them up and got Betty into her zookeeper position. Betty had trained the animals to do tricks; Larry the Lion can jump through a hoop of fire -- really a small hula hoop, but when I place

Piggy

it upright between some books it looks real. Ellie the Elephant takes the smaller animals on rides. Today she has Willie the Woodpecker and Seymour the Seal on her back.

Eventually, noise emanated from the living room. I leaned against the door and listened. The front door opened and the roar of an engine filled my senses and the neighborhood. After several revs, the sound faded down the street. Dan was hacking as I entered the living room.

"Can I watch TV?"

He nodded. "Keep it down."

Stepping over chip bags and strewn pillows, I assumed my regular position. Soon I'm lost in cartoons. Dan was in the kitchen when the phone rang. He answered on the third ring.

"Yeah."

"This is him."

"Huh?"

"Yeah, yeah, thanks. Who is this again?"

"Oh, I was meaning to call you."

"Yes, I'm Jane's brother, her only surviving family."

"Um, hmm. Yes, well since she's worked at that bank for a while, I just assumed her bank accounts were there."

"They are, great, how much we talking?"

"Can you get that info?"

"Yes, I've already called the 800 number and taken care of that. Is that also your bank?"

"Given her years of service maybe that deferment could be extended."

"Sure, see what you can do."

"About the accounts, can I get some cash now?"

"I don't understand; I'm her brother."

"Yeah, she's here. I'm watching her."

"Guardianship? What does that mean?"

"I'll certainly look into that. But I'm a bit strapped for cash now."

"Certainly, you can make an exception."

"He will? Oh, right tomorrow, I'm having Jane's friends over to celebrate her life."

"Yes, she was a great woman. We were pretty close."

"She didn't? These last few years, we sort of lost touch, but we're still blood."

"You sure I can't get any sort of advance? I don't want the kid to starve."

"Hmm, I'll talk to him, if you say, he can help get all the paperwork done."

"Yes, yes, it's just that I know she must have been a great worker and your friend, right? I thought something could be worked out."

"Fine, I'll see you tomorrow, goodbye."

"What? Her car?"

"I thought she was driving."

"Oh."

"Yes, I would like that. Can I come by later today?"

"Fantastic, is it in the lot?"

"You know, I'm not sure what she's been driving these days."

"I've got the keys."

"From her purse, the police gave it to me that night."

"There wasn't much money in her wallet; I think the cop snagged it."

"Of course, he's not going to say anything, but she only had forty dollars on her. I'm sure that was just a plant."

"You'd be surprised what people will do."

"No, no point in reporting this stuff, you ain't ever gonna win."

"Um, hmm."

"You don't need to be the one; anyone can point it out to me."

"Oh sure, it will be great meeting you in person to," Dan said rolling his eyes.

"Who? Oh, Heather's here, she's fine."

"I'll see you later today, thank you."

He hung up and whistled. Dan went back into Mom's room. Mom kept a small desk and file cabinet in her room. He emerged with several files and sat down at the kitchen table. For the next hour or so, Dan was immersed in the files. Every once in a while, he put aside a piece of paper.

"I'm hungry," I said as I entered the kitchen.

"Hmm?" he asked. "Okay, what do you want?"

"PB & J."

"What?"

"Peanut butter and jelly."

"Hell, kid, you gotta learn to talk in full words."

Dan made two sandwiches and we sat at the table to eat as Dan opened his first beer of the day.

There was a knock at the door and Dan got up. It was Ms. Parks and Susan. I ran to the door.

"Hi, Heather. I told you I'd be coming by," Ms. Parks said.

Turning to face Dan, "I hope you don't mind, Susan's been asking about Heather."

"Ah, no. That's fine. You want to take her and let them play?"

Ms. Parks' initial surprised expression softened immediately. "Sure. Heather, you doing okay? You want to come over and play with Susan?"

Susan and I were already planted in front of the TV with Betty in between us.

"Yes!" we screamed in unison.

"When do you want her back?"

"Whenever. What's the uniform for?"

"I wait tables at The Red Diner on Sloop Avenue."

"You working tonight?"

"No, I just finished the breakfast and lunch shift."

"Why don't you come over for dinner? I've got a fridge full of food." Dan said smiling wide.

"No thanks. I've got a lot to do tonight," she replied.

"Hey, a guy's gotta ask."

"I'll have her back by five-thirty."

Dan started back inside as we walked down the path.

"Hey, Barbara, is it? Can you do me a favor?" he yelled.

She turned and waited.

"Take me to Jane's car," Dan said as he approached.

"Her car? I thought she was driving."

"She was, just not her car. I guess someone got sick and she was driving them home in their car."

"So two people died?"

"Ah, I don't know. I didn't ask about the other one," Dan said realizing how cold that sounded. "I guess I've been focused on my big sis and how great she was," he quickly added.

"Right," she said. "Like you told Mrs. Davis, you two were real close. By the way, it's Kelly."

Dan looked down at her nametag.

"I don't like the customers at the diner knowing my real name."

"Good thinking."

"My car's right here, you got the keys?"

"Gimme a second," he smiled as he darted back into the house. A few minutes later, he was locking up the front door and whistling. He strolled up to Kelly's red beat up Ford Escort and opened the door. Susan and I were already in back. Kelly pulled away as soon as he shut the door.

"Nice car."

"Bull, it's a junker."

"What does Jane have?"

"A green sedan, I think it's a Ford. It's at the bank, right?"

"Yeah, somewhere in the parking lot."

We passed through the neighborhood in silence for a while before Kelly turned into the parking lot of the bank.

"This is it? I thought it was further."

"This is it."

Dan got out of the car and didn't give so much as a glance in my direction.

"Do you need me to wait?"

"Could you? I'll wave to you from the window if everything's okay."

"Sure."

"Is there a convenience store around here?"

"Up the street and to the left."

"Thanks, I'll wave," he said as he walked to the bank.

"Don't you want to say goodbye to Heather?" she called out to him.

He froze mid step and turned around. Walking back to the car, he had a big smile on his face. Leaning into the window, "I'll see you later, Heather. Tonight, we'll make another one of those casseroles and spend some quality time together."

I stared back at him confused by his change in tone. Kelly shook her head and looked the other direction.

"Say goodbye."

I tilted my head.

"Come on, say goodbye to your Uncle Dan," he said as sweetly as he could muster.

"Goodbye Uncle Dan," I dutifully replied.

We sat in the car with the motor running for a few minutes before Kelly saw Dan wave at her. Susan and I were playing our own form of patty cake in the backseat. We had a routine of slapping our hands together; first one who screwed up lost.

Back at Susan's, we played cards and had some snacks. I beat Susan, like I usually did probably because she's a few months younger than me. I'll be seven in June.

"Susan, why don't you get your dolls out to play?" Kelly asked.

Susan skipped to her room.

"Heather, how are you?" I looked up at her. "How's Dan?"

I shook my head.

"Did you eat last night?"

"We had a chicken casserole. It was good. Jay and Dan had seconds."

"Jay?"

"Dan called his friend to come over. Didn't you hear him?" I turned looking up at her. "He was dressed in all black leather with a black helmet, and he had a really loud motorcycle."

"How long was he there?"

"He left this morning."

Susan came back into the room and laid down her dolls one by one.

"If you ever feel uncomfortable, or scared, or anything, I want you to call me. Or just come over," she said. I picked up a doll with the pink and white dress on. Kelly gripped my arm and looked straight into my eyes. "I mean it, anytime you want come over. And I want you to tell me if he does anything?" I nodded.

Five-thirty came quickly and Susan and Kelly walked me back to my house. Music was blasting so Kelly banged hard on the door. The music stopped and Kelly banged again. Dan opened the door with a cigarette in one hand and a bottle of beer in the other.

"Hey, you made it back. Sure you don't want to come in and stay for dinner?"

"No, we're good. Heather, you gonna be okay?"

"Yep, thanks for the snacks, Ms. Parks," I said as I passed by Dan.

"You're welcome Heather, anytime." Turning to return home, Kelly looked back at Dan, "I'll see you tomorrow."

"Huh?"

"The wake. It's tomorrow. Mrs. Jones said to be up at 10 A.M."

Chapter 6

The banging on the door went on for over five minutes until Dan finally opened the door. Mrs. Jones stood alone on the front step in a new outfit. She had on a plain black skirt, black nylons, and black tennis shoes. On top was her usual turquoise sweater, but now with a silvery scarf around her neck and a black cardigan. She looked almost normal, except maybe for her orange lipstick. I sat watching from the kitchen while eating a bowl of Cheerios.

"Good morning, glad to see you're up," she said as she strolled in.

"Shit, you said ten, it's nine-thirty."

"I lied." Putting a large green bucket on the kitchen counter, she turned to survey her task. "This place is a pigsty. Don't you ever pick up?"

"I ain't good at housekeeping."

"That's apparent." Mrs. Jones looked at me, "Heather, good morning. Having breakfast I see." I nodded. "Let me know if you need anything."

She opened the cabinet under the sink and got out a large trash bag. Shaking the plastic to open, she began a flurry of activity buzzing around the kitchen and living room sweeping all kinds of things into the bag. It was filled with bottles in minutes. Placing the full bag on the outside front step, she turned her attention to the couch and picked up pillows and fluffed. Dan returned from a long trip to the bathroom arranged to avoid her, no doubt.

"Why don't you shower and shave?" She half asked and half told Dan. "It is your sister's wake after all. You could at least be presentable."

Dan grunted but did a one eighty straight back into the bathroom.

"Heather, I'll help you wash up when he's done. Do you want to go pick out a dress you want to wear?"

Piggy

I nodded, relieved for some order at last.

Passing the bathroom on the way to my room, I heard the shower running. Dan had complied, apparently afraid of Mrs. Jones' wrath.

I perused my closet for a dress. Out of my three fanciest dresses, I selected the one that Mom liked best. It had a full pink skirt with little yellow and white bows all over it. The top was ivory with some pink and yellow trim around the short sleeves and scalloped collar. There was a darker pink bow that tied in back. I laid it on my bed and searched for some white socks and matching barrettes. Reviewing my selection, I put the barrettes back and replaced them with a headband that had a pink bow on the side. Next I pulled out my black shiny shoes, the ones with the silver buckle. Satisfied, I returned to the living room. Kelly was there now vacuuming the living room.

"Make sure you get under the cushions, God knows what he's been doing out here," Mrs. Jones said from the kitchen.

Kelly nodded, "Hi, Heather. Good morning."

Mrs. Jones emerged from the kitchen. "You pick an outfit out?" she asked. I nodded. "Why don't you color while your Uncle Dan finishes in the bathroom?"

I didn't color; I didn't even open the book. Instead I sat at the table and watched.

Mrs. Jones was scrubbing the kitchen sink and counters avoiding a pile of drying dishes to her right. Once completed, she wiped down the cabinets and refrigerator door and then reviewed her work.

"Floor's next. Heather, can you go sit on the couch?"

She moved each of the four chairs into the living room and filled up the green bucket with soap and water.

"Did you bring a mop?"

"Ahh, no, I didn't," Kelly said.

"Let me run next door."

Opening the door, Mrs. Davis was there with trays in her hands.

"I still gotta do the floors, can you wait? Just put those down on the coffee table," Mrs. Jones said over her shoulder, as she headed to her house. "Or the counter!" she yelled in afterthought.

"Not as bad as I thought," Mrs. Davis commented.

"I've been here for half an hour and Ethel's been here for an hour," Kelly said. "I've already taken one huge trash bag to the curb."

"Good thing we got here early. Where is he?"

"In the shower." As Kelly answered, Dan walked by the archway.

"Hey, Kelly," he said raising his eyebrows as he paused in the doorway.

He was clean shaven with a bare chest and a towel haphazardly wrapped low on his waist. Our eyes immediately focused on the green and red snake tattoo that came down from his shoulder and curved around his chest. Its tongue was sticking out over his sternum. There was another smaller tattoo on his arm; some sort of sword or dagger.

Ignoring Dan, Kelly turned and coiled the vacuum cleaner cord.

"Good to see you, Dan. It's Jan. Jan Davis from the other day."

"Hey," he acknowledged Mrs. Davis as he walked back into Mom's room.

Once gone, Mrs. Davis looked at Kelly. "What was that?"

"I don't know."

"Unbelievable. People will never cease to amaze me," she replied as she went into the kitchen and laid the trays on the counter. "I've got more trays in my car," she said as she left for the driveway.

Mrs. Jones came back inside holding a mop. "Where is he?" she asked.

"Just got out of the shower."

"Heather, you want to get ready now?" Mrs. Jones asked. "Kelly?"

"Sure thing. Heather let's go," Kelly said.

Mrs. Jones mopped the kitchen floor, leaving Mrs. Davis to finish the living room. Kelly helped me strip out of my pajamas and ran the water for a bath. She squirted extra bubble bath in so that when I got in I could hide beneath the suds. Once clean, she combed my brown hair and tried to style it while it was damp. Placing some strategic clips into my bangs and a few sponge rollers at the ends, we returned to my room to get dressed.

"How are you feeling?"

"Okay."

"Is your Uncle Dan treating you alright?"

"He doesn't say much. He sleeps late and smokes a lot."

"Did you have dinner last night?"

"Another casserole but I didn't like it."

"Why not?"

"Too many peas."

Kelly laughed.

"Is Mom ever going to come back?"

Piggy

Kelly's smile dropped from her face. "No honey, I'm afraid she's not."

I was not sure from where but I started to cry. I had kept my crying to myself when I was alone in my room, but now it suddenly seemed more real. Mom wasn't coming back. I'm not really sure what that means for me, but I'm scared of what it could be. Life with Dan was an unknown. He ignores me, yells at me, but he also lets me watch all the TV I want. Kelly put her arms around me and squeezed. My tears subsided as we heard sharp voices in the living room. Kelly pulled my dress over my head and helped me step into my shoes.

Entering the hallway we heard Mrs. Jones say, "You're going to wear jeans?"

"Hey, this is all I've got lady. I ain't rich like you," Dan replied raising his voice.

"Calm down, don't get all testy, Danny boy. I've probably got a jacket from my late husband that will work."

"I don't need nothing; this is fine," Dan said as we entered the living room behind him.

Both Mrs. Jones and Mrs. Davis stopped. "You look so pretty, Heather."

Dan gave me a quick glance, but his eyes were focused on Kelly.

"I'll go get the jacket," Mrs. Jones announced.

"I said I don't need it."

"It'll make you look more respectable." Dan raised his hand in response. "People donate to respectable people," Mrs. Jones said as she walked out.

Kelly looked at Mrs. Davis who motioned with her eyes to the small table along the wall. A large Tupperware bowl sat prominently in the middle with a handwritten sign that read: *Donations. Please help out.*

The house filled up with neighbors and co-workers. I had met some of them before, but mostly I didn't know them. They all came up to me, patted me on my shoulder, and said they were sorry. Dan mainly stayed in the kitchen, next to the supply of cold beer. Mrs. Jones' husband's black blazer was big for him and the blue tie didn't match but it did hide Dan's loud plaid shirt. His jeans were a dark denim that made his thickly creased light brown boots stand out as if there was a spotlight on them. All in all, when the jacket was buttoned, Dan almost looked presentable. After eating as much as I could, I sat at the corner of the kitchen table behind a line of four banquet trays, and colored.

An impeccably polished man in a dark blue suit came into the kitchen. He was over six feet tall with light brown hair and a thin mustache. He confidently strode over to Dan.

"Dan? I'm Steve Forrester, Jane's boss over at Lancaster State Bank. We spoke on the phone the other day."

Dan looked up and took his outstretched hand.

"I'm very sorry for your loss. Jane was one of our best employees. We're going to miss her dearly."

"Yeah, thanks," Dan said as if participating in small talk was the most painful thing in the world.

"Our attorney, John, isn't here yet."

"Yes I am," a portly man said entering the kitchen. He was in a black suit with a bright red tie. The suit coat hung from his upper chest as if on a curtain rod; attempting to conceal the enormous girth that inhabited his waistline. He was bald, at least on top, with short cropped hair circling his head like a pair of earmuffs. His second chin wiggled as he waddled across the floor and there was a bead of sweat already coming down the side of his face.

"Dan, this is John Robertson, the bank's attorney. Jane was using him for her will and a while back when she established her trust. It's a perk we provide our employees," Steve said, smiling.

"Trust? She had a will?"

"Yes. Certainly in this day and age, you can't be unprepared. Especially not a single mother with a small child."

"What does that mean?" Dan asked. "I mean, I'm her brother, I'm all she had left."

"Dan, I reviewed the trust yesterday in case you had questions," John responded taking out a notepad from his jacket pocket. "Jane was in the midst of updating her will. Her mother had died," he said as he looked up. "Sorry, your mother had died. I am truly sorry for your losses."

"Got it. What about the trust?"

John paused, a bit surprised, and shot a look to Steve.

"These days, I recommend to all my clients who are parents, and especially the ones with minor children, to set up a trust. So the children, in this case Heather, are taken care of."

"Are you saying I'm not getting the money?" Dan retorted.

"Well... not directly. Assuming you become the guardian, that money would become available to you to raise Heather and take care of her. There are some limitations...," John said.

"How much?"

"I'm sorry? What do you mean?" John asked again shooting a look at Steve.

"How much is this trust thing?" Dan snapped as he set his beer down, next to the heaping ashtray and his cigarette pack.

"The trust is structured in a way to pay out over time, with a tiered approach..."

"How much?"

"Ahh," pausing as his eyes shifted to Steve. Regaining his authority, "With her life insurance proceeds, it's close to three hundred thousand on an upfront basis, with some reserves for later," John said.

"When can I get it?"

"As I said, it goes to Heather's guardian and is intended to provide for her."

Dan looked at him and waved his hand in a circular motion. "Go on," he finally said.

"Jane was in the middle of updating her will. She was struggling with who to select as guardian for Heather. Her original will, the one in place now, named her, well your, mother."

Dan stared at John.

"Given you're the only living relative, that falls to you. Therefore, you'd have to apply to become her guardian which should be a formality. There'd be some paperwork to sign, and I'd want to go through the details with you, but essentially that's it. It would be yours to manage on Heather's behalf." John said that last part slowly and pointedly.

"How do I apply?"

"Come down to the bank Monday, I can meet you there, and walk you through the paperwork. We have to file papers with the State and then the State has to formally grant you guardianship," John stated taking a step closer to Dan. "I'm aware Heather's father has passed. What about her grandparents?"

"What do you mean?"

"What about her paternal grandparents?"

"My dad is dead."

"Heather's father's parents."

Piggy

Dan's face dropped. Looking from side to side, he quickly said, "They're dead too."

"They are?"

"Yeah, I remember Jane telling me. They were old, died of some disease."

John looked perplexed.

"Dan, I think what John is saying is that you're a young single guy," Steve interjected. "Are you sure you're up to raising a little girl?"

As if a light switch was flipped, Dan immediately relaxed. "Me, ready? Why of course," he said. "Heather? Why don't you come over here?" Dan said motioning for me.

John and Steve quickly spun around. I got up from behind the banquet trays and slowly walked over.

"Dan, I'm sorry. I, we, didn't realize," Steve stammered.

"Yes, my apologies, this is better left for a private discussion," John reiterated gently patting his hand on Dan's upper arm.

"Listen guys, I get it. You're checking me out. Sorry if I was a bit direct back there, I've had some hard times recently, as I mentioned to Steve. There's nothing more I want to do then raise Heather. Why she's my only niece and my only reminder of my sister," Dan said as smooth as silk.

"Dan, we're not checking you out. If the State accepts you as guardian." Dan's eyes shot like lasers through John. "And there's no reason why they wouldn't," John continued resting his hand on Dan's upper arm. "Then you'll be entitled to access the trust."

"Great. And Steve, thanks for calling about the car. It's been a big help," Dan smiled. "Monday morning at the bank?" he looked at John.

"Yes, Monday morning."

"See you then. If you'll excuse me, I'm going to step outside for a smoke." Dan grabbed his cigarettes off the counter and reached into the refrigerator for another beer. Walking out of the kitchen, he froze. Regaining composure, he slowly turned around and looked at me. "Heather, you want to come outside with me?"

I looked back at him, not sure who this person was.

"Would you rather stay in here and color?" I nodded. "Okay then, Heather, honey, I'll be right outside."

Steve and John said the same thing everyone else had been saying to me all day. They were sorry for my loss and to let them know if I needed anything. I wandered through the living room, avoiding eye contact and the same speech and pat on the shoulder or head I'd had all day. Entering the hallway, I found some solitude in the corner across from Mom's room.

"He's a drunk. How is he going to raise her?"

"Did you see that tattoo? He looks like a convict."

"Is he?"

"I have no idea. Do you think he could be?"

"You knew Jane the best."

"She never talked about him! One time! One time, she told me she even *had* a brother. She said he was a deadbeat. But that's all I got." Kelly's voice rang out.

"We should look into that." I finally recognized Mrs. Jones' voice, but there was a third voice I didn't know.

"And then what?" Kelly asked.

"I passed by the kitchen and heard Jane's boss say something about guardian."

"Well, isn't he her only family?"

Piggy

"Best I can tell."

"Isn't family considered automatic guardians?" Kelly said.

"Not necessarily. I've heard of cases where a lawyer or family friend can be a guardian," Mrs. Jones stated.

"What are you suggesting, Ethel? Do you have someone in mind?" The third voice said.

"No..," Mrs. Jones said slowly.

"Hey, I'm barely making it with Susan. I've got an ex breathing down my neck as is."

"Don't look at me. I'm a happy grandma. I hand 'em back when they cry," the third voice said.

"I'm too old," Mrs. Jones muttered. "Look ladies, I don't think there's anything we can do to stop it. Not without any proof. Besides, maybe he'll rise to the challenge."

There was a murmur of agreement with Kelly exiting the bedroom. As hard as I pushed my back into the wall, I couldn't escape into the shadow.

"Heather, honey, what are you doing out here?"

Mrs. Jones and the Avon lady, Mrs. Davis, stuck their heads out.

"It's boring out there," I said.

"I think it will wrap up soon. Several people have already left," Mrs. Davis said. "In fact, I should probably get out there and host."

"You get enough to eat, Heather?" Kelly asked.

"Yeah, the yellow cookies were really good."

"They were lemon bars. Where's Dan?"

"Outside smoking."

"Excuse me for a minute."

Mrs. Jones bent down and looked me straight in the eye. Her silvery scarf flowed into my face; it was cold, as if it was made of plastic instead of fabric. She threw it over her shoulder like a cape. "Sweetie," Mrs. Jones said, "how's Dan treating you?"

"Okay, I guess. He lets me watch TV."

"Is he feeding you? Taking care of you?"

"Yes, but mostly he sleeps or smokes."

"Or drinks," Mrs. Jones said under her breath.

"He does that too."

"Anytime you want to talk, or need anything, you come on over to my house or to Kelly's, I mean Ms. Parks."

I nodded.

The guests were funneling out. A cool breeze blew through the door that was standing wide open. Several people lingered on the front lawn. Mrs. Jones was in the kitchen washing pots and pans; the smell of soap filling the room. I walked over to the TV and crouched down. Turning the volume down, I flipped through the channels.

"Yeah, Monday, that's good," Dan said as he walked directly to the side table with the donation bowl on it.

"As long as you don't think it's too soon," Kelly said following him in.

Dan was rifling through the bills that were left; putting them into one pile in his hand. "Huh? Oh, no, the kid's gotta go to school. Besides I got stuff to do on Monday."

"What about after school?"

Piggy

"What about it?"

"Jane had Heather in a daycare near the school. In fact, I think the school owns it because they would transport the kids there every day. Jane would pick Heather up each day after work."

Dan had a blank look on his face as he folded the stack of bills and slid them into his pocket.

"Not so fast, Danny boy," Mrs. Jones interrupted as her hand clamped down on his. "Where do you think all this came from?"

"What?"

"This food didn't come from nowhere, nor did the little housecleaning we did today."

"What do you mean? You ladies cooked it all."

"A lot of it, but some of it was purchased by me," Mrs. Jones said yanking a few bills out of his hand.

"Wait a minute, I didn't ask you to clean!"

"I'm not asking you to pay me for that, just pay me back for the food I bought," Mrs. Jones said as she moved her face close to Dan's. "Its forty bucks, you got a bundle there for doing nothing," she said as she backed off.

"Dammit!"

"Get a job!" she said as she returned to the kitchen.

"I'm between 'em at the moment!"

Speechless, Dan's gaze fell on Kelly, "Can you believe her?"

"Yeah, she's real inconsiderate," Kelly said pausing. "We did a lot, Dan. Anyway, I have no idea how much Jane is paid up at daycare, but if Heather goes there, you're going to have to pick her up each day."

"Can't you do it?"

"I don't use that place, so no, I can't. Susan goes to a small daycare a few blocks away."

"Can she go there?"

"You want to take her out of the daycare she knows?"

Dan's expression changed again like when he was in the kitchen. Smiling, he said, "Actually, from what you told me Susan is Heather's best friend. I wouldn't want her to be without her best friend all afternoon."

"I can ask tomorrow, but you'll have to pay."

The wheels turned in Dan's head. "Can't they bill me, given my circumstances?"

"Your circumstance is that you may have paid-in-full daycare that Heather knows and loves, and you want to uproot her because you're too lazy to pick her up."

"Don't get all testy. You're kind of cute when you get riled up," he said as he took a step forward.

Kelly immediately took a step back.

"Please, pretty please," Dan said with emphasis, "Check into that other daycare and let me know. Meanwhile, I'll pick her up from the other place."

About an hour after all the guests were gone, Mrs. Davis and Kelly walked out with various trays and pans. Exiting the kitchen, Mrs. Jones looked at Dan pointedly, and stretched out her hand to him.

He looked at her for a long time and then responded by shaking her hand, "No hard feelings."

Piggy

She pulled he hand back as fast as she could. "I want the coat and tie back, jackass!"

"Oh," Dan said undoing the tie. "Should have known you weren't being civil."

"Takes one to know one, Danny boy."

Tossing the blazer into her hands, "Good riddance, old biddy." Then he chuckled, "Hey, I rhymed."

"Keep telling yourself that," Mrs. Jones said as she turned and left.

Dan shut the door and punched the air and I returned to watching TV. Ten minutes later, Dan opened the front door. "I gotta go out to the store," he said without a glance back.

"Can I go with you?"

"Nah, it won't be any fun for you. I got a couple of places to stop at."

"Please."

"No, you stay here and be good. I'll be back in an hour or so."

Four hours later Dan returned, drunk and carrying more 'supplies'.

I intended to stay out of his way, but he set up shop in the living room and commandeered the remote. I had already made myself a sandwich with the leftovers from the wake. I sat in the corner, Betty by my side, watching Dan flip the channels. Running back to my room, I brought back a small puzzle and sat down on the floor. Quietly, I put down the piece of cardboard Mom kept near the bookshelf that I could use. I carefully opened the box and ran my hands through the pieces.

"You know, you got a pretty good thing here, Heather."

I looked up at him.

"I'm all you got left. Your mom is gone. Gone."

Something about hearing it out loud, hit me like a ton of bricks. A tear ran down my cheek.

"Don't start crying again," he said raising his voice. "And don't think I haven't been able to hear you at night, neither."

I had been able to put up a good front during the day, but at night, I missed Mom the most. Reviewing the events of the day, or lack of events, I would cry knowing Mom would never read me another story, would never cuddle with me, and would never wait until I fell asleep again. I had thought I had been quiet enough with my head under the covers, but somehow Dan had heard.

"I'm it. Without me, you know what would happen to you?"

Tears streamed down my face, but I held my breath to prevent a sob.

"Kids without parents are sent to orphanages. They're horrible, dirty, cold places where you get beaten every day, you don't see the sun, you gotta fight for food, and you're forced to do manual labor all day."

Fear replaced my tears. I thought about the conversation Mrs. Jones and Ms. Parks had earlier. They didn't want me, nor did the Avon lady. Mom had told me that my dad had gone to Heaven when I was two. I had never even thought about my grandparents on his side, but they were dead too. It had never occurred to me how alone I had been. I didn't realize until now that Mom truly was all I had.

"You understand me?" Dan muted the TV and sat up.

"I've had some friends who were in orphanages. Whoa, you should hear their stories. Like the time, a friend of mine wanted another slice of bread and the orphanage caretaker beat his hands so hard he couldn't make a fist for weeks."

"And that was when they had bread. He told me he ate bugs for months. Said cockroaches were the best, especially the big ones, juicy he said." Dan leaned back in the couch and looked up at the ceiling.

"Another friend said the place he was in had a gang. The gang picked up where the guards left off. When he wasn't forced to work for the orphanage, the other kids would beat him up every day. They took his food, made him do their chores, and made him sleep on the floor with the bugs. Took his clothes, made him do all that stuff naked."

"They'd jump him any time of day; especially at night when he'd just fallen asleep. Heck, the guy still isn't able to sleep for more than 10 minutes at a time to this day."

"And I'm talking about the friends that got out," he said leaning again in my direction. "They told me a lot of the kids," Dan looked to his right as if he was being spied on or was giving away a secret. "They told me a lot of those kids; they don't get out at all. Some of 'em are beaten to death, or die of starvation, or worse," he paused and stared at me for a moment.

"Some of 'em have been sold into slavery."

"Yeah, this isn't talked about out in the open. This is all kept secret because the people who run those places, they're real powerful. They protect themselves. They NEVER get caught. They'll keep doing whatever they want to those kids."

"I heard of one kid that was sold into slavery. She was kept down in the basement until she was twenty. Forced to eat dog food and clean these people's house."

"You're lucky to have me here. Otherwise, who knows what could happen to you."

Silence invaded the room, as Dan leaned back and lit another cigarette.

"Are you going to take care of me?" I asked squeezing Betty to my side.

"Well, that depends, don't it? I want to, but you gotta want me to too," he replied patting the couch seat next to him. I slowly got up and jumped into the seat. He put his arm around me and for the first time it felt like he meant it. Running his hand up and down my arm I leaned into him to feel his warmth.

"You and me gotta be a team."

"I can do that."

"That means when those neighbor bitches pull you aside and ask you about me, you tell them everything's fine."

I raised my head to look at his face as he lowers his.

"Yeah, you didn't think I knew about that, did you?"

"I know e-v-e-r-y-t-h-i-n-g. I heard you tell them I sleep all the time and smoke, and don't deny it."

"I, I.., I didn't mean it."

"It's okay," as he pulled me into his chest, "This time." He squeezed me harder. "Next time, you say I'm the best uncle you've ever had."

"And you know what I am. I'm the ONLY uncle you got. And don't forget it."

Chapter 7

Monday morning I awake to loud banging on the front door and Dan screaming "Heather!" I pull back the covers and Betty accidently drops to the floor. Tumbling out of bed, I pick her up and gently lay her on top the bedspread, near my pillow. Heading for the door, I'm nearly hit in the face as Dan swings it open.

"Get ready for school, quick."

Kelly is standing behind him. "Get in the bathroom, I'll pick something out," she orders.

Ready in ten minutes, Kelly and I are walking out, as she looks back and says to Dan, "Set the alarm next time."

Susan is in the backseat as I rush to secure my seatbelt. Kelly drives fast and we get to school in no time. "I'll pick you up as usual, Susan. Heather, you're going to your daycare today, like before. Dan's going to pick you up."

I look back at her through the open window. "Don't worry I'll call and remind him. Now, hurry, I'm late for work." Susan and I walk toward Pinewood Elementary School's front entrance.

School is the same, except for my teacher, Ms. Blake. She keeps patting my head and asking how I'm doing. She makes me feel like I'm back at the wake. It's strange that everything at school is unaffected, yet my life is so different. I don't feel any different, but everything at home is now foreign. Gone are the nightly dinners that appeared on the table without any discussion or assistance. Gone is any sort of routine in the morning or at night. Replacing the old routines is as much TV as I want to watch; something Mom would never let me do. Why hadn't Mom let me watch more TV? She had always encouraged me to play on my own or with Susan. Often, she and I would play games together or sometimes she would read to me. What had been my normal was now a distant past.

Class ends and I get in line for the shuttle to daycare. After four days of playing on my own, I'm looking forward to daycare. Mrs. Simpson immediately greets me and pulls me aside as I watch the other kids rush over to the bookcases full of toys. Patting my shoulder, she asks me how I am. I'm trapped by her concern. This is getting

Piggy

tiring, plus now the other kids will think I'm getting scolded for something. I'm anxious to play and valuable toy-picking-time has been squandered. Mrs. Simpson asks about Dan and I dutifully repeat he's the best uncle I ever had.

"Really, he's the greatest," I reiterate. "Can I go play now?"

Free to the world of play, I join a group in a board game. Later, as I roll the dice in what is likely my winning move, the game is interrupted. My opponents are being called away by their moms. I look up and the afternoon is gone. One by one potential playmates are summoned and shuffled into awaiting vehicles to take them home. Mrs. Simpson takes pity on me and engages me in a game of checkers. I'm the only one left and my thoughts turn to last week, the other time I was the only one left. Stealing a glance out the window for the red and blue lights, I eventually see the green sedan pull in. I grab my coat and join Mrs. Simpson and Dan near the front door.

"How are you holding up, Mr... I'm sorry I never got your name."

"It's Dan, Dan Howard. Jane's brother."

"Yes, of course. Well, we love having Heather here. She's such a joy. I want you to know I'm keeping an extra eye on her this week."

"Heather, let's go."

"Do you have any questions, Mr. Howard? Any concerns about Heather?"

Turning perplexed, "No, I'm good," he says looking at her. Dressed in her typical uniform of floral dress and cardigan, her glasses shield her eyes from view.

"How much does this place cost?"

"I'm sorry?"

"How much?"

"Oh, we charge by the month. We bill the 20th of every month. You should be fine until next month," she says as she checks a book open on her desk.

"Yes, you're good until April 20th and the cost is one-fifty per month."

"One-fifty? For what?"

"It covers all the toys, an afternoon snack with milk, two assistants who organize play, and myself."

"That's it?"

"It's actually quite economical. We're one of the more reasonably priced centers. We also do field trips with the group. We give you advance notice, of course."

"Can I get a refund?"

"Is there a problem?"

"This is highway robbery."

"I don't appreciate your tone. And no, we don't do refunds. Payment is in advance so that I can schedule workers and buy snacks and things."

"Consider this your notice," he states as he grabs my hand and leads me out.

Approaching the car, he unlocks it and we both get in. He backs out of the spot and enters traffic while I am still buckling my seatbelt.

"You like that place?"

"Yes."

"How about you go to the place where Susan is?"

Piggy

"That would be okay," I say but I don't mean it. I don't want Dan to be mad. I like my daycare. They have toys I don't have and there's a jungle gym outside to play on when it's warmer. In the summer, I'm there all day and they serve peanut butter and strawberry jelly sandwiches with chips. I don't like soggy bread, so Mrs. Simpson toasts my bread before making the sandwich. Plus there's story time and field trips to the zoo. I have been to the daycare Susan goes to. Once when Kelly was sick, Mom picked up Susan from there. It was a house in the neighborhood, a few blocks over from us. We both went inside because Mom wanted to check it out. We had to walk down a steep staircase to the basement. Crammed into a small room that smelled of bleach were seven kids. There were barely any toys and most were broken. Susan said she liked it, but Mom later said it was all Kelly could afford.

"Got good news today."

"What?"

"I signed the papers to become your guardian. So, it's you and me, kid."

I smile. "Thank you, Uncle Dan."

Dan is a bit surprised. "You're welcome. Remember we're a team. We gotta stick together. Now how about some McDonald's?

"Yes!"

He pulls into the drive through and lets me order what I want. A chocolate shake and a Happy Meal. Mom rarely took me to McDonald's and never let me have a shake with my meal. McDonald's was a special occasion only place. The smell of french fries fills the car as I sneak a sip of my shake. Dan pulls away and continues the drive home. Reaching for the bag between us, his hand pulls out some fries. I stare, shocked. He stuffs them in his face and takes a long drink from his soda. Mom *never* let me eat in the car.

Entering the house, the now familiar smell of cigarettes fills my lungs. We sit down at the table and finish our meal. I eat so fast a snort comes out of my nose and we both double over laughing. Dan finishes two beers before I open my Happy Meal toy. When I set it down with a burp and another snort, he snaps his fingers.

"Lemme show you something." He motions me to follow him to my room. There on the table by the bed, where my pink lamp and a few of my stuff animals sit, is an alarm clock.

"Now, I've set this for tomorrow morning. When it rings, you gotta turn it off and get ready for school. I don't want Kelly mad at me no more."

Ingenious. It certainly solves the problem.

"See, your Uncle Dan's been busy," he says triumphantly. "Remember, we're a team. You gotta do your part so we can stay together and that means stepping up and taking care of yourself."

I get into the habit of rising by seven each morning, getting dressed, kissing Betty goodbye, and leaving before Dan gets up. Ms. Parks takes me to school and each afternoon I go to daycare. While Dan eventually picks me up, I'm always the last to leave. Usually, he honks in front of the center so he doesn't have to come in. He hasn't said anymore about the other daycare and I hope the idea has passed. For the first few nights, we have McDonald's and Dan's mood is good. But after a few days, we go straight home and heat up one of the casseroles. Dan smokes and drinks beer or whiskey all night while flipping through channels. I either go to my room or stay in the corner out of his way. It isn't perfect, but it has become our routine. Ms. Parks walks over to take Susan and me to the park on Saturday or Sunday; whichever day she has off.

Eventually, Dan and I come home to an empty refrigerator. The empty pans, which I tried my best to wash, are stacked up on the far side of the kitchen table. This morning, there had been some leftovers from last night's casserole surprise, but Dan must have polished them off for lunch. Dan rummages through the cupboards and comes back with some crackers and a can of tuna fish. I stick with the crackers because the tuna fish smells awful.

All the beer is gone leaving whiskey as the only choice. Worse, the bottle is full. From Dan's short tenure, I have learned that beer is a slow drunk and he doesn't get too animated. But whiskey, whiskey is definitely no good. Dan's voice gets loud even if he isn't mad. He'll yell at me for anything – waking him up, changing the channel, complaining there's no food, even if I don't complain at all. Sometimes when he yells, he slaps the couch real hard or swings his arm in my direction. I've quickly figured out, the far corner of the living room is the safe zone. As Dan pours another shot, I contemplate going to bed early to avoid what I expect may happen.

Knock, Knock the door sounds.

Dan spins around surprised. Peeking out the side window, he grunts. Opening the door, Mrs. Jones is in her usual colorful attire standing on the front step.

"Howdy, neighbor," she says.

"What do you want?"

"For starters, can I have my pans back?"

"What pans?"

"The ones with the casseroles in them."

"Oh, they're on the table." He takes a step back as she walks in. Surveying the room, her eyes only take a second to land on the bottle of whiskey.

"Partying I see."

"What's it to you?"

"Try to set a good example, Danny boy."

"Stop calling me that."

"Oh, relax. I know your type. I was married to one of you before my Harold. You want everything, but give nothing. There's nothing but lazy bones in your body."

"Get your pans and get out of here."

"I'm going. Heather, how you doing, sweetie?"

"I'm fine, Mrs. Jones," I say as convincingly as I can.

"You eat? Are all the casseroles gone?"

"Yes, we had a good dinner. All the casseroles were great, but they're gone."

Looking over her shoulder at Dan, "Perhaps you can get off your ass and go to the grocery store."

"Drop dead. I'll do what I want."

"Oh, you'll be dropping dead before me, Danny boy. You're gonna drink yourself into the grave, just like my first husband."

"Don't you wish." With that, Dan pushes Mrs. Jones in the center of her back out the door and slams it shut.

"Bitch!"

I get as small as I can, despite the fact I'm already kneeling on the floor in the corner of the living room. Dan paces back and forth and I can see his anger intensifying; like a tea kettle about to boil. He walks into the kitchen and yanks open the fridge. "Shit!" he screams. Heading back to the coffee table, he pours a big glass of whiskey and drains it. He looks at me, eyes blazing and I feel a tirade coming on. The piercing ring of the phone interrupts the moment.

Dan swivels around, surprised by the ring. Looking at his watch, he gives me a quizzical look. Slowly approaching the phone as if he is being watched, he answers it.

"Hello?"

"Who?"

"Yes, John, I didn't recognize your voice. How are you?"

Dan is again transformed. His anger gone, replaced by Mr. Nice Guy.

"That's great news. So, the accounts are mine?"

"When?"

"Yes, but when can I access the money?"

"Any way I can do an ATM withdrawal tonight?"

"How do I do that?"

"Oh, I see."

"First thing tomorrow then."

"Huh?"

"Yes, yes, she's fine. I was just reading her a story."

"Which one?" he looks at me in fear.

I mouth the words 'Cat-in-the-Hat'.

"Cat in the Hat."

"Yes, it is a Dr. Seuss classic."

"Thank you again and I'll see you tomorrow."

He hangs up the phone and does a little two step dance by the phone. "Whoo Hooo!" he shouts.

I watch him, relieved and scared by his transformation.

"No more cracker suppers. I am now your official guardian."

Chapter 8

The next day is uneventful until Dan picks me up from daycare. He's early, and this time he comes into the center. He finished the bottle of whiskey last night and was snoring up a storm when I left for school. This morning, I only opened the door a crack so that Ms. Parks wouldn't see anything; luckily she didn't get out of the car.

"I'm sorry to hear that," Mrs. Simpson says as I approach. "Heather, it has been a real pleasure getting to know you over the last two years. I wish you the best."

Confused, I look at Dan, but keep my mouth shut.

On the way out to the car, I ask what happened.

"You're going to go to that other daycare with Susan from now on."

"But last night you said we were rich."

"Not exactly. I'm finally getting compensated for taking care of you. That ain't exactly rich. And this place costs a fortune."

I climb into the car thinking through what I can say.

Breaking the silence, Dan announces, "We got some shopping to do."

We trudge up and down the aisles of the supermarket. Dan buys three cases of beer and several bottles of whiskey. Going through the frozen food aisle, he grabs stacks of frozen dinners and tosses them into the cart.

"Can we get pizza?" I ask.

"Sure thing, but these are on special, see?"

I glance at the sign and watch as Dan clears out the refrigerated case. It takes a while to check out and load up the car, but soon we are home. Unloading the groceries, I hand several frozen dinners to Dan. Only half of the meals can fit in the freezer. Shrugging, he puts the rest in the fridge. Opening up a beer, he downs it like it was a bullet. After a long burp, he reaches for another and closes the fridge.

"Should we make one of the meals?"

"Nope, tonight, we're ordering pizza."

I jump for joy. "Can we get hamburger?"

"What kind of a pizza is hamburger? Hamburgers are for McDonald's."

"Mom and I always got hamburger and black olives."

"You let your Uncle Dan teach you about real pizza. Pepperoni, sausage, black olives, mushrooms, and peppers. It's the only way to go."

"Can I call?"

"Not now, it's too early. Besides, Jay's coming by. We'll order it then."

I quietly rub my stomach and don't mention I'm starving. I had dropped my afternoon snack in the dirt by the jungle gym. It was too dirty to eat.

There's a light knocking on the door. Dan rushes to open it and finds Kelly and Susan standing there. Susan is clutching a new doll in her left hand.

"Hi, Dan," Kelly says as Susan comes in and shows me her new treasure.

"Well, hello. How you doing?"

"I'm fine. Listen, we haven't talked for a while but Judith told me that you're going to start Heather there tomorrow?"

"Why yes, thanks for the recommendation."

"Do you still want me to take Heather to school?"

"Yep. Could you take her to daycare too?"

"Every day?"

"That would be great."

"I don't always pick up Susan. I rotate with another mom from work. Between the two of us, we get the kids from school to daycare during the week. We are on our own to pick them up."

"Couldn't you work it out with her?"

"You want me to ask another woman you don't know to pick up your niece a few times a week?"

"Don't say it like that, I trust you. If you trust her to pick up Susan, I trust her to pick up Heather."

Rolling her eyes, "I can ask her, but are you willing to do the rotation with us?"

"What do you mean?"

"You know, chip in. Once or twice a week, pick up two, I guess three girls now from school and take them to daycare?"

"How about I make it worth your while?" he says. "Five bucks a week?"

Looking from side to side, Kelly says, "Make it ten."

"Deal. Now let's get onto more exciting stuff. What are you doing tonight? I'm having a little party here."

"It's Thursday."

"So?"

"It's a school night. Plus, I gotta work."

"I thought you only worked the breakfast and lunch shift."

"I do, but I picked up another job. Bartending one night a week at O'Malley's."

"Maybe I'll be seeing you there."

"Maybe. Who's all going to be here?"

"Just my friend Jay."

"Quite the party," she says. "Susan, come on, we gotta go." Susan gets up and runs out the door.

It's a while before Jay gets here; although his motorcycle is heard for a long time before he pulls into the driveway. He's wearing the same attire, all black leather with a red stripe on the arm, but today he's got a green bandana covering his face like a bandit. Pulling off his helmet and clutching it between his arm and hip, he yanks down his mask.

"Jeez, it's dusty today."

"Nothing a few cold ones can't take care of," Dan says as they enter.

Pizza is finally ordered with another painstaking hour passing before it arrives. The pizza Dan said was going to 'change my life' didn't. It was too spicy for me. A large amount of phlegm builds up in the back of my throat right after I devoured three slices. This has been happening more and more. I discreetly cough but it's lodged in my throat. I end up sucking hard up my nose and then coughing as much as I can in an attempt to get it out.

"What the hell is that?" Dan sneers.

"Sorry."

Piggy

"Sounds like you're snorting something," Jay says.

"Go to your room if you're gonna do that. That's disgusting," Dan orders.

Soon after being sent to my room, I'm curled up in a ball on my bed; my stomach in the midst of a gymnastic routine. It doesn't take long for the pizza to come back up. Rushing to the bathroom, I slam into Dan who is stepping through the doorway. I could have made it if he wasn't in the way, but instead I let loose.

Catching my breath in between heaves, Dan yells and jumps back looking down at the lower part of his jeans and shoes. I've scored a direct hit. Taking tiny steps while still hunched over, I make it to the toilet for a few more contributions.

"You're cleaning this up!"

I can't raise my head and opt to lay it down on the cool toilet seat. I'm finally feeling better.

Eventually, I emerge from the bathroom and get a towel out of the closet. My head is spinning and I have to sprint back to the toilet for a few false alarms before I completely wipe up the spicy remains of what made me sick. When I walk into my room, Dan's soiled shoes are next to my dresser. I pick them up and return to the bathroom to rinse them in the tub. Wafts of cigarette smoke and loud heavy metal music emanate from the living room. I don't dare stick my head out there and risk Dan's wrath. Once everything I can see is clean and I have gladly changed into my pajamas, I amble down the hall to put Dan's shoes into Mom's room. He has been sleeping in there; at least he does when he doesn't fall asleep in front of the TV.

"How much did ya get?" Jay asks.

"I'm her guardian now but there's a grace period for all the paperwork to be finalized. For now, I've only got access to a few thousand, which is why I'm having this little shindig."

"A few thousand huh?"

"Okay, I knew you'd ask for it. Here," Dan says, handing something to Jay. "It's all there, you can count it if you want," he adds.

"Nah, I trust you man."

"Bullshit, you don't trust anyone," Dan retorts.

"Nor do you my friend," Jay says as they laugh.

"What you gonna do now that you're flush?" Jay asks after a long silence.

"I think I gotta lay low until everything's finalized. I don't want to jeopardize anything," Dan explains as he asks for another shot.

I hear sounds of pouring as Jay coyly says, "How much?"

"Enough." Dan snaps. "Enough to spot me more than five hundred when my mom died. Cheap bitch."

"Maybe we should get a poker game going?"

"Not a bad idea. But, not until it's final. I gotta play this one cool."

Their attentions turn to a sporting event on TV. I shiver as my chills return. I place Dan's shoes at the edge of the hallway so that they don't see me and go to bed.

The next morning, I feel better than I expected. Passing through the living room, Dan is stretched out on the couch with his boxers on. Jay is in the same place on the floor. A glance to my right and I see Dan's jeans hanging over a kitchen chair. There is no sign of vomit, so he must have washed them himself. It dawns on me I've only seen Dan in one set of clothes. I know he's washed them once because last week there were clean towels in the bathroom. I open the front door and wave to a waiting Ms. Parks. Thinking back to that night, Dan brought nothing with him. He had nothing in his hands when he came to daycare. Where are the rest of his clothes and things?

"Good morning Heather," Kelly says. "You get any sleep last night?"

"Yes. Some. I puked."

"You were sick?" Kelly asks as her hand goes to my forehead.

"I think the pizza made me sick."

"Was it green?" Susan probes from the backseat.

"No more red with some full pieces of pepperoni."

"That's enough girls. That's gross."

Susan and I giggle as we stick out our tongues at each other.

"You feeling better, now? You don't have a fever."

"Yeah, my throat's a little sore, but I'm okay."

Kelly leans over and sniffs real hard around me. "Do I smell bleach?"

"I had to clean up the bathroom."

"He made you clean up?"

Realizing how this might sound, I quickly recover. "Ah, I wanted to. I felt bad after puking on him."

"You puked on Dan?" she responds smiling broadly. I nod and keep my head down. Kelly put the car in gear and almost made it to the end of the block before she could no longer hold back her laughter.

Chapter 9

The school bell rings and I follow Susan to the pick-up zone. Ms. Parks is waving as she pulls up. A girl comes around from behind and pokes Susan in the arm.

"Sally, this is Heather. She's going to come with us from now on," Susan says.

We pile into the car and arrive a few minutes later at the house Mom and I once visited.

"Judith, this is Heather," Kelly says to the large black lady who opens the door. She has on navy blue velour sweatpants that are stretched to the limit and a pale pink sweatshirt. Curlers adorn her shiny black hair. I can already smell the bleach as she bends down to take my face into one of her enormous hands. I see something out of the corner of my eye causing me to pull back in fear of something stabbing me.

"Child, what you scared of?" she asks.

Looking at her hands, I identify what frightened me. Her nails are blood red and so long they curve. I've never seen anything like them before and I can't stop staring until I figure out if they're real or not.

"I'm Mrs. Johnson, welcome."

Susan and Sally dart down the steep stairs while I stand firm.

"I run a tight ship here. No screaming or running. You stay downstairs. No breaking out."

I can feel my shoulder length hair hit the middle of my back as my head leans back far enough to look at her face. The top of her head seems to brush the top of the door frame.

"You understand?"

"Yes, ma'am."

"Good. Now go on downstairs." Turning to Kelly, "You got my money?"

"No, didn't Dan pay you?"

"Not yet."

"Let me talk to him and tell him."

"Okay, but I'll need a full month by next Monday."

Once downstairs, I spend the first few minutes searching for all the light switches and flicking them up and down, only to realize all the lights are already on. It's a smaller group, only eight girls. I ask Susan why there aren't any boys, but she has no answer. I make the best of it, already missing my other daycare.

Five-thirty comes slow. Ms. Parks shows up and Susan and I are summoned upstairs. Kelly looks dismayed to see me. "Heather, come on with us. I'll take you home."

She gets out of the car in our driveway and walks me up to the door. She barely gets her hand up to knock when Dan opens it.

"Hello there. You missed a good party."

"I heard. Heard Heather got sick."

"Yeah she's a little puker." I push past Dan as he holds out his arms and tilts his head. "You like?"

"What?"

"My new duds." He isn't wearing jeans anymore. He has on some sort of black pants that shine at certain angles with the light. A striped blue and green buttoned shirt is on top and neatly tucked in behind a black belt with a large silver buckle. I can see something shiny in the shirt and identify silver thread in it. He has on new leather shoes like the one Mom's boss wore; black and shiny with no laces. Clean shaven, his light brown hair is slightly damp and combed back. I catch a whiff of what I know to be Mom's perfume.

"Oh, you look fine," Kelly responds.

"Fine or F-i-n-e?"

"Whatever Dan. You need to pay Judith up front a month. Then in two weeks you pay again, so that there's always a rolling two weeks."

Dan stares back at her still moving his eyes up and down encouraging her to give him the once over. "And you need to pay me upfront as well. Fifteen bucks."

"I thought we agreed on ten," Dan says as his arms drop immediately and his face tightens up.

"That was before I realized I'm picking her up each night."

"That was the deal."

"No, the deal was transport to daycare from school. Now you want me to bring her back and don't forget I'm not charging you for the drive each morning to school."

"Don't get your knickers in a bunch." He reaches into his back pocket and pulls out a wallet. It must be new since I'd never seen it. Counting out the money, he hands the bills to Kelly.

"And another fifteen for next week. I want a rolling week too."

"Now?"

"Yes, I'm not going to keep hounding you."

"Fine, fine," he says as he pulls out more money. "Now, why don't you come on in for a drink?"

"No thanks." Turning to me, "Heather, Susan's with her dad this weekend so I won't see you until Monday, alright?"

I nod.

"Now you gotta come over for a drink. I wouldn't want you to be all alone over there."

"Don't worry about me. I picked up double shifts this weekend," she replies and walks back to her car before Dan can say anything else.

"Do you like my new clothes?" Dan asks me, shutting the door.

"Yeah, you look good. Where's Jay?"

"He's got this motorcycle club thing this weekend, so he's not coming over," he states. "I'm going out and may not be home until late. Keep the door locked."

"You're leaving me?"

"I've been cooped up in this place for weeks. I gotta get out."

"What about dinner?"

"You're a big girl. You can heat one of those frozen dinners we bought." Grabbing the car keys, he smiles and opens the door, "See ya later, alligator."

I stare at the door listening to the car pull out of the driveway. Silence envelops the house and I notice all the little noises the house has to offer. I lock the deadbolt and turn on the TV for some noise. Next I get Betty. She'll be here with me. I walk through the entire house, like they do in cop shows, to make sure no one is hiding anywhere. Resigned that I am the only one here, I enter the kitchen and turn on the stove.

I hadn't noticed when Dan bought them, but there were only three varieties of frozen dinners – Salisbury Steak, Turkey and Gravy, and a few Chicken Pot Pies. There may be different ones in the freezer, but something tells me that frozen dinners in the fridge won't last long. I opt for the steak, not sure what Salisbury is.

I hear it sizzling when it comes out. As I peel back one corner of the foil, steam gushes out and the sauce on the meat is boiling. I let it sit for a few minutes before peeling off the lid, or at least almost the entire lid. The upper center compartment, there are four compartments total, has its own foil lid. On top it reads 'chocolate pudding' and I now notice the label -- *Do Not Heat*. Touching it, I burn my fingers. The pudding is in its own foil container that is supposed to be lifted out *before* cooking. I'll remember that next time.

I assess the rest of my meal. The steak compartment is the largest of the four and spans the length of the tray. Overcooked, the meat is a dark brown and quickly hardening to stone. The upper left corner has a dollop of mashed potatoes and the upper right hand corner has the greenest peas I've ever seen. Mom always bought canned peas which were light green and mushy; these are almost neon green and hard. Not rock hard, but you can feel the skin squish when you bite into them. They taste funny too. I eat what I can and throw out the rest. Despite not eating since lunch, my stomach is still queasy from last night's pizza incident.

I watch TV with Betty until nearly 11 P.M. and wait for Dan. Eventually climbing into bed, I lie wide awake for another hour and still nothing.

The sun is shining through my curtains resulting in a shadow dance I haven't seen in days when I wake up. It's quiet. Tiptoeing down the hallway, I peek around the corner expecting to see Dan sprawled out on the couch. Nothing. Turning to my right, I gently turn the knob to Mom's room and slowly ease the door open. Nothing. He isn't here. A key is inserted in the front door lock and I spin around in surprise. Frozen, I'm not sure who will come in. The knob jiggles but doesn't turn. Banging ensues.

"Heather, open up," Dan shouts.

Running to the door, I undo the deadbolt and open the door.

"Howdy," Dan slurs. His shoes are scuffed up and everything is wrinkled. His untucked shirt is incorrectly buttoned with the right side hanging down lower than the left. His brown hair is a mess and I can see a hint of stubble along his chin.

"Water," he says as he stumbles to the kitchen.

"Where were you?" I ask loudly.

Piggy

He spins around quick, so quick I don't see his hand coming. The slap is hard and across my face. I stagger back and fall slowly to my left. Shocked it takes me a moment before the tears well up.

"I don't answer to you! I can come home whenever I please."

I can't help but go into full-fledged crying. Normally I can stave it off until night time when I think of Mom, but it's been a few days and the floodgates have opened.

"Stop crying!"

I suck my breath in, comply, and remain on the floor.

"You cry all the time. I hear you, squealing all night long. If you're not crying, you're snorting. You're like a little pig!"

I pull my feet in so that I can take my weight off my hand.

"You're a little piggy, that's what you are. Piggy, piggy, piggy!"

I stand and he lunges at me with his arm extended aimed to slap me again.

I drop back on my butt and put my arms over my head. He doesn't follow through and instead chuckles. "You scared? You scared, little piggy?"

I nod hoping this is the response he wants.

"Well you should be. I'm all you got and you go on and treat me like I'm your slave. Asking me where I was. It's none of your fucking business where I was, you understand!" he screams.

"I'm sorry."

"You gotta let me have my space. We're a team, but I'm the boss." He stands up straight and sways. Sitting down at the kitchen table, he pulls out his smokes from his upper pocket. "Now, make me some coffee."

"We don't have a coffee pot."

"Heat up the kettle; I got instant."

I do as asked and eventually pour a glass of orange juice for me and Dan. Setting his down in front of him, he picks it up and drinks. Standing on one of the kitchen chairs, I find the instant coffee packets and place some on the table. I move the chair to the stove and pour the water after it's boiled into a mug and bring it to Dan with a spoon. I go back to my room with hopes of avoiding him the rest of the day.

Chapter 10

My wish comes true, but for more than Saturday. Dan slept a lot over the next few weeks. When he wasn't sleeping, he was out. I subsisted on Salisbury steak after depleting our supply of chicken pot pie which I found to be my favorite. I mastered cooking the steak without burning it and remembered to save the pudding from the oven. The pudding was the only part I liked. The peas went into the trash along with whatever portion of the steak I couldn't choke down.

Ms. Parks takes me to school every day and brings me home from daycare each night. Whenever she asks about Dan, I lie and tell her he's fine and treats me well. I never tell her he's out, certain that would bring upon his wrath. The first weekend Dan stayed out, I told her he was taking me to the zoo; afraid he wouldn't be home if she came over. On the second weekend, I rouse the courage to surprise them around lunch time on Saturday.

"Heather, are you okay?" Ms. Parks asks when she answers the door.

"Dan sent me over to play," I reply hoping I hadn't missed lunch.

Following her into the kitchen, Susan is finishing a piece of pizza at the table.

"Do you want a slice?" Ms. Parks asks.

"Yes, please."

Setting a plate down in front of me, Ms. Parks asks, "When do you need to get back?"

I shrug and reply, "Whenever," before devouring the cheese pizza.

Susan and I play dolls and board games for the rest of the afternoon. As the sun sets, Ms. Parks picks up the phone to call Dan despite my pleas that he's taking a nap. After a minute or so, she hangs up. "You can stay for dinner and then I'll walk you back after."

Piggy

I eat as slow as possible, but I can't put off the escorted walk home. My plan has backfired. I had thought I'd be able to walk home on my own, but now I'm in trouble. 'Please be home, please be home' I chant in my head.

Glancing back at Ms. Parks, I pull the key out of my pocket. I slide it into the lock but the door opens before I turn the key.

"Where have you been?" Dan snaps.

"Ah, I was playing over at Susan's like you said I could," I say with a straight face.

"Hmm. Go on, get in."

I walk toward my room, but glue myself around the hallway entrance so I can eavesdrop.

"I called earlier but there was no answer."

"I was out."

"You alright with Heather coming over?"

"Sure, I said she could." I smile; he backed me up.

"She was starving; ate nearly three slices of pizza for lunch and a big dinner. Are you feeding her enough?"

"She's a little pig and yes, there's plenty to eat. I think she's gonna be one of those fat girls."

"I don't know about that. She was just really hungry. Anyway, I've been meaning to ask you about next week. School's out; do you have plans for Heather?"

"Plans?"

"You realize you always answer my questions with a question?"

"Is that what draws you to me?"

Piggy

"No," she says exhaling loudly. "Meaning, she won't be in school all day. I won't be coming over to pick her up in the morning."

"What are you doing with your kid?"

"Well, *Susan*," she says pointedly, "Goes to the same daycare all day on Monday, Wednesdays, and Fridays. It's usually all week, but this summer I've got some extra cash to put her in an art program on Tuesdays and Thursdays."

"Can Heather do that?"

"Does she want to do that?"

"Sure she'll love it."

"Did you think to ask her? Or are you going to follow any parenting decision I make so that Heather's no bother to you?"

"You say it so mean. I'm a single parent, I'm doing the best I can," Dan says as his voice changes into the smooth talker he can be when he wants something.

"Right. I can do the same thing I have been for Monday, Wednesday, and Friday, but I'll have to check if there are any more spaces in the art program. It's two-fifty for the eight weeks."

Whistling, "That's steep."

"Actually, it's pretty cheap. But what's the alternative for you? Are you going to take Heather to Judith's on Tuesdays and Thursdays? Or are you going to have her sit here with you all day?"

"You know, maybe she'll stay home with me those days. We're real close, Heather and me."

"I'm sure you are. Do you want me to ask if there's availability?"

"Nope. No cash just now."

"Tell Heather I'll see her Monday."

Piggy

Dan shuts the door. "You hear that Heather? She'll pick you up Monday," he says in a normal voice.

I peer out from the hallway and look at him

"Didn't anyone tell you, you shouldn't eavesdrop?"

"I'm sorry. Sorry about going over there. I thought it'd be okay and you weren't..." I stop myself before I say 'here' hoping I haven't lit the fuse.

"You tell her I wasn't here?"

"No, I said you were home. I didn't tell her anything."

"Good, keep it that way. Nobody needs to know where I am or what I do." Dan walks into the kitchen to get a beer. I pause and assess Dan's mood so I know what to expect tonight. Surprisingly, he passes by me and enters the bathroom with his beer. "Pick this place up, I'm having people over. When I get out of the shower, I want this place clean," he instructs.

I pick up as best I can and get the vacuum out. The place isn't that dirty since Dan's barely been here for two weeks. When he gets out of the shower, he's whistling implying a mellow mood. Stepping out into the living room doorway, he's got a towel around his waist and is rubbing his head with another one. I stare at the serpentine tongue on Dan's chest that I rarely see.

"Did I tell ya? It's official. Word came in the mail; I'm your legal guardian."

"Great."

"You and me, kid. We watch each other's backs. We're a team. Otherwise, who knows what could happen to you."

The music starts blaring around 10 P.M. I've been in my room for an hour already. Before the music, there are several loud voices

Piggy

amidst the stream of loud engines pulling into the driveway or around the house.

I want to peek out and see who is there, but I don't dare. The bathroom becomes a revolving door of people. Sometimes more than one person is in the bathroom at a time. I crawl into my closet to put my ear against the wall to see if I can hear what is being said. A few words pop out, but mostly, the voices are muffled. I twist around to crawl out of my closet and sit on something that breaks. Flipping over on my knees, I inspect what I've broken. It's a plastic yellow egg that has opened up to reveal a piece of chocolate. Mom hid this here.

Easter was the last holiday before she died. She always went all out for Easter. We dyed eggs together. She would use rubber bands and stickers to create decorations on the dyed eggs. As the eggs were drying, she would watch me as I searched for all the hidden eggs and candies throughout the house. It was my job to find them all. She would give me bonus prizes if I found five items in the first five minutes. And I always seemed to get the bonus prize. I remember our tradition of saving the big hollow bunny for last after the little chocolate eggs were all gone. And how Mom would make egg salad sandwiches for lunch with a side of jelly beans. A wave of missing Mom comes over me and I crawl onto my bed and hug Betty until I fall asleep.

The next morning, the doorbell rings in a consistent pattern. Every thirty seconds, it is hit again. I stay in my bed not wanting to venture out. I finally hear the front door open with Dan yelling something. He falls silent, and then screams "Stop ringing the bell."

When I can't hold it anymore, I stumble out of my room and into the bathroom. The place is trashed. The toilet seat is up, something I've become used to with Dan, and the bowl is filthy. There's no toilet paper and all the towels that had been hung up are lying in a pile in the corner, soaking wet. I take a few Kleenex tissues out and carefully put the lid down.

When I leave the bathroom, Dan is stirring in Mom's room. I hear him mumbling to himself. I steal a look at the living room and am surprised to find it empty, of people, that is. There are bottles and plastic cups everywhere, along with pizza boxes and bags of chips. One of the couch cushions has a large dark wet spot on it. I smell something foul and glance to my left. Someone has vomited on the

Piggy

floor near the bookshelf. Disgusted, I study the bookshelf which has had several books moved or taken out. My eyes zero in on the middle shelf, home to Mom's butterfly collection. Broken pieces of glass lay haphazardly among the pile of figurines. I hurriedly step closer and inspect the collection. Horrified, I find some figurines are broken, but several appear intact. My examination is interrupted by the doorbell which rings again. Dan storms out of the bedroom, past me, to open it. No one is there.

"You old biddy, stop ringing the doorbell!"

Mrs. Jones' voice is faint but distinguishable in the background. Dan goes outside. I walk to the threshold and peer out. Lined up on our front porch is a never-ending row of beer bottles and a small pile of broken brown glass. There's a note taped to one of the bottles '*Keep your trash to yourself*'. Dan nearly tackles me on his way back into the house.

"Hey, watch this door and don't let anyone ring that bell again," he says as he enters the kitchen. Filling up a glass with water, he looks at me. "You hear me? I need to get some sleep. Don't let anyone ring that bell."

I nod. For the next hour, I sit with the front door cracked open shivering and standing guard of the doorbell. Afraid to leave my post, my mind races with thoughts of the broken butterflies. I decide that once the place is cleaned up, I can scrutinize their damage and see what glue can do to salvage them. Next, I survey the cleanup job that awaits me. I tally the beer bottles, but keep getting distracted and losing count.

Mom's bedroom door opens followed by the bathroom door closing. Now that Dan is up, I'd better start cleaning. I go into the kitchen for a garbage bag and find the fridge wide open. Dirty plates and glasses are all over the kitchen counters, table, and floor. There's a creak behind me and I spin around. She's tall and thin with black mascara smeared under her eyes. Wearing a Harley Davidson tank top and a short jean skirt, her blonde hair hangs down and nearly covers a rose tattoo on her shoulder. She's carrying her shoes and walking barefoot through the living room.

"Morning little girl, you be real quiet for your dad," she whispers. Slipping out of the front door, she's gone.

Piggy

Back to my task, I start with the bottles and trash first, then onto wiping everything down. I poorly plan my clean up, and go through all the kitchen towels in the first hour with most being spent on the carpet. I nearly puke myself a few times at the stench. I carefully place the third full garbage bag in the kitchen and then wash the dishes. Once I can see the countertops, I return to the living room. I pause at the bookshelf and lay down my towel. Carefully scooping up the broken glass pieces, I move them to the newly wiped coffee table. Of the twelve butterflies, eight appear undamaged, two have small pieces broken off, and the remaining two are shattered. I return the unbroken eight back to the bookshelf. Next, I separate the pieces into two groups – the figurines with small breaks and the figurines that are shattered. The latter pile looks impossible. I get the glue out of the junk drawer and set on repairing the purple and yellow butterflies that each have their wings broken off. I carefully reattach the wings and place them in the center of the coffee table. Satisfied with my progress, I get a zip lock bag and sweep the fragments of the remaining two butterflies into it. When I have more time, I will sort the pieces and see if glue can bring them back together.

Dan walks in, coughing and hacking. He closes the front door. Without saying a word, he goes into the kitchen and turns the kettle on for coffee. I get the vacuum now that he's up and plug it in.

"Can you do that later?"

"I'm cleaning up."

"I know, but just do it later."

Returning the handle to the upright position, I walk into the kitchen. "Can you help me take the trash out, so I can do the floor?"

He looks at me and walks over to the bags and grabs one. Opening up the front door, he's confronted by the beer bottle line up. "Christ," he says under his breath. "Get me another bag."

I hand him one and he puts all the bottles into it. "Get a broom for this too."

Sliding the two other garbage bags to the doorway, I retrieve the broom. Dan has carried out all the bags to the curb. He passes me as I sweep up. The TV turns on.

"Why is this cushion all wet?" he says loudly.

"I tried to wash it."

Dan sits on the other side. "Make me a cup of coffee, will you?"

With a full dustpan, I enter the kitchen. A crack of glass comes from the living room. "Shit!"

I run back into the room. Dan has put his feet up on the coffee table and disturbed the drying figurines. Both are laying on their sides in more pieces than I started with.

"You broke them!"

"What are you putting them on the table like that for?"

"I was fixing them. Your friends broke them."

"Well, whatever, they're broken now. Clean them up."

I stare at him in disbelief. "You're not even going to say you're sorry?"

"What do you want? You put them on the table. You ask me they're all ugly anyway."

"They were Mom's!"

"I didn't know!" Pointing at the bookshelf, he continues, "Besides, there's still some over there."

I throw the broom handle at him and turn to walk away. He grabs my wrist and twists me around.

"Don't test me, Piggy, I didn't break them so don't blame me. Got it?"

He lets go of his grip and I pull my hand to me and rub my wrist.

Piggy

"I'm the one in charge here, not you. You do as I say." He's sitting up with his feet on the floor and looking directly into my eyes.

I nod and stifle a cry.

He leans back, then quickly forward. In one swift motion, he picks up the broken purple butterfly and whips it at the bookshelf. As if he was a major league ball player, he scores a direct hit of the shelf with the remaining collection. More glass breaks. My eyes dart to the shelf in shock and then back at Dan. I run to my room.

Crying into my pillows, Mom fills my thoughts. I miss waking up knowing she was already up and making breakfast. I miss waffles, eggs in a frame, and grilled cheese with ham and pickles. I miss Easter egg hunts and the games we played together. I have so little left of her and now even less.

Time passes and my hunger overpowers me. I sneak back into the kitchen passing Dan along the way. He's watching basketball and occasionally screaming at the TV. I quietly get something to eat although there is little left in the fridge. As the game ends, Dan's agitation grows, when the phone rings.

"Yeah."

"No shit. Where'd the defense even come from?"

"No, no, I got it. How about we double it?"

"What can you give me on the Mavericks?"

"Ten points? That's it?"

"Okay, I'll take it. Yeah, yeah, I know the drill. I'm good for it."

Hanging up, Dan joins me in the kitchen. I look down as if mesmerized by the peanut butter and crackers I'm eating. Dan opens up cupboards and the fridge in search of food.

"I'm going out to get something to eat," he announces. I look up but catch myself and remain focused on the crackers. I refuse to show him any emotion. "Do you want to come with me?"

I remain silent.

"Suit yourself," he says as he walks out the door.

When I hear the car start, I get up to inspect the damage to the butterflies. Five remain intact. Luckily, my favorite, the royal blue monarch with gold trim has survived. I examine its wings – the pattern a mixture of brown veining with light tan and blue in between. A thick band of gold lines the edges of the wings and the tips of the antennas.

I put two more broken butterflies into a new bag and add them to my project list. I glue the remaining three as best I can but there are pieces missing. Putting them in my room to dry, I spend the next several hours sorting out one of the zip lock bags that I believe hold the parts to two butterflies, but eventually give up. The pieces are too small. The surviving five butterflies are now safely stowed in my room on my bookshelf, next to the three glued and partially whole butterflies.

I go to bed before Dan comes home. When I wake up the next morning, there is a new butterfly figurine on my bedside table with a note saying 'Sorry'. It isn't as pretty as Mom's and is made of plastic, not ceramic. I leave it on the coffee table before heading to school that morning and never say a word to Dan about it. The butterflies can't be replaced and Dan doesn't get it.

Chapter 11

It's the last week of school and we mostly play games all day or pack books away for storage. On the last day of school, instead of daycare, Ms. Parks takes Susan and me to get ice cream sundaes to celebrate. We are now second graders. When she drops me off at home, she insists on coming to the door with me. I insert my key and yell for Dan. No one comes.

"Is he here?"

"I'm sure he's sleeping. You can leave," I say to her.

"I want to see him first," she says as she marches into the house and looks around. She walks back to Mom's room and bangs on the door. It swings open and nothing.

"I'm not leaving you here alone, Heather."

"It's okay. He'll be back soon."

"We'll leave him a note and he can get you later."

"Let me get Betty," I say as I rush to my room; happy that I'm not going to spend another night alone, but scared of what will happen when Dan gets back.

Susan and I fall into our regular play. After our typical rotation of dolls and hopscotch, we come inside to play a few board games since the outdoor lights aren't so bright. Bored with Susan's slow pace at a game of Sorry, I watch Ms. Parks carefully cutting cheddar cheese in the exact shape of the bread. Then she slathers butter onto slices of bread. My mouth waters when I smell the cheese melting. Ms. Parks expertly flips the sandwiches which are golden brown. I quickly take out Susan in our game. Gloating, I head to the kitchen with Susan close behind me.

"Almost ready," Ms. Parks smiles.

We sit at the table as our plates are set in front of us. Ms. Parks has cut off the crust of my sandwich just like mom used to do. A tear starts to well up in my eye, but is squashed by my hunger as I greedily eat my meal.

Piggy

After dinner, we watch some TV. Ms. Parks eventually gets Susan ready for bed and lends me a pair of pajamas. Inspecting my clothes, she asks, "When was the last time these were washed?" I shrug. "I'm going to run a load, if they're not done when Dan gets home, I'll run them over tomorrow."

She walks to the washer and I follow her. I watch intently as she starts the washer knowing this will be a new task for me. I've been washing underwear in plain water and bar soap for weeks and only after wearing them several times. If I want clean clothes, I'm going to have to wash them myself.

Another half hour passes and the roar of a motorcycle passes by the house. Ms. Parks looks out the window.

"Come on, he's home."

Taking me by the hand, we walk across the street to the house. Jay and Dan are milling about the driveway.

"Heather's with me in case you were worried," she says loudly from the sidewalk as Dan turns around and looks surprised.

"When were you planning on coming home?" she continues as Jay sticks his head out of the doorway.

"What are you talking about, I'm home now."

"It's nearly ten o'clock. I drop her off from daycare at five."

"I got held up."

"And you didn't think to call?"

"Call who?"

"Me, Mrs. Jones, anyone."

"I knew she was with you."

"You can't leave her alone in the house by herself."

Piggy

"I was a little late. It's no big deal."

"I'm fine, Ms. Parks," I say walking inside. "Thanks for dinner."

"See, she's fine," he says.

I immediately go to the kitchen table to get my certificate for completing the first grade. I hold it proudly to my chest as I stand next to Jay in the doorway.

"We're gonna have a couple of beers, why don't you join us?" Dan says outside.

"No thanks," Kelly says before storming home.

Dan whistles and turns to look at Jay. Raising his eyebrows, "See what I mean?"

"She's hot alright. You think you got a chance?"

"I'm working it. Taking my time." Looking down at me, "What you got there?"

"I finished the first grade today," I say.

"Congratulations, only eleven more to go."

I smile broadly.

"Now go onto bed," Dan says patting me on the head.

My smile falls flat as I slowly walk to my room. It has been over a week since the butterfly incident and Dan's been nicer to me, although I expected more than just a pat on my head for my achievement. I wait in my room for a few moments before resuming my place in the hallway where I can hear their conversation.

"I saw Dex, the other day," Jay comments cracking open a beer.

"What's that asshole up to?"

"He looked good. Got himself a new bike and had cash to buy me a few."

"Where's he getting the money?"

"I had heard a few months back that he was selling drugs," Jay states.

"Is that what he's doing?"

"Not exactly. At least not the way I thought. He's selling geriatric drugs to retirement homes."

"What?"

"You heard me. He sells prescription drugs to old people. Says he has a connection at a few nursing homes."

"He's working a regular job?"

"Nooo. Shit, we're talking about Dex."

"I don't get it."

"He's selling stuff to these places under the table, you know cheaper than they can normally get them."

"How?"

"Dex knows a guy whose brother is in charge of buying the medicine and supplies for a retirement home. Dex sells him cheaper medicine than the place can order. The home doesn't know any different. The medicine is the same and they think they're paying the same rates as before, but instead this guy is getting stuff a lot cheaper from Dex." Jay takes a long drink of beer followed by a loud burp. "They split the profits. I guess he's got the same sort of deal at a few other places."

"Shit, so he's selling fakes?"

"No, he says he's not. Says even he has a conscience. Can you believe it? He actually said that with a straight face." They laugh.

"Where does he get the drugs?"

"He says he takes them from the hospital. He goes in late at night and swipes what he can."

"You're shitting me."

"Nope, nope, that's what he said. Anyway, we should call him."

"Why?"

"He had a lot of cash on him. He's ripe for a poker game."

Dan is silent for a moment. "Piggy, you aren't listening are you?"

Quickly and quietly I rush back to my bed and jump in. Folding the covers back, I hear nothing. Dan isn't coming down the hallway. I continue to fake sleep until I fall asleep.

Chapter 12

Summer starts with no fanfare. Ms. Parks picks me up three times a week for daycare. Twice a week, I stay home, often with Dan sleeping through the day. Our house becomes party central when Dan is around. Jay sleeps on the couch several nights a week. There are a handful of regulars that come to the parties, but mostly the faces invading my home each night are new. I get proficient at cleaning. I have it down to a routine - every Tuesday, Thursday, and Saturday. I have also mastered the washing machine and revel in clean clothes.

My birthday comes and goes when I turn seven. Ms. Parks remembers and has cupcakes for Susan and me after daycare, but that's all. Mom always made my favorite cake – chocolate with chocolate frosting. I would help her stir the batter mix, licking the edges of the bowl when she wasn't looking. When it came time for the frosting, I would stir as much as I could, whipping powdered sugar out of the sides of the bowl. Mom would take my lumpy frosting and whip it smooth and silky. She would let me have the spoon she stirred with to lick while she expertly used a long spatula to evenly frost the cake so it was perfect, just like a magazine photo. Then, I'd lick any remaining frosting out of the bowl when she was done.

Dan didn't come home until late the night of my birthday, but he did buy me a new stuffed animal which he placed outside to my door. Later, I found out that Ms. Parks had reminded him of my birthday.

In the middle of the summer, when the heat is no longer curtailed by the setting sun, Dan throws another party. Music blares late into the night and the sounds of beer bottles and smell of smoke fill the house. I stay in my room hoping the cleanup won't be too bad. My quiet play is interrupted by Dan in the hallway. He's talking to someone so I jump off the bed and put my ear to the door.

"I'll get you the money," Dan says. "I got shitty luck. Who would have thought the Lakers would lose?"

"No more credit until I see cash," a man says with a voice that almost growls.

Piggy

"Don't worry, I got it," Dan responds as a siren bellows outside. "What the hell?"

The hum of voices shuts off like a light. The music stops and there isn't a peep out of anyone. I press my ear to the door. Nothing.

There's movement and I feel a gush of air. I can hear some rumbling outside. The loud roar of motorcycles begins, and then fades into the night as they drive down the street. After a while, the front door slams and Dan is pacing in the front room. I wait; wait for Dan to come into my room so that I can ask him what happened, but nothing. The TV turns on and Dan doesn't make a sound.

The next morning, I'm up early and go out into the living room. Mom's door is shut. I eat breakfast and clean up. After completing all the quiet cleaning tasks, I turn on the TV.

At noon, Dan gets up. He doesn't seem angry but I stay out of his way all the same. After he has his coffee and a few smokes, I enter the kitchen.

"Can we go to the store? There's not much to eat here."

He grunts. Getting up, he walks to the sink and pulls back the curtains. He sees something and quickly opens a closet and grabs a bottle. Brushing by me, he reaches for his smokes and heads for the door. Before closing it, he leans back inside. "Stay here."

I immediately move the kitchen chair to the sink and peer out the window. Mrs. Jones is outside gardening. Dan is on our side of the rose bush talking to her holding the bottle out of sight. She looks up and shakes her head. I can't hear what she's saying but she talks for a long time, eventually standing up and putting her hands on her hips. Dan is standing calmly at the hedge not moving. Taking a drag from his cigarette, I see him flick his ash into Mrs. Jones's yard. Her face reddens as she starts shouting something. Dan tosses the lit cigarette into her flowerbed causing her to scramble to get it. Throwing it back at Dan, they are now as face to face as they can be with a two foot wide rose bush between them. Mrs. Jones is animated and shouting at Dan while pointing her finger.

Dan coolly uncaps the bottle and lifts it up for her to see. He slowly pours out the bottle along the hedge as if he's coating something in paint. Mrs. Jones screams and lunges for the bottle, but Dan keeps passing it back and forth out of her reach. Mrs. Jones rushes to the gate and onto the sidewalk as Dan empties the bottle. She runs at him in an attempt to tackle him but he steps aside and she collides into her rose bushes. Stumbling, she gets her balance and slowly pulls back from the hedge, careful to pick the prickly branches out of her sweater. There are red marks on her face where the rose bush has scratched her. Dan is laughing. She glares at him and garners her strength.

He takes a quick step forward and in one fluid motion, pushes her chest. She immediately falls backwards onto her butt; her mouth gaping open. She stays on the ground frozen as if unable to move. Then she sucks air in and coughs. He's knocked the wind out of her. She puts a hand out on either side of her as if grasping for something. Dan watches her and lights up a cigarette. She tries to ease herself up from the ground, but isn't successful. After a few more attempts, she looks up at him with tears in her eyes and says something. He bends down, grabbing her upper arm and yanks her up. She howls in pain. Without stopping, he half walks and half pulls her around to the gate and through her yard. She continues to howl as her right leg drags behind her between hops. Dan pushes her through the open front door and all I can see is her hand on the door frame. He leans in and says something to her.

Then he turns around as if nothing happened and walks back to our driveway. Picking up the empty bottle on his way, he tosses his unfinished lit cigarette into her yard. I hop off the chair and drag it back to the table as fast as possible. I make it back to the table seated in the chair, hoping Dan won't detect my spying. Breathing hard, I endeavor to look innocent.

Shutting the door, he utters, "Nosy bitch." Sauntering over to the kitchen trash can, he lifts the lid and drops a bottle from his raised hand into the trash can; the word *bleach* emblazoned on the side.

The phone rings.

"Yeah."

"I told you, I got your money. You'll get it tomorrow, don't worry," he says slamming down the phone.

Piggy

Dan walks over to the couch and turns on the TV. Switching on a game, he doesn't say a word. I retreat to my room to stay out of his way. No matter how hungry I am, I can tell he's in no mood to hear it.

A bit later, I hear a siren. Sneaking down the hallway into the living room, Dan is asleep in front of the TV. I quietly walk back to the kitchen window and see Mrs. Jones being taken out of her house. She's pale with a mask over her face and strapped to a gurney. The ambulance lights are flashing and a few neighbors from across the street are standing out front. I look over at Dan but he doesn't stir.

Chapter 13

Monday comes and Dan's not up when I leave for daycare. Ms. Parks picks us up a bit earlier in the afternoon than usual because Susan's dad is taking her to a baseball game tonight; a fact that she hasn't been able to shut up about all day. On the ride home, Susan describes her snacking plans for the third time, debating between a hot dog, nachos, and caramel corn combo, or a corn dog, nachos and a sundae feast. My stomach growls at the thought of any one of those snacks.

"See you tomorrow," Ms. Parks says before coming to a complete stop. Jarred, I undo my seatbelt. "Heather, can you hurry?" she asks.

"Sorry," I stammer.

"Sorry to rush you. I want to go visit Mrs. Jones tonight. Did you hear? She had a stroke and broke her hip."

I jerk my head to face her, then quickly lower my eyes and shake my head before getting out of the car.

Entering the house, Dan is on the phone.

"John, I've been trying to get you all day. I can't seem to get anything from the account."

"I realize it's monthly but I need a little extra now."

"No, that's gone already. You know I had to move here and drop everything to take care of Heather."

"Yeah, but I had expenses to get set up here. I left a lot of loose ends."

"I thought you said there was a lump sum after six months?"

"Oh, I thought there was a big payout."

"I see. Can't I get an advance on that?"

Piggy

"Why not?"

"I understand that, but I need some more. Certainly we can work something out."

"Jane wouldn't want her to starve."

"It is an emergency."

"Oh, I see, like what then?"

"Ah huh," he says shaking his head and mentally taking notes.

"That's why I'm calling, that's exactly why I need more."

"The car had some trouble. I had to take it to the shop. And you know I use that to drive Heather around. Plus, I enrolled her in this fancy art school that she attends on Tuesdays and Thursdays. You ever see any of her drawings?"

"I think she's got a real talent. And you know Jane had no eye, not like me. I've done some art."

"Yup, I paint landscapes. Or I did, before taking over here for Heather. But I know a lot of creative types."

"Anytime, sure thing. Of course, I had to leave most of my stuff behind when I came here."

"Uh-huh. Yes, and she also needs new school clothes and supplies, it's starting up in a few weeks."

"Hmm. How much is that?"

"That's all?"

"I see. Can I get the money now?"

"Fine."

He slams down the phone, "Shit!"

Piggy

Looking around, he grabs his keys. Heading out, he freezes. Turning around, he studies me for a moment. "You're going with me," he orders while motioning with his hand.

At the bank, we don't see any of the people I remember. Dan even asks for Steve, the bank president, but he isn't there. He talks himself up to the teller who seems to have no idea who he or I am. Going on and on about being a single parent, taking care of his dead sister's kid, he lays it on pretty thick. In the car, he slams his hand on the steering wheel knowing that our little show has been wasted on an uninterested audience.

We hit McDonald's and even sit outside to enjoy it. Dan is staring off in space and I decide not to spoil the mood. He suddenly gets up and I follow.

"I gotta find a game."

I look at him uncertain what he means.

We drive for about thirty minutes and pull into a warehousing area. Large semi-trucks are all around, shielding a row of sedans and pickup trucks that are parked outside an entrance on a large rectangular building. The entrance is dark and appears closed; as do all the buildings around the yard. Dan pulls into a parking spot next to a tan sedan.

"You gonna be okay in the truck?"

"Can I come in with you?"

"No, no kids in there. And it's best if you don't make yourself known out here, you understand?"

I don't respond and hide my uneasiness of sitting in a car alone. I tell myself that while he's been in a good mood, it is only a matter of time before it changes. That helps me to conceal my fear as he shuts the door, locks the car, and motions with his hand for me to lie down on the seat. I nod indicating I understand not to let anyone see me in the car and to crouch down. Over the next several hours, I review all the paperwork and maps the car has to offer, chew the last piece of gum that is wedged in the console, trace the outline of the stereo with each of my fingers, and count the air ducts slats. Every time I hear a sound, I duck down. As it gets darker outside, more cars pull up and sometimes people come outside to talk. I can't understand what is said; only that there are men talking around the car. When the light fades away with the sun, there is nothing to peak my attention so I fall asleep.

I awake when Dan opens the door. "Whoo hooo!" he says beaming.

Groggy, I sit up and fasten my seatbelt. He pulls out of the lot and drives. "You should be real proud of your Uncle Dan, I hit it big."

For the next twenty minutes, Dan recounts the plays of note and gives some pointers on what I eventually discover is the game of poker. He's in a good mood and I want to keep him that way so I let him talk, asking follow up questions as appropriate. He pulls into McDonald's and we order again, but this time we eat in the parked car because it's a bit chilly out and Dan can't smoke inside. I have to go to the bathroom so I climb out of the car.

"You're going to wait for me, right?"

"Yes."

I go as quickly as I can and when I return to the parking lot, Dan's car isn't there. I take a few steps off the curb and look around panicked. A loud honk prevents me from tears. I run to the car door and get in. Dan's looking at me and smiling. I smile back. He points ahead of us. I turn to see a large sign across the road, 'Bayside Hospital Emergency Entrance'.

"Let's check this out," he says.

I don't understand, but I go along. He pulls into the back of the lot where a street light has burned out. We walk toward the entrance but hang back twenty feet and stand by a tree. Dan watches the entrance for a while. Eventually, we head in.

"Stay close to me," he says.

We walk through the double doors that automatically open. Going from the darkness of outside to the fully lit up hallway takes some adjusting. There's no one around as Dan and I take careful steps forward. About fifteen feet inside, we pass by an open door with an empty wheelchair in it. Dan motions to me to get in.

"Just play along and don't say anything."

Wheeling me out of the room, we move even slower than before as Dan checks each open door before passing it. At one door, he goes inside leaving me out in the hallway. Returning, he's wearing a white coat on and has a towel to cover my legs. Now we go much faster. Dan pauses at a few signs and decides on our direction. A few people in white coats pass, apparently oblivious to our unlawful intentions. As we approach a nurse's station, Dan fixes his eyes straight ahead and increases speed to pass by quickly; I glance over but see nothing. Once down the corridor, Dan randomly enters rooms. Sometimes he comes out with things – pill bottles, syringes, and small packets, and other times nothing. He snags a blanket from a cleaning bin and drapes it over my lap, an improvement from the towel. He goes back to the bin and searches for something else in the dirty laundry. Finding what he wants he shoves it under the blanket.

We return the same way we came in, although Dan is much more relaxed. He even nods authoritatively to a fellow white coat wearer. Rolling me out to the parking lot, he orders me into the car. He collapses the wheelchair, tosses it in back, and closes the trunk. Looking around the lot a final time, he jumps behind the wheel and drives as fast as he can home.

Pulling onto our street, we pass a car. It's Kelly. Dan pulls into our driveway and watches Kelly park her car. She's alone and seems unaware we have driven past her. Dan watches her intently, but I'm too exhausted. I immediately go to into the house and to bed. The car isn't the most comfortable place to sleep. I'm grateful tomorrow is Tuesday and I can sleep in.

When I get up around eleven, Dan is on the phone.

"Lemme show you want I got to sell and you tell me how much."

"The one over on 76th? Got it, see you soon."

Piggy

He hangs up and sits down to put on his shoes. "I gotta go out."

"Do you want me to come with you?" Although I'm still groggy from the night out, I'm not relishing another day alone.

"Nah, I gotta meet a couple of guys. I'll be home later."

I'm shocked when the front door opens around 4 P.M. Dan is smiling and carrying two bags of groceries and a bag from McDonald's. I rush to help him excited at the prospect of food. My eyes spy a happy meal with an extra side of fries plus a chocolate shake.

"I thought you might be hungry," he says as I grab a handful of fries and shove them in my mouth. "Slow down, Piggy," Dan chuckles.

He goes into the bathroom and eventually the shower is running. I eat my extremely late lunch and then unload the groceries. A fresh supply of Salisbury steak dinners doesn't even invoke the familiar turn in my stomach. I wait on the couch for Dan. He emerges clean shaven, hair combed, and dressed in nice khaki slacks and the white coat from last night.

"How do I look?"

"Good."

Holding up a printed cotton dress with ties in the back at the neck and waist, he says, "And this is for you."

"I like my footie pajamas."

"It's for tonight. We're going back to the hospital. I'm on a streak!" he says. "You know that stuff we took?"

"The pills and needles?"

"Yup, I got some major cash for them. This is gonna be our new gig."

I look at him not certain what to say.

"You did real good last night. You just have to keep it up. Just sit in the chair and look sick. Don't say anything and don't look at anyone. Follow my lead, okay?"

I nod. With a full stomach and Dan happy, I don't care what I do or what I wear. I fall asleep in front of the TV and awake to Dan's shake at eleven.

"We gotta go."

I get dressed and we replay the night before but this time, Dan has more confidence. He shuffles from room to room taking whatever looks valuable. My lap is overflowing with pill bottles and plastic wrapped instruments so Dan places a basket under the wheelchair for additional stash-space. After an hour or so, we approach the exit and Dan inches forward to ensure the coast is clear. We take advantage of the emptiness and make our way back to the car and high tail it out of the parking lot.

As we pull off the main road into the vicinity of our neighborhood, Dan keeps looking in the rear view mirror. He pulls the car over and faces me. A sedan behind us passes and again, it's Kelly. Dan shuts off his lights and follows her at a distance through the neighborhood and onto our street. He pulls next to a curb a few houses down from her house and watches as she gets out of the car alone and goes inside. We wait another fifteen minutes, staring at the dormant driveway. I yearn for sleep and can't figure out why Dan is so intent on watching nothing. I remain silent as I've learned to do with Dan. A few minutes into our impromptu stakeout, Dan starts the car up again and completes our journey home.

The next day drags on but I'm able to nap at daycare. Ms. Parks picks up Susan and me like clockwork and our trip home is uneventful until we pull into my driveway. Mrs. Jones is being wheeled through her front door in a gurney. Susan doesn't notice, barely looking up from the book she is reading. I follow Ms. Parks out of the car and to Mrs. Jones's front door.

"Ethel? How are you?" Ms. Parks calls out through the open doorway.

Piggy

A young black woman with a head full of braids and a pink jumpsuit comes to the door. "Mrs. Jones is under a mild sedative. You should come back later if you want to visit," the nurse says.

Before Ms. Parks can respond, a middle aged balding man replaces the nurse in the doorway. "Can I help you?"

"I'm Kelly Parks from down the street. I didn't realize Ethel would be coming home today. Is she alright?"

"Oh, I'm her son, Roger. She's as good as you can expect after a stroke. She hasn't regained her speech or much of her motor skills, but the doctors are optimistic. Are you two close?"

"No, not very close. I'm just concerned about her. Will she be staying here?"

"Yes, she made me promise years ago that I would never let her stay in the hospital too long. My father died in the hospital so she's always been leery of them. I've made arrangements for full time care here."

"Is there anything I can do to help?" Ms. Parks asks.

"Not right now. I'm staying here for the next few days to make sure she's settled, but then I've got to get back home. I live in Dallas."

"Do you know what happened?"

"Best we can tell, she had a stroke, collapsed, and broke her hip. Mailman found her and called 911."

"How awful. Please let me know if there is anything I can do. I'm just down the street."

"Thank you. I'll tell her you stopped by; although honestly, I'm not sure she understands much. Most of the time, she's confused," he says.

They say their goodbyes and we turn and walk to the gate, passing the dead flowerbeds.

Piggy

"Oh, her poor roses. Without her, they all died," Ms. Parks says.

Yeah, I'll bet the bleach didn't help much either, I think.

Approaching my door, I search my pockets for my key as Ms. Parks knocks. Dan answers on the first knock, surprising both of us.

"Hello," he says smoothly. "Would you like to come in?"

"No, I can't stay. Listen, I wanted to tell you that next week, I'm not going to be able to take Heather to daycare."

"Oh, are you going somewhere?"

"Susan's dad has her for the week, but I'm going to work."

"I see. You've been working a lot lately."

"Yeah, well times are tough and tips aren't what they used to be."

"You still working at O'Malley's?"

"Good memory. Yes, still there."

"Maybe I'll stop in for a drink sometime."

"It's a free country."

"It is that."

"And after next week, I'll be able to take Heather to daycare everyday if you want. Susan's art class is over. Plus, school starts soon."

"Yeah, that would be great. Same arrangement for when school starts?"

"Yes, still fifteen a week?"

Piggy

"Yes."

Ms. Parks turns around before pausing and pivoting back to Dan. "Oh, and have you noticed Heather is bursting out of her clothes?"

"What?"

"She's a kid; she's growing. She can get away with the pants for a little while, but after September, she'll be ridiculed. And..." Kelly looks at me on the couch. "Heather, how are your shoes?"

I shrug.

"Are they tight?" she asks taking three steps into the house and bending down at my feet. Placing her thumb on the toe of my shoe, she presses down. "Yeah, she needs new shoes too."

Dan begins to close the door.

"Hey, don't close that." Getting up quickly, the door swings back open and Dan's hands are up in the air like he's a cowboy being held up.

"Don't get all jumpy, it's a bit cold out."

"Anyway, if you want," she says standing in the doorway, "I can take her with Susan and for an extra sixty, I'll get all her school supplies too."

"Sixty bucks? That's crazy."

"Twenty is for school supplies. The rest is for me to take her shopping for clothes. The clothes and shoes are extra."

"What school supplies does she need?"

"The school sent out a list two weeks ago." She stated. Shaking her head in defeat, "Never mind, I'll bring you a copy. Yes or no, do you want my help?"

"Here's cash for the supplies. I'll take her to get clothes."

Chapter 14

We fall into a routine of late nights either scouring hospitals and the occasional clinic, or having the living room transformed into a poker parlor. Dan has started up a regular game at our house. As much as I didn't like Mrs. Johnson's daycare at first, I'm excited when Susan is back from her dad's and we can play every day.

On the Saturday before school starts, Dan is up around ten. The night before, he won big at poker and he's in a good mood.

"You said you were going to take me shopping for new clothes."

"Huh?"

"New school clothes? It starts Monday."

"Right. Let's go."

Dan drives us to a strip mall that has a Goodwill store and a 7-11.

"Why are we here?"

"You wanted to go shopping."

"Mom always took me to JC Penney's."

"You're a growing kid, why buy new stuff? You're only going to grow out of them again." I look at him, not sure what to say. "Besides, the stuff they have here was sold at a fancy department store once. It'll be just like new."

We enter the store and take in the floor plan which is full of clothing racks. Dan spots an older woman in a Goodwill smock. She's overweight with bright yellow sweatpants on that are stretched so tight, the seams are begging for relief. Turning toward us when she hears the bell on the door, she waddles in place to shift her girth around and position herself behind the counter.

Piggy

"Hello there. I was wondering if you could help me and my niece," Dan says sweetly. "First day of school is Monday and she's growing like a weed. Can you help us find some new outfits and shoes for her?"

She studies Dan up and down for a few moments before pointing, "The racks for her size are over in the far left corner."

Dan smiles at her, but she's already looking down. His charms aren't working, so he tries again, "You know I don't know what's in fashion these days."

She looks up and laughs, "Fashion? You're in the wrong place for that." Smiling, there's a large gap between her two brown-as-dirt front teeth. I wonder if she ever brushes. Her bottom teeth are no better, crisscrossed in several directions with a large chip on one that makes it look like a fang.

"Can you please help us out, I'm lost in a place like this," he smiles broadly again and this time she's looking at me.

Sighing, she says, "Follow me."

We walk over to the corner where she pointed and I survey the overstuffed racks of shirts and pants. The older woman rifles through one rack and occasionally glances back at me, sizing me up.

"Come here," she says motioning for me. She spins me around and pulls at the tag in my waist band. "That's a popular size, there's not going to be too much here."

"She's growing, maybe a size up that she can grow into?" Dan offers.

She continues searching and placing potential items on her arm.

"I'm gonna go to the 7-11 to get some smokes, you two going to be alright?" he asks.

"Don't you care what she gets?"

"Of course I do, but I'm thirsty. You want something?" Dan asks smoothly.

Looking at him over her eyeglasses, she pauses for a moment. Staring right into him as if deciding whether to take a swing at him or answer. "Large cherry slurpee," she says finally.

"Me too," I say hopeful that I can tag onto her order.

"Three slurpees it is. I'll be right back."

Dan is gone for thirty minutes. In that time, I try on all the pants and shirts the grey-haired, brown-toothed woman has found for me. Most are too big, but there are a few I like. There's a Coca-Cola T-shirt that looks new and a pair of jeans that are big in the waist but long enough to touch the ground.

"Here's a safety pin," the woman says as she pins together the waistband to keep them from falling off. "There, those look good."

I smile at myself in the mirror. My dark brown hair is pulled back into a pony tail. It's a bit greasy since I now only wash it on Wednesdays and Sundays. My face still has a smattering of freckles across my nose and cheeks, but my skin is pale. Despite a hot summer, I've been inside most of it – either downstairs at daycare or sleeping the day away at home. I twirl around in the mirror as the woman waddles back with two pairs of tennis shoes and a pair of brown boots. The bell rings at the door and we look up to see Dan back with the drinks.

"You look good," he says inspecting my new outfit. I point to the fitting room door where another shirt, a hoodie, and a sweater are hanging, along with two pairs of corduroys.

The woman is sucking down her slurpee as if it's the first one she's ever had. Coming up for air, she says, "Mmmm, hmmm. Nothing like a slurpee on a hot day is there?"

Dan nods and wanders over to the men's section. I sit on the floor after taking a long drink and try the shoes on. The boots have a big buckle on the side and a zipper. The toe is rounded but they still look a bit cowboy to me. I put them into the pile near the other clothes I've selected. Maybe Dan is right, Goodwill isn't so bad. I decide to

Piggy

wear the tennis shoes since the ones I've come in with have pinched my toes for weeks. The woman and I bring up the items to the counter. Dan is there looking through the glass case at some pocket knives and lighters.

"Can I see these lighters?" he asks as we approach.

The woman walks around the counter and pulls a key from her waist that's attached to a chain. Pulling out a tray which is overflowing with lighters, she sets them on the counter. Several have logos on them for cigarette or whiskey companies. There's one with a turquoise inlaid pattern surrounding a red round stone in the middle. Dan picks that one up and holds it. He bounces it in his hand and then flicks it to light. The flame springs up.

"How much?"

"It's on the bottom."

Flipping the lighter over, "Twenty bucks!"

"I don't set the prices," she says as she fills out an invoice listing the items we've brought to the counter. Dan puts the lighter back in the tray. I make a loud slurping sound as my drink has come to an end.

The woman starts to ring up our total and mentions, "I'll throw in the boots for free 'cause of the slurpee."

"Is that a flask in the case behind you?" Dan points behind her.

She turns to follow his finger. Dan moves swiftly. With his other hand, he palms the lighter and slides it into his pocket. I open my mouth to say something and he glares at me.

"You want to see them?"

"No, just wondering. We'll take the clothes here," Dan says shelling out some bills. Pocketing his change, the woman hands him a plastic bag filled with our purchase and the clothes I came in with.

"Thank you for my new clothes," I say to both of them, smiling.

Chapter 15

School starts and I'm ecstatic to be back in a routine. Dan drags me to various hospitals two nights a week. We get more adept at our larceny. It takes us just a few hours to make our score. Dan trusts me more as I've gotten to be an expert of spotting unattended high-dollar value items from the hallway. He says I'm a natural.

By the end of the September, our visits stop. Poker games and parties replace our hospital thievery. Dan is flush with cash even though he always seems angry after watching sports on TV.

I focus on school, cleaning up around the house, and staying out of Dan's way. I talk him into getting groceries when he's in a good mood and hoard food in my room for the stints when he's not. As the weather turns colder, I'm glad for my boots. My winter coat's sleeves come up to my mid forearm and on a ride home from daycare, Ms. Parks asks about it. When I can't come up with a response fast enough, she pats me on the leg and says, "I'll talk to him."

That night, she walks me up to the door. There are four Harley Davidsons in the driveway and an old beat up blue pickup truck at the curb. Pounding at the door to announce her presence, Dan eventually answers and a rush of smoke comes out when he opens the door. Mixing with the cold air, it turns white and clouds his face for a moment. Inside, the poker table is set up and apparently going strong by the number of beer cans and bottles around the table's perimeter.

"It's five o'clock on a Tuesday and you're playing poker?" Kelly asks.

"Hold your horses, there. Nice to see you, too," Dan says.

Inside, a few of the guys whistle and we overhear, 'What a hottie' and 'Firecracker.'

"It's a school night. What kind of place is this to raise her?"

"Its okay, Ms. Parks, I'll stay in my room," I say attempting to diffuse the tension.

"I don't tell you how to raise your kid; don't be telling me how to raise her."

Piggy

Opening her mouth, Kelly holds back her words and sighs loudly. "She's cold, this barely fits her anymore," she says tugging at my sleeve. "Get her a new coat."

Dan grabs me by the arm and pulls me inside. I take a few steps toward the kitchen but stay within earshot. The guys are laughing, 'You're getting told off by that little thing?' one says.

"Who are you to tell me anything?" Dan snarls.

"What's that supposed to mean? I happen to care about Heather."

"Why don't you focus on your own situation? I'll deal with her."

"Fine," she says shaking her head. "Halloween is this weekend; why don't you let her spend the night and trick or treat with us?"

"Halloween?"

"Yes, it's a big holiday for kids. Besides the neighborhood goes all out. Everyone decorates their front doors and walkways and hands out candy." She stops mid-sentence, "Maybe you should leave your lights off that night. I suspect no one is going to trust candy from you."

"Fine by me. I don't want to be bothered by all the rug rats."

"Great." Ducking her head down to look directly at me as I stand under Dan's outstretched arm, she says, "Heather, I'll see you tomorrow for *school*," she says loudly. "Try to get some sleep through all this," waving her hand at the table.

I nod and walk to my room. It's probably best to not stick around after this confrontation. Dan doesn't talk to me much the rest of the week. He's either enthralled in a baseball game or passed out on the couch. When I come home from daycare on Thursday, there's a baby blue ski coat on my bed. It has a few rips and stains but it fits.

Halloween comes and I race over to Ms. Parks' house around two in the afternoon. Her sewing machine is out in the front room and there are fabric and yarn pieces all over the floor.

"Close your eyes," Ms. Park instructs as Susan is smiling wide next to her.

When I open them, Ms. Parks is holding a pair of light blue overalls with a red and white plaid shirt and matching hat in front of me. Susan is holding a similar outfit but hers is a dress and she has a red yarn wig on her head.

"I thought you two could be Raggedy Ann & Andy," says Ms. Parks.

I'm so happy I cry. We spend the next few hours helping to finish the costumes and painting our faces to look like the dolls. Ms. Parks makes us look almost like twins.

As it starts to get dark, there's a knock and Susan runs to answer the door.

"Susan's dad is going to trick or treat with us," Ms. Parks tells me.

Built like an athlete, Mr. Parks strolls into the room with a green tracksuit on. Tanned with shiny black hair that's cropped real short, he has the whitest teeth I've seen. He looks like the guy selling the tooth whitening paste on TV. An aroma fills my nostrils. It's him who smells so good. Dan always reeks of cigarette smoke and is rarely clean shaven let alone having fresh breath or white teeth.

"Who's this?" Mr. Dreamy asks.

"This is Heather, Jane's daughter."

"Oh, yes, hello Heather. You probably don't remember me, but I met you when you were real little," he says as he bends down and I breathe in his cologne and gaze into his blue eyes. If there is such a person as Prince Charming, I think he'd look like Mr. Parks.

"She's coming with us tonight."

Piggy

He nods not looking at Kelly. Leaving the house exactly when the street lights come on, we knock off one whole side of the street before seeing another kid. We cross the street and head to my house. Susan and I are already discussing future candy trades when we pass by my house. There are no outdoor lights on but you can see a sliver of light behind the curtain in the front room. As we walk past, I see someone looking out. We continue down the street passing Mrs. Jones's house which is also dark. She's still bedridden and Ms. Parks told me she hasn't improved much.

Footsteps echo behind us. "Where's my little Heather?" Dan says. We all turn around as Dan gives me a hug and takes a look at my costume. "How cute," he says in the fakest tone I've heard out of him. "Thank you so much, Kelly for getting Heather here a costume."

Kelly is speechless. Finally, Mr. Dreamy extends his hand to Dan. "I'm Pete, Kelly's ex-husband."

"How do you do? I'm Dan, Heather's uncle."

"Kelly told me about Jane. I'm sorry for your loss."

"Yeah, what a shame that was. But you know, God's got a plan."

Kelly and I exchange looks trying to identify who this person is in front of us. Remembering my role, I take a step toward Dan so he can put his arm around me. 'Go along with whatever I do' he always tells me on our hospital trips and something tells me this is one of those times.

"You here to trick or treat with your little one?"

"Yeah, I don't get to see her very much so any opportunity I can, I take."

"Hmm. Well, I best be getting back."

"Do you want to join us?"

"Yes, Dan, wouldn't you like to join us so you can see your little angel trick or treat?" Kelly chimes in.

"Thanks. Thank you both, but when Kelly told me about the sleepover, I thought I'd enjoy a night out on my own. You know how little time you have with little ones at home."

"I sure remember when Susan was little, and I'll soon be familiar with that again."

"Oh?"

"My second wife is expecting our first."

"Hmm." Dan stares a bit too long. "Congratulations, that's great news."

"We should get going. I don't want to keep the girls out too late," Kelly interjects.

"You all have a great night. Bring her back anytime tomorrow, Kelly," Dan says as he turns around.

We canvass the next two blocks before returning home and taking inventory of our loot. Mr. Dreamy leaves almost as soon as we get back. Susan and I stay up late as we sort our candy into piles and then trade the kinds we don't like with each other.

Chapter 16

It's mid-November and Ms. Parks drops me off from daycare as usual. I pull out my key to insert it into the lock. Dan whips the door open and pulls me inside. Slamming it shut, he slaps me across the face.

"Who'd you talk to?" he screams.

I fall against the curtains clutching my cheek. Another blow brushes by the top of my head as I slide down the wall. Putting my hands over my head, Dan's rant continues.

"Who'd you tell Piggy? Who!"

He grabs my wrists and pulls me up. His face is beet red and there are droplets of spit at the sides of his mouth. I cry shaking my head.

"What did you say!"

"I'm sorry," I say, not knowing what any of this is about.

"Who!"

"I don't know what you're talking about."

He yanks my arm hard and shoves me down on the couch. Getting right in my face, I can smell the cigarettes and whiskey on his breath. He places his hand on my chest and pushes me into the couch, leaning with all his weight. I gasp for air.

"Who!"

"I don't know, I don't know, I don't know," I plead, mouthing it the last few times because I can't get any sound out.

He leans back and grabs his smokes. Lighting up, he sits in the chair across from me and glares.

"You have no idea?"

Piggy

I shake my head and rearrange myself from the uncomfortable position he's twisted me into. He looks out the window, staring at the curtains. I mentally make myself invisible, a skill I've gotten good at. Eventually, Dan's face returns to a natural color.

"Well someone," he says, "*Someone* called social services on us." I stare back at him and make my expression as blank as possible.

"Social services, you hear me?"

"They knocked on the door today, out of nowhere. Sat out there for twenty minutes ringing the bell. I had to hide here all day."

"You listening? Social services can mess up what we got here, Piggy. They can send you to an orphanage. You'll be a slave, beaten every day, forced to work for nothing. No clean bed or nice warm house like here. You won't be able to do what you want. No food neither. No one will ever see you again."

"You'll just disappear," he said flickering his fingers upward.

"You want that?" he asks. "You want to be forced to live in a dungeon? Be a slave?"

"I didn't say anything to anyone," I protest.

"Who did?"

"I don't know."

He stands up and dictates, "Here's what we're gonna do. You're going to clean this entire place up so that it's spic and span. I don't want to see one speck of dirt anywhere."

"They're coming back?" I ask.

"Of course they are. Those people don't just go away. I had to call them and tell them we wouldn't be home until Saturday."

"When are they coming?"

"Saturday, you fool! What'd I just say?"

Piggy

"That we wouldn't be home until Saturday."

"You watch, they'll be here. Coming around to check on us. I know these types. They want to surprise us. Try to catch me in something. Well, you're gonna wash up and look presentable. We're gonna fill the fridge with food and we're gonna be the happiest fucking family that we can be."

I nod.

"And you're not gonna say one word to fuck this up!"

Saturday morning arrives and Dan shakes me at 6:30 A.M. I stick my head out from under the seven blankets I've used since Wednesday. Dan has left the windows open to air out the smoke.

"It's freezing," I moan.

"I turned the heat on and closed the windows. Get up and get ready."

The house has been spotless since Thursday and the fridge is full. I slowly get out of bed and immediately wrap a blanket around me. Trudging to the bathroom, the cold tiles leech through my two pairs of socks and footie pajamas. I wash up and brush my teeth, thankful I took a bath the night before. Dan comes in and combs my hair into pigtails and ties a ribbon on each side.

"It's the details, kid. Always focus on the details," he says.

He's clean shaven, wearing his nicest pants and a shirt and tie he got at Goodwill. We went Thursday after school and Dan got me a new dress for the occasion. When Ms. Parks saw Dan pick me up from school, I thought she was going to swallow a bug, her mouth was open long enough.

We sit in silence. I finish my bowl of cereal and wash the bowl. Dan is on his third cup of coffee. His leg is bouncing on the ground like a jackhammer. He looks over to the kitchen drawer at regular intervals. His smokes are in the drawer. There's no trash in the trash cans and last night, Dan took the stuff we had in garbage cans to the McDonald's dumpster. He wanted no hint of a beer bottle in sight.

His bouncing leg and frequent yearning looks to the forbidden drawer are soon accompanied by his fingers rattling on the table. He gets up for the fourth time and I think he's going to take off his tie again. He's taken it off and put it back on two times already. Instead, he goes to my bedroom and returns with a coloring book and crayons.

"Here, look normal."

There is only one uncolored page in the book, but I don't say anything. I color the used pages, saving the one page for when they come. Another hour passes and there's a knock at the door.

Dan jumps up pausing to take a deep breath at the door. Once last piercing look at me and he opens the door.

"Yes, can I help you?"

"Mr. Howard? I'm Janet Shandling from Health and Family Services. Can I come in?"

She's young, maybe twenty-five, with short curly red hair. She's wearing a navy blue skirt with a matching blazer and an ivory collared shirt underneath. The skirt hits at her knees showing off shapely legs. She takes two steps into the house, the heels of her black pumps sinking into the carpeting. Under different circumstances, Dan would be all over her.

"It's a pleasure meeting you," he says shaking her hand. "I got your card the other day when I got home. Sorry I wasn't here when you came by."

"That's okay, it was in the middle of the day."

"What can I do for you?"

"I'm here on an informal visit to see how you and Heather are doing."

"Heather, honey, meet Ms. Shandling."

Piggy

I dutifully walk over to her and offer my hand, just like Dan taught me. "How do you do?"

"Isn't that sweet, I do fine and yourself," she smiles.

"Where are my manners? Can I get you a cup of coffee or anything?" Dan swoons.

"No, thank you."

"Please, please, sit down."

We take our places on the couch. I sit next to Dan and kick my feet back and forth slightly. Dan said it looked cute when my feet couldn't touch the ground. Ms. Shandling sits in the chair across from us.

"This is an informal visit?"

"Yes, my agency is responsible for the welfare of children and anytime we have someone in a new situation, such as yourself, we like to check up and make sure everything is okay."

"It isn't new anymore. I've been living here since end of March. And I've been Heather's legal guardian since May," he says looking down, pausing for effect, and then adding, "Since my dear sister, Jane, passed away."

"Yes. Please accept my condolences. It was a car accident wasn't it?"

Shaking his head in agreement, he squeaks out a tear. "Yes, horrible, horrible situation."

"Can you tell me how things have been going since March?"

"Sure. Well, I won't lie; it was a bit of an adjustment for me, but a great one at that. You know I'm single and never so much as had a dog, let alone a little angel like Heather. But things are great. We're in a routine now and things are just fine."

"Are you working now?"

Piggy

"Oh, no not right now. I want to be here for Heather. Make sure she gets through this transition."

"Heather, could you go to your room for a minute so I can talk to your uncle?" she asks.

Dan feigns surprise and then graciously pulls his hand away from me. "Go on, go play with your toys."

"Nice to meet you," I say as I walk to the hallway. I open and shut my door before returning to my spot around the corner from the living room.

"Any issues with Heather?"

"No, she's doing good. I couldn't have asked for better. And as for my sister Jane, she's taken care of us, so I don't have to go to work yet. But when Heather is more settled, I'll find something," he says. Then quickly adding, "Something flexible which allows me to be here for her."

"As you said you're a single guy, any parties or late nights?"

"Oh, no, I'm not one for that anymore. Maybe the occasional friend will stop by but they're gone by eight."

"I reviewed a police report and it shows that they answered a disturbance call at this address."

"Ah, it must have been a mistake."

"No this is the address on the report. The report shows the call was answered after midnight on July 10th. It goes on to say that there were forty people in the house, there were several open containers, and loud music."

"Oh, July. Yes that was a celebration for a dear friend. I'll admit my guests stayed too late, but that was months ago. And school was out."

"No other parties?"

Piggy

"Nope."

"No poker games, perhaps?"

Taking a while to answer, Dan finally says, "How does your agency work exactly?"

"I told you we're concerned with the welfare of children."

"But for those in foster care or something else, right? I'm her legal guardian. I'm family. I don't remember anything about the guardianship being under the review of Family Services."

"Ah, in some cases," she stammers.

"What about my case is some cases?"

"Ah, um. Actually, we got a report from a concerned party."

"Really, who?"

"I'm not at liberty to say."

After a long pause, "Oh, yes, I did have one poker game. I'd forgotten about it as it wasn't supposed to be here. My best friend from high school turned thirty-five and some other friends and I threw him a surprise party. It was supposed to be at my other friend's house, but he had a plumbing issue. At the last minute, we had it here."

"I see, and Heather?"

"I had a sitter for Heather that night; she wasn't supposed to be here. But then the sitter got sick or what was it again.... Anyway, it was a coincidence that she came home and the game was still going on. But we wrapped it up early."

"Oh."

"I'm not much of a poker player. I always lose. Nope gambling is not my thing. You gamble?"

"Ahh, no."

Piggy

"Yeah, I only did it for my buddy because it was his birthday. But since you brought it up, I'll make sure that doesn't happen again. Now, is there anything else?"

"Can I get a tour of the house while I'm here?"

"Absolutely. My sister, she bought a fine house. Real cute."

I'm at my door quietly turning the handle and barely get inside when I hear their voices enter the hallway. I pull out several stuffed animals and plant myself on the floor. The door swings open.

"This is Heather's room. How you doing, Heather? You playing?" Dan says as sweet as pie.

Ms. Shandling is taking notes.

"It's pink. What little girl doesn't like pink? And down here is my room, well it was my sister's room."

Their voices fade into the living room. The front door opens and I sneak back down the hallway.

"Nice meeting you. I hope I answered all your questions."

"Yes, thank you for meeting with me," she says as the front door closes.

I peek around the corner and Dan's back is to the door. I start to say something but he puts his finger to his lips to keep me quiet. We listen for a car door and the sound of it pulling away before he speaks.

"Bitch!" he shouts looking across the room. Moving his gaze to me, "I don't want you talking to Ms. Parks anymore!"

"Are you going to take me to school from now on?"

His face is tight with anger and he stares at the ground for a moment. "No! But you say nothing. Just hello, goodbye. Nothing else. Nothing you hear!"

Piggy

    I nod, stepping back into the hallway not wanting to stir anything up. Dan goes to the curtains and pulls them back to look out. Grunting into the glass, he turns and immediately gets his smokes out of the drawer. He opens the fridge then slams it shut. Grabbing his keys, he leaves without a glance back.

Chapter 17

The familiar sounds of snoring fill the living room as I walk down the hallway on Sunday. Dan hadn't come home when I went to bed. A kitchen chair is in front of the picture window facing out. Dan is sprawled out as much as he can be on an upright chair; head flopped back, snoring up a storm. The curtains are open and the morning sun is streaming in. There's a gurgling sound, followed by a lapse in his breathing, as his head suddenly jerks forward and into the sunshine. It only takes a few moments before the bright sun wakes him up. Groggy, he sits up straight and looks around.

"Start the kettle," he orders.

I comply; also getting a glass of water and bring it to him. He takes it but isn't awake enough to know what to do with it. Gazing at me, I reach down and pick up his cigarettes and hand them to him.

"Thanks, Piggy."

A few minutes later, pulled together, Dan joins me in the kitchen and fills a mug with instant coffee in preparation for the hot water. I'm polishing off the last bowl of cereal.

"Anyone come by yesterday?"

"No. And I wouldn't open the door if they did. You told me not to."

"Good." Rubbing his neck and rolling it from side to side, his bones creak. "I'm gonna lie down in the bed for a while. Don't answer the door."

Monday morning, Ms. Parks is out front, honking her horn. Dan has instructed me to wait in the kitchen until he allows me to leave. The honking continues until finally there is a knock on the door.

"Heather, it's me."

Dan opens the door.

"Oh, ahh... Where's Heather?"

"You got time to talk now?" he says as I stand out of sight near the kitchen doorway. I can see her through the door crack.

"No, sorry, I'm in a hurry."

"Certainly, we can chat for a few minutes."

"Listen, sorry about the other night, but O'Malley's is swamped on Saturdays."

"You got anything to tell me?"

"I really got to run."

"It was you, wasn't it?"

"What?"

"You called social services."

She loses all expression from her face. "I gotta go, is Heather here?"

"You called them and told them to come check up on me." The muscles in his hand flex against the edge of the door. "Didn't you!"

"Look, Dan."

"Who do you think you are?"

"Dan, let me explain."

"Fuck your explanation, bitch. Don't you ever say another word to them again."

"This isn't a good environment for her. You've never raised a kid, maybe she should be in a different place."

"Shut up, you listen to me. You don't say another word to them or to anybody."

"Dan."

"They call you, you tell them you were mistaken. Everything's fine. I'm a great uncle, you hear!"

"Dan, I'm not going to lie for you."

"Don't get up on your high horse and say shit like that. You ain't better than me."

"I gotta go, is she here or not?"

"What do you think your ex would say if I told him you're working nights and leaving little Suzy home alone?"

Color drains from her face as if a plug has been pulled.

"Yeah, scared? You should be. You think I haven't noticed?" He opens the door a bit wider revealing me in the kitchen doorway. "I've seen you coming home late, heck, we've both seen you. And no babysitter comes out neither."

She is moving her lips a little but nothing is coming out.

"That's like child endangerment, isn't it? Leaving a little kid in a house at night all alone. I bet Petey would be real interested to hear that."

"Noooo," she stammers, "Please don't tell him."

"Yeah, well you didn't keep your big mouth shut, why should I?"

"I need the money, please."

"Petey and his little wife would probably love another kid at home. Heck, like a built in babysitter for them. I'd betcha he'd make it worth my while if I told him."

"No, please, don't!"

"Not to mention what kind of accidents can happen to a little kid..... alone.... in a house.... at night."

"No! Please don't!"

"Don't what?"

"I'll call them back and tell them I was mistaken," she says.

"What else?"

"I'll tell them that I lied and that we had a fight over something. I'll tell them that you're the best uncle."

"Don't go overboard."

"Whatever you want me to say, I'll say it."

"And you keep picking her up," he nudges my shoulder, "Taking her to school and daycare for nothing."

"Okay, please, please, don't tell him. I can't lose Susan."

For a long time, he stares directly at her. No emotion on his face. "Go on, get to school," he says pushing me out the door. Leaning toward Kelly, "Don't you forget this. Don't fuck with me or I'll fuck you over and your kid too."

Kelly turns and quickly walks to the car. She beats me inside. Shaking, she bursts out into tears.

"What happened, mommy?" Susan asks.

"Nothing honey, nothing, mommy got something in her eye."

"Mommy?" Susan whines looking back and forth at me and her mom.

"Its fine, sweetie," Kelly murmurs after a few blocks.

Chapter 18

Thanksgiving weekend, Dan and I are out doing the hospital tours again. It's been over a month since we've gone. I had thought we were done with it, but when I got home from school Wednesday, Dan was on the phone.

"*I understand your concern, John, but raising a little girl is expensive. Can't I get another advance?*"

"*What do you mean there's no more?*"

"*Oh, what about the other account?*"

"*Certainly, I could get another advance, or even a loan, against that.*"

"*I see.*"

"*No, no. I'm sure it's temporary.*"

Hanging up, Dan punched the wall, causing a dent and cracking the paint. The next morning he told me we'd be going out again. Instead of eating a roast turkey drumstick with hazelnut and cranberry stuffing, I'm shivering, in a lightweight cotton wrap with a flimsy robe that hangs down just above my knees. Dan won't let me wear anything under the pajamas. "Details" he says.

There are a few hospitals that yield better results than others, so we go to those first. Normally, it's dead quiet as we cruise through the hallways, but tonight the emergency room is jam packed with families, often one person is holding up a bloody towel in their hand; an apparent carving knife accident. Initially, Dan is nervous, seeing all the people, but the first room we check, we score two big handfuls of pill bottles. Dan quietly unloads our take into the black canvas bag, which Dan has affixed under our wheelchair. The bag holds a lot more than the basket ever did.

"Orderly!" an unfamiliar voice says from behind. Dan picks up the pace. "Orderly!" Turning the corner, a nurse taps him on the shoulder. She has caught up to him. Short white hair with cat glasses that hide her eyes, she is close to sixty.

Piggy

"I need you in Exam Room Five," she says.

Dan looks at her then down at me. "I'm taking this girl to X-ray."

"She looks fine, is it urgent?" Dan pauses not sure how to respond. "I can take her," she says.

Reaching for the handles, she carts me down the hallway. Stopping after a few steps to look back at Dan, "Clean up the floor and exam table and do a round for linens."

I look back at Dan uncertain what to do. He has a terrified look on his face and mouths something to me that I don't get.

"How you doing, honey?" the nurse asks.

"Okay," I answer now wishing I had pretended to be asleep before she saw me.

"What's your name?"

"Susan," I reply per Dan's instructions.

"What are you getting X-rayed?"

What? My eyes scan the floor, walls, and ceiling as if there is an appropriate answer written somewhere. "I don't know," I manage to say.

Slowing down at the elevator door, "Where's your chart?" she asks running her hand on the back and sides of the chair.

"I don't know," I answer as I sense her bending down to look under the chair. "Aw!" I scream.

"What is it, Susan?" the nurse says popping back up.

"My stomach hurts," I say using what had been my 'I want to stay home from school voice'.

Piggy

"That's why you're here, to get better," she says as my mind races through escape plans.

"Sara, help!" a voice down the hallway hollers. Saved, I turn to see another nurse in yellow scrubs, wheeling a cart into a room.

"Code Blue!" the yellow clad nurse yells again.

The older nurse rolls me to the room that the cart has disappeared into. Parking me outside, she locks down the wheels. "Stay here for a minute, sweetie."

Once out of sight, I grab the wheels and push, but nothing happens. I run my hand around the top of the right wheel and find the lever that is tightened across the wheel. Releasing it, I push the wheels forward again. This time, spinning the chair around, but still stuck in the same spot. My breathing becomes shallow and the slightest sound is amplified. Frantically looking for the other lever, it feels as if ten minutes has passed. Then it hits me, I can walk. I get up to make a run for it. Suddenly, Dan is behind me pulling me back into the chair by my shoulder. Throwing a bag onto my lap and unlocking the brake, he pushes me fast, so fast I nearly fall out around the corner. We head down the hall following signs for the exit.

Once in the parking lot, we throw the chair and bags into the trunk and peel out with the doors still ajar and no seat belts on.

"Whew, that was close," Dan says laughing.

He's enjoying this? I think.

"We won't go back to that place. Did you say anything to that nurse?"

"Nothing."

"Good, good thinking. You're good at this."

I look intently at him. Sniffing, I smell urine. Opening my robe, I reach under my gown and feel a wet spot.

"Got good stuff. Got a lot of stuff," Dan goes on not noticing me.

"One more stop," he says.

"No!"

"What's your problem?"

"I peed."

"What?"

"I peed."

"You can't see it in the chair."

"I can't go out like this."

"Sure you can. Besides it's almost like you're in character."

"No."

"One stop. I promise it'll be short. Then we'll go wherever you want for dinner. You name it."

It's pointless to fight. I won't win.

The next hospital yields a modest score before we pull into Wendy's for a Frosty shake and fries and call it Thanksgiving dinner.

Piggy

Chapter 19

Ms. Parks won't come near our house. I walk to and from the curb each day. We barely talk in the car and now I only see Susan during the week; our weekend play dates cancelled.

The hospital visits have become a twice a week chore, but we're much more seasoned now. Dan has gotten a clipboard so there's a chart when asked. I'm not sure whose paperwork he's taken for my cover and I wonder whether someone isn't getting the right medicine because their chart can't be found. I've taken to wearing my hair different ways and sometimes putting a bandana on. I avoid eye contact at all times.

It's more comfortable to get around the hallways now. Even though we rotate the hospitals, not visiting any location more than once every two months, every hospital seems to have the same basic floor plan. The real risk is getting in and out of the hospital without anyone asking why an orderly would bring a young sick girl out to the parking lot.

We've got our expeditions down to a routine so that it only takes an hour or two each night. Often, Dan leaves me in the wheelchair by the supply room. He then goes and plays orderly. Spilling something near the nurse's station only to have to clean it up which, of course, requires access to the supply room for cleaning materials. His favorite is spilling half full specimen cups which roll all over the place and take a long time to clean up. He says it's like herding cats and people can't keep their eyes off someone running around like an idiot. As soon as the supply room door is open and the staff has become our intended spectators, I sneak in and swipe the good stuff. Dan has shown me what to look for and what's worth the most -- mainly pills, vials, and needles.

The weather has gotten colder, but then California never gets that cold. There is a decoration domino effect in our neighborhood, as house after house puts up Christmas lights and gets a tree. At night, I admire the neighbors' decorated trees lit up through their picture windows. I don't want to provoke Dan and something tells me, asking for a tree would do it. Staring out the window, I am startled by a set of eyes looking straight back at me. I jump away from the window.

"What?" Dan says. He's in his usual position on the couch watching TV.

Piggy

"Someone is out there."

"Who?"

"I don't know. This guy. In a car."

Dan goes into the kitchen to look out a different window. The lights are off in there but he still eases the edge of the curtain up. Dan stands up quickly.

"Who is it?"

He doesn't answer me; instead he stares at the ground thinking. He walks to the sink and puts his cigarette out. "Get all them bottles cleaned up and in the trash. Hide 'em."

I grab the bottles closest to me as Dan walks out the front door. He doesn't close it all the way, instead leaving it ajar. I help it out with a nudge and it swings wide open. I don't care about the loss of heat; I want to know who this is. Dan is making a beeline to a four door black sedan parked across the street. A large man gets out when Dan is nearly at the car. They shake hands and turn toward the house. I ramp up my cleaning efforts as I see they are headed this way. Dragging the full trash can into Dan's room, I shut the bedroom door. I throw the dirty dishes and fast food containers under the sink. Next I run the circuit with a damp towel to wipe off the surfaces, grabbing the overflowing ashtray and Dan's smokes in the process. I hear them at the doorway, just as I've made it to the kitchen with the paraphernalia.

"Heather?" Dan calls out to me.

"Yes, Uncle Dan?" I say walking into the living room.

"You remember John, ah, Mr...?"

"Mr. Robertson," John interjects. "How are you Heather?"

"I'm great."

We engage in a brief staring contest.

"I thought I'd stop by and say hello." Looking at me, John says, "I haven't seen you since, ah, well since your mom's service."

"Uncle Dan and I are getting on fine," I say realizing when I said it, I wasn't asked yet.

"Go on, now. Go to bed, I'll be in a few minutes to read you a story," Dan says.

"Good night, Mr. Robertson. It was nice of you to stop by."

"Aren't you the little hostess? It was nice seeing you. Good night."

"What can I do for you?"

"Just checking in. Everything going okay?"

"Yep."

"Car's running?"

"The brakes are a bit skittish."

"I thought you replaced those a few months ago."

"I did. But I gotta take it back to the place and have them take a look. I think they did something wrong, it doesn't feel right. You want a cup of coffee or something?"

"Sure."

"Let me put the teapot on, all I've got is instant."

"Oh, no I don't want to be any trouble."

"Fine. I won't. You're probably saving me from being awake all night. Have a seat." Dan says.

"I can only stay a minute."

Piggy

"Anyway, the service station will take care of me," Dan continues. "They'll fix the brakes if anything is wrong. Of course, I was thinking of having them check the tires while I was in. You know bald tires are an accident waiting to happen."

"You should definitely have them take a look."

"Of course, they may cost a pretty penny to replace."

"Dan, I didn't come here to give you more money."

"I know, I was just saying."

"Dan, there is no more money. Except for the monthly checks, that is."

"What do you mean?"

"You choose to take what was discretionary as a lump sum when you first became guardian."

"Yeah, and that was the only way I could settle my things and move here."

"I thought you lived in Victorville."

"Outskirts, but that's still sixty miles away."

"Then you took out a big chunk of the emergency account, when you had the car problems."

"Yeah, but I didn't get it all."

"No. No, there's still some emergency fund left. About three quarters of it, but it's coming up on nine months since Jane died. That fund has to last you until Heather is eighteen."

"But the checks still come."

"Yes, until she's eighteen, you will continue to get a check as long as you're her guardian."

"What do you mean, as long as I'm her guardian?"

"Nothing. I'm just stating the facts."

"Uh huh. So why'd you come?"

"I came to see how you were doing. And to make sure you understood the situation. You've run through a fair amount of the trust already. I want to make sure you're going to be able to make what's left work out for you."

"I can make it work. But you know, kids are expensive, especially girls."

"Yes, they can be. But Jane more than provided for Heather. I'd hate to see her denied anything once she gets into junior high and then high school."

"We're doing great. Don't you worry. I can make do on that monthly check."

"It's just that, to date, you haven't. Are you sure you can do it going forward?"

"Yup, besides, now that we're through the transition, I'm going to look for a job after Christmas."

"You got anything in mind?"

"Construction probably, that's what I've done before."

"Really? I didn't know you worked construction."

"Yeah, yeah. I'm more the general contractor."

"Great. I don't know anyone in that industry, but I'll help out in any way I can."

"Of course, as a general contractor you really gotta be set up in your own business to make any money. And that takes capital."

"Dan, there is no more money."

"This wouldn't be an advance or anything, more a loan."

"No, the terms of the trust allow for some emergency funds but start ups aren't covered."

"Don't worry about it. I'll get a job on the bottom. You know, work myself up the ladder. I've done it plenty of times."

"Good." After a long pause, John continues, "I better be going. My wife is waiting for me."

"Thank you so much for stopping by. I really appreciate it."

"Sure thing. You take care." John says as the door shuts.

Chapter 20

Christmas break was filled with poker games, parties, and football games. Dan was happy and we skipped a few hospital trips because he was flush with cash. He even got me some new puzzles, a board game, and coloring books for Christmas. There they were wrapped silver paper with a bow on each box one morning when I got up. Sure it was the day after Christmas, but he still got me something.

Dan's winning streak continued both for football games and poker into January. That all changed during the playoffs. Dan started to lose and his intensity grew with each game. Single win stints were briefly celebrated before his focus quickly shifted to the next game.

Dan invited Jay over to watch the Super Bowl. I was told to be quiet, not to ask questions, and to never walk in front of the TV. When I wanted a soda, I was to walk the long way around the couch to the kitchen. We ordered pizza but Dan didn't eat much. His anger was on a steady incline throughout the day. When the team he bet on lost, he threw his beer bottle at the wall. Unfortunately, it hooked to the right and smacked dead center into the TV screen. Sparks flew everywhere and the room went completely dark. Dan's rant continued despite Jay's efforts to calm him down.

After the fuse box was found and light was restored, Dan and Jay split a bottle of whiskey. I overheard Jay say things like 'Stu will be wanting his money tomorrow' and 'I thought you had the cash'. Most of the time I couldn't decipher their mumbles.

The next afternoon, I return from school to an empty house, a regrettably common event. I get the vacuum out and drag it into the living room. Dan hadn't done a good job cleaning up after the game and I can see glass still in the carpet. Just as I finish vacuuming, I hear his car pull into the driveway and I retreat to my room.

Entering, he is silent except for the sounds of his coming home routine – keys clinking on the table, door slamming, fridge opening and the popping sound of a bottle cap.

"What the hell?" he says loudly.

Piggy

I freeze; mentally flipping through images of the living room. I try to remember anything I may have put out of place, anything dirty I've left out, but I come up with nothing. What had I done? What was he angry about? I hide in my closet hoping he'll think I'm still at daycare. Then nothing. Not a sound. He isn't coming down the hallway; he isn't doing anything.

Rustling up courage to enter the living room, I find him staring into space on the couch. There's a letter in his hand.

"Do you want me to heat up some dinner?" I ask.

As if I've broken the trance, he glances my way. "Sure."

"Anything particular?"

"I don't care," he says. Adding, "No chicken," when I'm in the kitchen.

I bring the meals to the coffee table as Dan hates getting up. I glance at the letter, its two pages long and looks official. The State of California Seal is at the top. Dan notices my overt looks and picks it up, folds it, and places it between the cushions.

I wait until the next morning to look for it. Pulling up all the cushions, there's nothing but finely ground potato chips. I pause at Dan's door; he sleeps like the dead in the morning, maybe I can pull it from his pants. My search is interrupted by Ms. Parks' car honking.

When I come home from daycare, Dan is out so I scour the house but still can't find the letter. I settle in for what I think will be a night alone. I bring out my stuffed animals and Betty into the living room to play, when a loud bang makes me jump. Someone has punched the door, not the typical repeated knocking. I go to the curtains and peek out. He's big. His head is nearly level with the outside light. Black leather vest with a black T-shirt underneath, the guy's gut sticks out far. He's got a stringy beard that's long, hitting the middle of his chest. Sunglasses shield his eyes, I guess from the streetlight glare.

"Who is it?"

"Get Dan."

"He can't come to the door."

"Kid, open up."

"Please come back."

"Dan!" he screams and strikes another blow on the door.

"Please come back, he can't come to the door."

"Let me in!"

"He's in the shower."

"I don't give a fuck if he's taking a shit, I want to see him."

"Please come back," I repeat all of my memorized phrases. I take a step away from the window in hopes that he'll leave. Instead, he launches his body against the door. Repeating the blow a few times, the door swings wide open and a piece of wood goes flying. I scream and run back to my room and into the closet.

I hear him going from room to room. Eventually swinging open my door, the door knob finds its familiar indentation in the wall, which has undoubtedly been made bigger by this guy. I can't help but cry out in fear. A thick hand reaches into the closet and drags me out.

Crying, I scream, "He's not here."

"Where is he?"

"I don't know."

"Where is he?"

"I swear, I don't know."

"Why'd you say he was here?"

"He told me to never tell anyone I was here alone."

"Shit." Looking around, "Get up."

Walking back to Dan's bedroom, he rifles through the drawers and tosses furniture around. "What does he have?"

"What do you mean?"

"Does he have a stash of cash, anything of value?"

"He keeps all the cash with him."

"Any idea where he is?"

"I don't know where he goes."

He stares at me.

"He's gone to a poker game before."

"Where?"

"I only went once. It was in a warehouse area."

"What was around it?"

"I don't know. We drove on the freeway for a long time."

I follow him out to the living room. Cold air blasts through the door that is hanging, diagonally, from one hinge.

"You tell him. Stu was here. Stu." I nod. "Tell him Stu wants to see him."

Chapter 21

Dan comes home a few hours later. I've propped a chair against the door but it isn't close to shut. I'm in my room, huddled under the covers when I hear him call out to me. I run out to the living room.

"What the hell happened?"

"Stu was here," I stammer.

Dan's angry expression vanishes.

"He was big."

"What'd he say?"

"He grabbed me."

"What'd he say?"

"He wants to see you."

Plopping down on the couch, Dan stares at the broken TV, "Get me a beer, would ya."

"He ripped apart your room."

Dan isn't fazed. Emotionless, his stare is unbroken. "Did he take anything?"

"I don't think so," I say slowly. Why wasn't he upset?

"Go to bed. You gotta get up for school tomorrow."

"I don't have school tomorrow; it's Saturday."

No answer.

"Dan?"

"Go to bed," Dan commands.

The next day, Dan fixes the front door. The door basically falls off when you open it, but at least now it shuts. He's real proud as I follow him outside to review his accomplishment. Smiling, Dan reaches for the knob. It spins around, but does nothing.

"Shit! Go around back and crawl through the window," he orders.

I run along the side of the house and in a few moments, I'm opening the front door, pleased with the speed I make it inside. Dan's attention is down the street. He's watching Ms. Parks packing up a pickup truck with furniture and boxes. There's a short muscular man helping her, but it isn't Mr. Parks. Dan walks slowly to her as if a magical string is pulling him. I follow him, keeping out of sight. Reaching her house, I hunch down behind her mailbox and survey the scene.

"What's going on?" Dan asks approaching Kelly.

She looks up as the unidentified man disappears into her house.

"I'm taking a load over to my sister's."

"You moving?"

"Yeah, end of the month. I only have this truck so it's going to take several trips."

"Why are you moving?"

"My sister lives across town. She's got a spare room for me."

"But why?"

"It'll work better for me."

"You still gonna pick up the kid?"

Piggy

"The kid? You know, she has a name. By the way, thanks for your concern."

"You gonna pick her up or not?"

"For the next week."

"What about this place?" he actually sounds like he's just been dumped.

"I think I'm going to rent it out, if I can. Money's been tight for a while. I had to pick up a second job, as you know."

She walks up to him and stands real close, "But this way, my sister can watch Susan at night, while I'm working, and I don't have to worry about an asshole like you breathing down my neck."

"Fuck off, you turned me in first."

"Screw yourself. You're a horrible person. Who the hell knows what's going on over there? You have no business having a child anywhere near you. And you threaten me?"

"I could still tell him."

"Go ahead, I've solved the problem. Besides, it would be your word against mine. And who do you think Family Services is going to believe?"

"Don't you fucking call them."

"Don't you say a word to my ex and maybe I won't."

The small muscular man returns, "Everything alright?"

"This is my brother-in-law, Stan," pointing back and forth between them, "Heather's uncle, Dan."

Dan turns and storms away before Stan can utter a word. He nearly kicks me as he turns out of the driveway and stumbles upon me.

Piggy

Monday morning comes with the familiar honking from Ms. Parks' car. Susan looks sad as I close the door.

"We're moving," she says.

"Susan! We were going to tell her together this afternoon," Ms. Parks says.

"Sorry, mommy."

"I know. I saw you packing."

"Heather, I'm sorry, but it's better for us. And we're still going to be in town, so we can still see you."

I look down. I know it is because of Dan. He's already run Mrs. Jones off and I didn't even like her; now, Ms. Parks.

"Listen, instead of daycare today, I'm taking you two out for ice cream. Then we'll talk about it."

I can't focus the entire day. My teacher, Ms. Blake, checks my forehead a few times for a fever. She finally gives up calling on me as I take up too much time asking what the question was and then not having an answer anyway. Finally, the bell rings. Susan and I walk to the pick up point. Ms. Parks pulls up a few minutes later and takes us straight to the ice cream parlor. I order my favorite -- chocolate ice cream with marshmallow topping.

"Heather, I want you to know this wasn't an easy decision. It has nothing to do with you. And I don't want you to think you're not going to see us anymore. Susan is still going to be at your school. It's just that, my sister has a spare room and it will be better for us, to move in with her."

I look down to hide my eyes which are filled with tears.

"Heather, we'll still see you every weekend."

"Mommy, can't Heather come with us?"

My eyes brighten.

Piggy

"I wish she could but I can't swing it."

The marshmallow topping turns sour in my mouth.

"Heather, is there anything you want to tell me about Dan?"

"We're fine," I say.

"Is he hitting you?" she says grabbing my wrist.

"No."

"Is he touching you in anyway? You know that you don't like?"

I shake my head.

"I've seen you come home late. Where do you go?"

I can't tell her about the hospital trips. "Probably just McDonald's," I offer.

"At midnight?"

I shrug.

"Can we go to McDonald's?" Susan asks oblivious to the tension.

"No sweetie," turning to me, Ms. Parks says, "Heather, I wish things were different. Your mom was always kind to me. She was the only friend I could count on. I wish I could do more, but I can't."

"Dan gets money for me."

"What?" she asks.

"He's my guardian. He gets money."

"Hmm. I was wondering how he did it without a job," she said finishing her coffee. "Okay girls, we should go."

Piggy

Before dropping me off at my house, Ms. Parks turns to me one last time, "Here, take this and hide it. It's my sister's phone number. Don't let Dan have it. You ever have a problem with him, you call me."

I slide the piece of paper into my pocket and nod politely. I'm never going to call her. She doesn't want me. I heard her say it at Mom's funeral. She's only saying she cares. No one cares about me. I'm on my own. I knew I was on my own the minute I saw Dan almost a year ago. Mom was gone, just like Grandma, and I was alone.

Entering the house from the operable back door, Dan is on the phone in the kitchen.

"So what does this mean anyway?"

"Letter says get paperwork."

"How much?"

"What do you mean all of it?"

"I don't keep stuff like that."

"What else will work?"

"Shit. You called them didn't you?"

"Normal, my ass, you turned me in."

"Why? I don't know, maybe you want the money for yourself," he says seeing me walk into the kitchen. "I gotta go," he says hanging up.

"What are you doing home so early?"

"Ms. Parks took us out for ice cream."

"She did?"

"Yeah."

"She probably feels guilty for leaving you. You know, she doesn't give a shit about you."

"Are we ever going to get the TV fixed?"

"You think I'm made of money?

I walk to my room.

"Rest up. We're going out later. Probably around ten," he shouts.

Chapter 22

Our hospital expedition doesn't yield much. As we pull onto our street, our house lights are on and the door is wide open. Dan drives by without slowing down. He drives to a park that is a few blocks away and stops.

"Let's sleep here," he instructs.

"Who was at our house?"

"Go to sleep."

"Shouldn't we call the police?"

"No, go to sleep."

"Who was there? Was it that guy?"

"I don't know, but I'm not gonna find out."

Reclining his seat, Dan leans back to sleep.

"I'm freezing," I say.

Dan's got jeans, boots, and a coat on. I'm wearing a flimsy cotton gown with socks and slippers. Normally we go home and I jump into bed. Dan leans forward and shimmies out of his coat and hands it to me. That along with a hoodie in the back seat are my blankets for the night. Time ekes by until the morning birds are in the midst of their songs. Nudging Dan awake, he turns the ignition starting up the heat.

Around six, we head back to our house. Dan parks down the street and tells me to wait in the car. I see him walk cautiously through the yard and into the house. Eventually he comes out and waves at me from the front lawn. It takes me a moment to understand he's not coming back to the car. I quickly walk home hoping no one sees me in my cotton gown with no back.

Once inside the place is trashed. The couch has been turned over and all the cushions have been slashed. The cushion stuffing is strewn throughout the living room. There are numerous holes in the wall and any pictures have been smashed. The bookshelf has been upended. The TV remains untouched, but it was already broken. A large sign hangs in front of the screen, 'Pay me.'

Looking around in horror, I turn to inspect the kitchen. Every cabinet is open and empty. The pantry door is ajar, but I know that it is empty. The pantry's contents of chips, crackers, cereal, and baking supplies are scattered across the floor like debris. There are mustard swirls covering the piles of glass and food. The far wall, near the open refrigerator door, is covered in something brownish black and it takes me a while to figure out that all my beloved pudding has been smeared on the wall. I see the frozen dinner boxes and feel sick at the sight of the coagulated Salisbury steak on the floor.

"Pack a bag," Dan orders.

I tiptoe to my room, careful not to cut my feet on any glass since my slippers don't offer much protection. Shockingly, my room looks pretty good. All the drawers are turned out on the floor and my clothes are in a pile in the center of the floor but it almost seems neatly ransacked. My bookshelf has been moved away from the wall with most of the stuffed animals on the floor in front. I scan the butterfly shelf and spot the blue monarch with gold trim on its side; unscathed from this latest assault. I frantically sort through the piles of animals on the floor and find only one other surviving butterfly – the small yellow and white butterfly. If I had to rank the collection, the yellow one would have been my least favorite; it was small with no detail in the wings. The wings were a solid pale yellow with a white stripe splitting the wings and forming the body. Seeing it now, I decide it one of the most precious and beautiful butterflies of the collection. The rest of the butterflies are smashed into bits and pieces. I carefully transfer the two surviving butterflies to the edge of my bed which I've cleared off for packing.

Next, I search for Betty and find her in a corner. Hugging her, I exhale in relief. I sort through my clothes. I can't find the jeans that fit best and instead put on a pair of corduroys and as many warm clothes on top that I can find. Sliding my boots on, I walk into the hallway and head to the coat closet. Dan emerges with a full trash bag.

"You packed?"

"I need my suitcase."

"No suitcase, use a trash bag."

"But I have a suitcase," I say envisioning my Hello Kitty roller bag.

"Get a trash bag, it'll be less conspicuous."

He goes into the kitchen and finds one for me. Handing it to me, "Hurry, we gotta get out of here."

I create a pile of 'take' items on the bed. Extracting a sweater from the pile, I wrap my two favorite butterflies in it and gently place them in the bag. I then fill the bag with more clothes and shoes but quickly run out of space. My 'take' pile barely has a dent. I review my stuffed animals realizing I can only take a few. I choose Larry and Ellie. I carry them, Betty and my bag into the living room. Dan is looking out the window as I enter the kitchen intent on getting a second bag.

"Ready?"

"I need another bag."

"Nope, just one."

"But I have more clothes, all my books for school and…"

He storms to me and sees my trash bag. He grabs it. "You're already packed."

"No! There's still more stuff I want to bring."

"One bag, let's go."

"But… Another whole pile has to come too," I whine.

"This must be the important stuff because you packed it first," he says walking out.

Grabbing Larry, Ellie, and Betty, I freeze in the living room. Are we ever coming back? I frantically turn and scan the living room. I look at the pile that was once the bookshelf and search for the picture of

Mom and me that was on the top shelf. I stumble on the debris as I sort through books and couch stuffing.

"Let's go!" Dan yells.

"I need the picture of Mom!"

"You ain't gonna find it in that pile. It's gone."

"No!"

He pulls me away. "No!" I scream again but this time with such a shrill that he lets go. I quickly grab Betty and Ellie, and anxiously review the area. I stand up straight in the midst of chaos.

"Let's go," Dan orders in a voice that necessitates my compliance. I follow him out as he pulls me along, Betty and Ellie in my arms. I'm unable to grab Larry off the floor. We step onto the front porch and walk with our heads down in silence to the car. The neighborhood is coming alive with commuters and daily life but no one notices us.

We drive for about an hour with Dan circling an area full of roadside motels. He selects one and unlocks the dimly lit room around 8 A.M. There are multiple spots on the threadbare carpet. I think of the carpet cleaning commercial that talked about 'high traffic zones' and wonder what's been going on in this room. The blue floral bedspreads on the twin beds match the blackout curtains which Dan opens when we enter. There is almost a shine coming off one bedspread when the sunlight hits it as a cockroach scurries out of sight. I set Betty down, along with my trash bag on the little table near the window. Dan has thrown his trash bag on one of the beds. I go into the bathroom and encounter a strong smell of cigarettes and Lysol. Looking back at Dan, he hasn't lit up since we got home so I know this smell is from the previous tenants. There is a yellow ring around the tub and hair in the drain. I pee not letting my butt touch the seat. Coming out, Dan is pacing and smoking.

"Let's go across the street for some food."

"What about school?"

"Huh?"

"It's Tuesday."

"No school today."

We cross the street to a diner and have breakfast. It's the first time I've had waffles since Mom. Dan sits and smokes for a long time, drinking countless cups of coffee. The waitress is kind enough to bring me some crayons so I quietly color while Dan broods.

It's almost eleven by the time we return to the motel. I barely turn on the TV when Dan announces he's going out.

"Don't open the door for anyone," he says shutting the curtains tight.

I fall asleep as soon as he shuts the door. I don't know what time it is when he returns but its dark out and the news is on the TV. He's got McDonald's and a six pack. Polishing off one Big Mac by the time I'm fully awake, Dan starts on his second.

He smokes and finishes his third beer while I eat the cheeseburger and fries he has gotten me. "We're not going back home again," he says decisively.

"Why not? We can clean it up."

"It's not that. We can't go back. And I don't want you calling anyone."

"Why?"

"We need to stay out of sight for a while. I know you had to leave a lot of stuff behind, but we can't go back. It's too risky."

I take a drink of my soda.

"You bring your hospital stuff?"

"No."

He slaps me on the side of my head, "Stupid, why not?"

"I didn't know we weren't going back."

"Fine, we'll get another hospital gown tonight."

"I thought we had to stay out of sight."

"We'll go further than we normally do. Besides, we're not hiding from the hospital people."

"Who are we hiding from?" I say, pausing, "Stu?"

"Yup. I owe him some money so we gotta score big this week."

Dan is staring at the TV over my shoulder. His attention is taken by something on the screen, but when I turn around, a commercial starts. It's as if a light switch went on because Dan is suddenly full of energy.

"Get ready, I gotta make a stop first."

Dan stops at a gas station and buys a few things. Throwing them in the back, we go on driving for about an hour before pulling into a hospital parking lot. Dan goes in first and comes back about ten minutes later with a dirty hospital gown and robe. I keep my T-shirt on, but Dan sees it and orders me to 'get into character'.

We go through our normal entrance routine, watchful of any unwanted stares. Strolling freely in the corridors, Dan spots a gurney. Pausing for a moment, he has me lay down and covers me up with the sheet that had been on the bottom. He parks the wheelchair in an empty room and we start our quest for sellable items.

When we're completely alone, I ask Dan, how I'm going to be able to steal anything while lying down. He tells me not to worry. He turns the corner and approaches a door labeled 'Supply Room'. I stare in disbelief as Dan pulls out a set up keys and unlocks the elusive door we've always tried to get into.

He rolls me inside and shuts the door. A light automatically goes on as we enter.

Smiling, "I lifted some keys off an orderly," he says. "Sit up."

Piggy

Almost without pause, he relieves the shelves from everything they have. He carefully places the boxes in a row between my legs and then has me lay down so that he can continue putting loot around my body. Covering me with a sheet, he grabs a linen bag near the front door, empties it, and fills it up with more pill bottles and boxes. This is like a four week heist all in the span of one trip. Fully loaded, Dan peeks out the door and then pulls me out. The linen bag is slung over Dan's shoulder but the sound of the pills rattling in their bottles is too obvious. Dan lays the bag above my head and pushes. He has to put some muscle into the first shove before the wheels engage. He quickly traces back our route to the room with the wheelchair.

"Follow me in that," he orders as he helps me off the gurney. "When we get close to the door, slow down and let me get ahead of you."

I do as he says, expertly wheeling myself in the chair. I've picked up some skills during our little visits and can now turn on a dime. As we approach the exit doors, there is still no one around. Dan motions me to stop. The doors are about twenty five feet in front of us, but we have to pass through an intersection first. Dan sneaks up and squats down as if tying his shoe. His head leans into the intersection and looks both ways. Jumping up, he's excited and can't contain his smile.

"Quick, get to the car," he whispers.

We dash out and I actually beat him back to the car. I've already collapsed the chair by the time he's unlocked the trunk. Working as a team, we alternate tossing our bounty in. Squealing the tires a bit out of the parking lot, Dan is laughing and smiling.

"Whoo hooo! We scored big!"

My laughter is interrupted by a scent. Sniffing more intently, "What's that smell?"

Dan tilts his head up and breaths in. "Shit!" Dan yells, pulling the car over.

Opening the back door, he reaches for a can labeled gasoline. Up righting it, he feels around the back of the folded down seat.

Piggy

"I think only a little spilled," he says.

Wedging the can behind the driver's seat, we continue our drive. An hour later, Dan's pulling into our neighborhood. Dan goes past our street and turns right at the alley.

"You missed the turn."

"No. We're going around back. I just got to get something."

"Can I get my...."

"No!" he yells. Lowering his voice, "No, you stay here. Don't leave this car."

I'm a bit surprised at how sharp he is after we had such a good haul. I watch him walk between the houses cutting through the backyards of several neighbors. It's after two in the morning and dead silent. He's gone for a while and I grow concerned. Maybe Stu is here. Maybe Dan's been jumped by Stu. I open the car door and hold my breath, straining to hear as much as possible. Nothing. Complete silence. I get out but don't shut the door completely.

Following Dan's path, I trace the edge of the garage that sits behind Mrs. Jones' house. I get to the back fence separating our house from our neighbors and look for the gate. It's pitch black; I'm under a tree which blocks any moonlight. There's a crackle of branches on the other side of the fence. Next I hear a thud and Dan is in front of me. I scream startled by the surprise, but he slaps his hand across my face. Forcing my shoulders around, he pushes me down the path. Back at the car, he drives out, careful not to squeal the tires or turn on the lights. As we pass our street going out of the neighborhood, I see a faint hint of orange in our front window.

"What did you do?"

"What?"

"You said you had to get something. What did you get?"

"Ahhh, I... I couldn't find it."

"What did you do?"

"Don't worry about it."

"What did you do?"

Stopping the car, he grabs my arm. "Don't worry about it. You saw nothing."

Piggy

Chapter 23

We stay at the motel for a few days. On the third day, Dan leaves me alone most of the morning as he unloads all the hospital loot. Back with cash, his mood has lifted. He takes me to a late lunch and then we drive to an office building. Exiting the elevator, Dan pauses at the signs. Heading to our right, Dan opens the third door down 'Harris at Law' the plaque reads.

The blonde haired girl at the front desk looks about twenty and is pretty enough. "Can I help you?"

"I need to see Mr. Harris," Dan says coolly.

"Dan?" a chubby man with a striped shirt and polka dot tie says leaning out of a doorway. "Randy Harris," he says extending his hand.

"Pleased to meet you. I'm Dan Howard and this little cutie is my niece, Heather."

Seated across the desk in Mr. Harris' office, Dan tells him why we are here. He goes through Mom's death and his guardianship and then pulls out the letter I'd been looking for.

"In May, I officially became guardian, and I got this letter a few weeks ago." Handing Mr. Harris the letter, he reads it.

"This seems relatively standard."

"Relatively?"

"I don't see it that often but the State does have the right to audit trusts and technically, it is a trust."

"The thing is, we're homeless now."

"Excuse me?"

"Our house burned down a few nights ago."

My mouth gapes open and I glare at Dan. Placing his foot over my toe, he applies pressure to squelch my protest. Mr. Harris studies

Piggy

me for a moment as Dan leans forward applying more pressure. My intended scream turns into a cry of pain, although Mr. Harris can't see the cause of my discomfort.

"She's still upset, as you can imagine."

All Mom's things, the figurines I couldn't carry, my stuffed animals, and any photo of her, gone. My sobs continue as Dan releases my toe.

"That's horrible. I'm so sorry."

"Water under the bridge. We survived, Thank God."

"I'm still not clear how I can help."

"Two things, really. First, the audit is going to focus on paperwork that I don't have and second, I fear there have been some unsavory characters in my sister's life. I think the lawyer that helped set this trust up is intent on taking over guardianship of Heather and I can only assume it is for the money."

"I see. Let me answer your first question. We can apply for an audit extension which will give you time to contact your bank and credit card companies and get copies of any bills or statements. That should be enough proof that the money went for guardianship related expenses."

"That's another problem. I'm not proud to say this, but I've had some issues with my credit in the past," Day says, pausing for effect, "I had a bit of a gambling problem, I'm ashamed to admit."

"This audit would only be for the months since you became guardian."

"Yes, but what I'm getting at is I didn't have a bank account or credit card. I've been dealing in cash for the last several years."

"The trust is in a bank account."

Piggy

"Yes, the lump sum is there, but I'm only allowed to access a portion of it. I've been withdrawing what I can to pay bills and what not."

"You don't have any receipts or records?"

"All I had burned up."

"I can file for an extension and submit extenuating circumstances which will buy a bit more time. Then we'd have to piece together a list of typical expenses and show them to the State."

"List of expenses?"

"You know, we'd list out an average grocery bill, gas, utilities, etcetera. That total should come close to the monthly withdraw and then show that to the State. There have been cases like this before, usually it's older people who were raised in the depression and don't trust banks. But you can start saving receipts now and we should have several months by the time the audit happens to support our claim."

"How long would the extension be? I mean, what's the maximum we can ask for?"

"Six months is the max and with your recent fire, we should get that easy."

"Great. Another thing the account automatically makes the mortgage payments, can you stop those?"

"Well," Mr. Harris leans back, "it may seem odd, but you actually want to stay current on the mortgage. Until the insurance claim is settled at least. Otherwise the bank could foreclose."

"I'd rather stop paying until I make my claim."

"I'm sure you could contact the bank and do that."

"Could you take care of it?"

"Yes." Mr. Harris says slowly. "But I'd advise against it."

Piggy

"Uh, huh. What about this lawyer, I mentioned, trying to take over?"

"Do you have any proof?" As Mr. Harris says this, the receptionist comes through the doorway carrying a tray loaded with a coffee pot, two cups, sugars and a small pitcher of cream. Mr. Harris waves her into the office with his hand.

"Here you go, thought you all would like some coffee," she says setting down the tray.

Dan's face tenses up at the interruption.

"And you, young lady, why don't you come with me and pick out a soda?" taking my hand, I'm pulled along with her, "We've got orange, grape, and strawberry, plus the regular stuff."

I select an orange cream soda and turn to walk back to the office, but she is intent on keeping me company. She draws a tic-tac-toe square on a piece of paper and prompts me to play. Every time I look over my shoulder near the door, she draws another game. Fifteen minutes later, Dan emerges from the office saying his goodbye.

We walk down the hallway in silence. Entering the elevator, I kick Dan in the shin.

"Why did you do it?" I scream after the doors close.

Grabbing me by my ponytail, he yanks my head back into an uncomfortable direction upwards.

"Don't kick me!" His face is close to mine, and his eyes are staring straight into mine.

The bells dings and the doors open as he releases me. There's an elderly couple getting on as we exit. They don't seem fazed so I assume they saw nothing.

Once in the car, my anger is renewed. "Why did you do it?"

"I had to! The place was trashed. And we couldn't go back there again anyway. Not with Stu breathing down my neck."

Piggy

I stare at him in disbelief.

"This buys us some time to get away and maybe collect on the insurance."

"All mom's stuff was there."

"I had to do it. And don't you say a word to anyone about it."

I turn and shake my head.

"You want to go to the orphanage?"

"No," I say shaking my head.

We drive for a while before I have the courage to speak. "Where are we going to live now?"

"The motel for now."

"Do people know where we are?"

"No, and don't you tell anyone. Or call anyone."

"But what about school and Ms. Parks?"

"No school for a while."

"But Ms. Parks and Susan."

"She doesn't care about you. She was already moving away."

"Do they know we're alive?"

"I saw her yesterday when I was there. She saw the house; she didn't even come over to ask about you. She's happy not to have to deal with picking you up every day."

"You were there?"

"Yes. I had to file the report. Jesus, kid, sometimes you don't think."

"Report?"

"I had to talk to the cops and the firemen. Make sure they know it was an accident."

"Am I ever going to go back to school?"

"Not right now. I got to get stuff straighten out. You think I want you hanging around all day?"

Piggy

Chapter 24

The next week, I spend all day at the motel mainly on my own. Dan is gone most nights and doesn't get back until early morning. Sometimes we go out for breakfast, but more often it's a late lunch. He has instructed me to not answer the door or phone so the room is dirty since I haven't let the maid in for several days.

I sit at a chair that I pulled up right in front of the TV so I can keep the volume low. Dan's snoring since he just got home an hour or so ago. The phone rings. On the second ring, I nudge Dan awake. He picks up on the fourth ring and it takes him a while to figure out who it is. It's Mr. Harris, who informs Dan that the audit extension has been accepted. Dan immediately gets up.

"Get ready to go," he says entering the bathroom.

Stunned by seeing more activity in ten minutes than I've seen from him all week, I am slow to change out of my pajamas. Next, I go to the sink to wash my face and fix my hair. The door opens and a wall of steam comes out before I see Dan. He pushes me aside from the sink to shave. I stare at him as the shaving cream is perfectly removed in strips from his face.

"You packed and ready?"

"You want me to pack?"

"Yes, we're going."

"Going where?"

"I haven't decided yet, but we're getting out of here."

I walk over to the dresser and pull out my clothes. I go through the same ritual to pack up the butterfly figurines as I had done before; carefully rolling them up inside a sweater. Putting it in the middle of the trash bag, I top my bag with Ellie. Spinning the bag around to make a handle, I take Betty in my arms and sit on the edge of the bed waiting for Dan. He brushes by me and throws a few things into his bag and walks out the door. I hurry to follow him knowing not to wait for any other sign that he's leaving.

Piggy

We drive to the bank. Dan tells me to wait in the car and I watch him as he approaches the teller line. I lose sight of him in the sun's glare for a few minutes only to see him storm out the front door. Mr. Forrester from the bank is jogging behind him to keep up. They say a few words and then Dan continues walking. Mr. Forrester follows him, they stop, say a few more words and then Dan continues walking. This goes on three more times before they are standing in front of the car and Mr. Forrester catches sight of me. Walking over to my window, I push the button to lower it, but the car isn't on. Mr. Forrester opens the door and takes a good look at me.

"How are you Heather?"

"I'm fine."

"I'm so sorry to hear about your home. You weren't hurt or anything?"

"No, we weren't there," I say as Dan closes the driver's door.

"We had gone to see a friend of mine and spent the night. Lucky us," he interjects.

"Yes, that was lucky," Mr. Forrester replies as his eyes take inventory of the contents of our car.

"We've got to get going."

"Why aren't you in school, Heather?"

"I took her out for a while, 'cause of the fire."

I remain silent and become fixated on Betty.

"Certainly, it's been long enough that she needs to get back into a routine."

"She's fine. But thank you for your concern," Dan says as he smiles. "Now if you don't mind, we really have to be going."

"Could I get your current address?"

Piggy

"As you know, we're kind of between places at the moment."

"Yes, but, ah, for your bank statements. So we can send them to you."

"I'll put in a forwarding address with the post office when I have one."

"Certainly, that will work. But if you could let me know where you're staying now, I know a lot of people are worried about you two. You've been through so much."

"We're fine, aren't we Heather?" I nod and smile.

"You know I ran into Ms. Parks and I know she'd like to offer her help."

"You talked to her?"

"Yes, I stopped by your house when I heard about the fire."

"What'd she say?"

"She's real concerned and wanted to know if I had any contact," he says slowly.

"She don't need to worry about us. We're fine," Dan says putting the car in gear and nodding his head to the door.

Mr. Forrester steps back. "Goodbye Heather, I'm glad you're alright," he says as he closes the door. Dan wastes no time pulling out.

We immediately get onto the freeway and I assume I'm in for my role as sick kid in a wheelchair, but after an hour, Dan still hasn't pulled off the freeway. The lull of the road causes me to drift off because when I wake up, it's dusk and Dan is pulling into a gas station. I spot a few Arizona sweatshirts and ask Dan where we are. He tells me not to worry. We drive for several more hours. When I see signs for New Mexico, we pull into a motel for the night.

The next day, Dan is up early and after a quick stop at a drive-thru, we're on the road again.

Piggy

"Where are we going?" I ask for the umpteenth time and finally get a response.

"Texas."

"Why?"

"I used to live there."

That's all I get for the rest of our drive.

I'm shaken awake by Dan and its dark out. We're at the drive through of a burger joint and Dan is asking me what I want. When I stare back at him uncertain where I am and who I am, he tells the microphone he wants a cheeseburger meal. We don't eat in the car because the motel is right next door. A sign on the front door says 'Voted Amarillo's Best Value'. After checking in, we're off to our room to eat.

No sooner is Dan's soda making a slurping sound when he's out the door with the familiar 'stay here' command. I make the best of my new room but quickly realize we hadn't unloaded the car before Dan left. My pathetic excuse for a suitcase is in the back seat. Luckily, Betty is with me. I hop on the bed and switch the TV on and get lost in re-runs.

Dan returns around midnight and informs me we're going out to a hospital. Despite knowing no one here, Dan is confident he'll find a buyer for anything we take.

"Gotta keep the cash flowing," he says.

We score a modest take but the ease at which we got it is astonishing -- no guards anywhere and very few nurses or orderlies. We take our time to picking out the items we steal and leisurely pack up in the parking lot. If only the place had better stuff, we could get away with a weekly visit. Dan is happy and we stop for a very early breakfast at I-Hop. He leaves me at the booth while he goes over to the counter to talk up the waitress. She's laughing and I begin to think we're going to have a guest tonight, when Dan walks back to the table alone. The sun is coming up and the place is beginning to fill up. Dan motions for us to go.

He's in no hurry pulling out of the parking lot. Turning right, we barely drive one block before Dan slows the car down. Eventually pulling over, he's staring at a sign 'Wanted: Apartment Manager' and then underneath 'Apply Unit 1'. The two-story light blue building has staircases on either side heading up to a balcony before the second floor apartments. There are multiple dark tan doors with numbers on them facing outward. I can see eight doors on the front side – four on the bottom and four on the second level. There is a sidewalk through the middle of the building that leads to a courtyard which I later find is surrounded by more apartments. Dan taps his hand on the wheel, and then properly parks along the curb.

"Let's go apply," he says with his hand on the door handle.

Dan pulls a tie out of the back and fixes his hair in the side mirror. Taking me by the hand, we walk up the sidewalk and spot Unit 1 on the far left. Dan gives me the look; the look that says 'go along with whatever I say' and 'don't say a word' all in one expression. He knocks gently but confidently on the door.

A few moments pass before an older man who's hunched over answers the door. His slicked back hair is as white as snow along with the matching stubble of facial hair. He's got on light grey pants with a thin belt tightened to the last hole. The fabric is bunched up under the belt but it still looks like his pants will fall down. His collared striped shirt is buttoned all the way to the top and I can clearly see the white T-shirt through the thinning fabric.

"Yes."

"I'm here about the Apartment Manager position," Dan says.

We're invited into a medium sized living room with a kitchenette off to the side. It is much smaller than Mom's house with a little table and chair in the corner next to a small stove. The off white walls blend into the small patch of tan speckled linoleum in the kitchenette and into the tan carpet of the living room. The living room has two overstuffed upholstered chairs positioned in front of a large TV and with a little table in between. From the looks of the table top, this is where the old guy eats all of his meals. An archway to the hallway sits exactly across from a bathroom door.

Piggy

Dan recounts our sad story which has gotten sadder by the day. Not only has Mom died but apparently she was married to Dan's best friend and he died in the accident as well. The story of woe continues with Dan being just the best Good Samaritan ever. He adds new aspects to his tale. Unbeknownst to me, he's played nursemaid to his parents and to his dying friend from church, all of which has interfered with his career ambitions. Dan rambles on about his fictitious church to the point I think we've moved here as part of a religious quest. Finally, the old man interrupts him.

"I am sorry to hear about your troubles. But I'm not sure this is going to work out for you. This is a temporary job, until the summer."

"The sign didn't say anything about timeframe."

"No, I only put that in the paper. I just put the sign up today. Normally, I move back to New Jersey in June, when it gets too hot here. I've got a guy who takes care of the summer for me; stays until I'm back in October. But this year, I gotta get back a little earlier. My sister took a spill and I gotta help her out."

"That still gives me little over three months; that'll really help to get us back on our feet."

"Plus, this is a one bedroom, not ideal for the two of you," the old guy says as he extends his arms and takes a few steps backward to the hallway. Grasping the bedroom door knob, he opens it to show the size of the place. I can see a small bed in there, not much else. Dan follows him and sticks his head into the room, blocking any view I had.

"What's that door there?" Dan says pointing down the hall past the bathroom.

"It used to be a two bedroom," the man says walking in the direction of Dan's pointed finger. A door opens and I can hear the rhythmic sound of a dryer. "But I converted the second bedroom into a laundry room," the old guy says as his voice goes out of range. A few seconds later, they both emerge from the hallway.

"You'd be amazed at what tenants will do in a shared laundry room. I just had it," the old guy says.

"I think it's perfect for the two of us. I don't need space and you know kids, always getting dirty and needing clean clothes. This would actually be great."

Dan continues to sell the old guy on our suitability until he caves.

"I put in the paper a start date of March 15th, but if you're ready, I can be out of here in two days."

"Perfect."

"Let me get your name and details. My guy will run the necessary checks."

Dan's face falls for a moment, but then he reaches into his back pocket for his wallet. He's totally busted but he seems so calm.

"You know, I left my license in the car," Dan says, "Let me go get it."

I turn to follow him out to make our escape, but Dan stops me, "You stay here," he states.

I freeze. Is he dumping me with this old guy? My mind runs through my options. If he leaves me, I'll be sent to an orphanage for sure. But why leave me? I've done everything Dan has wanted. My heart races and my breathing becomes rapid. A few moments later, after a few uncomfortable smiles to the old guy, I'm shocked, but happy, when Dan walks back into the slightly ajar door. Handing the old guy a card, the man takes it and copies down the information.

"Didn't you say your name was Dan?" the man questions raising his head to look at Dan.

"I use my middle name," Dan answers coolly.

"Oh, you got a number I can reach you at?"

"Let me take yours. We're currently at a motel now."

Walking back to the car, I wait until we're out of range. "What did you give him?"

"Why, were you a little scared?"

"I didn't know what you were doing."

"Scared I was going to leave?"

"Yes," I say hoping my show of fear will induce him to explain. I don't know where we are; I don't know anyone here; and there's no place left back home. And now I'm not sure who Dan has said he is.

"Well you should be scared. I'm the best thing you got and don't forget it," he says turning the ignition. "I gave him an ID I swiped. From now on, you're Karen Jackson and I'm your uncle, Larry Dan Jackson."

I nod and pick up my pace as he walks much faster than me.

"I got a lot of tricks up my sleeve, Piggy."

Chapter 25

Two days later, we're moving in. Moving in our two trash bags, that is, it takes all of five minutes. The haul from our recent hospital visit was nearly as much as our luggage. The old guy left us most of the furniture but he took the big TV. We move the little TV from the bedroom into the front room. The laundry room is tight with the washer and dryer taking up one entire wall. There's a little desk opposite the washer and a small lamp. Dan puts down a yoga mat that he found in a dumpster next to the desk. Adding an extra blanket and pillow the old guy left, he announces my room is ready. It actually isn't uncomfortable, but one smell of the carpet tells me at some point, the old guy had a dog.

We head out for a celebratory lunch at I-Hop when we nearly tackle a middle aged woman about to knock on our door.

"Oh, where's Mr. Simpson?"

"He's gone for the summer. I'm the new manager," Dan says.

"So, I deal with you now? Or do I call him?" she asks, adding, "It's regarding the rent."

"Yup, you deal with me."

"I was going to tell him that I'll have the rent in two days." She stares at Dan waiting for a response.

"Okay."

"That's not a problem then?"

"Nope."

"I'm sorry, where are my manners? I'm Jessica Capshaw in Unit 7," she says as we introduce each other and she asks about our background. Dan goes through his abbreviated spiel, leaving out some of the more Mother Theresa moments.

"So you'll be enrolling in Prairie Lane School."

"Huh?" Dan asks.

"What grade are you in, Karen, third?"

"Second," I reply.

"Oh, how old are you?"

"Seven, but I'll be eight in June."

"You may be in my class. I teach the second grade."

Dan and Jessica discuss the school more and she offers to help me get enrolled. Dan sweet talks her as soon as he realizes she drives to school every day. Vying for a similar arrangement to Ms. Parks, Dan pushes her to agree on carpooling adding it's only fair since he wasn't making a fuss about the late rent.

The next day, Dan, Jessica, and I are at the school completing the paperwork for my enrollment. Dan nearly calls me Heather before correcting himself. I'm happy he's made the mistake first. It's been nearly three weeks since I was last in school and I'm excited and terrified at the same time. School and daycare had been my refuge into normal this last year, but walking these new halls and not seeing any familiar faces scares me. I wish Susan was here. Or Betty. Dan wouldn't let me bring her, he said I needed to be strong.

It's surprising how quickly Dan and I get into a routine. Ms. Capshaw picks me up each morning. I'm careful to watch out the window for her; coming out of the door before she has a chance to knock and find out Dan's still sleeping. Prairie Lane is a K through six school with an after school program for working parents. When school is over, we're shuffled into the gymnasium to play, similar to extended recess. Ms. Capshaw is also the music teacher so she stays until 4:30 for choir practice, before bringing me back to the apartment. Dan makes a good show of it the first week, ready at the door around 4:45 so she can see he's home. But as soon as our routine is set, Dan goes back to normal.

It takes several weeks for Dan to unload the hospital loot we got our first night. He said he had to cultivate a buyer. In Lancaster, he told me he sold everything to one guy who had several buyers lined up. Unfortunately, Dan couldn't find anyone in the area so he had to create the market himself. Impressed with himself, he detailed his strategy one night when we actually spent some time together. Dan said he'd hung out in bars around hospitals and retirement centers looking for a suitable employee. He had successfully pitched his proposal and would sell our stash the next day.

But something happens and he never mentions it again. The pile of items remain the next day when I come home from school and Dan's mood is sour. It takes two more weeks, but eventually the pile is gone. The end result is no more hospital trips which I am happy about. Dan focuses instead on gambling, either betting on sports games or poker.

In May, I skip through the door, excited to show the permission slip in my pocket. My class would have a field trip to the zoo for our graduation celebration. I run through the apartment, but there's no sign of Dan. I amble to my room and sit cross legged on my sleeping mat. Picking up Betty, I tell her my news. Then I hug Ellie and put her next to me as I focus on Mom's butterfly figurines. The Monarch's royal blue wings with gold edges glimmer when the light hits it. I had placed the Monarch and the smaller yellow butterfly on top the small desk; the only decorations in my room and the only things I have left of Mom's. Bored, I come back into the front room to watch TV and wait for Dan.

Glancing at the front door, I notice our mail chute is full. I pull the mail out and lay it all on the table. It's mostly grocery store ads and flyers from maid services; but one letter stands out. It's from Lancaster State Bank. There's a 'please forward' stamp on the front and our address is handwritten next to it. The original address, an Amarillo post office box, is crossed out. Dan has told someone we were in Texas. I hold up the envelop to the light but can't see anything. The door knob turns and I quickly drop the letter and push the stack together.

"What are you doing?" Dan asks carrying a twelve pack.

"Nothing," I say.

"What's that?" he asks pointing to the table.

Piggy

"I got the mail. Do you want me to heat something up for dinner?"

He walks to the table and pushes me aside. "You don't need to get the mail," he says. Seeing the letter, he sets down the beer and rips it open. "I gotta go," he says after reading it and checking his watch.

I inspect the envelop after he's left; but there is nothing in it. He took whatever it was. I put the beer in the fridge and wait for him again. He's back in fifteen minutes and much happier. I present him my permission slip and tell him about the field trip. He signs the slip without acknowledging anything I've said. I continue telling him about my teacher and how we're going to tour the zoo and see the new baby giraffe, but he doesn't even glance in my direction; while I'm in mid-sentence, he goes to fetch a beer and turns the TV on.

I shut up and sit quietly in the corner, watching Dan more than the TV. A knock at the door interrupts us. Dan looks over at me to see if I know who it is. I shake my head. Dan opens the door to reveal a young guy with long brown hair pulled back into a pony tail. He's got a full shaggy beard and is wearing a plaid shirt and jeans. He introduces himself as the resident of Unit 13.

"The hot water is out."

"So?" Dan replies.

"So, can you fix it?"

"Why you asking me?"

"You're the super right?"

A light goes off in Dan's head. We've had zero interaction with anyone but Ms. Capshaw. It is a rude awakening to remind Dan that he actually has a job now.

"Oh, right," he says walking over to our kitchen sink and turning on the faucet. "We got hot water here."

"Well, I don't. I'm in the other building."

"Okay, I'll call the plumber."

"Aren't you even going to take a look?"

"Are you lying about the hot water?"

"No, but Mr. Simpson would always check it out. You know, maybe the pilot light is out or something."

"Well, I'm gonna call the plumber."

"When?"

"Tomorrow, I guess."

"I can't go without hot water that long. Can't you call him now?"

"I can, but it's after six. He probably doesn't work nights."

"Great. How about a break on the rent for this?"

"Not going to happen."

"Shit. Just fix it then as soon as possible. Unit 13," he says walking away and to the curb.

"You're going out anyway," Dan shouts after him, "You're not even using the hot water."

Tuesday morning, Ms. Capshaw is early. I jump out ready for school, but she puts her hand on our door and steps partially into our apartment. Calling out and knocking for Dan, I race back in to get him, telling her, he's in the shower.

Dan is not happy being awoken this early. I tell him it's Ms. Capshaw and he rolls out of bed in his dirty T-shirt and boxer shorts.

"Yeah?"

Piggy

"Oh, did you just get up?"

"What do you need?" he asks evading the question.

"The dumpsters are full and have been for several weeks. I don't think the garbage truck has been here. Can you look into it?"

"Ah, sure," Dan says.

"Karen, let's go," she says as we walk to her car.

Over the next few days, the young man that had come to our door becomes a frequent visitor. He complains that the handyman didn't fix the water heater and that the water, while warmer, isn't hot enough. He has also taken up the crusade of the garbage. Citing it is a health risk. Friday night, he comes over again to complain.

"Did you pay the garbage bill?" the young man finally asks Dan.

"What? Of course, I paid it," Dan says as he glances over at me. Something in his glance tells me he didn't even know about the bill.

"Get it taken care of or I'll call the city," he says storming off again.

The phone rings and it's Mr. Simpson.

"Hello, sir," Dan says. *Another ten minutes passes before Dan says another word. I can only imagine that someone has complained about him.*

"I'll take care of it. Sorry you were disturbed."

"What?"

"Yup, I'm on it. I put ads in the paper and I'm screening people now."

"Three? No it's two."

"Oh, right, I did know they'd given notice."

"It's that time of year. Memorial Day is next weekend, lots of people move around then."

"I understand, don't you worry, I'll get it done this weekend," Dan says hanging up.

The next day, Dan is up early. He's put up signs in the front and over at the I-Hop parking lot about vacant apartments. By Sunday, he's got a few prospective tenants looking at the places. Escorting a young woman into our apartment, he tells me to go to my room while he has her fill out some paperwork. I don't hear much, but he says congratulations before she leaves.

"Whoo hooo!" he shouts. "One down, two to go!" He sticks his head in the laundry room and dictates, "Hey, go next door and get me a turkey sandwich."

Handing me a twenty, I go to I-Hop and order two turkey sandwiches to go. Dan is out front when I return looking at everyone who passes by. We sit on the stoop and eat while he gleefully recounts his progress. He's got a few people interested but only one place rented. He seems confident that he'll get them all rented by the end of the week.

Excited, I jump into the conversation and tell him about the zoo again. I'm certain he wasn't listening before.

"We're going all day Thursday and then school's done on Friday."

"What?"

I tilt my head up high and say, "I'm going to finish the second grade this week."

"Is that so?"

My face falls at his lack of excitement.

"That's good, we're moving on Sunday anyway."

Piggy

"We're not staying here?"

"No. You knew that. We only had this place 'til June."

"Where are we going?"

"Don't know yet."

"Can't we stay here?"

"Not in our current place," he says as he realizes I'm upset. "Don't worry, we'll find a place," he adds as he pats my back.

As the last week of school winds down, Dan is jittery. He informs me on Tuesday that he's still got one apartment to rent, which I would have thought would have made him happy, but instead he's agitated. The young man from Unit 13 stops by again, but Dan refuses to answer the door. The young man pounds on the door and yells 'garbage' a few times before leaving.

The phone rings a while later and Dan waits to hear who it is on the answering machine. It's Mr. Simpson who is repeating this is his third message and to call him back. Dan erases the message as the phone rings again. He grabs the phone in anger; "I was gonna call you back," he snaps.

Gearing up for another terse comment, Dan's face relaxes.

"Oh, hello. Sorry I thought you were my ex," he says chuckling.

"You are, great. It's still available, although I've got another guy interested."

"When can you sign?"

"Tonight would be better. First come, first serve."

"First thing then. I'll be here."

"See you tomorrow," he says.

Piggy

When he hangs up, he actually does a little hop. His jitters have vanished. Grabbing a beer, he turns on the TV and searches for the right channel; a basketball game appears. Checking his watch, he leaps up and grabs the phone.

"Hey, it's Dan."

"Still open on the Lakers game?

"What's the spread?"

"Put me down for five."

"Yes, I'm good for it. I paid you back last week," he snarls.

"Just put me down," he snaps a final time before hanging up.

The game goes into overtime and the Lakers win but Dan shows no signs of happiness. I stay out of his way, and head off to bed.

The next day when Ms. Capshaw drops me back home, Dan is waiting for me. He's sitting on the couch with our two trash bags.

"We gotta go."

"No! You said end of the month."

"Things change."

"The zoo is tomorrow."

"Shit happens. Let's go."

"No, please, please, can't I go tomorrow? I want to go to the zoo."

"Nah, I want to be on the road tonight."

"Please, please, let me go."

Piggy

He pauses for a moment and I think maybe I've persuaded him.

"No, that means we're here all day and I can't risk that."

"No!" I scream and run to my room.

"Don't 'no' me! We're going."

I see Betty in the corner. Tucking her under my arm, I reach for Mom's Monarch as Dan's hand seizes on my upper arm. He yanks me hard to him and I stumble backwards. The Monarch is in my hand against my waist, unscathed. Dan pulls me up as I cry out in pain.

"Okay, I'll go!" I scream, standing up. "Let me get my stuff."

Dan lets go of my arm. "Gee, thank you for seeing it my way."

I snatch the yellow butterfly and strain to pick up Ellie. I squeeze Ellie trying to make her smaller as Dan repeats the urgency to leave. I scan the room to see if there is anything else, but he's gathered up all my clothes. I walk slowly back into the front room and he shoves me a bit as he brushes by me. I drop the yellow butterfly and step on it before I realize it. I suck air in and look up at Dan in horror.

"Let's go!" he screams.

Picking up the two bags, he turns to look at me. I'm frozen in place wanting to scoop up the butterfly for later repair. Dan drops one trash bag and takes a step toward me. I clutch Betty in one arm, have Ellie under the other arm, and am gingerly holding the Monarch in my hand. I think he's going to grab my arm but instead he snatches the Monarch from my hand. I scream. Jumping up to his raised hand, I cry for its return. Ellie and Betty fall to the floor as I hop unsuccessfully to the Monarch.

"When I tell you to do something, you do it. No questions," he says as he grips the butterfly. Squeezing, small glass parts fall out of his grasp. I jump again but I know it's pointless. Dan drops the butterfly to the ground and stomps on it before I can reach for it. Sinking to my knees, I cry as I inspect the destroyed figurine that had been Mom's favorite. Dan picks up both trash bags and walks out to

Piggy

the car. Minutes pass when I'm jerked out of my gaze by the car horn. I wipe my nose on my arm, grab Betty and Ellie, and head to the car. I'm nearly at the car when Dan points back at the apartment.

"Shut the door, idiot!"

I jog back to close the apartment door and return to the car that Dan has already started. He pulls out before I've shut my door and we're gone.

Present Day

Chapter 26

A gush of wind whips dirt across my face as I smooth back the hair that has come out of my ponytail. I look down at my new Betty, dirty, but still how I remember her. It seems so long ago. I don't remember the last time I've thought about Mom. Most times, it's too painful.

I gently place new Betty into the wagon along with other handpicked items from my latest junk patrol. Wheeling it back, I stop a distance from the van. Dan and Warren are still sleeping off their Grand Slam comas. Reviewing the yard, yesterday's delivery remains only half sorted. I had promised Dan I'd get through it today in exchange for the Denny's trip. I pick up new Betty and walk quietly to the van, careful not to step on anything that will make a sound. The side door is open and I lean in. Placing Betty down on my side, I cover her with my brown blanket to keep her safe.

I go back to sorting the junk and a few hours later, Dan and Warren stir. Standing and stretching, they take turns walking to the pee hole. I'm actually glad they're awake. A 'tidy bug' has gotten into me and instead of sorting the delivery, I'm sifting through the entire yard and grouping things. The automotive section is by far the largest covering twelve by fifteen feet easy. I tell myself this will make Dan happy and be better for sales. Plus, future deliveries will be easier to sort. Dan is staring out into the field and I wave my hand like Vanna White at him, but he gives me no indication he sees me. Disheartened, I convince myself that once he sees the junkyard all organized, he'll understand the genius of my strategy.

I continue creating four main sections – automotive, furniture, housewares, and personal items. Within these sections are subsections of like items. There's a lamp aisle inside the furniture section and a row of books next to the personal item section. My head is racing as I envision signs that could be placed in each section.

"What have you done?" Dan says behind me, making me spin around in surprise.

I smile and extend my arms on either side. "I organized it all."

Piggy

"Looks like it. What's the stuff over there?"

"The automotive section," I say proudly.

"Yeah, most of it is," he says walking to it. "But a lot of it ain't car parts."

"I put anything in that section that looked like a car."

"Nah, you got some lawn mower parts and other machine pieces."

"Oh."

"Here, make another pile, and I'll point out what's what."

"Okay," I say thankful for the interest in my project.

We spend a surprisingly enjoyable hour creating three separate piles that ultimately become subsections to either housewares or automotive. Dan never says thank you or any other word of appreciation, but the fact that he's shown interest is enough.

We head back to the van where Warren has been watching us.

"We're low on beer," he says.

"Already?"

"Yep."

"Shit, you drink like a fish," Dan says.

"Nah, I only had four, maybe five, you had the rest."

"Where's the other twelve?"

"That's what I'm talking about, only two left."

"Shit. Where's the whiskey?"

Piggy

"You got some?"

"Bought some with the beer."

"Fan-tas-tic! We're in business baby."

"Nah, I want more beer," Dan says.

"Piggy, get some kindling for the fire."

The sound of two cans opening in unison fills the air behind me as I gather twigs. Returning, Dan is propping up the logs like a teepee.

"You get this going, I'm getting another twelve," Dan says.

"I can go," Warren quickly offers.

"No, I want to stretch my legs."

"I'll do the same," Warren says. I know why he's being so accommodating. He wants a hot dog or something at the store. That's why Dan really wants more beer. They just aren't inviting me to the snack fest. Fine, Dan must still be pissed about lunch yesterday.

"Piggy, you get the fire started so we can find our way back. It's getting dark."

I nod and catch the matches Dan tosses at me. Once I get the fire going, I retrieve new Betty, a bottle of water, and the jam packets from this morning. I had hoped to save these for a while, but I know they're not going to bring me back anything to eat. Sucking down the packets, I throw the wrappers into the fire.

My attention turns to Betty. I wet my hands and rub them together to get them as clean as possible. With my damp hands I scrub her face and limbs. Next I restyle her hair, but I really need a comb and all I have is a brush. I make a mental note to see if Kathy at the grocery store has a comb I can borrow. Then I get my toothbrush, douse it with water and scrub the stains out of Betty's dress. It works okay, but not great. I clean my toothbrush under a rinse of water and intermittently rubbing my hand against the bristles.

Sitting in front of the now roaring fire, I review my effort. She's in better shape but still beat up. Not like my original Betty. I think about all the times I played zoo with my Betty. All the times I cried into her hair and held her tight while I slept.

"Looky here, she's got herself a dolly," Dan says coming into the fire light.

Startled, I jump up and run to put Betty back. I hadn't meant to let him see her.

"What are you now, Piggy, fourteen, fifteen, and you still need a doll?"

I know my face is red, but my rising anger can't compete against the tears that come.

"Ah, shit, you ain't gonna cry now are you? You cried forever when you lost that last doll. I can't go through that again."

I jump into the van, close its side door and hide behind it. Dan and Warren laugh. "What a baby."

Clutching new Betty, I don't remember the dreams I had when I was six. I'm certain it wasn't to be a drop out living in a junkyard. Dan had made me quit school in the sixth grade. I'm fifteen and a half and have nothing, except the seventeen dollars I've squirreled away when Dan wasn't looking.

I get under the covers, suddenly cold as my body grieves for the loss of heat from the fire. Dan and Warren continue to hoot and holler as the clink of the whiskey bottle being passed back and forth becomes the background noise. I must have dozed off at some point because a loud crack wakes me up.

Dan is on a rant about how hard his life is.

"I could've been a dealer in Vegas by now!" he shouts at the sky. "Wasn't for her, I would've gotten a casino job and worked my way up. But noooo! I gotta lie low."

He goes on for a while longer but I can only make out a few words. I've heard it before, he's stuck with me. He gave everything up

Piggy

for me. Without him, I'd be rotting in some orphanage being forced to work as a slave and to eat shit. Or worse, I'd be raped every day. Kathy tells me I can leave when I'm eighteen. As I contemplate my limited choices, the van door swings open. Dan is swaying at the open doorway. His eyes fall onto me before he grabs new Betty.

"No!" I scream as I scramble to get up.

"I ain't listening to you cry no more. I'm sick of it. All I've done for you and now you want to play baby? I don't think so."

I have one foot outside, when without hesitation, Dan throws new Betty into the fire. My heart sinks to the ground taking my body with it. I stay down, motionless with my mouth wide open and for several moments, I do not breathe. At some point the need for air overwhelms me, but I can't seem to remember how to suck air in or blow it out. A long gasp comes out of me as I regain my bearings. Standing, I watch the plastic face fold in on itself. I curse my ability to make a good fire. The tears are coming down like a faucet has been turned on but I'm not sobbing.

I turn to Dan and howl, "Why?"

He's laughing at me. The anger wells up inside me and my face is on fire. I want to lunge at his throat and rip his face off with my bare hands. But I'm no match for him. Instead, I turn and run as fast as I can. Since it's dark and the ground is uneven, my sprint is more of a jog. I hear Dan's voice laughing for far longer than I can stand. I finally hit the gravel pathway and speed up. I run in hopes that my pain will go away. But it doesn't. My panting replaces the hole in my heart for a moment as I approach the gas station.

I sit down by the empty gas pumps and catch my breath. My eyes focus on the scratched up pump that has rust holes near the base. For a long time, I rock back and forth and consider my options when suddenly my plan of action solidifies in my mind. I rise, brushing the dirt off my jeans, and walk inside where Kathy is at the register.

"What were you doing out there?"

"Thinking."

"'Bout what?"

Piggy

"Dan pissed me off again."

"What did he do?"

"I don't want to talk about it. Can I hang out for a while and watch TV?"

"Pull up a stool."

We sit behind the counter and watch E.R. Kathy's got on her usual attire -- jeans and a sweatshirt. This time she's got a second sweatshirt over the first since it's getting colder out. My eyes are scanning the place whenever she turns her head. There is a stack of corrugated boxes near the counter so I know a shipment of stuff has come in. I see what may be of help and excuse myself to go to the bathroom. I take a few steps to the boxes and palm the box cutter in my hand. I casually slip it into my pocket before turning around and feigning my forgetfulness to Kathy. She hasn't even glanced at me so I reach behind the counter and grab the community key. Once inside the bathroom, I yank out the semi-full trash bag and find another item. The janitor puts extra bags at the bottom. I swipe a few. Unfortunately they're white, not black like I had hoped. Outside the bathroom are the employee lockers. I quietly open the door and peek at Kathy. She's ringing up someone who must have pulled up. I quickly check all the lockers but they're empty except for the one with Kathy's purse and it's got a lock. My idea of swiping money from Kathy is a bust. The bell rings as the customer exits and I walk back around the corner.

We resume our TV watching positions and I wait until Kathy is engrossed in the program before looking for other money options. I get lucky as a half hour later two cars pull in and one guy comes in to pre-pay. Kathy rings him up but as she's handing back change the other guy sticks his head into the station.

"Pumps broken."

"You gotta jiggle it."

"I tried. It's broken."

"Christ," Kathy says under her breath and she follows the pre-pay guy outside. She hasn't shut the register drawer so I know this is my chance. I crouch down and move under the register. I reach up

Piggy

and feel for the twenty compartment. There's a big stack so I take a handful, leaving some. Next, I feel for the ten compartment but there aren't any. I know she keeps the big bills under the drawer so I raise my head up and lift the drawer up. I keep an eye to the outside to make sure no one is looking at the register. With one hand, I lift up the drawer and with the other, I feel a smattering of paper under it. I try to gather the papers up one handed but they slide all over. Seeing Kathy turn to come back inside, I grab what I can and shove it down the front of my shirt. I drop the drawer down and run my hand across the other compartments. The only other one with a stack of bills is the dollar slot. I snatch a handful and shut the drawer as the bell at the door dings. Dropping to my knees, I crawl back over to the stool.

"Piggy?"

After planting my butt down on the stool, I lift my head up to counter height. "I'm here. Just tying my shoe."

We watch TV for the next hour. I'm torn between fleeing and not looking guilty. Dan has always told me you gotta be cool when you steal. It's when you flee that they catch you. I've actually got to pee and wish I would have done it when I was in the bathroom before. But I have to wait as I don't want her to get suspicious. The wad of cash is tickling my chest and the box cutter is digging into my leg but I remain seated and pretend to be interested in the TV show.

A car pulls up before eleven when the show is ending and I steal away to the bathroom. There, I can pee in peace and arrange my loot. Walking out, Kathy is with a customer.

"You leaving?" she asks. I nod. "You can take my flashlight if you want."

"Thanks," I say as I take it out of her hand.

"Bring it back tomorrow," she shouts at me as I'm exiting the door.

I don't have to run home, now that I have the light. I feel bad about stealing from Kathy. She's always been good to me, but my plan is set. I've had enough of Dan. How could he do that to Betty, to me, all these years?

I turn off the flashlight as I approach the fire. Warren is sacked out and snoring up a storm and Dan is not in sight. I make it up to the van and see Dan passed out in back, door wide open. I slowly take out one of the trash bags and open it up. I drag my clothes slowly across the blanket mattress so as not to wake him. Stuffing them into the bag, I also snag Dan's coat and baseball hat. I look around for anything else and add the bottle of water to the bag. Spinning the top of the bag around, I knot it and place it by the front tire.

I know it's time but my stomach is doing jumping jacks inside me. I swallow and taste something sour. As I reconsider my plan, I remember that I haven't eaten anything, except for jam packets, since the breakfast at Denny's over twelve hours ago. I'm not tasting fear, but my stomach bile from yet another night going hungry because Dan is pissed off. Rage rises inside me and I tell myself over and over, 'Do This'.

I remove the box cutter from my pocket and gingerly place my foot in the van. I slowly put my body weight on it. Once both feet are inside and I'm bent over so as not to hit the roof, I take a few short steps over to Dan. I very slowly bend my knees until they touch the blanket, reaching out one hand for balance.

Now over him, on my knees, and with box cutter in hand, I look at where I'm supposed to cut. The throat is the vulnerable point, which I learned on E.R. His neck is fully exposed as he lies on his side. I have a clear shot. All I have to do is swipe him across the side of his neck. The jugular, the show calls it. One swipe and he's dead, or so the show indicates. I swallow hard and take a deep breath. My mind races through all the times I've gone to bed hungry and all the things Dan has made me do. Placing the blade just over him, I pause for a moment. Then in one swift motion, I cut.

The blade easily enters his neck and I immediately see blood. This is followed by a howl I have never heard before. Dan grabs his neck and turns his head to me as he howls a second time. He sees me, then sees the blade, then looks back directly at me. My eyes feel like they are going to pop out I've got them open so wide. I fall backwards and partially roll to the door, but not before he grabs my collar. I ram my right elbow back as hard as I can, hitting something and then swivel around on my butt, impulsively swinging my arm with the blade completely extended. I swipe at air. Dan has fallen against the side of the van to evade my swing. I stand up outside and open the passenger door. Grabbing the bat Dan keeps for protection, I now

Piggy

have two weapons. Dan is at the door when I shove the top of the bat into his sternum. He falls back howling again.

Warren rouses at the ruckus. His eyes are wide open staring at me. I quickly identify the bat is a better weapon for me. I look at the box cutter, but don't know how to get the blade to retreat so I throw it down next to my white trash bag. Dan is now exiting the van and I switch the bat handle to my right hand and take a swing. He side steps the full impact with the bat tip brushing against his upper arm. He loses his balance and hits the ground; blood streaming from his neck wound. I take a step back to assess what my options are. I see Warren out of the corner of my eye. He's still under the little blanket he sleeps with and his eyes are half shut. I'm not sure what he's doing. Maybe all those times he stared at me he was really feeling sorry for me. Maybe he's letting me have my due with Dan. No, I think. I can't trust him -- Dan's been his sugar daddy for some time now. There's no question which side he's really on.

I shake my head and focus on Dan who is now rushing at me. I take a big step to my left and he grazes by me. I twirl around and take an unguarded swing at his back and make contact. He stumbles forward and falls. His outstretched hand falls onto the bricks we use to line the fire pit and he howls again. Rolling over to his back, he gets up again as I take my time to swing at him good. His hand reaches up and intersects my bat and we're now in a tug of war. Getting to his feet, he pushes the bat back at me and it hits me hard in the stomach. Letting go of the bat, I fall to the ground biting the inside of my lip on the way down. He jostles the bat in his hands and spins it around to take the handle. I roll to my knees, jump to my feet, and run.

Dan slams the bat against the van as he runs after me.

"What the fuck are you doing?"

I continue around the front of the vehicle, buying myself time to think.

"Bitch! You NEVER hit me!"

"You're gonna get it now!"

As I turn the corner, Warren is looking right at me but still sitting in his chair with his blanket. Distracted by his eyes, I don't watch my footing and trip on something. As I fall down, I get a glimpse of Warren shutting his eyes and faking sleep. Dan is gaining on me. I quickly roll onto my back, knees up and perched on my elbows. Dan stops and takes a slow step to me.

"Well, aren't you fucked?"

I look from side to side. I'm trapped. I'm between the fire to my right and Dan's chair to my left. Dan takes another step when I see the tent pole. I kick it and the tarp falls down in front of Dan's face. I scoot backwards and turn onto my knees. Dan brings the bat straight down on top the tarp and the tent pole snaps as I frantically crawl to Warren edging the fire. The impact of the bat grazes me. Getting to my feet, I yank the other tent pole thinking it will aid in my escape. Instead, it drops the other side of the tarp down and Dan and I are looking straight at each other. Warren stirs, now covered by the tarp. I guess even he knows he can't convince Dan he's still asleep.

Dan points the bat at me and moves quickly to me as I pull to get the tent pole free. I can't get it free, but I'm able to twirl it around to block his path. The pole hits him full on at his neck. Coughing, he stumbles and loses his balance. He falls in slow motion backwards. There's a thud, then silence. Dan's face is no longer angry -- it's frozen with a surprised look as his mouth gapes open. His eyes are full of fear and then I see it. The other tent pole. The one he snapped with the bat. It's sticking out of him. I see the blood glisten in the fire light. I suck air in and remain standing. I've done it. I've killed him. Oh my God, I've killed him. Suddenly, my plan doesn't seem well thought out. Now all the police dramas fill my head. They always find the killer. That's what I am, a killer. I look around and Warren has pulled the tarp off of him. He's staring back and forth between me and Dan.

"Shit, Piggy! I thoughts you two were just going to have it out."

With that, I run. I run as fast as I can. I go through the junkyard the long way so as not to pass by the fire again.

"Piggy! You get back here!" Warren screams.

But I don't turn around, much less slow down.

"Piggy!" I hear Warren scream one last time.

Chapter 27

I run faster when I hit the pavement. I see the lights on at the gas station and keep running. Kathy may have already figured out the money's gone. I approach the highway on-ramp and slow down to catch my breath. Jogging, I continue up the ramp. I look down, shit, I forgot the trash bag. All my extra clothes are in it. I'm hot now, but I know I'll be cold later. Entering the highway, I continue south on the shoulder. There are cars headed northbound, but none so far going my direction. I keep watch knowing that if Warren gets into the van, he could easily find me. I consider walking in the dirt ravine next to the shoulder, but decide I'm making better time this way.

A driver going north flashes his brights. I turn around to see if he was flashing at me. A car driving southbound with one headlight is approaching. I put up my hand, but it doesn't even slow. I walk backwards because I can see more lights in the distance. Two semis pass me, but a third pulls over. The cab blows out hot air when I open the door. I take a good look at him. Sixties maybe seventies with a trimmed grey beard; he's got thick glasses that hide his eyes. A fleece jacket with sheepskin frames his neck.

"You getting in or not?"

I nod and climb in. With my head pointed downward, I stare at my shoe. "Thanks," I murmur.

"Where you headed?"

"South."

"Obviously. Where south?"

"Just south for now."

"You running?"

My head snaps to him and I can't disguise my look of discovery.

"Calm down. I don't give a shit."

Piggy

I remain silent and focus on the song on the radio hoping he's not a talker. It's a classic tune that Dan would listen to, but I can only remember the chorus – *Here comes the Sun, do do do do, Here comes the Sun...*

"I'm headed to Springfield. Been driving for a full day now," he offers.

I remain silent.

"There's a coat behind you if you want."

I reach back and find a large blue hoodie that smells of gas. I put it, grateful for the warmth. We ride in silence listening to the radio. I see a sign for Madison and let my eyelids droop. The rhythm of the truck lulls me to sleep.

A burst of cold air wakes me up as the old man gets out at a gas station. It's very early in the morning and the sun hasn't come up fully yet. The old man heads to the bathrooms. I soak in my surroundings. There's the freeway to my far left, a pitch black two lane road to my right, and a handful of gas stations and fast food joints surrounding the vicinity. The McDonald's across the street gets my stomach growling. I think about going over there for an Egg McMuffin when my hackles are alerted. He's been gone for a while. Maybe he's turning me in. Maybe there's an all point bulletin out for me already. He knows I'm running. At the very least, he could turn me in for that.

I take a quick look around the semi's interior and swipe a handful of change from the ashtray. Snagging a baseball hat from behind the seat, I climb down from the cab. Ducking down, I walk to the gas pump and hide behind it. I steal a look at the minimart. He's at the counter. I'm not taking any chances. I run crouched down across the driveway and street to the McDonald's. My hand is on the door when I think that this would be the first place they'd look. I turn and run to a Burger King that's on the other side of the freeway. I run as fast as I can under the overpass, glad that the sun's not up. A truck getting off the freeway honks at me as it passes by. I suspect I'm hard to see. I reach my destination and go straight into the bathroom. It's empty so I jump into the first stall and lock it. I stand on the toilet and wait.

Ten minutes later, I decide to risk taking a pee. Squatting on the toilet seat isn't comfortable but I make do. Feeling claustrophobic, I

Piggy

exit the stall and go into the handicap accessible stall. I see the diaper changing table. I pull it down and situate myself on it. Finally, a moment of privacy. I pull all the money out of my pockets and sock and tally it up. Some of the money isn't money. There are several checks and one lone hundred. This must have been what was under the drawer. I had hoped to get more, but this isn't bad, three hundred sixty-seven dollars. Along with the hundred, there is two-forty in twenties which I carefully fold flat and divide into three separate pockets. The change I swiped turns out to be nearly three dollars and I put that along with the twenty seven ones in my front right pocket. I wait another ten minutes or so, but no one comes in and I don't hear anything out in the hallway.

I come out of the stall and wash up. Wetting my hands, I run them through my hair that is in bad need of a wash. I reset my ponytail putting the hair through the hole in the cap that I place on my head. I tighten down the hat but it is still loose. I decide the hood up looks more natural. I fold the hat and shove it under my coat.

I head straight for the counter and order two croissant sandwiches and hash browns. I treat myself to orange juice and coffee. Once finished I survey my location and figure out my next move. The sun is nearly completely up now. Morning commute is not the time to hitchhike. Too much risk of being turned in as a delinquent.

I grab the free newspapers at the front entrance and come back to my booth. Leafing through, I think I'm actually in Madison. The two maps I find don't help me so I go to the counter.

"Is this Madison?"

"Outskirts. It's about five exits up the freeway."

"Are there any roads that can get me there?"

"Freeway's fastest, but if you turn left out here," the girl says pointing, "Go down about a mile and then turn left onto Rossmore. That goes on for, ah, I don't know, but it goes 'til you hit Madison limits. Maybe eight miles, or twenty. I don't know, I've always taken the freeway."

"Thanks," I say and walk out. Eight to twenty miles, I think. It's morning, I should be able to do that before dark. Hoping for eight, I

Piggy

walk out of the parking lot and pass another gas station. On the side, there are dumpsters and I catch sight of a wheel. There's a bike behind the dumpster. I adjust my path looking over my shoulder to see if anyone's watching. Grabbing the bike, I see the unused chain coiled around the seat and locked. Too bad. I wheel out and pedal hard down the road.

It's not a great bike but it gets the job done. I ride nearly twenty miles before I reach what must be Madison, slightly before noon. By guess I turn onto streets that look like thoroughfares. I see signs – Madison Cleaners and Madison Ford.

I go in what seems to be circles before I come across a strip of retail shops. At the end, is a post office. I wheel my bike inside not wanting someone to steal my stolen goods. The old lady at the counter gives me directions to the bus station. I embark on my journey and around three I pull up in front. I'm yelled at by a security guard when I take my bike inside. Outside, I place the bike in the rack and uncoil the chain as much as I can given the unused lock is firmly connecting the chain. I drape the chain around the front tire in hopes that the casual observer will think the bike is locked.

It's a small bus station with the ticket office inside. The person at the ticket counter tells me it's better to buy a ticket to Chicago then buy the one to Los Angeles there. That's where the major station is.

I fork over cash for the ticket.

"You need a tag for your luggage?" the man asks. Shaking my head, I walk over to the benches to wait the five hours for the next bus. The wait goes fast enough, I spend time flipping through magazines in the convenience store.

Soon enough I'm seated in the middle of the bus, next to the window, watching the trees on the side of the road whisk by. Dan and I spent some time on the outskirts of Chicago. Dan ran the apartment scam a few times there before we had to leave the area. He'd use me and our sad situation to get the manager job which meant free rent and much better facilities than the motels. We'd usually stay for three or five months, before the tenants complained too much. I made it through the third and fourth grade that way; changed schools six times.

Piggy

Once Dan had enough of a place, he would wait for a few apartments to become vacant. He'd have a fire sale one weekend and get prospective tenants to pay first and last rent at a discount; of course, getting them to write the check out to 'cash'. Once all places were 'rented' and he had pilfered what he could from the manager slush fund and laundry change machine, we'd be on our way to a check cashing place and onto a new gig.

The bus enters Chicago city limits at dawn and meanders through the empty streets to the bus depot. Getting out, the wind whips through me like a knife. The thin hoodie, which I'm wearing like a double breasted jacket, is no match for the cold wind. I rush into the station and immediately go to the ticket counter. The booth is closed and I glance at the clock, five-thirty in the morning. I look around the station and see pockets of people. I pick the safest looking group and sit on the benches near them. As always, my eyes are scanning the area and ground for anything of value. Once I found a five dollar bill, but mostly I find spare change. Now, I'm looking for duffle bags. Duffle bags that are easy access and may have something warm inside.

The coffee cart opens and is swarmed by passengers. I spot a few bag candidates but there are too many people around. Instead, I head to the ticket counter.

"Where to?"

"Los Angeles."

"Downtown or someplace else?"

"Ah, downtown."

"Direct?"

"Yes."

"Two thirty-five, plus taxes and fees."

"Is that the cheapest?" I ask doing the math in my head. I've got just over three hundred in three different pockets, but only about twenty in my front pocket. Buying this would leave me less than a hundred left.

Piggy

"We ain't supposed to do this, but you could buy a ticket to Omaha which will get in around six P.M., then spend the night in Omaha and take the morning bus to Grand Junction. Spend the night there and then again in Vegas. Then onto LA. You're basically buying four tickets. It's cheaper since you're not going overnight and we don't have to pay the drivers as much. Plus those are all busier routes. However, you are not allowed, officially that is, to sleep in the bus depots. So the cost of even the cheapest motel will eat up any savings."

I take in all the information but he's a fast-talker. "How much to Omaha?"

"Fifty-six, plus taxes and fees. Total is sixty-one fifty-two."

That would leave me with over two hundred. "I'll do that," I say taking the crisp hundred out of my back left pocket. Glad that I'm getting rid of that bill, the man hands me my change and ticket.

Walking back to the benches, I laugh remembering the two months of school I had in Winslow. They assumed since I was new that it would take me a while to get up to speed. I saw it in their faces, the familiar 'she's not too smart' look that the teachers gave each other when Dan went through his spiel to enroll me. If it was English class, I would have agreed with them or even science, but math class? That was always my strongest subject. Further the week I started, the third grade teacher had set up fake cash registers in a fictitious store to teach us how to make change. Heck, I was counting back change and slipping bills under the drawer like a pro. The teacher was shocked and asked me where I learned how to do all this. I kept a straight face and said 'lemonade stand'. Dan and I laughed all night after I told him that one. Smiling at the memory, I quickly remember that I'd killed him. I'm a murderer. I tell myself. Dan was mean to me, especially when I didn't do what he said. But kill him? Sitting in the breezy station shivering, it comes to me; I'm never going to see him again. Shockingly, a few tears well up and I shake my head hard to stop them. What am I doing? I hated Dan. Why am I suddenly feeling the pangs of missing him? Don't you be sorry for him, I remind myself. Then I go through all of the shit he did – the beating, the starving me for fun, working me to the bone, and forcing me to steal. Plus, there's no question in my mind, he burned down the house.

The loud speaker calls the bus to Omaha and I board with the other passengers. It's a nine hour ride with one stop. I sit with two

Piggy

younger women for lunch at our stop. They recount their entire sightseeing trip to me. They had ridden bikes along Lakeshore Drive and seen the Shedd Aquarium as well as spending too much time on Rush Street. I listen patiently while sizing up what could be in their bags. They're closer to my size than anyone else on the bus. On the second half of the ride, I tell them about my father who died in a car accident and how I was coming back from seeing my Nana in Chicago. I told them how hard it was for Nana to say goodbye to me and how much I missed my mom. They bought it all.

When we get off the bus in Omaha, they go to the bathroom, together of course, to freshen up. One of them leaves me their bag to watch. Mistake. I catch a local bus outside the station and head downtown. I follow a group of people off the bus and find myself in an old downtown area. I walk around and find a place where I can use the bathroom.

I totally score. There are two pairs of jeans, shirts, underwear, and a brand new sweatshirt that says 'Chicago' on it. I wet a tank top from the bag and return to the stall. I strip off my clothes that are sticking to me and pile them in the corner. I wipe myself down as best I can getting the chills as the cold cloth touches my body. I put on clean underwear and socks and the jeans. Long and a bit loose, I cuff the bottom and select a shirt. Repacking the bag, I grab my dirty clothes and shove them to the bottom of the trash can in the front of the bathroom. I still yearn for a real shower, but this is the best I've felt in a long time. I take a good look at myself in the mirror. Brown mousy hair slicked back into a ponytail, the hint of dark circles under my sunken eyes. I've got a fresh row of zits across my forehead, no doubt a gift from the filthy baseball cap I wore while sleeping on the bus. My nose has a smattering of freckles across it and seems too big for my face. The pale tannish yellow of my teeth results in closed-mouth smiles whenever possible. My new outfit looks good although the crotch hangs down a bit more than it should. The checkered blue shirt has cool snaps instead of buttons and the thick sweatshirt is warm, almost too warm. Next, I've got to find shoes.

I walk around for another two hours and find a place to eat cheaply. Eventually I come back to the place the bus dropped me off and wait. Soon enough a bus is there and I return to the station four hours after I left it, and buy my ticket to Grand Junction. Sixty more dollars down, I'm left with a little over one-fifty. I find a bench along the wall near some other passengers who are also waiting for the bus. I survey the scene as midnight approaches and the station empties out.

A security guard does his rounds to all remaining people in the station. Whether he's supposed to or not, he lets anyone with a ticket stay, kicking out anyone else. Planting himself near the entrance, he locks the doors and takes his seat at the guard desk. I lean back and close my eyes, my duffle bag clutched tightly under my arm.

Chapter 28

The ride to Grand Junction drags on. I've never been to Colorado and the scenery is beautiful along the drive. Staring out the window, I think about what my predicament. Dan probably had six different IDs on him; maybe the cops won't be able to identify him. Then I remember Warren. He'll tell them. He'd tell anyone anything over a six pack. If they figure out who Dan is, they can figure out who I am. He's my guardian so there must be some record. A new thought occurs to me, maybe Warren hid Dan somehow. Maybe he's taken over the junkyard. Who would really know if Dan disappeared? A few gas station clerks and junkyard regulars? If Warren was smart, he'd be able to talk himself out of any questions raised. Of course, nothing about Warren makes me think he is smart.

My thoughts turn to my story. People always want you to have a story. I decide I'm going to visit my dad in Los Angeles. But I dismiss that for anyone besides people on the bus or cashiers. Next, I decide I'm in college. No, that won't work. I'm a senior in high school. Yeah that's a little better. I'm pretty sure I look older than I am but it's a stretch to say eighteen. Maybe I say I'm seventeen but I took the GED so I could move in with my dad. That's good, I decide as the bus enters the depot around five o'clock.

I step off the bus with an entirely new identity in my head. Walking confidently, I enter one of six sets of double doors into the main hall. The depot is a single level building with expansive two-story ceilings. The main hall is nearly as wide as the ceiling is high. Most of the floor space is open except for the middle which has a large grouping of wooden benches in perfect alignment. There are also benches along the walls in a kind of outline to the hall. The walls are covered in murals depicting western motifs like stage coaches, cattle runs, or the pony express.

Hoping for a McDonald's, all I see is a diner near the main entrance. I exit the depot and look up and down the street, nothing. I'm starving so I walk back in and sit at the counter.

A slim twenty-something, fresh faced waitress sets a glass of water and a menu in front of me as she continues her walk down the counter. Her long blonde hair is pulled back tight and braided down her back. She's got a zip up the front uniform on with heavy nylons and tennis shoes. I watch her as she skillfully picks up plates, refills

Piggy

coffee, and takes orders. It takes a while, but eventually she gets to me.

"What can I get you?"

"Cheeseburger and fries."

"Anything else?"

I shake my head.

"Medium?"

I tilt my head unsure what she means.

"You want your burger cooked medium?"

"I guess," I say still not sure what it means.

I watch her while I wait. She's the only waitress here and the counter is full, along with five tables. She doesn't miss a beat and is always moving. There's a manual glass washer behind the counter so when she's not pouring coffee, making change, or bussing plates, she's washing the dishes. She's pretty with a clear, clean face and not a hint of makeup. Most women I've seen pile the makeup on. My burger comes and I devour it, surprised at how hungry I am. By the time she comes to claim my plate, only a handful of tables remain.

"You done?"

"Yeah," I say looking down at a nearly clean plate.

"How about some dessert?"

My mouth waters. "How much do I owe you so far?"

"Nine dollars with tax, so under ten."

"Let me think about it."

"Where are you going?"

Piggy

"What do you mean?"

"You're at a bus depot. Where you off to?"

"Nowhere," I say completely forgetting the story I had conjured up.

"How old are you?"

I pause for a moment. "Eighteen."

"Hmm," she says before getting interrupted by customers standing by the register.

I sit at the counter nursing my water and dreaming about ice cream. Regardless of how cold it is outside, my taste buds are churning as I flip through the plastic menu with the pictures of all the types of sundaes you can get.

The waitress returns. "You want to order something?" she says looking at the menu in my hand.

"No."

"I'm Sam," she says offering me her hand to shake, "Its short for Samantha."

"Nice to meet you."

"What's your name?"

"Susan," I reply without hesitation.

"Well, Susan, I'm beat. You mind if I smoke?" she asks. I shake my head. "I've been here since ten and it is finally letting up. I think this is the last of the dinner rush," she says pointing to the remaining tables.

"You the only one here?"

"Yep. Just me and the cook. But he's Mexican. I can barely understand a word he says. I'm doing a favor for my boss. He owns

Piggy

another diner closer to town which is where I normally work. He was shorthanded today and called me."

"Yeah it looked like you were running around all over the place."

"What he didn't tell me was I'd be working lunch and dinner alone. Jeez. I ran around like a chicken with its head cut off. The customers aren't happy when they have to wait, and then I get lousy tips."

She continues to lament her troubles for the next hour. The place is open until nine but no new customers have come in since I sat down. She does most of the talking. She tells me about growing up in Grand Junction, about her high school, and about her ten year reunion coming up next summer. About an hour later, she disappears into the kitchen and brings out a chocolate sundae with whipped cream and a cherry.

"Here, it's on the house," she says.

I gobbled it down and lick the spoon for any remaining chocolate.

"What are you going to do, spend the night here?" she asks.

Surprised that Sam has surmised my plan, I think of a plausible answer, "No, I'm waiting for my dad."

"Really?" raising her eyebrows. "When was he supposed to be here?"

"Ah, about now."

She leans on the counter to me. "The last bus arrived twenty minutes ago. This place, and the station, closes down in thirty minutes, and you've been here for nearly three hours. C'mon, tell the truth."

"I'm taking a bus to Los Angeles tomorrow."

"Why you going to la la land?"

Piggy

"No Los Angeles, it's where my dad is."

"I lived in San Francisco for a few years and everyone there called L.A. la la land. Get it? Anyways, is your dad alright with you spending the night in a bus depot?"

"Yes," I say garnering the most confident voice I have. "Where's the bathroom?"

"It's down at the end, but wait here for a minute," Sam says. I watch her walk through the empty restaurant and to the entrance. She pulls down the gate and goes into the kitchen. A few minutes later, she's behind the counter running something on the cash register.

"This will only take a few minutes," she yells to me from the other side of the counter. I sit and wait, not sure if I've been locked in or not. The cook comes out and hands her some keys. He goes back into the kitchen. Sam locks up the cash drawer in a cabinet along with a long tape of paper. She motions for me to follow her. I jump off my stool and walk to the gate turning to follow her into the kitchen.

"Exit is back here," she says.

We go out through a nondescript door at the back of the kitchen and then we're inside the main hall of the depot.

"If you're going to stay here tonight, and I really don't think you should, don't go to the bathroom alone. Out in the open, there are usually enough people and there's a security guard that patrols, but the bathroom is too isolated."

We reach the door and open it. The smell of stale urine is overwhelming.

"Yeah, it's bad," Sam says. "Lots of times the bums come in here because the men's room gets even worse. Just hold your nose."

We both enter stalls, side by side, and I unzip my jeans. I pull down my underwear and sigh in surprise. I'm bleeding, but I don't know from where. I unroll a handful of toilet paper and wipe but with only marginal success.

"You okay over there?"

"Ah, yeah."

"What's wrong?"

"Ah, nothing."

"You hurt or something? You don't sound right."

"Ah, I'm not sure."

"What do you mean? What's wrong?"

"I'm.. I'm bleeding. I mean I guess it's stopped but I bled."

"You got your period?"

"What?"

"Your period? Do you need a tampon?"

"I don't know."

"Susan, you're bleeding between your legs right?"

"Yes."

"Have you gotten your menstrual period before?"

"I don't know."

"Hold on," she says outside my stall door. There's a crank and then the sound of a candy bar coming out of a vending machine. A box appears under the door.

"Here. If your underwear is messy, wrap it with toilet paper and then put this pad on between your legs."

I do what she says having a harder time getting the jeans back up. Opening the door, I walk past her to the sink to wash my hands.

Piggy

"Don't worry, I'll explain," she says. "Why don't you come home with me tonight? What time is your bus tomorrow?"

"I didn't buy the ticket yet."

"Then it's settled. You can crash on my couch. This is no place for a girl," she said holding the door open for me. As I pass by her, she says, "Eighteen, my ass."

Outside the wind whips at us as we jog to her beat up blue and rust colored Chevy Nova. Getting in, she starts it up and puts it in gear. It's a manual transmission so I watch her seamlessly shift the gears. She explains what a period is and after several questions I finally ask, "This is every month?"

She bangs on the steering wheel in laughter, "Afraid so. Little Auntie Flo comes every month." Turning to me with a serious face, "And when it doesn't it means you're pregnant."

Sam's apartment complex is a three-story rectangular building with long dimly lit hallways that smell of smoke. She unlocks her door and turns on the light. I enter and see a small kitchen to my right with black and white checkerboard tiles which immediately reminds me of Mom's house. In front of me, the living room has a cozy and over-stuffed light brown couch with a small coffee table and a rocking chair off to the side. There's a door to the left that is half opened which I assume is the bedroom. Plain ivory drapes cover the few windows and are closed tight.

"You got extra clothes in here?" she says pointing to my bag.

"Yes."

"Bathroom's in there. Why don't you change and I can wash your jeans."

I turn realizing the door I saw was really a bathroom. The bedroom is across from it. I turn the light on and enter a baby blue bathroom. Baby blue tile, baby blue toilet, and baby blue walls surround me. There's a darker blue cover on the toilet seat and a matching rug around the base along with blue towels. There are even little baby blue Dixie cups on the counter.

"If you want, take a shower," Sam says through the door.

It hadn't crossed my mind at first, but I gleefully strip off my clothes and crank the hot water. She has shampoo and condition that smell like lavender and soap with little grains of sand or something in it. If I scrub too hard, it hurts my skin. I must have stayed in there for an hour because my skin is all wrinkly and the entire bathroom is moist and steamy when I pull back the curtain. I rifle through my bag and put the other pair of jeans on. They fit much better and I wonder why I didn't wear these to begin with. I put on the same shirt because I like it better than the one with flowers. Opening the door, I follow a burst of steam into the living room.

"I thought you were going to die in there."

"Sorry, I haven't had a good shower for a while."

She grabs my dirty clothes and places them on top of a basket before exiting the apartment. "Be right back," she says, adding, "Make yourself at home."

I have a few minutes to really check the place out. Glancing at the kitchen floor, I flashback to the many times I mopped the kitchen floor at home. The kitchen cabinets are a light brown wood with a coating of clear polyurethane and little silver knobs. The counter tops are a speckled white, black, and tan formica. I open the fridge and it's full. There's beer, soda, milk, a bag of apples, Tupperware containers filled with the unknown, a carton of eggs, some English muffins and a loaf of bread. I reach for a soda and search for an opener.

Continuing my inspection, I walk back to the bathroom and enter the bedroom. It's a modest size room with a bed in the center. The quilted bedspread has a square for each state in the US. I read and count the number of states I've been to when I remind myself, my time is limited. There are two matching bedside tables with a small lamp on one. I see a handful of photos on top the dresser. Sam is in most of them; there's an older couple with her at what must be her graduation, one of Sam and a young man on a beach, and then two others that must be family vacations. I hear the key in the door and I pop back out and turn off the light. Walking back into the living room, I brush my wet hair with my fingers so that it looks like I just came out of the bathroom.

"Remind me in forty minutes to switch it to the dryer," Sam says as she walks into the apartment and into the kitchen. "You need anything?"

"Thanks, I'm good," I say raising my soda. "It's very nice of you to let me sleep here."

Sam comes and sits in the rocking chair with a beer and her cigarettes. She motions for me to sit on the couch.

"Tell me about yourself, Susan."

"I already told you, I'm going to Los Angeles to stay with my dad."

"How old are you really?"

I pause, knowing she didn't buy eighteen. "Sixteen and a half."

"And you never got your period before?"

"No."

"Most girls get it by fourteen, some at eleven. I got mine at twelve," she says rocking slowly back and forth. "Where were you before this?"

"Nowhere," I quickly say. She seems to know more about me than I know I've said.

"You had to come from somewhere. You a runaway?"

"No."

"Listen, I know you're lying. I don't care; I'm not going to hurt you or anything. But I'm not letting someone sleep here if I don't know them at all."

"I'm running away from my dad," I say wishing I could take the words back as soon as I say them.

"Then who is in Los Angeles?"

"Ah… Ah, my mom. But she doesn't know I'm coming," I state recovering from my mistake.

"Hmm. Tell me why you're running."

"He hits me sometimes and is real mean. I couldn't take it anymore."

"Where were you?"

"Omaha."

"Did you grow up there?"

"Yeah, around there."

"Why aren't you with your mom?"

I need a new story; but I have no time to think of one; she keeps peppering me with questions. Why wouldn't I want to be with my mom? My mind goes blank.

"Why aren't you with your mom now?" she asks again.

I look back at her blankly.

"You think too much before you answer, I know you're lying."

I can't do it anymore. I'm too tired. I can't think of anything to say. The silence is deafening as Sam sits across from me staring deep into my eyes. Gnawing at my fingernail, I give up. "My mom died when I was little. I've been living with my dad ever since. But he does hit me and he is mean," I say keeping some of my half-truths to myself. "We lived in a shit hole; I was always hungry; I wasn't going to school; I… I…. I just needed to get away."

Piggy

"I think that's the first thing you've said that I've believe. Now, how old are you really?"

"Fifteen and a half," I admit. "My birthday is in June next year."

"I guess you're a late bloomer. Are you hungry now?"

"No, I had that sundae."

"What are you going to do tomorrow?"

"I don't know."

"What is in Los Angeles for you?"

"Nothing, I guess, it's just far away," I say remembering I had already said I grew up in Omaha.

"You know it's dangerous to travel on your own. And Los Angeles isn't the safest place. You sure you want to go there?"

I shrug.

"How about this. The guy I work for has a waitress opening at the other place where I work most of the time. You ever wait tables?"

"No."

"It isn't that hard. You could work there with me. It's nearly the holidays so the tips will be good. Then you can think about what you want to do next."

"I don't know."

"Why don't you come in with me tomorrow and we'll see if you can get the job? You can stay here on my couch and we'll work out some sort of rent later. Agreed?"

"What's in it for you?"

"Not much, but it will help me with the rent."

"Why are you helping me?"

"Because I've been there too. My mom's second husband was an asshole. As soon as she met him, she forgot about me and always took his side. I didn't run away, but I think I know what you're feeling," she said. "And sometimes when someone offers help, they mean just that – help."

Chapter 29

The diner is much nicer than the one at the train station. There is a long counter with a row of men taking up all the cushy red stools. Across from the counter is a large open space filled with a mix of metal tables with stainless steel chairs or red upholstered booths. It's at least twice the size of the bus depot location. The lights are daylight level bright and there's a wall of mirrors on the far side. The place is half full and there are two waitresses running around.

It's nine-thirty and I'm following Sam, wearing an extra pair of tennis shoes she had. They are a bit big but in much better shape than the ones I had. 'Breakfast shift' she says over her shoulder as we stroll in. We go straight into the back and into an office.

"Lou? Got a minute?"

A balding man with a few strands of hair on the top of his head looks up. He's pale as can be and pudgy with a white short sleeved shirt that is transparent to the T-shirt underneath. I'm finally warming up after a freezing drive here, yet he's sweating. The hum of dishwashers is all we hear as he slowly picks up his glasses and puts them on.

"What?"

"This is my cousin, Susan, from Omaha. She's interested in the job."

"How old are you?"

I pause not sure what to say. Luckily Sam chimes in. "Seventeen next month. She's staying with me for a while."

"Got any waitress experience?" the man turns to me to ask.

I follow Sam's lead, "Yeah, I worked at the Denny's back home."

Lowering his head, "Fine, you're training her. She can start tomorrow."

Piggy

"Thanks Lou. Can she shadow me today to learn the menu?"

"Sure," he says as she grabs my shoulder and pulls me with her. "But I ain't paying her for that," he yells as we enter a small room filled with lockers and mops.

Sam opens a closet and pulls out a uniform. Holding it up to me, she returns it and digs for another. Handing me the second one, she tells me to change in the bathroom. Dressed and ready to go, I follow Sam to the hot food line where she orders two omelets 'the way she likes it' from the cook. They're full of creamy, gooey cheese, although I could have done without the peppers and mushrooms. I clean my plate and Sam punches in showing me how the time card works.

I follow Sam for the entire day, helping her as best I could. First, we prep the back station – cleaning ketchup and mustard bottles and 'marrying' them with the less full ones, filling the ice bins, napkins holders, and straw holders, and setting up what seems to be a hundred pieces of lettuce tomato combos. She says they're used as garnish on all the plates and that we're to help out the kitchen staff.

Ten forty-five and Sam gets her first table. She tells me that she starts taking them before eleven so the early shift doesn't get stuck staying with a lone table that never leaves. Besides, she says, you always want to do favors; you never know when you'll need one. I am literally Sam's shadow as she waits on tables. I say nothing but watch intently. She has some way of taking orders that I haven't figured out yet. An abbreviated mess of letters is what it looks like. She's always moving and no matter where I stand, I'm in her way. After the lunch rush dies down, she tells me to deliver two sodas to a table to see how I use a tray. I hold the tray in two hands, shaking, until she orders me to the back of the kitchen to practice walking back and forth, one handed with the tray.

Before I know it, the dinner rush starts. Sam calls them the early birds which doesn't make a lot of sense to me, since most are really old. Several have walkers or canes which means it takes them forever to get in and out of their seats. Around seven fifteen, Sam stops taking tables. We order dinner in the kitchen and I feast on a delicious double cheeseburger, fries, and an icy soda. We never actually got lunch, but I guess breakfast was a bit late.

"You think you can do this?"

Piggy

"Yeah. I got to practice with the tray more."

"You need to learn the menu more and I haven't shown you how to make change."

"I know how to do change," I say with a smile, and then add, "I used to work in my dad's business sometimes. He had a pawn shop."

"Great, that's usually the hardest thing to train. You ready to go home?"

We watched TV the rest of the night and she didn't pressure me with more questions.

The next few weeks fly by. I get the hang of waiting tables quickly and can take over an entire section by the end of my second week, even during lunch rush. I'm amazed at the tips I earn -- forty-two dollars in one day -- although Sam says they'll get better. Sam helped me fill out the paperwork for the job. When I asked what a social security number was, she rattled off hers as an example. I must have had a blank look on my face because next, she suggested a number I could call to get mine. I quickly lied and said I knew it. Using the first three digits she recited, I randomly filled in the rest of the boxes.

Sam and I have been inseparable, a likely product of working every day. Sam wants to work as many shifts as possible over the holidays, which she says is the best time for tips. We eat at the restaurant for breakfast and dinner and then come home and crash in front of the TV. Sam usually falls asleep soon after we get home, but I don't feel tired at all. The couch is comfortable and warm, so much nicer than what I'm used to.

When Halloween comes, Sam says we have to dress up. We plan to go shopping after work and bring street clothes with us. It's Friday night and Sam says there's a good secondhand store for costumes that's open late. I'd been living in her sweats or my uniform for two weeks so I hadn't noticed that I've gained weight. In the bathroom, where we change, I have a hard time zipping up my jeans. Sam notices.

"Maybe you should get some clothes that fit, while we're out," she says while fixing her hair. "And more stylish."

She leaves and I'm alone at last. I head into a stall and perform my daily ritual of combining all my money and counting it; I have never been without it. I've got quite the wad of bills now; almost four hundred and since I don't want any bills over twenty, it's a fat stack. Transferring the money from my uniform, I have to squeeze the wad into my front pocket. The creases of the bills stab into me and I'm fairly certain I'm not going to be able to sit down. Sam calls out to me and I grab my uniform and walk out.

The shop has a neon sign of brightly lit letters across the awning, 'Out of the Closet'. There are a handful of parked cars and we find a spot in front. Walking in, Sam suggests that I dress like a cowgirl since I've already got the shirt.

"I don't have a cowgirl shirt."

"Yes you do. That one you were wearing when I met you. It's hicksville."

"Really? I like that one."

Rolling her eyes, she pleads, "Please let me help you pick some stuff out that was made in the last decade."

The shop is long and narrow with three rows of clothes in the middle running the entire length of the store as well as on either side of the outer wall. We walk up and down the long aisles as Sam pulls out items for herself and me. This place does have better stuff than Goodwill. Sam hands me six pairs of jeans and too many tops to count. Rounding the last aisle, we approach the shoes and accessories section. She hands me a belt and tells me to find shoes that fit. I look at the pile of shoes on the floor that may have been neatly arranged on the shelves at one time, but not anytime recently. Realizing the big handwritten sign reading '7' refers to size, I sort through the pile and find a pair of black tennis shoes that fit and a pair of brown walking shoes. Carrying my discoveries to Sam, she's holding up a red felt cowgirl hat and a red bandana under her arm.

Approving of the tennis shoes, she nixes the brown ones calling them geriatric wannabes. She takes a few steps to the pile and kicks at the edges with her foot.

"Let's try this stuff on, and then we can hit Payless."

Piggy

Sam does have taste. What looked okay on the hanger, looks great on me. Two pairs of jeans fit and aren't too short. There's a coral colored cashmere blend sweater that I love. It has a big snag on the ribbing around the wrist, but the sleeves are too long for me anyway, rolling them up you can't see any flaw. A thick sweatshirt with 'Go Bulldogs' seems appropriate given how cold it is here.

"Lemme see," commands Sam.

I yank back the curtain and step out in my coral sweater, new jeans, and a sweatshirt coat that has fake sheepskin fleece on the inside. Twirling around and happy, I gaze at myself in the three way mirror. I look good. I can't remember the last time I had clothes that I liked. Dan always bought me what was cheapest and often too big so I'd grow into them.

"Looks good. Try on the blue shirt and some other jeans."

I continue my fashion show and in between outfits, Sam's hand appears in the fitting room with more options. On my last outfit, she places a much needed ski coat over my shoulders. I put on my favorite outfit and look through my buy pile. Two pairs of jeans, a pair of black tennis shoes, three sweaters, a sweatshirt and pants, the fake sheepskin fleece sweatshirt, a ski jacket, and two shirts. Tallying up the cost, I put back two sweaters, one shirt, and decide on the fake fleece over the ski jacket. Sam tries to convince me to buy more adding that the tips will get better. I decline saying I don't want to spend too much.

"The clothes are better, but the prices are higher," I reply while at the register and sadly forking over my money. If I hadn't nearly frozen on the way into work this morning, I probably wouldn't have bought all I did. Of course, if I was here on my own, I wouldn't have bought anything, I would have swiped it all. But with Sam watching me, I knew I couldn't steal anything without her calling me out.

"You gotta get the coat. You have no clue how cold it gets here," Sam pleads.

"This will be fine."

"You'll be sorry."

We walk out and I look down, she's not carrying anything. "What did you buy?"

"Nothing."

"What about a costume?"

"I can wear what I did last year. I've got a black robe, it's more of a cloak, that I cinch around my waist and then using a few white paper plates and coffee filters, I can make it look like a nun." Continuing after we get into the car, "Last year I stuffed a pillow under it and said I was pregnant, but the cloak is so big on me, most people didn't notice."

We drive a few blocks and pull into Payless to look for boots; no luck, plus I don't want to buy anything that I'm going to wear once. We see Goodwill on the drive home and find a pair of red faux boot clogs. Slip on clogs with no backs, the toes are pointy like a pair of cowboy boots. They're five dollars and Sam buys them for me since I didn't want to waste the money.

It's late when we get home and we immediately go to bed. We have to be up early because we're doing the breakfast shift.

Dressing in the morning, I don't feel like I'm in much of a costume until the bandana and hat are put on. I stare at the shirt that Sam calls hicksville in the mirror. I still like it. Sam emerges from her bedroom with an enormous black tent over her and a black napkin on her head. She pops into the bathroom and with some skillful placement of bobby pins the napkin transforms into a habit. Next she pulls a small stack of paper plates out of her bag. She cuts one into a long curved strip and using a piece of tape to complete the circumference, she creates a collar. Next, she cuts a half moon shape and wedges it next to the collar securing it with bobby pins in either side. In a matter of minutes, she transforms into a nun.

It's not even five am and we're off to work where we hit the ground running as soon as we walk in. The closing shift didn't set up the tables so we have to scramble to lay out napkins and silverware. Since its morning, Sam has me add coffee cups which adds to the chaos. Sam is still moving at twice my speed even though she's encumbered by her bulky costume.

Customers stream in and I'm swamped. People eat slower at lunch with a table turning maybe once every forty-five minutes; but at breakfast, seats are turning every twenty minutes. The tips are about the same as lunch time, although Sam says that's because of our costumes, otherwise, she says, we'd get a buck a plate.

Once the rush fades, we steal a few minutes to eat before the lunch rush. I order a cheeseburger because I can't look at another egg. I eat about half of it before being called to a table and finish the rest, one bite at a time as I'm in the kitchen. The day flies by and Sam's right, the tips get much better. I play up my character deciding I am Annie Oakley which gets a lot of laughs. Sam's costume is still better. We recount our best and worst customers on the ride home. I barely have enough energy to pull on sweats before passing out from exhaustion.

The next day we sleep in on a much needed day off. It's Sunday and I awake to church bells ringing out eleven chimes. Sam hasn't stirred so I take the opportunity to count my money. I made nearly a hundred dollars in tips yesterday and I can't believe it. I made back all that I spent on clothes. I turn the TV on and set the volume low as I channel surf. Sam gets up after noon and joins me on the couch too tired to talk or shower. Before we know it, the sky is darkening. We order a pizza and only get up off the couch to pee or get a soda. I think about all the times I watched TV with Dan. Why wasn't it like this? We're sitting here, cozy, not bothering each other; and Sam hasn't yelled at me or laid down the law on what we'll watch. The only annoying thing is her smoking but even that is less than Dan's habit. I shake my thoughts out of my head and relax into the night.

Chapter 30

Monday morning, we're back to our regular schedule of lunch and dinner shifts. Starting next week, we'll have every Monday off instead of Sunday. Sam says we've been covering for Janet which is why we've been working nonstop. After clocking in, Lou steps out of his office. I've barely seen him since I started although occasionally he runs the counter if we're shorthanded. He calls Sam and me over and hands us envelopes.

"You gonna work Thanksgiving for me?"

"Is Julio making the good stuffing this year?"

"I haven't thought that far ahead, just trying to cover the holidays. Sally's raising a fit about working too much again."

"If Julio makes the good stuffing, we'll both work and we'll work Christmas Eve and Christmas too."

"Seriously?"

"Hey, I got no family in town and I'm saving up for a new car. The one I have may not make it once it really starts snowing."

"Works for me, thanks," he says retreating back into his office. As we walk back to the prep station, he pokes his head out of the doorway, "Hey kid, good hustle out there."

I smile with pride as Sam pats me on the back. "You must be doing good; he never says anything nice."

Handing her my envelope, she won't take it. "Open it."

"What is it?"

"It's your paycheck."

I rip open the envelope and stare at the check – two hundred forty-two dollars and sixty-five cents. My gaze slowly climbs up to meet Sam's eyes. "Really?"

Piggy

"We don't just work for tips," Sam says with a laugh. "Don't get too excited, soon enough you'll be wondering why the check is so little. Plus, one-fifty of that is mine for letting you stay with me."

I nod as a tear comes to my eye. This is the most money I've ever had. I've seen poker pots this size but those weren't mine. This is the best job ever. I can't believe that a few weeks ago I was begging Dan for a few dollars. Why didn't he get a job waiting tables? We wouldn't have had to sleep in a van. It's so easy to make money. I'm not even tired and I think I've made over five hundred dollars since I started. I cry and look at Sam who is studying me.

"Thank you."

She hugs me. "I'm glad I could help."

Partially wiping my tears on her shoulder, I lean back. "I.." I begin before being overwhelmed by a sob that requires me to catch my breath. "I,.. I...," continuing my attempt, "I want to go back and get the coat."

Laughing, "Sure thing we can go back. Right now, we've got tables."

Before I know it, it's Thanksgiving and the stuffing was as Sam demanded -- excellent. I haven't been able to remember what Mom's stuffing tasted like, but I know I loved it. Over the years with Dan, we'd mostly make it to a shelter or soup kitchen for Thanksgiving; on rare occasions, we'd go to a sit down restaurant for the feast. Dan always remembered Thanksgiving; he loved mashed potatoes and pumpkin pie. He didn't hold any of that same fondness for Christmas. Eating the stuffing Julio made surpassed it all. I ate so much I felt like I was going to throw up. Sam laughed and told me to drink plenty of water to kill the starch bomb I had ingested.

Sunday morning after Thanksgiving, we get into the cold car to drive to work.

"Hey, so everything is going good, right? You know staying at my apartment and stuff," Sam says.

"I'm fine. Thank you for letting me stay."

"Do you think you'll be okay being in the apartment by yourself?" I nod looking at her.

"I'm going out tonight with some friends. We're going to a bar in Grand Junction and you're not old enough."

"I'm fine on my own."

"I know but it's the first time you're alone here. And honestly, I don't know how to explain you to my friends."

"Don't worry about me. I'll be fine."

"I haven't pressured you about your past or why you're here. I figure you'll tell me when you're ready. But until then, I'm not going to give you a key." She turns to look at the expression on my face.

"That's fine," I say not exactly knowing why she's making such a point out of this.

"So you'd be trapped at the apartment Sunday night. And if I spend the night with my friend, maybe until Monday morning too." I remain silent. "That okay?"

I nod.

That night, I sit with Sam in the bathroom, watching her get ready. She applies a layer light brown foundation all over her face. This is followed by concealer and then a powder. Her eyes take the most steps with three different color shadows, a dark black eye liner, and mascara to finish. The result is stunning. I had thought she was attractive, but now truly see her as beautiful. She styles her hair down so that it's full and wavy from scalp to tip. I'm so used to seeing her in a braid, I barely recognize her. Dressed in slimming jeans and an animal print top, she walks to the door for her coat.

"You look good," I say.

"Thanks. I will probably spend the night so that I don't have to drive. I may not be home until noon."

"Don't worry about it, I'm going to watch TV and then sleep in."

The door shuts and I turn the TV on and wait thirty minutes before I search her apartment. There's really nothing I haven't seen. She's got a stash of cash in her sock drawer all the way in the back. I count out five hundred dollars and carefully place it back where it was. There are some pieces of jewelry in a small box on top her dresser. Nothing of much value although I like the blue feather earrings. The bottom drawer has another box with a small diamond necklace in it, along with some pearl earrings that appear dated in style. There's also a locked file cabinet that I try for ten minutes to pick. The spring must be angled weird because I can't get it open and fear I'll scratch the cabinet. I decide to look for the key in Sam's purse next time I have the chance.

I put on some of her clothes but she's taller and a bit wider than me. I walk around the living room in a few pairs of her high heels and then resign myself to TV and a night of whatever I want to watch.

I wake up in a sea of broken potato chips from the night before. Feeling restless, I decide to explore the neighborhood. I rummage through the kitchen junk drawer and find some duct tape. Cutting off a piece, I lay it across the door latch. Now the door swings open freely. I tie a piece of string on the inside door knob and thread it around the door jam, it's just enough tension to keep the door shut.

Outside, I walk the sidewalk that borders the apartment building. It's a basic three story rectangular building with entrances on the front and back and additional fire exits at the ends. The parking structure entrance is in the back with the cars in two levels underneath. There is one elevator at the far end from our apartment.

When I complete the loop, I decide to expand my perimeter walk. I walk to the far curb away from the parking entrance. As I'm stepping off, I see Sam's car slowing in front of the parking entrance. I wait for her car to enter the garage, gluing my body to the small tree that is nearby. I don't see her head turn so I'm fairly certain she hasn't seen me. Once out of sight, I run to the first door I can and beat Sam back to the apartment by a few minutes. Enough time to dispose of the tape.

Chapter 31

It snows at the beginning of December and I'm grateful for my rescued ski coat along with the matching gloves, hat, and scarf I also splurged for. Dan and I usually went south for the hard part of the winter so I'm not used to the cold and wet that comes with snow. Tips get better as Christmas approaches and I find they get even better when I tell them my mom has passed. I play up my sorry situation. I even have a sigh down that is on the edge of a squeak which works nearly every time and garners me extra heavy tips.

Sam is happy and continuing to chip away at her goal for a new car. She is cashing my checks for me and handing me the amount less rent every two weeks. After a while, I resort to carrying a small purse because my growing wad of cash won't fit in my pockets and I remain adamant that only small bills will do. My purse never leaves my side except at the diner, when I lock it in my own locker with a heavy padlock that I got at the drugstore.

Sam continues going out on Sunday nights with her friends and gets home later and later on Monday morning. This arrangement gives me time to explore the neighborhood and Sam eventually trusts me with a spare key. I find two different strip malls a few blocks in opposite directions of the apartment. One has a Subway and a convenience store. I eat Monday breakfast at Subway as a substitute for McDonald's Egg McMuffin which I really crave.

The other strip mall is centered on retail with a small jewelry store, a hair salon, and my favorite, a Tuesday Morning store. I spend hours perusing the aisles with particular attention devoted to the aisle full of figurines. It's segmented by type starting with a clown section, a sports section which has cartoon characters holding baseball bats or golf clubs; next is a princess section, and then an animal section. At the end, after the puppies, cats, and bird collectibles, is a small group of butterfly figurines. Mom's butterflies were individual; most of these are perched on a branch with flowers making the butterfly only a part of the figurine, not the entire thing. Only two are individual – a little blue and white butterfly with no unique markings and a gold and brown Monarch that reminds me of the one I saved from Mom's house only to have Dan break it in anger. About the size of my palm, the Monarch has gold veins throughout the wings and a gold body. The base is small giving the illusion the butterfly is in flight. With a slight movement of my head, my eyes check the ceilings and walls for cameras or mirrors. I plan my next move taking into account the large mirror the

Piggy

shopkeeper uses to see people in the back of the store. Turning my shoulders slightly, I quickly snatch the Monarch and gently drop it down my shirt. I continue shopping roaming through several more aisles while arranging the Monarch in a position under my shirt that can't be noticed. I leave the store ten minutes later when two women enter. My plan is to get the blue butterfly next Monday.

Christmas Eve and Lou is working in his office. At one pm; he puts on his overcoat and shuts his door. Walking over to us at the counter, he has a piece of paper in his hand.

"You got my number if anything happens, right? You're locking up and opening on your own tomorrow," he says to Sam, who is nodding her head. "You memorized the alarm code?"

"Yes," she says in a tone that highlights her annoyance.

"Thanks for working, both of you." Turning to me, he says, "Susan, I got this letter from the government. Says the social security number you gave me isn't valid. Can you fill this out again so I can file it?"

I nod not knowing what else to do. Sam steps in for me, "She probably transposed the numbers," she says.

"Great, slip this under the door when you're done. Merry Christmas!" he shouts as he waves to us and the cooks and walks out.

I stare at Sam and open my mouth, but nothing comes out.

"Let's talk about it tonight," she interrupts.

Throughout the day, we work in silence only discussing tables when necessary. I know I need to get a social security number. Sam's going to pressure me again about it. I run through ideas and land on stealing someone's ID. Problem is, the only females here are me and Sam. My only option is a customer and I calculate my risks. Get caught and likely get fired. Probably lose my place to stay. Don't get an ID and get fired for no valid number. Sam's got that look in her eye like she's going to have it out with me and press me to search for my real number. We've had the conversation once before. Sam told

Piggy

me that someday, I'd have to get the number, which basically meant she knew I lied before. I tried to convince her that I never got one and I should apply now, but she said it was automatic at birth. If I can get a valid number, I'll tell her I had it the whole time. I was just too afraid my dad would find me. That sounds good. Next, I scan my tables looking for targets.

There's an elderly couple by the corner that may work. The man has a walker parked nearby and seems to be dozing so maybe I can distract his wife. I grab the water pitcher and walk over. Their water glasses are full as I dart my eyes around the seat for her purse. It's small and on her other side. No good. I stroll through my tables filling water and scouting for an opening. There's a mother with two young kids on booster seats whose purse is wide open. I head for their table grabbing a stack of napkins off a nearby table.

"More water?"

Her back is to me wiping goo off the boy's face. "Yes, please."

I spy her wallet and pour. "I thought you might need some extra napkins." I say dropping half the stack on her open purse before she turns around. The others, I place next to her hand. She looks up and me.

"Thank you. I just don't understand how dirty he can get."

I continue pouring until the glass is over flowing in front of the boy and the water goes straight for him. The mother flashes me a look and then attacks the spill with her newly acquired napkins. I reach down, grabbing the set of napkins I dropped on her purse and clutch a big handful. I pull my loaded hand to my front apron pocket dropping the wallet inside. Once secure, I offer the stack of napkins to the woman.

"Here's some more. I'm sorry. I guess I shouldn't do two things at once."

"Don't worry about it, the water actually helped get the goo off. Thank you."

"Let me go get you a clean towel," I say as I spin around and walk into the kitchen. I make a beeline for the bathroom and inspect my prize. Flipping through the pockets, I don't find a social security card, but I do find an insurance card that lists a nine digit number as the member ID. Score. I shove the card into my smaller upper pocket and walk out of the bathroom carrying the wallet. I swipe a kitchen towel and cover the wallet before entering the kitchen area and walk back through the dining room to the table. When I approach the table, I fake a little trip and fall onto her open purse with my hand. Gripping the edge of the table with my left hand I regain my apparent loss of balance and raise the towel up, sans wallet, and hand it to her.

"I'm sorry about that. I'm a klutz today."

"Wait 'til you have kids. It gets worse," she says with a smile.

"I'll bet. Merry Christmas," I say as I return to my ignored tables and finish out my shift.

Chapter 32

Sam says little as we lock up and walk to her lone car in the parking lot. I consider how to bring up my newly found number. Sam pulls out of the parking lot and we make the familiar trek home.

"You're going to have to tell me the truth. It's been a few months now, and I haven't pressured you at all. I need to know now."

"I have one," I blurt out steering the conversation.

"What?"

"I have one already."

"You have a social security number?" I nod. "And you're telling me now?"

"I thought if I told you my number you'd try to reach him or something," I say making it up as I go. "I can't go back to him."

"I wouldn't do that without talking to you first."

"And I thought maybe he'd find me if I used it."

"Hmm. That's possible. When are you sixteen?"

"Next June."

"I don't know what the rules or laws are but I think if you're over sixteen you may be able to choose where you stay."

"Really?"

"Well, I don't know *know*, but I think you have more say." We turn the corner and head into the neighborhoods. "That's six months from now and there's a chance he wouldn't be able to find you for a…" she stops talking while slowing the car down. "What's going on?" she mumbles under her breath.

Sam always takes the back roads through a few neighborhoods to get home. Her car has a taillight out so she avoids the major roads and the scrutiny of the cops. Tonight, the intersection, where she crosses from one neighborhood to another, is blocked off and there are policemen standing in front of the barricades waving us off. She pauses and then snakes back a few houses in reverse, before backing into a driveway and turning around. I suspect she's avoiding advertising the back of her car. She drives further down the main thoroughfare of the neighborhood we're in. She looks to her right, at each intersection, to see when the coast is clear, but every street has barricades at the other end.

"What the hell?" she questions out loud. Then, slapping the steering wheel, "Oh, its Santa," she says. "This neighborhood does a holiday parade with Santa on Christmas Eve and we must be hitting the route." She continues driving on the main thoroughfare. I strain to see the parade. She notices me looking. "I think the parade ended at nine."

I remain silent looking down each street we pass.

"Anyway, I don't know the particulars but I think we gotta give Lou your real number."

"Stop the car," I say softly at first. "Stop the car!"

Turning to look at me, she obeys and pulls to the side. I'm out the door walking back in the direction we came. She jumps out and follows.

"Susan!"

Catching up to me, I've stopped on the sidewalk in front of a navy blue house with white trim and a wraparound porch. There are icicle lights hanging from both stories of the house – on the pointed peak of the upper level as well as the lip of the roof covering the porch. There are six steps up to the porch which is bordered by a simple white railing with spokes every foot or so. The railings are draped in brilliant blue icicle lights. There is one lamp lit in the front window, but otherwise the house is dark. A large evergreen wreath tied with a red velvet bow is centered on the bright yellow front door. The house looks like it belongs inside a snow globe.

"What?" Sam asks.

Piggy

I can't speak; my eyes fixated not on the house, but the pine cone tree in the front yard. The tree is ten feet tall with branches cascading down into a perfectly symmetrical pyramid. It's covered with big round gold ornaments that reflect the multicolored lights wrapped around it. The tree is dusted with snow on the tips of its branches. There's a gold angel on top which is somehow lit up as if there is a spotlight on it. It looks like Mom's tree, except she used multicolored bulbs and white lights. I focus on the angel who is peacefully resting on top.

"My Mom used to decorate our tree this way. She always got the tallest tree that would fit in our house. We spent the weekend before Christmas decorating it with ornaments and tinsel. This one doesn't have any tinsel, but we used the stringy kind that makes it look like icicles," I say turning for a moment to look at Sam next to me. "The angel… The angel looks just like I remember. It was my grandmother's. Mom kept it in a cushioned box so that it wouldn't break. It was blown glass with a gold tint and little sparkles around the angel's dress." I can picture it so clearly now. "We used to play Christmas music for the entire month and sing along when we decorated. She gave me…" My voice cracks at Betty's name and I can't finish my sentence. Instead, I slowly sob. I haven't thought of the tree for so long and now I think of all of the decorations that burned up in the fire. I continue weeping as Sam puts her arm around me.

"I miss her."

"How did she die?"

"Car accident when I was six. After that, my uncle became my guardian and everything changed. No more Christmas trees, no more Christmases, no more birthdays. Heck, I was lucky to be fed. At first I was in shock. Mom had given me the death speech when my Grandma died so I knew she wasn't coming back. I hoped Dan would be a substitute for her. But he barely talked to me in the beginning. I thought if I was good and got him to like me, things would be like they used to be. But they never were."

"I'm sorry, Susan."

I stop and hold my tongue. What am I doing? Sam's been good to me but I can't be found. She can't try to find him; the cops would find me for sure. I'll end up in an orphanage at best and prison at worst. You can't just kill someone, even Dan didn't do that. My mind

Piggy

replays what I've already said. I never said Lancaster or Red Bluff, Wisconsin. So that's good. But now she knows he's my uncle and my guardian. No, I can't tell her anything else. But I've got her listening. Dan used to say, 'once you drop the hook and they bite, you can just reel 'em in.'

"What did he do to you?" she asked.

"My uncle wasn't a nice man; he used to beat me all the time. He smoked and drank, treated me like a slave, withheld food, and wouldn't let me go to school," I say realizing most of this is actually all true. He didn't regularly beat me but there were times he hit me. I recount other examples when Dan was mad, but when I see Sam's eyes aren't completely sympathetic, I embellish my story. Dan has taught me; a sad story told right, has the other person on the verge of tears. I continue weaving my tale of woe until I see what I want to in her eyes. Of course, I omit any part that doesn't paint me as the victim. We talk the rest of the way back to the apartment and she's buying it all. At the right moment, I rattle off the memorized social security number telling her that I was too afraid to use it before.

Around midnight, I can't talk anymore and Sam goes to bed. I stay up reviewing all I've said and done this evening. Sam promises she won't contact Dan in anyway, not that I've ever said his real name. Lying on the couch, a pang of guilt washes over me. Sam has been the one good thing that has happened to me since, well, since I can't remember. Maybe I should tell her the truth. I mean, not the entire truth; I'm not going to tell anyone I killed him. But maybe I could tell her a bit more. Life is good right now and I want to keep this going. I rationalize that a lot of what I said tonight was the truth, just a little tainted and embellished in some parts. Heck, Dan wouldn't even call any of it a lie. He always told me, 'the truth leaves you no options.' My mind scrolls through all the lessons Dan has taught me.

Suddenly, I'm in my pink bedroom with Betty waking up in Mom's house. It's dead quiet. Outside, the sun hasn't come up yet. Excited, I woke up when I wanted. I climb out of bed and tuck Betty under my arm. Gently turning the door knob, I tiptoe down the darkened hallway and drop to my knees careful not to make a sound. The Christmas tree lights in the living room are on. Mom always left the lights on so that the tree would shine and could be seen from outside. I slowly peer around the corner and spy on the tree. The room is empty and the front window is pitch black so I know it's the middle of the night. I crawl to the tree and our faux fireplace. Mom

Piggy

said that Santa would come even if we didn't have a fireplace. But I wanted to be sure, so she gave me a piece of cardboard and some poster paint. She outlined the fireplace and drew in the bricks and mantle. She even drew in the logs, but no fire -- Santa won't come down a chimney that has a fire I told her. Mom let me paint what she had drawn, so I made it the most colorful fireplace ever with red, blue and yellow bricks. When it was dry, Mom moved the TV stand over to place the 'fireplace' next to the tree. Now we were covered, Santa would definitely come.

      I steal a glance to the coffee table and the three cookies and glass of milk are untouched. I crawl to the TV stand and pull the rocking chair in front of me. I wait. I wait for Santa. I'm certain I didn't fall asleep but when I hear Mom call out to me, I'm covered with the quilt from the back of the couch. Popping my head up, the milk and cookies were gone, and there are three packages under the tree. Mom walks into the room and I see her. I see her...

Chapter 33

I jerk myself awake, covered in sweat. I've been dreaming. Dreaming about Mom. I squeeze my eyes shut and recount the dream but it fades away as soon as I remember it. Its Christmas morning. The click of the bathroom door tells me Sam is up. And now my mind is completely blank. I've lost Mom again.

We're at work by five fifteen. The cook is in the parking lot waiting for Sam to open up, so it takes a while for the kitchen to warm up. The first two hours of breakfast are dismal. You could hear a pin drop in the restaurant with only two single old guys showing up. Around nine, the breakfast rush starts but it's a significantly reduced crowd. Sam plays tricks on me -- suggesting tea with honey and lemon to my tables. Hot tea is such a pain to serve. She has enthralled several old ladies with the idea and it takes them the longest time to pick out their tea flavor. I'm too tired to retaliate having gotten less than four hours sleep.

The lunch rush comes through with a smattering of travelers who are apparently bouncing between relative's homes. I mindlessly perform my duties as my thoughts keep shifting to Mom and home. When I first ran, I was set on going back home. I didn't really think about it. I knew I had to get far away and Lancaster was the only place I could think of. If it wasn't for Sam, that's where I'd be. But what is there for me? The house burned down. I didn't even have a picture of Mom. Ms. Parks moved away. There's nothing back there for me. As long as Sam lets me stay, I've got a good thing going.

Then it hits me, I never *saw* the house burn down. I mean Dan said it burned down and I'm certain he set a fire, but what if some things were saved? Like Grandma's Christmas angel or any picture of Mom. Ms. Parks moved to another part of Lancaster, she could still be there. Maybe now that I was older I could live with her and Susan. Susan, the person I'd become. It was the first name that popped out of my mouth when Sam asked me. I wouldn't tell them about that. The images of the fantasy filled my head -- I'd live with them and maybe I'd get a job at night and go to school again. I wanted to go to school. I got through a little of the sixth grade before dropping out. If I stayed here, I couldn't expect to go to school. Not with Sam.

"Hey, I called Lou," Sam says from behind making me jump. "He says we can close at seven if it stays like this. I thought we'd make good tips today but boy, was I wrong."

"Can I take lunch now?" I ask.

She nods and I order my usual from the cook. Sitting at the small table by the store room, I eat alone. I recognize the cook as the breakfast guy during the week. He must be the only one Lou could get to work. I make a mental note to tell Lou, not to do that again. My cheeseburger is like a hockey puck and the fries are soggy.

Sam comes up when I'm finished and lays down the form in front of me. "I filled this out for you. You should check it and slide it under Lou's door."

I nod.

"Susan, I'm glad you told me the truth last night. So don't take this the wrong way, but I gotta be sure. I'm going to confirm that this social matches your name." I freeze and keep my expression blank. "Don't freak out. I want to help you and I'm not going to try to find this guy, but I can't have you living with me and still not be sure who you are."

"It will match," I say coolly staring directly into her eyes.

"I'm sure it will, but I have to be sure."

I pick up the paper and walk to Lou's door and slide it underneath.

"Good," she says a bit surprised.

"I didn't lie to you last night." That was almost true. Most of what I told her was Dan's level of truth, although I have lied about other things like my name, where I got the social security number, a few precise details about where I lived as a child, and some of the more sensational parts of my stories last night. But somehow I rationalized that what I had said was mostly true.

"Good. Let's be honest with each other from now on," she says turning to go back out into the restaurant.

My senses are heightened and I run through my options. Why had I slide the paper under the door? Dan always said sometimes the best thing to do was to call a bluff, but when he did it, he always had a

Piggy

way out. Sam and I aren't working tomorrow. There's no way I can get in here and retrieve the form before Lou sees it.

I could pick the lock. No, it's not busy enough, the cook and Sam are constantly around here. Plus, one of them would see me for sure, Lou's door is like center stage.

I could tell Lou I made a mistake and use tomorrow to get another number and this time, a matching name. I'll level with Sam and tell her I was scared. But would she ever believe me after this? Or would she check up on whatever story I tell her.

Maybe she won't search. I think for a moment before discounting it. She will, I can tell by how she looked at me. If she doesn't, Lou could. Besides he may be suspicious of me.

Its four o'clock, I've got three hours to decide. As soon as the deadline enters my mind, I know what I need to do.

I go into the locker room and take out my purse. Opening it, I check my money is still there, as I always do. I've got a little over two thousand. I would have had more, but Sam upped the rent when she saw how much I was making in tips. I look over my shoulder and swiftly unlock Sam's locker. I sneaked a peek at her combination weeks ago. The spare key I use on Mondays is back at the apartment. I open her purse and grab her keys. Pulling off the key to the apartment, I replace the others. I flip through her wallet and see about two hundred dollars which is likely yesterday's tips. My hands are on it when I think of all she's done for me. I shut her purse with only the key in my hand. Grabbing my coat, I stick my head out of the doorway and see the hallway is empty. I quietly walk out the back exit.

I know the route back to the apartment. It's a fifteen minute drive, so I figure a forty-five minute walk. Over an hour later, my fingers are frozen and can barely hold the key still. Once I enter the apartment, I rub my feet and hands until I feel life come back to them. The phone rings and I know it's her. Three rings. I need to get moving.

I change out of my uniform into my warmest outfit and look for a bag to take with me. I see a Macy's shopping bag on the top shelf of the coat closet and grab it. I load it up with the rest of my clothes. Just as it's full, I toss it all out. I head to the kitchen for a trash bag and place all the clothes in there. Then I stuff the trash bag into the Macy's bag. I don't want to advertise that I'm carrying all I own.

Next, I kneel down and reach my hand under the couch. Carefully tapping the small box to me, I pull on the corner that peeks out. I open the box and inspect my treasures. There the gold and brown Monarch lies. Next to it is the blue and white butterfly. I place the box on the coffee table and find some newspaper to roll each in. Next I go into the kitchen and grab a Tupperware container and safely place my pieces inside. I pack the Tupperware into the Macy's bag, shoving over the trash bag to make it fit.

The phone rings again. Sam's trapped at the diner; I know she can't leave. On the fourth ring, the machine answers but the person hangs up. I rush into Sam's room and have my hand on her stash of cash before dismissing the idea for the second time. I can't steal from her; she's been too good to me. A pang of guilt rushes over me for leaving this way, but I know it is what I've got to do. I do a quick survey of the rest of the apartment pausing at the kitchen. I grab a pen and paper intent on leaving a note, but as soon as they are in my hand, I can't think of what to write. Staring for a long time, I finally scribble 'sorry' and walk out the door. I place the key under the mat in front of her door assuming she'll look there.

I jog the six blocks to the bus stop and jump on. The clock on the bus says five thirty-two. Panting, I breathe a sigh of relief, thankful I scoped out this bus weeks ago. Dan always told me you got to have a way out. I had planned my route back to the bus depot in case something happened. Now something has. I close my eyes and slow my breathing. Relax, I tell myself, I'll be at the depot by six. I pull off my coat that has gotten too hot and stuff the scarf and gloves into the pockets.

Checking the clock, its five fifty-three, but when I look out the window, we aren't near the station yet. I make my way up to the driver.

"Doesn't this bus go to the depot?"

"Yes."

"Aren't we supposed to be at the depot by now?"

Piggy

"Be there at six twenty," he says after referring to the schedule in front of him.

"I've ridden this bus before, and it was faster."

"Holiday schedule. We combine some bus routes on holidays," he says taking a good long look at me in the mirror. "Please step back behind the line," he orders.

Six twenty, that still gives me forty to fifty minutes before Sam can get there. By now, she knows I left and she's likely pissed if there was a dinner rush. She'll figure out I have her apartment key. The question is will she go home in search of me or come straight to the depot? It was smart of me not to take her money. That would have got her chasing me for sure, but if she thinks I'm robbing her apartment, I may be in trouble. She may come straight to the depot. It's ironic, I think, for the first time, I actually do something against my instinct – and not steal from her -- and I still may be in trouble.

The depot comes into view and I'm the first one off the bus. The diner in front, where I met Sam, has the gate down and is dark. The station is full of people, bums really, not actual passengers from the looks of them. I reach the ticket counter and ask for a ticket to Los Angeles.

"Next bus leaves at seven tomorrow," the cashier says, leaning down into the light, to reveal his full beard and curly hair under this cap. "But there's a bus at seven forty-five to Vegas."

"Vegas?"

"Yep. Gets in at five twenty am. You can catch a bus to LA from there."

"Thanks, I'll do that."

Handing me back my change and ticket, "Merry Christmas, young lady," he says with a smile.

I circle the seating area to find an open and quiet place to wait. I decide the main hall is too out in the open and patrol for a better location. Walking out to the departing area, I read the signs and determine where my bus will be. The bay is empty now. There are

Piggy

square concrete pillars between each bay about two feet wide, which shield me from the depot doors' view. I lean my back against the concrete, but the cold seeps through my coat in minutes. I quickly decide this will be my spot at seven fifteen in case Sam comes, but for now I need warmth.

    I enter the main hall and find an empty spot on the floor that is far from anyone else. Before I know it, seven fifteen comes and I force myself to exit the building to wait the rest of the time in the cold. Time is now passing slowly as I sneak glances back at the depot doors. I convince myself that I can see the front entrance from the exit doors so I return inside which feels warmer at first, but the cold draft whistling through the doors makes me feel like I'm outside again. I keep checking the front entrance for Sam. The doors behind me open and cold air blasts through. Ten to fifteen passengers, all carrying baggage, pass by me. My bus has arrived.

    I run out to the bay and nearly tackle the bus agent who is helping the driver unload the luggage beneath the bus. I waive my ticket, but am told I can't board until it's been cleaned. I return to my spot inside the doors and keep a watchful eye. Still no Sam. Every five minutes, I check back with the bus agent. Finally at seven thirty-five, I'm the first to board the bus. Selecting the seat at the far back, I pull the curtain over the window. I wait for what seems like forever. A handful of passengers board and find seats. The driver stands at the front and announces the bus's destination and walks the rows checking tickets. A few moments later, he's pulling out of the bay. I scan the parking area as we drive through. Still no sign of Sam. A hint of sadness wells up inside me. I had thought I would really miss Sam and yet, she likely won't miss me. It's seven forty-seven. She must have gone to her apartment to make sure I hadn't robbed her. She doesn't care about me. She didn't even try to look for me. I should have taken the cash and jewelry she had in her dresser.

Chapter 34

It's pitch black when the bus pulls into the Vegas bus station. Unlike Grand Junction, this station is a one-story nondescript building with low ceilings. The waiting area is small with two distinct rows of couches on either side of the hallway in front of the ticket counters. Closest to me as I walk into the hall, is a rowdy group of younger men that are standing by the vending machines. A security guard barely glances at me as he watches the group with interest. Sprinkled throughout the seating area are a few older couples situated on the dark green upholstery. At the far end of the row, there's a group of four Hispanic women sitting and knitting something. Past the couch area, there are some benches lining the walls and a smattering of people sprawled out in slumber, likely homeless. At the front entrance, furthest from me, is a second man, dressed in a navy blue uniform, which I assume to be a security officer.

The ticket counter is dark and there is a sign indicating it is closed until six am. Turning to hunt for an empty and quiet seat, I notice a man standing alone along the wall. Young and slim, he's dressed in jeans, a nice white oxford shirt, and a black blazer. His blondish brown hair is parted on the side with a swath of long bangs falling into his eyes. He looks like one of those magazine ads for cologne. He catches me looking at him and smiles.

Identifying a few seat options, I turn my attention to the bathroom and walk to the sign. The sign is above a doorway that enters into a long hallway where I can see the men's room door and I suspect that the women's room is around the corner. I remember what Sam said about the bathroom at Grand Junction so I pause and see if anyone is following me. No one is behind me but the lone man is watching me and I feel the weight of the second security officer's eyes. I take a step to my right and lean down for the water fountain. Taking a long drink, I turn around and choose a seat near the hallway. I wait hoping for a woman to approach the bathroom.

Sitting on the thinly cushioned couch, I habitually feel for my money that I've spread among my pockets. The bulk of my stash remains in my green canvas purse with a top zipper which I've had clutched in my hand since leaving Sam's apartment. My hand is beginning to ache from my tight grip and I need to get something with a strap or better, a lock.

Piggy

I sense the proximity of a person and look up to see the man from against the wall. He casually sits down next to me with barely five inches between. I shift my Macy's bag between my legs.

"Man, I hate waiting," he says to me. "I'm headed to Hollywood and I got myself up early to catch the bus and now they aren't open, doesn't that suck?"

I remain silent not certain what he wants.

"I spent the last two days with my mom and grandma out here. I bought them a little condo out here for the summers, but they like it year round. I try to get out to see them two or three times a year, even when I'm on location," he says with barely a breath between sentences.

"There's nothing like Christmas at home and all that good food – turkey and all the fixings, and of course, the pies. My mom made an apple and a pumpkin pie for me. Pumpkin, though, that's my hands down favorite, and my mom she does it right – candied pecans on top, a real homemade crust, not that stuff you buy and roll out, and real whip cream. It's like heaven," he says kissing his fingers. "What's your favorite pie?"

"I don't know," I answer.

"You don't know! Haven't you had pie before?"

"Yes, but I guess I didn't like it that much."

"Then, you've never had a good piece of pie before. You know, you're in luck, there's a coffee shop a block away from here that sells pies almost, *almost* as good as my mom's. I go there all the time and get pie and hot chocolate with extra whipped cream."

"Sounds good," I say plainly as my mouth waters.

"Where you off today?" I look at him. "Where you going?" he repeats.

"Los Angeles."

Piggy

"Hey, we're probably on the same bus. I'm heading back to Hollywood. I'm in the middle of this movie and it's crazy busy right now."

"Are you an actor?"

"I used to be, but now I produce and direct."

"Really? What movies?" I ask. I've never met anyone famous before.

"I can't talk about what I'm working on now. The studios get so protective and all, but have you seen The Godfather?"

"Only the first one, on cable. You made that?"

"I did all of them and Alien, too."

"Do you get to hang out with the stars?"

"Sometimes, although, I'd say they get to hang out with me. I'm Jack, by the way."

He extends his hand and I reach for it, it's warm and soft. "I'm, I'm Heather," I say not positive why I used my real name.

"Nice to meet you, Heather. That's a pretty name and such a pretty face. Anyone ever tell you that?" he says while tilting my chin upwards with his finger.

"No," I laugh. No one has ever given me a second look.

To my right, I see three women approaching the hallway. He glances in the direction I'm looking as I stand up.

"Where you off to?"

"Just the bathroom."

"You want me to watch your stuff?"

Piggy

"No, thanks."

"Hey, I looked at the schedule before I sat down. First bus to LA is at eight thirty. Now that you got me thinking of pie, I'm going to go down to that coffee shop and get me a slice. You interested?"

"Yeah. Pie sounds good," I say.

"I'll wait right here for you."

I follow the women down the hallway and enter one of the bathroom stalls. I've been holding it for so long, it almost hurts and takes a long time. I hate using the toilets on the bus; they always stink. The women are talking in a language I don't understand but I listen anyway. Emerging from the stall, I see the last of them shutting the door. I wash my hands and face and yank out a pile of paper towels to dry off. Rinsing my mouth out to get the fuzzy goo off my teeth, I spit and check my teeth. Returning to my seat, Jack is standing waiting for me.

"Come on, we got to go get that pie," he says.

"Sure," I say following his lead. There are more passengers filling up the main hall and I notice a line at the ticket counter.

"I don't have my ticket yet," I say to Jack. "Do you have yours?"

"No, but look at the line. You stand in that, we'll never get pie. Let's get our tickets when we get back."

I look at the three people in line and watch a fourth join them. "Nah, I'd rather get it now. The line will only get longer."

"No, it's always longest first thing. It'll be shorter when we're back. Trust me."

A fifth person now joins the line. I stand for a moment trading looks between the entrance at the far side of the station, the ticket counter, and the clock. It's six now, so there's over two hours before the bus leaves. Plenty of time to wait in line when we get back.

Piggy

"C'mon, let's beat the breakfast rush," Jack says with his hand under my elbow beginning to guide me out. I follow his lead and take several steps to the doors.

About twenty feet from the door, I slow and look at Jack. "Breakfast rush isn't until seven."

"Then we'll really beat the rush."

Now I stop as he tugs on my arm. "Do they serve pie this early?"

"Sure, all day."

He seems so insistent.

"Everything alright here?" a deep husky voice says from behind us. It's the man in the navy blue uniform which I thought was a security guard. Instead, he has a name tag on the upper left pocket of his uniform, 'Samuel', which is sewn directly under an emblem for the bus company. He's a tall and bulky black man with just the hint of stubble on his chin.

"You alright, miss?"

"Yes. Does the line get worse or better the longer we wait?" I ask pointing to the ticket counter.

"It's pretty good now, only three people in line."

I spin around to look.

"Heather, we can get your ticket after," Jack says.

"Where you off to?" Samuel says pointedly to Jack.

Jack's face tenses. "Just out for a bite. She can get her ticket now if she wants."

"I'll be fast," I say as I jog over to the line. Looking back, Samuel and Jack are still talking. Jack looks uncomfortable and takes a few steps backward. As I move to the front of the line, he turns around and leaves the station. I quickly request my ticket to Lancaster.

"You want Los Angeles," the ticket cashier said. "From there, you can catch a local bus to Lancaster."

I shell out the required amount.

"Bus lines up to your left and leaves in twenty-five minutes," the cashier says.

"When does it leave?"

"Six-thirty."

"I thought the first one out was eight-thirty."

"Nope, every hour starting at six-thirty."

I jog back to the doors to Samuel.

"Do you know which way he went? We were going to the coffee shop a block away," I say to Samuel.

"There's no coffee shop around here."

"We were going to get pie; Jack said there was a coffee shop." I say as Samuel shakes his head. "Do you know where he went? There's an earlier bus than he thinks."

Samuel bends down to look me square in the eye, "He's no good. Stay away from that guy."

"Jack?"

"There isn't any coffee shop around here. He wanted to get you outside. He was conning you."

What? My mind considers what he said but it doesn't add up.

Samuel turns and walks back to the entrance.

Piggy

I run through my conversation with Jack. He approached me. He started talking to me. What did he say? Then it clicks and all makes sense. How did I not see it? Normally I see cons a mile away. I guess I've been away from Dan too long. I've gotten soft. I walk to the bus bay where the cashier had pointed to. I think back at what Jack said. Hollywood, movie star, director, hmm. He said just enough. Dropped enough crumbs to keep me interested but not suspicious. He was good. I do a quick check of all my pockets and sigh relief.

Chapter 35

      The bus is half full for the seven hour drive. Seated in a row to myself, I doze for most of the trip. Around eleven, voices three rows behind me arouse my attention. Over the course of thirty minutes, their volume rises as their sentences get shorter. The last audible phrase is 'lazy bitch' which results in me getting a seat mate. I pull my Macy's bag close and clutch my purse. I sit next to a middle aged man with a bushy mustache and a tattoo on his neck. He stares straight ahead and doesn't say a word but I still sit tensely awaiting the slightest touch of a pickpocket. As we pull into Union Station, he returns to his prior seat without a word or a glance.

      I exit the bus first and walk into the station. Union Station is even grander than Grand Junction with three story ceilings and a large hall with clusters of comfortable chairs along the walls and several rows of dark wooden benches lined up like pews in the center. The benches are positioned in front of a long row of ticket windows, maybe twenty in all. Each window has etched glass with the word 'ticket', and is surrounded by dark wood that has been carved with images of people and horses.

      I make a beeline for the bathroom, which is full of patrons, and wash up. Exiting, I find a diner near the front and sit down for a much needed cheeseburger and fries. I splurge for a chocolate shake without batting an eye, knowing I've got over two grand to spend. I critique the waitress confident I can do better. Around two fifteen, I approach the ticket counter where I'm directed to a bus stand outside. Leafing through the schedule handed to me, I identify the bus number that will take me to Lancaster but I'm not certain how to actually get home. I remember the address because I had memorized it years ago at the insistence of Mom. But I don't know the right bus stop to get off at. I run through my brain trying to remember the busiest street that was near home as I see my bus pull up.

      Forty-five minutes into the ride, I ask the bus driver if I've missed a stop, but he tells me Lancaster is the next four stops coming up. I study the route the bus is taking looking for street signs that may jog my memory. No good. The first stop comes and goes as does the second. On the third stop, the bus driver calls out city center and looks me in the eye from the rearview mirror. I get out and do a three sixty to decide my next step. I spot a post office and head to it. The friendly clerk, who has to trade out her regular glasses for her reading glasses to study a city map with me, gives me a series of directions that I

Piggy

attempt to memorize. Looking at me for a moment, she grabs a piece of paper and scribbles out the directions. I follow the route she has laid out.

It is dusk when I approach my neighborhood and a chill is in the air. As I turn the corner onto Clark Street, I do a double take on the street sign because nothing looks familiar. Most of the houses are decorated with Christmas lights that haven't been turned on yet. I remember staring at the house across the street that always went all out with decorations. Nothing on this street reminds me of that house. I strain to recognize anything as I spot a house number and cross the street to the even side. The houses pass by and I wonder if I didn't recall the address incorrectly. I nearly pass my house. The number is the same, but it looks nothing like what I envisioned in my head. It's two stories tall with a small porch and two windows on either side of the front door and three on the second level. I can see a Christmas tree in the window but it's not lit yet. The black door stands out against the beige house with white trim. There's a white picket fence surrounding the front lawn and I put my hand on the gate before changing my mind and dropping it to my side. This isn't it.

Turning to my left, I look at the house next door. It's smaller with a recognizable hedge fence bunting up to the sidewalk. I take a few steps to it. The garden is dormant given the time of year, but I can visualize Mrs. Jones's roses. As I stroll by, the house becomes more familiar. Facing the front, a wreath is proudly centered on the gate with a small sign 'Merry Christmas from the Jackson Family'. Jackson? Am I remembering Mrs. Jones's name wrong? It hits me as a car's front lights hit my face. It's been nearly ten years. Mrs. Jones was old, maybe she died. The car passes with the driver taking a good look at me.

I walk back to where my house was before it burned down. That's why I'm not recognizing the house. No angel to recover now. A car door slams and I turn in the direction of the sound. It's a woman walking into Ms. Parks' house. I only see her from the back but it's her. She must have moved back, maybe after money got better or maybe her sister moved away. I jog down the sidewalk, looking both ways as I cut across the street. I come up the driveway and slow to a walk as the front light flickers on. I pace a few moments outside not sure what to do if she doesn't recognize me.

I set down my Macy's bag and muster up some courage. I raise my hand to a knocking position, when the door opens. Startled my hand hovers at eye level not sure where to go. She's younger than I remember and taller. Her long blonde hair is down in gentle waves that frame her face. She doesn't have any makeup on and I wonder if she just washed her face.

"Can I help you?" she says.

"It's me," I force out.

"I'm sorry?"

I can't hold back the tears. "It's me, Heather," I struggle to say.

"I'm sorry; I think you have the wrong house."

My sobs become uncontrollable and apparently frightening. She partially closes the door. "Listen, I'm sorry. I know it's the holidays, but I don't have any money."

"Don't you remember me?"

"I'm sorry, no. I can call you a cab if you want."

I can't believe it. Has it been that long? I was seven when we left. She's playing dumb and I can't blame her after what Dan did to her. She wants no part of me or anything to do with him. "I'm sorry, Ms. Parks," I say turning to walk away.

"Kelly Parks?" the woman says.

My sobs stop for a moment as my face twists around and nods.

"She's my landlord."

Chapter 36

My face relaxes as I look back at her. She is taller than I remember; taller because it isn't her.

"Wait here for a minute," the woman says.

I dry my eyes with my scarf and discreetly blow my nose in the corner of it. A few minutes later, the woman returns with a phone to her ear and waves me inside.

"No, we'll be here. See you soon." Hanging up, she closes the door.

"Have a seat, you look tired and cold."

"Thanks."

"I'm Maureen; I rent this place from Kelly. I have for years."

"I'm Heather."

"Yes, I know, Kelly was telling me about you. She's driving here."

"She's coming here?"

"Yes, to get you."

"Where is she?"

"She lives about twenty-five minutes from here near the Air Force base. Can I get you something to drink or eat?"

For whatever reason, the cheeseburger seems a distant memory. I ask for a snack and a soda. I focus on the chips and dip she brings me not certain what to say to her. Luckily, she does all the talking. I hear about her job at the hospital and the few unpleasant patients she's had today. I evade any of her questions which keeps her jabbering on about her job. At long last, headlights pull into the driveway. A car door slams and there's an immediate and insistent

Piggy

knocking at the door. Maureen answers the door as I stand up. Kelly runs into the living room and nearly tackles me in a hug.

"How are you?" she murmurs.

She nearly squeezes the wind out of me in her embrace and I choke a bit on a chip that must have been wedged between my teeth. As I move my arms up from their dead position at my sides, I cry deeply. The kind of crying that you don't even realize you're doing until your face is all wet and you can't breathe. I cry for everything and for nothing. I cry because she remembers me and more importantly she wants to remember me. After a few minutes, Kelly takes a small step back to give us both some air and sits down on the couch next to me. She's crying too, as is Maureen, although I'm not sure Maureen knows why she's crying. I wail with my head in my hands as Kelly puts her arm around my shoulder and rubs my back.

"I looked for you," Kelly said.

I stop and look up. Maureen is walking back into the living room with a box of Kleenex. Both Kelly and I take one. "You did?" I say between blows.

"Yes. Where did he take you?"

"All over," I say.

"I want to hear all about it. First let's get you home."

We say our goodbyes to Maureen who is still wiping tears out of her eyes. Kelly gives her a big hug and we walk out and get into Kelly's blue sedan. It's a much nicer car than the beat up red Chevy I remember. This car has heated leather seats and is still warm from the drive over which instantly makes me feel good.

"So are you okay, I mean healthy, you're not hurt?" she asks as we pull out of the neighborhood.

"I'm good."

"Did he hurt you?"

Piggy

"No," I say not certain what she means.

"Tell me what's happened since you left."

"I.. I... Where are we going?"

"We're going to my house. Susan is there, you remember her?"

"Yeah. So, you did move away."

"Eventually. I didn't move when you left. Once Dan was gone, I stayed for a few more years hoping you'd come back. I tried to look for you, but he covered his tracks."

"You stayed?"

"Yes. I was only moving because Dan was threatening to tell my ex that I left Susan alone at night."

"He was?"

"There's a whole bunch you don't know. Let's get you home and settled, then we're going to have a long talk."

"Susan will be there?"

"Yes, and if you don't mind, I want to leave her out of this. I sheltered her from it all when you left and I don't think she needs to know any of it."

"Why didn't she come with you?"

"Oh, well, lots have changed with me. I've got two more kids now. I met a guy, Captain Bryan Jenkins. He's with the Air Force. I met him six years ago and we got married almost right away. I moved into his house near the base and that's where we live."

We merge onto the freeway as she recounts how she met Bryan, what their wedding was like, and the birth of her two boys.

"I'm not waiting tables anymore, but I do work part time as a bookkeeper at a small construction company. Justin and Jason keep me real busy, but I need time out of the house."

We slow to drive through an open gate with an empty guard house. Kelly continues driving along a windy road for a bit before houses appear. Catching my curious expression, she explains the empty guard house. Apparently, the neighborhood voted to reduce costs and now there is no guard, just a neighborhood watch program.

"What does your husband do?" I ask.

"He's a pilot; he flies fighter jets although mostly he commands a troop. He's overseas now."

"He's not here?"

"Nope. He's on some training mission. We got to talk to him yesterday to wish him a Merry Christmas. It was the first one we've spent apart. The next scheduled call is in two weeks."

She pulls into the driveway of a home three times the size of her one on Clark Street. We pass a large front lawn that is sparsely decorated for Christmas; a few strands of lights around a small tree in the yard and some lights bordering the two front windows. Entering a two car garage, it's loaded with bikes, strollers, sporting equipment, and another car, a white Jeep Grand Cherokee. We enter the house from the garage into a small hallway.

"We're home!" Kelly yells out.

Shutting the interior garage door, I follow Kelly down the hall.

"I just put them both down," I hear as my eyes rest on Susan who is standing in front of Kelly. She doesn't look at all as I remember her. Her long dark brown hair is pulled back in a headband which appears like a halo around her face given the back lighting. Her perfectly shaped dark eyebrows are complimented by her lush eyelashes and full mouth. The light green leggings show off her slender figure and the form fitting top accentuates how filled out she is. I touch my flat chest briefly before shamefully dropping my hand.

"Hi Heather," she says as she walks to me uncertain what to do.

"Hi."

"You're taller than me," she says.

"Yeah, I guess so," I say entering into an expansive great room that has a large screen TV on the far left wall and a comfy-looking light brown couch 'U' across from it. There's an open kitchen to the right that has a bar with seating in front of it. Along the wall across from me is a dark brown dining table with six high back chairs. There are china cabinets on either side of the table and two extra chairs neatly lined up against the wall. In front of one of the cabinets, wedged in the corner, is a tall noble fir tree covered in ornaments of all shapes and sizes. There is a silver star on top which matches the rope of tinsel that encircles the tree. There aren't enough lights on it and those that are on are flickering as if about to go out. Underneath, is the aftermath of Christmas morning with open boxes and stacks of wrapped clothing and a pile of used wrapping paper.

"This is home," Kelly says startling me out of my inspection. "It's a mess right now."

Susan is looking back and forth from her mom to me. "You want to watch a movie?" she asks.

"Why don't you watch one in your room, I want to talk with Heather," Kelly says.

"See you later Heather," Susan says looking relieved.

Kelly walks over to the coffee table and grabs the remote. Alone and now dead quiet, she turns to me. "Want anything? Coke? Hot chocolate? Cookies?"

"Hot chocolate sounds good."

"Sit up here while I make it," she instructs pointing to the bar counter facing the kitchen. The tiled countertop is cold to the touch and the metal bar stool is difficult to pull out. Wedging myself into the chair, I face her.

Piggy

"Tell me everything."

I recount my story from as far back as I remember. I tell her about Stu coming over and scaring me and about when Dan and I came home to a trashed house. That was why we had left -- fear of Stu. I tell her about Dan coming back and sneaking into the house and then learning later, the house had burned down. I conveniently leave out the hospital robberies.

"The fire was horrible. It nearly spread to Mrs. Jones's place," Kelly interrupts. "Mrs. Jones had to move into a nursing home while they dealt with the smoke damage. She never came back, she died a few months later. The two places sat there for the longest time. It wasn't until the next day, that we found out you weren't in the fire. At first, we thought Dan had fallen asleep with a lit cigarette. Weeks later, we found out it was arson. No one saw Dan that night, but he was the only one anyone suspected."

"Was there anything left?"

"Nope, the place burned to the ground. I sifted through some of the ashes in hopes of finding something, but the fire department wouldn't let me look until their investigation was done, and that took six weeks. By the time I could look, what the fire didn't destroy, the wind and the rain did."

"Whose house is there now?"

"I've never met the new owners. The lot was vacant for years. The bank had it cleared for safety reasons, but it sat as an empty lot until three years ago."

I continue my story, telling her I had finished the third grade in Texas and that Dan bounced from one apartment manager job to another.

"After Texas, we went to Arizona. We stayed there for the summer, but then Dan moved us to Albuquerque, where I went to the fourth grade and started fifth. That was the best we had it. Dan managed this apartment complex that was really nice. It had a pool. He met a woman there; started hanging out with her; even got a part time job at a warehouse. But it didn't last. She turned out to be worse than him, violent and angry, plus she did drugs. We left and went to

Wyoming, then Oklahoma. I actually got through the fifth grade, but I had to cheat on a few tests to do it," I say looking up to see if she was flinching. "We moved to a few different towns in Oklahoma from apartment complex to complex."

"Why did he keep changing jobs?"

"Oh, he wasn't really working. Eventually the owners would wise up that he wasn't doing anything. Or the tenants would complain. Before he would get fired, he had a 'fire sale' rental weekend. He'd do it fast, get tenants in to rent any vacant apartments. He'd offer a huge discount and then ask for cash up front for first and last. The rents were so cheap, people would pay him, and then we'd take off with the money."

"Wasn't he ever caught?"

"Nope."

"How did he get the jobs?"

"Dan was smart; he never used his real name. He'd pickpocket IDs and give the apartment owners those names. He'd get the job based on someone else's credit and background. It would take a while for anyone to figure out something was up. By that time, we were long gone."

"Then what?"

"We moved to Nebraska near an Indian reservation and Dan got a job at a casino. I got to enroll in the sixth grade, but I didn't finish. One night, Dan got beat up bad. Turned out to be one of Stu's guys although I never knew how he found us. I don't know how Dan got away, but he did. He showed up at home all bloody and limping. I cleaned him up, packed, and left. I didn't know where to go. Dan passed out as soon as I got him in the car, so I drove for as long as I could and we eventually made it to Illinois."

"You drove?"

"Yeah, Dan taught me."

"How old were you then?"

"Twelve."

"And no one pulled you over?"

"I drove only at night. Rested at a motel during the day."

"Then what?"

"Dan said Stu would have people looking for him, so we had to lie low. We ended up on the outskirts of Chicago for a while. Dan collected stuff in the back alleys and resold it to junkyards and pawn shops. He said he couldn't gamble anymore because Stu would find him and any job in a casino was too risky. We eventually made it up to the middle of Wisconsin and Dan found a small piece of land that had been a junkyard. It was abandoned. Dan took it over and that's what we did."

"Did what?"

"Found stuff people were throwing away and resold it at our yard. Sometimes Dan would swipe something, but usually he picked up what people put out."

"Where did you live?"

"Dan had traded the car for a van so we could hold more stuff. We slept in that."

"Did you go to school?"

"Not since the sixth grade."

"Why did you stop?"

"I stopped going when we were in Nebraska. When we moved to Wisconsin, I wanted to go again, but Dan said it was too much trouble to take me back and forth. We lived pretty far from any town."

"What made you stop in the first place?"

"I just stopped wanting to go."

Piggy

"Do you want to go now?"

"Could I?"

"We can see after Christmas break what to do. I don't think they'll let you enter the sixth grade given you're almost sixteen, but there must be something we can do."

"How do you know how old I am?"

"Heather, your birthday is June 9th. I've thought of you every year since you left."

"Really?"

"Yes, I searched for you, but I was too late. I'm sorry; I wish I wasn't so scared back then."

"What do you mean?"

"Heather, I was barely making my mortgage payments and my ex wasn't helping out much. He wanted sole custody of Susan so he made it hard for me. If I had had the money, I would have fought for you sooner. I would have reported Dan a lot earlier than I did."

"You reported Dan?"

"Yes to social services, but it went nowhere. Then, after he threatened me, I decided to move away. I thought if I could remove the one thing he could damage me with, I could challenge him for guardianship. But it was too late. He took you away before I could do anything."

"You wanted me?"

"Yes, Heather," she says leaning forward to touch my arm. "I always wanted you. Your mom and I had talked once before the accident about having me be your guardian, but it was one conversation and the accident happened shortly after. When she died, I couldn't afford to take you on. I didn't know she had a trust set up."

"A trust?"

"Yes, Dan got money for you every month."

"Oh, right. But he told me it stopped when we moved to Arizona."

"That's because your mom's lawyer had requested an audit of the trust. Dan must have been scared of the audit, because he left before it could happen. Plus, we suspected he had burned the house down, but we couldn't find him. He never came back for the hearing. I was going to challenge him in court and try to win guardianship. But he never showed. My one complaint to social services was inconclusive. Barring any proven allegations that he wasn't a fit guardian, there was nothing we could do until we found him."

"Did he still get the money?"

"No, it did stop. Your Mom's lawyer, John Robertson, you remember him?"

I nodded thinking back to the time he had visited our house.

"He got the trust frozen until the audit could take place. Then the audit was postponed until Dan came back. In the meantime, Dan couldn't withdraw any of the money. From what I'm told he never tried."

"Could Dan have gone to jail?"

"He still can. Where is he now?"

"Ah, I don't know."

"How did you get away?"

My face froze. I have linked myself to the junkyard. Why did I say that? I felt so comfortable with Kelly; talking to someone I *knew*, that I had said too much. But I couldn't tell her I killed him, I'll go to jail. If Dan is wanted by the cops, they could look for him and find out what I did.

"We were driving to Chicago," I say. "Dan stopped for gas and I ran away."

"Where was he going?"

"He didn't tell me. We were driving south for the winter," I say realizing its Christmas and we did go away each winter.

"We can worry about this later. It's late, why don't we get you settled and then we can deal with Dan," Kelly states.

I glance at the clock; it's nearly midnight. "Yeah, I'm tired."

Pointing to my Macy's bag that is next to my feet, "Do you have laundry to do?"

I shake my head.

"Is that all you have with you?"

"Yes."

"We've got a futon in the office. That will be your room from now on," Kelly says as she crosses the living room and heads up the stairs. "But I'll get it set up with a real bed and figure out a better place for the desks and computer. You need pajamas?" she says turning to see me still sitting on the couch. Motioning for me to follow, I stand snatching up my Macy's bag and purse.

Upstairs consists of a long hallway with six closed doors on one side and the top railing of the stairs on the other side. Kelly opens one door to give me a tour of her master suite. It's a big room with a king sized bed and matching bed side tables with lamps. There's a stripped down bassinet shoved against the far right wall. Alongside the opposite wall, a bookshelf is next to the entrance to a large beige bathroom with a Jacuzzi tub and glassed in shower. We exit as Kelly points to Susan's room and a linen closet. Gently opening the boys' bedroom door, Kelly puts her finger to her lips as we walk in. Against one wall is a small twin bed that is shaped like a locomotive. On the exposed side, there's a metal railing coming out from under the mattress and creating a wall on the side of the bed.

"Justin falls out of bed so we use this," Kelly says pointing to the device. Behind the bars, Justin is sleeping soundly with a teddy bear tucked under the covers.

Piggy

The crib sits against the window and next to the other unused locomotive bed. Kelly leans in and adjusts the blankets. There, Jason's tiny head protrudes out from under a blue blanket that is surrounded with stuffed animals. We tiptoe out and Kelly points to the bathroom that I'll use before opening up the last door.

Set up like an office, there are two desks. One with a computer and a large monitor on it; the other covered in papers. Across from the desks and under the only window, is a yellow covered futon. Kelly leans down and gives the bottom a yank and it falls flat into a bed. Once the sheets are on and I'm snug in a pair of Kelly's sweats, we say good night before Kelly shuts the door.

"I'm glad you're here," she says.

"Me too."

When the door shuts, I roll over and flick on the lamp Kelly has set up next to the futon. I go through my nightly ritual of counting my money and putting the entire purse inside the pillowcase. Exhausted, I fall asleep as soon as I turn off the light.

Chapter 37

I awake to Justin's screams, who I determine is getting a bath. Rising, I'm well rested having slept for over ten hours. Walking out of the office, the bathroom door is open. Kelly waves me in as Justin splashes wildly in three inches of water surrounded by multiple ducks and boats.

She points to a toothbrush on the counter and informs me there is a breakfast feast downstairs. I brush my teeth taking advantage of what has, at times, been a luxury. Plodding downstairs, Susan is watching TV. Jason is in a small chair-like cradle on the floor in front of her. As she waves at me, the phone rings. I meander into the kitchen and inspect the spread. I load up a plate with fruit, cinnamon rolls, and a chocolate donut. Washing it all down with two glasses of orange juice, I'm stuffed and feel a bit sick after digesting so much sugar.

"Want to go shopping?" Susan asks as Kelly carries Justin down the stairs.

"Do you want to, Heather? I thought we could get you some more clothes and things," Kelly says.

"I've got two other pairs of jeans and some tops," I answer.

"You're going to need more than that. Besides that coat you have is a bit torn up."

"I've got Christmas cash burning a hole in my pocket," Susan chimes in.

"Why don't you get ready and we'll go to the mall?"

An hour later and after a very long loading period for the double wide stroller and various bags of supplies, we're on our way to a large shopping mall which boasts having over fifty stores. Susan has been talking non-stop about her high school where she's a sophomore.

"Mom says you're going to enroll so I'll be able to show you around instead of just telling you about it," Susan states.

"Honey, I'm not sure she's going to be in your school," Kelly says looking in the rear view mirror as she pulls into a parking spot.

Piggy

"Aren't you a sophomore?" Susan asks.

I'm not sure what to say.

"We're going to have her tested," Kelly says.

"What? Why do you need to be tested?" Susan says as she jumps out of the car.

"Drop it, Susan," Kelly commands.

"Fine. Where are we meeting?"

"We're staying together today."

"C'mon it's going to take you forever to get them out and strapped in."

"We're staying together," Kelly says looking up at Susan's face.

Susan and I watch as Kelly unfolds and snaps the stroller into shape. Susan doesn't offer help and I don't want to get in the way.

"Where did you go before now?" Susan asks turning to me.

"What?"

"What school were you in before?"

"I wasn't."

"You weren't in school?"

"No."

"How come?"

"I lived out in the country and didn't go."

"There weren't any schools?"

Piggy

"Susan," Kelly says with emphasis.

"Fine, you didn't go to school. You still with your uncle?"

"Not anymore."

"He sent you out here?"

"Susan!" Kelly yells. "Get the diaper bag from in front."

Returning with the bag in hand, "What?" Susan says to Kelly.

"Heather is going to stay with us for a while. She's not with her uncle anymore and we're not going to talk about it until she's ready to. It's complicated, okay?" Kelly says.

Susan makes a face and rolls her eyes. "Can we go now?"

We weave through the parking structure and enter the mall. The place is bustling with shoppers. I walk behind Kelly who has a hard time with the wide stroller. I've been in malls before, but usually not to legitimately buy anything. We make our way to Susan's favorite store and she wildly rampages the racks. She has seven tops in her hands before I make my way through the first ten feet of the store. Kelly points a few things out to me, but I shake my head after seeing the price tag.

"It's my treat. Think of it as a belated Christmas present."

I pick out a blue sweater and go to try it on. Susan is whipping through outfits in the fitting room next to me.

"Here let me park this in your room," I hear Kelly say to Susan in the midst of her protests about the dressing room being too small.

When I emerge with the plain blue sweater, Susan is in yet another outfit and posing in front of the three way mirror as Kelly is coming around the corner; her hands full of options for me. Kelly has a better eye than Sam did with most of the clothes fitting and making me look slimmer than I feel. I usually buy clothes a bit on the baggy side but Kelly has my size pegged.

Piggy

Kelly and I make it to the cash register with seven items in my hands followed by Susan who has three items. The clerk motions for the next in line and we walk to the counter and place my stuff down. Susan throws her items on top. Kelly immediately grabs Susan's items and hands them back to her.

"You have to pay for these with your Christmas money."

"What about her stuff?" Susan asks.

"I'm buying this as her Christmas present."

"That's not fair!"

"You got all those presents and money on Christmas. It's more than fair."

Pouting, Susan takes a step back and looks over her three items.

Kelly takes out her credit card and pays for my items as Susan makes frequent glances to me and the clothes. We step aside to allow Susan to get rung up. She pulls out a gift card and some cash. Pushing aside one of the items, she pays for two of the items and we leave the store.

Re-entering the mall, Susan has our route predetermined as we bounce from store to store. We spend a great deal of time at a young teen store where Kelly buys a few things for the boys and I get a new coat and a purse with a long strap. A quick stop at a discount shoe store, and I've got two new pairs of shoes. Our last stop is the main department store.

Susan isn't interested in stopping here but Kelly puts her foot down and we enter the store through the perfume section. Kelly skillfully maneuvers us to the lingerie section. She selects a pair of flannel pajamas and holds them up to me checking the length of the pants. Susan wanders out of the department.

"Pick out some underwear and bras while we're here," Kelly says to me as she chases after Susan.

Piggy

I see a few tables covered in underwear and pick out two pair. Kelly returns with the stroller and Susan.

"These the kind you like?"

I shrug.

"They're granny underwear," Susan says over Kelly's shoulder.

"How about these?" Kelly says holding up a pair of much smaller panties. I shrug and she holds them across my groin. Confirming my size, she picks out three pair and tells me to find six more in the same size.

"What size bra are you?"

I freeze at her comment.

"I can check the tag if you want," she says coming to me.

"I'm a medium."

Giving me a quizzical look, Kelly runs her hand up and down my back.

"You're kidding! You don't wear a bra?" Susan says too loudly for my comfort.

"Susan! Go take the boys and sit over there. I don't want to hear another word," she orders.

Turning to me, Kelly says, "Don't worry about her. Go ahead to the fitting room and I'll be right in."

Susan chuckles as I pass by her. I'm reminded of Sam's hicksville comment about my clothes. I don't dare tell them I only got my period three months ago.

Kelly knocks on the door with a handful of bras and a tape measure in one hand. After a brief staring contest, I realize she expects me to take off my shirt in front of her. Twenty minutes later, we emerge from the dressing room and see Susan ignoring the boys as

280

Piggy

she watches the small TV the store has in the waiting area. Kelly points over to the far wall and tells me to get five pairs of socks. I walk over as Kelly has a one-sided conversation with Susan.

Susan is quiet on the ride home. I know she's mad about Kelly buying me stuff. I keep casually looking at her hoping to catch her eye but she's stoically staring into the night.

"Let's order a pizza," Kelly says entering the house. "Susan, get a large of whatever you want and a medium hamburger and cheese." This perks Susan up. Turning to me, "Why don't you try on your new outfits?"

I go upstairs to my room, *My room*, I think. I have a hard time carrying all the bags. I put on the bra and new underwear first. Sliding into the jeans and green plaid sweater, I twirl around in front of the mirror that's on the back of the linen closet door. I hold up my arms and let the price tags dangle like earrings. Kelly comes up the stairs and watches me for a while.

"You look so pretty, Heather."

I spin around surprised by her voice. "Thank you," I manage to say before I burst into tears. She walks to me and we hug. "Thank you so much. I've never had so many new clothes before." Pausing to breath, "I've never had new underwear."

"Never?"

"Dan made me shop at Goodwill."

Exhaling loudly, "Those days are over," she says. "Try on the rest."

I let her go and run to my room to change.

"Tomorrow, let's get your haircut, too," she says as her voice fades down the stairs.

I take a long look in the mirror. My mousy brown hair is pulled back in my usual ponytail. I've lost my freckles from lack of sun and feel pale. But my clothes match and fit and don't have any holes or stains. The clothes Sam found me were good, but not as nice as these. I neatly fold my new things and place them on top the desk that Kelly cleared off for me. The doorbell rings and the aroma of pizza wafts in. I wear one of my outfits downstairs.

We watch movies all night with Susan controlling the remote. She barely speaks a word to me and Kelly seems too busy with Justin and Jason to notice. I'm not sure what to do to make her like me.

Piggy

Chapter 38

The next morning, I get up earlier and walk downstairs. Justin is eating at a kid size table set up in the corner of the kitchen and Jason is in a high chair sweeping cereal pieces from side to side. Kelly acknowledges me and I open the fridge to get some juice.

"Kim invited me to come over today," Susan says descending down the stairs.

"Heather, do you want to go with Susan?"

Susan's eyes bulge.

"No, thank you. Maybe some other time?" I say.

Susan's face relaxes. "Definitely. I'm going to change and then walk over," she says running up stairs two at a time.

"Good, you and I can talk some more," Kelly says to me.

After helping clean up the kitchen, I follow Kelly upstairs to watch her dress the boys.

"How are you doing so far, Heather?"

"This is great, thanks for letting me stay."

"What do you want to do?"

"What do you mean?"

"Would you like to stay here with us? Go to school?"

"Yes," I reply with my eyes lighting up. "Can I?"

"Yes, I want you to stay; I'm making sure that's what you want."

"Yes, this is the best place I've ever been in."

"I'm glad you like it. And I'm glad you're here. I wish I could change the last eight years."

I look down at the ground at Jason who is keeping busy with a stuffed bear. Justin is tugging at Kelly's shirt.

"Do you have to go potty?" Kelly asks Justin. "Can you watch Jason for a minute?" she says as she takes Justin by the hand and walks down the hallway.

I look around the room. There are two twin locomotive beds with big smiley faces representing the head of the engine car. The pale beige carpeting is offset by pastel blue walls with a mid-level strip of dancing zoo animal wallpaper encircling the room. A bookshelf, full of books and stuffed animals, leans beside the crib and reminds me of my pink bedroom and all the stuffed animals I left behind.

"Let's go downstairs," Kelly interrupts my thoughts. "Can you carry him?"

I nod following her down. Depositing Justin near the coffee table, Kelly lays out some coloring books for him. I put Jason in his bouncy seat next to the couch.

"Heather, I'm glad you want to stay," Kelly says joining me on the couch. "But in order for you to be here, we are going to have to find Dan."

"What? Why?"

"Don't get scared. He can't hurt you now. We have to do this legally."

"No."

"Listen to me. The lawyer, Mr. Robertson, he came by after the fire, after you left. He told me to contact him if I ever saw you again."

I pull my hand back from her grasp.

"You haven't done anything wrong. In fact, I suspect you're in better shape than you think. The trust has been sitting there untouched."

"Is that it? You want the money?"

"No, the money isn't for me, it's for you. And besides, unlike when you left, I'm much better off now. That money is for you, for college, for a new life."

"No, not if it means trying to find Dan."

"It's not only the trust; I may not be able to enroll you in school if I'm not your guardian. Let's talk to Mr. Robertson. He'll know what to do. I'd like to become your legal guardian so that you can live here and I can look after you."

"And take the money."

"No. If it makes you feel better, I'll specifically request that the money doesn't go to me."

"Then why look for Dan?"

"Because we have to legally change your guardianship in order to enroll you in school, take you to the doctor, everything."

"You're not going to find him."

"You may be right. I don't know how hard the lawyer looked before. He said he hired a private investigator when you first left."

My mind rolls through my options. If Warren was smart, he would have buried Dan so that no one would ever find him. More likely, Warren ran, in which case Dan's body has been found or will be. If Kelly or the lawyer look for Dan, they could find him, dead, with an unsolved murder case to boot. I'd be linked to it right away. Warren would testify that I did it. Or a new thought pops into my head. I could say Warren did it. There was no one else there. It would be my word against his. I could say it was a drunken fight or a fight over money. That could work. Kelly's stare rattles me out of my thoughts. I decide I'll have to think through a scenario that frames Warren tonight.

Piggy

Touching my arm to ensure my attention, "I'm not going to do anything without you knowing about it," Kelly continues.

I nod.

"Now, let's go have some fun today. School isn't until next Tuesday, so we've got time to talk more. You ready to go?"

"Where?"

"It's a surprise."

We get into the car after the long loading procedure from yesterday is replicated. It's a nice day, warm, not like December at all. Kelly drives to a strip mall. Unloading, I help with the stroller, snapping it into place quickly.

"Wow, you're fast. It took me weeks to figure this out," Kelly says pointing to the double wide.

"Guess it makes sense to me," I say realizing my days breaking down and setting up wheelchairs has paid off.

Kelly wheels into a glass door that says Hair Salon. Inside, there are two banks of mirrors on either side with chairs in front of them.

"Surprise! You're getting your hair cut," Kelly announces.

I'm shown to an empty chair and a cape is placed around me. The stylist is a short dark-haired young woman with multiple piercings in her ears and nose. Standing behind my chair, we stare at each other in the mirror. She smiles and another piercing peeks out of her mouth -- a solid silver dot in the middle of her tongue. I can't help from squirming at the thought of the pain it must have caused.

"How do you normally get your hair cut?" the stylist asks as she runs her hands through my hair revealing her heavily tattooed arms.

"I've never gotten a haircut before," I say.

"Sure you have," Kelly says.

Piggy

"No, never."

"Your hair isn't that long," Kelly says lifting it up from below my shoulders.

"Mom cut it for me in the kitchen a few times, but never since Dan."

"Did he take scissors to you himself?"

"No, I've never gotten it cut," I say, not understanding the disbelief.

"Heather, you've got to be honest with me. Your hair is at your shoulders, you're nearly sixteen, if you had never had a haircut, your hair would be down below your butt."

I look at her.

"At least," the stylist offers. "Hair grows one to two inches a year."

"Maybe you've forgotten," Kelly offers.

"No, I've never had it cut," I confirm while racking my brain on why I'm so sure. When I remember why, my face drops and I look down at the floor.

"Why are you lying, Heather?"

"I'm not. Can we talk about this later?" I say with tears welling up in my eyes.

"Okay. It's okay," Kelly says while rubbing my shoulder.

"How do you want it cut?" the stylist says impatiently.

"Any ideas?" Kelly asks me. I shake my head. "I think maybe some long bangs with some layers. Keep it long. What do you think?" Kelly says to the stylist.

"Yeah, that will look good. I can make it fit her face better. You want highlights?"

"Yes, just a touch," Kelly says smiling at me.

The next hour and a half my hair is washed, pulled and parted, painted with white stuff that smells, and left under a heater until it's done. Next, I watch my locks fall to the floor followed by a painful period of pulling my hair out with a round brush. I'm asked to close my eyes to the end as the stylist finishes me off and sprays a dose of hairspray. Spinning around to the mirror, I am allowed to open my eyes.

I barely recognize myself. My hair is light and fluffy with waves on either side gently framing my face. There's a hint of blonde at the tips that turns my mousy brown to beautiful. A smile grows on my face.

"You look so beautiful," Kelly says at my side.

I turn from side to side admiring my looks. I whip my head in one direction and watch my hair fly like in the commercials.

"I love it!" The stylist is smiling back at me. "Thank you, thank you!"

We walk out of the salon as I catch a glimpse of myself in every mirror. Kelly drives to a restaurant where we get situated and order hamburgers and shakes. Jason sleeps after a bottle and Justin is busying himself with crayons and toys Kelly has brought with her.

"You look great," Kelly says as I smile and take another look in the mirror that is next to us.

"Do you want to tell me about the haircut?"

"I didn't lie."

"Then what?"

I contemplate what to tell her. I think up a different story but then think that maybe the truth will help convince her not to look for Dan.

"Dan shaved my head when I was ten."

"What!" she shouts leaning forward in disbelief. "Why?"

I pause trying to figure out a way to explain without stating my involvement, but I can't. And looking at her, I want to tell her.

"Dan and I used to rob hospitals," I say studying her face for reaction. She stares at me emotionless. "It started when I was still living here. We'd go into a hospital late at night and he'd take medicine and stuff."

"What for?"

"He'd sell it. I'm not sure to who. There was someone here who would buy it all. When we started traveling, Dan would find someone new or as he said cultivate someone."

"What does that mean?"

"He'd find people who worked in retirement centers and talk them into buying the medicines he stole for a discount. They'd scam the center together and split the difference."

"I don't understand. What did you do exactly? Just walk in?"

"At first, then Dan stole a wheelchair and costumes. I was the sick patient and he was an orderly wheeling me around for some late night test. We'd go in after midnight, and look at what was left in rooms and take it. Sometimes we'd get access to a supply room and then we scored big."

"Did you steal?"

"Dan taught me to. Told me I had to help him."

"And you never got caught?"

"There were some close calls, but no."

"Why'd he shave your head?"

"He said that I wasn't cute anymore. I'd gotten older and he thought it was a harder sell for people to believe I was sick. He held me down one night while I was asleep and shaved my head. Told me I'd look sick that way," I pause and look at Kelly.

"That's why I dropped out of sixth grade. I was too embarrassed to go. It was bad enough when the other kids made fun of me wearing the same clothes every day, but I couldn't hide my bald head."

"Heather, I'm sorry to have doubted you. That must have been terrible."

"It was what it was," I say. I can't even cry anymore about it.

Chapter 39

New Year's Eve and Susan is going to Kim's house for a party. Kelly pushes her to take me. We walk the half block in silence. I've got on my favorite new outfit – jeans, black flats, and a green plaid sweater. My hair looks almost as good as the day I got it cut.

"Susan, are you mad at me?" I ask as we reach Kim's house.

"No why would you think that?" she says shortly.

"For starters, you seem mad right now. I want us to be friends like before."

Stopping, she turns to me. "It's just that you're mom's favorite now and I'm tired of it."

"I didn't mean to get in the way."

"It's not you, it's her. For a long time, it was me and her. Then Bryan came along and it was better. My dad moved away so I don't get to see him as much and Bryan made things better. But then Justin, Jason, now you. She picks her favorites and I get nothing. No time. No attention. Nothing."

"I'm sorry."

"Listen, my mom told me you've had it hard. But I've had it hard, too. Remember the daycare we'd go to?"

I nod.

"What a dump. I hated that place, but she had to work."

"I remember you liking it."

"Well, I didn't. And now, now she's home most of the day with Justin and Jason. She never stayed home with me."

I'm not sure how to answer.

Piggy

"And what's up with you anyway?" she says turning her anger to me.

"What do you mean?"

"Mom said you've been through a lot and I'm not supposed to ask you about it. But what was so bad? You were poor, so what? We were too for a while."

"I bounced around a lot."

"No different than a military family. Kim's lived in four places and she's only fifteen."

I don't know where to begin or if I even want to explain.

"What did your uncle do? Did he beat you?"

"He wasn't good to me."

Rolling her eyes, she takes the last few steps to the front door and knocks. A short Hispanic girl answers, introducing herself as Kim. She's gorgeous with big brown eyes and long brown hair. She's got boobs like Kelly and I try not to stare. We follow Kim into a great room that is very similar to Kelly's. Two long couches form an 'L' across from the TV which is blaring music videos. Tables are pushed against the walls and chairs are lined up like a waiting room; all to make a dance floor. Fifteen girls are spread throughout the room either dancing, eating, or doing their nails.

"Hey, everyone!" Susan shouts, "This is Heather, she's staying with me for a while."

Everyone turns to wave quickly and then return to what they are doing. I can't stop thinking what 'for a while' means. I stay on the sidelines slowly inching my way to the crowded table covered with snacks and drinks. A new song comes on and several girls scream -- a call to the dance floor has been made telepathically. The snack table is now vacant and I graze at my leisure.

Satisfied, I take a seat near the nail polish station.

"Hi, I'm Judy," a thin small redhead says to me. I can tell by looking up at her that I dwarf her by at least a foot. She's pale with lots of freckles spread across her face and neck.

"Want me to do your nails?"

"Sure," I say letting her take my hand.

She removes polish from my unpolished nails I suspect because she can't understand why anyone wouldn't have their nails done. Next she pushes back my cuticles.

"Where are you from?"

"All over."

"Where was last?"

"Chicago."

"I've always wanted to go there."

"Yeah, it's nice," I say falling into the role I think she expects.

"What grade are you in?"

"I don't know."

She looks up and squints her eyes.

"I've been out of school for a few years. Lived out in the country. I have to see what grade they'll let me enroll in."

"The country of Chicago?"

"On the outskirts. I didn't live in Chicago proper."

"I've lived here all my life. Lancaster that is. We've moved a few times within town, but no place else."

"Do you like it here?"

Piggy

"Yeah, it's alright. Better now that we're in this neighborhood. Our last place was kind of a dump."

"Is your dad in the Air Force too?"

"Both my parents are. My dad teaches flying and my mom works on the base."

"What do your parents do?"

"My mom died when I was young. I never knew my dad. I've been with my uncle ever since." I'm astonished by how easily my life flows out. Kelly and I have been talking about the last eight years all week so I guess it has gotten easier to talk about.

"Hold your hands out, like this, for twenty minutes. You can wave them, but don't let them touch anything," Judy instructs as she gets up to get a snack.

I look down at my newly pinked nails.

Returning with a handful of M&Ms, Judy plops back down on the couch.

"What's your favorite band?"

"I don't have one. I didn't listen to much music."

"You really did live in the country."

We talk more about music as Judy rattles off all the bands she likes, what their songs are, and what CDs she has. I listen soaking in this new culture I've found myself in. This is what normal life is like? You have friends over, you shop, you play music, and you go to concerts. You don't beg for food or eat the scraps off Dan's takeout when he doesn't even think to get you something. You don't hide in the shadows avoiding an angry tirade or hide money in your shoe.

Judy is pulled away and I head to the bathroom, assuming it's in the same location as Kelly's house. Around the corner, I hear Susan's voice.

"I don't know what her story is. She used to live here and now she's back. Some sob story of a hard life. I mean she did look like white trash when she arrived. She was wearing this horrible sweater and a coat with huge tears in it. Her hair was greasy and puke colored when she arrived, but mom took her to get her hair done, which is why she looks at all presentable. Plus, my mom bought her a ton of clothes."

"She's kind of pretty," a voice interjects.

"She's okay. My mom says she's staying with us indefinitely, but who knows? Get this; she didn't even wear a bra when she showed up. Looked like a deer in headlights when my mom asked her what her size was. I mean, not that she needs one, she's as flat as a board."

"Bathroom is to your right, Heather," Kim's voice says behind me. I turn to look at her. As I take a step, Susan's face, along with two other girls poke out of a doorway. Giggling, they each pass me on their way back to the party.

I relieve myself and spend more time than I need to in the bathroom. What was I thinking that I could fit in? That someone like me could be normal. These girls pout over broken nails and not getting what they want. I'm never going to be like them. I can't tell them what I used to do, they'd ridicule me.

I open the door and see the coast is clear. I make it to the front door without anyone so much as glancing at me. I shut the door and walk back to Kelly's.

The first floor is empty as I make my way upstairs. Kelly has moved one of the desks into her bedroom which leaves me with more space. It is feeling more like my room every day. My clothes are neatly hung in the closet or folded on the shelf below. I've even taken out the butterflies I swiped in Colorado and set them on the window sill. I look at them every morning as the light streams through and makes them look like they are flying.

Once in my pajamas, I flip through some magazines until midnight when I hear muffled screams celebrating the New Year.

Chapter 40

"We need to talk about Dan again," Kelly states.

The whole family, except Susan, had gotten up late and had brunch together. Susan strolled in around eleven. She went straight up to bed saying they had stayed up all night. Kelly shouted after her, "Get your rest, school is at eight tomorrow."

"I left a message for John to call me," Kelly says as my face drops. "I didn't tell him anything, only said I needed to talk with him."

I relax. "I don't want to find him."

"Hear me out. For you to stay, legally, I need to become your guardian. For that, we need John, Mr. Robertson. Let's let him tell us what the next steps are. Maybe it will be like the hearing. But now that you're here, you can tell the court what Dan was like. Whether we find him or not, the court has to rule in our favor and everything will be solved. I promise you won't see Dan if you don't want to."

I *know* I won't see Dan again. I like it here. It's the first time I've felt safe for a long time. I don't want to screw it up. I offer, "We can talk to Mr. Robertson. But.."

"Don't worry; it'll be fine," she says looking into my eyes. "Now, tomorrow morning, I'm taking you down to school. Susan's school is grade 10-12 but the junior high is a few blocks over and that's where the main administrative offices are. After I drop her off, we'll see about what grade you could start in."

The next morning, I get up early excited and scared about school. Susan monopolizes the bathroom and I'm left with ten minutes to wet my hair down a bit and hope for the best. I had already laid out what I was going to wear the night before. I race downstairs after I hear Kelly calling for us to go. Grabbing a pop tart from Kelly's hand, we head out to the car. Kelly has thankfully already loaded the boys up, a task I've grown tired of quickly.

"Pee-yew!" Susan says waving at her nose.

Piggy

"Grow up, Susan," Kelly snaps at her.

"She didn't even take a shower!"

"I'm sorry, I didn't have time," I say, with the bubble of my perfect day already burst.

"Maybe we need to set a bathroom schedule for you two," Kelly says, staring harshly at Susan who has, once again, claimed the front seat. I'm wedged in between the two car seats in back.

We drive in silence until Kelly pulls into Susan's school. The car has barely slowed when Susan jumps out with a quick bye before slamming the door shut.

Kelly continues onto the junior high and completes the unloading ritual surprisingly fast. We enter Washington Junior High, a two story building with lots of windows across the front. Weaving around the hallway full of kids that are going in every direction, we make it to the front desk. I sit outside on a wooden chair watching the two boys as Kelly goes into an office to talk with an older lady wearing a light green skirt and matching blazer. A half an hour later, Kelly leaves me in the care of Mrs. Adams who has short brown hair reminiscent of a helmet.

Mrs. Adams walks me into an empty room and tells me to wait. A while later, a teacher's aide comes in and hands me a test. She sits in the room as I complete the seven pages which cover a wide range of topics.

At lunch time, Kelly is back, without the boys, to pick me up. First, Mrs. Adams pulls Kelly into her office. After a moment, Kelly waves at me to join them. The small office is surrounded by bookshelves teeming with books. One middle shelf has a row of paperbacks stacked two tall and two wide, making it essentially four rows of books. Stacks of folders and more books are placed in front of the bookshelves creating a second wall of clutter surrounding the small space. Wedged in the center is a desk that Mrs. Adams carefully walks around to take her seat. Kelly and I have to jockey the tight space to get into the two guest chairs.

Mrs. Adams gives an overview of the test I have taken as Kelly and I peer over piles of folders on the desk and politely look interested.

Piggy

Bored, my eyes flick around the desk and the room. Resting casually on top a pile of papers on her desk is a blue Monarch butterfly paperweight. I'm drawn to how close in blue it is to the one Mom had; the one I eventually lost to one of Dan's angry rants. Kelly stands up to reach a brochure that Mrs. Adams is handing her and without hesitation, I grasp the Monarch in my hand. No time for inspection, I casually drop it into the pocket of my coat. I reengage eye contact with Mrs. Adams to make sure she hasn't noticed, but she is undeterred in her monologue.

"How did you feel you did, Heather?" Mrs. Adams asks me.

"I don't know. I think okay."

"You did exceptionally well," she says as Kelly clutches my hand. "You tested in the seventh grade for math which is excellent. Reading comprehension was a bit below average and then a fourth grade level for science."

"What does that mean then?" Kelly asks.

"With a tutor to bring her up in the weak areas, we may be able to enroll her next fall."

"In tenth grade?"

"That will depend on how hard you work, Heather. I'd say ninth is more likely, but if you really apply yourself," she says looking between Kelly and myself, "If you're able to get her the tutors, it's possible you can get into the tenth grade."

Kelly and I clap hands simultaneously.

"Don't get me wrong, it's going to be a lot of work," Mrs. Adams warns.

"This is great news, thank you, Mrs. Adams," Kelly says standing.

"Here's a list of tutors we recommend. I don't know how many have time during the day."

Kelly folds the piece of paper and stuffs it into her purse as she continues her goodbye to Mrs. Adams.

Getting into the car, I ask, "Where's Justin and Jason?"

"There's a daycare I use when I have to work afternoons. I have to pick them up by five," she says starting the car. "How about a quick lunch and then we go see John?"

"What?"

"He called while you were taking the test. I didn't tell him much," she says leaning to me. "Just that you're here. He has time today at two-thirty."

Kelly drives into the underground parking of a six story building. Riding up the elevator, the damp air makes me shiver. We find Mr. Robertson's office and wait in a small room for ten minutes before he's ready for us.

"Mrs. Jenkins, good to see you again. Heather," Mr. Robertson says extending his hand, "It is nice to set eyes on you again. I was worried about you."

I shake his hand not knowing the shaking protocol and sit down next to Kelly in front of his desk.

"How are you?"

"I'm fine, Mr. Robertson."

"Please, call me John," he says with a smile. He's lost weight. His double chin is gone and I can see the chair around him. I remember a roly-poly brown haired man who waddled when he walked. Now, the uniformly dark brown hair is throwing me off as this guy looks fairly slim from what I can see under his shiny black suit.

"I'm glad you're doing well as is Steve, Mr. Forrester, from the bank. We were concerned about you. Do you want to tell me what happened? Or what you remember?"

Piggy

I'm not prepared for the question and look blankly back at him. From out of nowhere, I begin talking. "I think Dan owed money to this guy, Stu. He was a big biker looking guy who had come to see him a few nights before we left. He had terrified me but Dan didn't seem too scared. A few nights after his visit, we came home late and found the house trashed. The front door was torn off the hinges."

"I don't remember that," Kelly says to my left.

"Yeah, well, that's what happened. When Dan realized you were moving away, he seemed antsier. We ended up staying at a motel for about a week. I wasn't allowed to go out but Dan did. Then Dan got a call and we went down to the bank."

"Yes, Steve was the last person to see you that day. Do you remember that?" John said.

I nodded. "That night, we left town. Before we left though, Dan made a stop back at the house. I didn't see him set the fire, but I smelled gas on him and I'm pretty sure it was him."

"Good, we can use that," John says.

"Use it?"

"In the case against him to challenge your guardianship."

"Oh. After that, we went to Texas, then a bunch of other places."

"She doesn't have to go through all this again, does she?" Kelly asks.

"No, not now at least."

"What we want to know is what do we do now?"

"Well," John says leaning back in his chair. His coat falls open exposing his stark white shirt and clown red tie. I can see he is as slim as I had surmised. "We have to open up the complaint again. That's some simple paperwork. I think we should separate it from the trust audit. Since he hasn't drawn on the money for so long, there isn't much to audit. We'll raise the complaint to Family Services," he says leaning to me, "And we'll need a list of reasons why he's not been a good guardian from you."

"A list?"

"It won't be hard. You and Kelly can sit down with my assistant and tell her some stories about what he did. Kelly says you lived in a van for a while?" he says. I shoot a look at Kelly who had said she didn't tell him much, but apparently enough to get to the van detail.

"Heather, it won't be hard. He didn't feed you, you didn't go to school, and you lived horribly. That along with the arson and what I witnessed should be enough," Kelly says placing her hand on my arm.

"Actually, what you witnessed is irrelevant now. Too much time has passed. But we do need to notify the authorities about a lead in the arson case."

"A lead?" I say.

"The fire department certainly has Dan as a suspect, but we need to notify them that he may actually return."

"What do you mean, return?" I retort.

"When we file the complaint, we're going to have to make an effort to find Dan and serve him. We're the requestors, so to speak, so it's up to us to make a diligent effort to find him and notify him of his requirement to attend the hearing."

"I thought we wouldn't have to find him," I say pointedly at Kelly.

"I said I wasn't sure we had to."

"We have to make a diligent effort, that's what the law says, which means we have to send notices and process servers to his last known address or location," John says.

Piggy

"You're not going to find him," I say quickly. "I mean, I don't know where he is and if he was smart enough to hide from you for eight years, he's smart enough to stay hidden."

"It's more of a formality, Heather. And you won't be required to see him if you don't want to. I can file a restraining order against him."

"What happens if you don't find him?" I ask.

"The case will take longer, but eventually we'll be able to argue it. In the meantime, we can easily petition for temporary guardianship with Kelly."

"Why can't we do that now?"

"We can, but the temporary guardianship is only valid if it is contingent on another proceeding."

"What if we do nothing and I just live with Kelly?"

"You won't be able to access the trust," John replies.

"I'm fine with that."

"And Kelly will have no legal authority over you. The State won't allow a minor to live without a valid legal guardian so you'd be sent into foster care."

"Can't Kelly be my foster care?"

"She could petition for that. It would take some time and there's no guaranty she'd get it. And no guaranty that if she became a foster home, you'd be sent to live with her. Even if that worked out, the State would do the same sort of searching for Dan as we have to do."

"They would send out an investigator," I say narrowing my eyes as I feel I've found a solution.

"No, probably not. Since you're nearly sixteen, they'd probably send letters and alert their counterpart agencies in the states where you think Dan could be."

"Let's do that."

"But again, you may be forced to live in a foster situation without Kelly. And you can't access the trust. Do you know how much the trust is?"

I look at him.

"It's been sitting untouched, earning interest. It was set up to pay out until you were eighteen. There's over a hundred thousand of back pay, not to mention the monthly fifteen hundred would start back up."

"How much?"

"You heard me. You're financially well-off for a young lady. And that's not the best part," John says smiling, confident he has won the argument. "Your mom also set up a college account. When you turn eighteen, there's a hundred grand for you to attend college. You must use it for tuition and board, but it's yours. If you choose not to attend college, then the money transfers to you at twenty-one."

"Wow," Kelly says.

"Wow, is right," John states.

I glance between John, Kelly, and whatever is on John's desk. I can't be linked to Dan. I'll get caught for sure. They don't let prisoners have money. Any linkage and I lose it all.

"Do I get direct access to the monthly payments?" I ask with three follow up questions on the tip of my tongue.

"Your guardian does."

"John, I have already told Heather that the money is hers. Can we set up some secondary trust or account so that the money doesn't go to me?"

John considers it for a moment. "Yes, we can do that. But it would still likely have to have a minor clause in it."

Both Kelly and I must have questioning looks on our face as John continues. "Meaning that you won't really have direct access until you're eighteen at the earliest. The account can be joint, but it would still require your guardian to co-sign any withdrawals."

"When I'm eighteen, I get all this back pay?"

"Ah, yes, you would."

"That's what we'll do," I say definitively.

"Do what?" John asks.

"Request temporary foster care and don't look for Dan. Then when I'm eighteen, I'll still have enough money for college."

"But you may not be able to live with Kelly until then."

"I lived in worse places."

"Heather, don't let your fear of Dan keep you from making the right decision here," Kelly says.

"I don't want you to look for him."

Kelly and John exchange curious looks. John is the first to break the tension.

"We don't have to decide anything this minute. You can think about it some more. My recommendation is to challenge the guardianship. It is by far the fastest way to get completely away from Dan and full access to all that is yours. The way you want to go will take more time and has risks on where you would live and such. Realize this may not work out like you want."

"I'll take that chance," I say rising from the chair.

"Why don't we touch base in a few days after you've had more time to think about it?"

"I don't need more time," I say flatly.

"Even if we go your way, it will still take me the week to do the paperwork so we have time either way."

Kelly stands up. "Thank you for fitting us in today. We'll talk more later," she says shaking his hand.

We drive home in silence stopping to pick up Justin and Jason. Once home, I'm saved by the boys' screams and needs. I sneak away to my room for a few hours until Kelly calls me down for dinner.

Chapter 41

That night at dinner, Susan yammers on about her friends and how much they got for Christmas implying she's impoverished with only a few articles of clothing to show for the holiday. Kelly is simultaneously feeding the two boys and eating herself as I successfully avoid making eye contact with her. I volunteer to do the dishes in hopes Kelly will get busy with the boys' baths.

When I'm done cleaning, I join Susan on the couch who is simultaneously on the phone and watching TV. I don't pay attention to what we watch and I'm not sure I could with the number of times Susan changes the channel. She doesn't even glance in my direction. Around eight-thirty, Kelly descends the stairs and tells Susan to go to her room and do homework.

"I don't have any," she says defiantly.

"I'm sure you do. Now go on."

Rising alongside Susan, I begin my escape but Kelly puts her hand on my shoulder and waits for Susan to make it up the stairs.

"Let's talk."

"I don't want to look for him," I say cutting to what I know is her topic of choice.

"I don't get it. He can't hurt you. I'll protect you."

"I don't want to."

Kelly takes a deep breath and sits down across from me. She starts from the beginning making her argument and outlining all the reasons that my decision isn't in my best interest. She brings up various medical situations where I'll need a guardian to look out for me.

"I don't even know if I *can* apply for foster kids," she says at last. "I have to talk to Bryan about this and our next scheduled call is in ten days. I can't apply to be a foster parent without talking to him first."

I remain silent but not hostile.

Piggy

"Even if we got it, I don't know how long it would take *or* if I'd be able to request you. Maybe they'd make me take someone else which is a situation I don't want." She pauses looking at my face for any signs that she's convincing me.

"I don't want to see him."

"That can't be the only reason. What did he do to you?"

"Nothing."

"Did he touch you? Force you to do something?"

"I already told you he didn't."

"He didn't hit you much, he didn't molest you, don't get me wrong Heather, I know you've been through a lot, but what is frightening you?"

"I just don't want to see him," I repeat forcing some tears and running upstairs to my room. I had thought I created enough drama to be left alone, but Kelly follows. Now approaching my door, I have to actually produce some tears.

"You're going to have to tell me," Kelly says behind me.

Opening the door, Susan is there, my purse in one hand and a wad of money in the other.

"Give me that!"

Startled by my scream and then by my merciless shove, I grab my purse back and Susan falls onto the futon.

"Where'd you steal that from?" she shouts.

Kelly is looking at me as I quickly examine the money to ensure the bulk is there before stuffing it into my purse.

"Heather? Where did all that come from?"

Piggy

"Yeah, you little thief. Not such a good kid after all," Susan snarls.

"Susan, go to your room," Kelly orders.

"Mom!"

"Go!"

"She may have stolen this from me!"

"Go," Kelly says with finality.

Shutting the door, Kelly sits on one of the chairs as I fall back onto the edge of the futon. Kelly continues to stare, not saying a word.

"I earned it," I say.

Kelly raises her eyebrows.

"I did!"

"Did you steal that from Dan? Is that why you don't want to find him?"

"No."

"Where did you get it?"

"I told you I earned it."

"Heather, that looked like a lot of money. You told me Dan starved you and withheld money. That," she says pointing to the purse I had slid next to me out of her sight, "doesn't look like he withheld money."

Kelly sighs and breaks her stare. Glancing around the room, debating her next avenue of questioning, her eyes fall onto the window sill. I follow her gaze and freeze. The blue Monarch that I had swiped today is proudly displayed in the middle. I play it cool, just like Dan taught me; don't offer an explanation before it's asked for. Although, I think, I violated that rule a few moments ago. Kelly stands and takes the three steps to the window and picks up the paper weight. Bouncing it in her hand slowly, she turns to me.

"This was on Mrs. Adams' desk, wasn't it?"

"No, I had that."

"Really? I'm certain I saw it on her desk today."

"No, I've had that since Mom. It was hers."

Pausing and looking up to the ceiling, "I forgot about that. Is that why you have these? These butterflies?"

"Yes."

"I remember her collection. She had like fifteen or something?"

I nod.

"A couple were from her mom, right?"

"Yes."

Tilting her head downward, she leans in, "But, her collection was all Mirakasi. This doesn't even have a brand on it."

Snatching it from her hand, "It was hers!"

"Heather, don't lie to me."

I get up and run out of the room. I trip over Susan who has been eavesdropping at the door. Continuing down the hallway, Justin has gotten out of bed and is blocking the top of the stairs. One glance at him and he shoots that guilty look that kids have when they're caught doing something naughty. The only open door is Kelly's so I run in there thinking I'll lock myself in her bathroom. I trip on a pile of clothes near the bookcase that is adjacent to the bathroom doorway and go down. Looking back, Kelly is picking up Justin so despite my fall, I have time to make it to safety. As I move my head around, I see her.

Piggy

She's smiling widely with her arm around Kelly in the backyard of our house. Its summertime and she has shorts on and is wearing sunglasses, but her smile is unmistakable. Her shoulder length light brown hair is layered to feather back from her beautifully tanned face. She's wearing a short sleeve shirt that was unbuttoned to show off her long neck and diamond pendant. I had forgotten about her necklace. It was a perfect round diamond on a thin silver chain that would nearly fade into her skin so that the diamond appeared to float on her chest. I want to see Mom's eyes, but her sunglasses are too dark.

"That's your mom and me in your backyard," Kelly says above me.

I nod, tears streaming down my face. Kelly drops to the floor and pulls me up to sit and hugs me as I cry harder than I ever remember crying. And not the fake crying that I've learned to do when I need to. Catching my breath between sobs, Kelly releases me.

"I'm sorry, I forgot about the pictures. Do you have any?"

I shake my head.

"Let me look, there may be another one I have with you and her."

"I killed Dan," I blurt out under my breath

Kelly glares at me and then calmly shuts the bedroom door.

"I killed him. Did you hear me?"

"What do you mean, you killed him?"

"I killed him, that's why we can't look for him. I'll be caught. Put away for murder. That's why we can't, we can't look for him."

"Calm down, let's talk this through. What exactly happened?"

Swallowing hard, I wipe my eyes and nose on my sleeve.

"We got into a fight. He was mean to me and he burned something I wanted. I don't know why that day, what he did, what he did to me any other day; why that day I just couldn't take it anymore, but I couldn't. I knew I had to kill him. I got a knife, a box cutter really. And after he passed out, I was going to cut his throat."

Kelly was rubbing my leg as I continued.

"I was going to do it. I had the box cutter in my hand and leaned over him, but I guess I didn't cut deep enough and he woke up. So I ran. I mean I was planning to run afterwards, I had packed my stuff up. But now I had to run from him. He was bleeding and chasing me. I fell down near the fire and he was above me. I thought for sure he was going to kill me so I tried to get away. I kicked the tent pole and he must have fallen backward on it. Next thing I know, he's got this bloody stick coming out of him; trying to catch his breath."

"It was an accident."

"No, it wasn't," I confess.

"He fell onto the stick."

"I cut his throat and kicked the stick that he fell into. I killed him," I state without emotion. "I wanted him dead. I planned to kill him."

"What happened then?"

"I ran. Hitched a ride, got to Chicago and caught a bus."

"Where did you get the money for the bus ticket?"

I hesitate but I've said so much already. "I stole it from this convenience store near us. It's where I got the box cutter."

"Then what?"

"I made it to Grand Junction and met a really nice girl, Sam. She let me stay with her and I got a job and, and that's where I earned the money. I didn't steal that. That's mine."

"When was this?"

Piggy

"In October, but then I left to come here."

"Why didn't you stay?"

"They knew my social security number was phony. And Sam was asking questions. I knew she or the guy I worked for would find out who I was. So I left."

"How do you know Dan was dead?"

I nodded. "He's dead. He had blood coming out of his mouth."

"Would anyone have helped him?"

"Warren may have, but he's kind of stupid."

"Warren?"

"He was this black guy that started hanging around with us. He was scamming food and booze off of Dan."

"Do you think Warren helped him?"

"I doubt he could have done much. Besides we were in the middle of nowhere."

"Let me think about this a bit."

"We can't look for him. They'll find his body or an open murder case. I'll be put in jail."

"Let's sleep on it."

Chapter 42

The next morning I stay in my room, not wanting to see Kelly and not certain what to say. Kelly finally sticks her head in to ask me to watch the boys as she drives Susan to school. I reluctantly go downstairs and come face to face with Susan who looks like a cat who conquered the bird cage. She flips her hair at me and walks out to the car.

I enter the kitchen to find Justin quietly playing with his cars in the corner and Jason dozing. I make some toast for myself but I can't eat it. Thoughts of prison enter my mind. Bread and water, that's what you're fed. I toss out the toast and reach for a yogurt instead. I review my options. I could run again. That would solve most of my problems. I could come back when I'm eighteen for the money. I can't assume I'll be safe here. On the other hand, I've been here barely a week and I feel at home for the first time. If I run, I won't be able to go to school and I'd be alone.

The door opens and I'm startled by Kelly coming back much faster than I expected.

"How are you feeling this morning?"

"Good."

"Let's call John."

"What?"

"I've been thinking about this all night. Let's call John and ask him how long we can hold off even applying for temporary guardianship. I would imagine that will buy us some time. In the meantime, we can search if anyone has found Dan's body and whether there are any investigations going on."

"How?"

"There are records that have to be kept. We should hire a private investigator and have them search death certificates and police reports in Wisconsin."

"I don't know. Couldn't that get traced back to me?"

Piggy

"I won't tell him anything about you and I'll pay in cash. I won't tell him why I want to know."

"Maybe I should leave. Come back when I'm eighteen."

"No. I don't want that and it's not a good idea for you to be out there on your own."

"I've done it before."

"For two months. Two and a half years is something else. Besides I'm still not convinced it wasn't self-defense."

"I attacked him."

"Yes, but Heather, you've been a victim of mental and verbal abuse for years. You can't think straight about this. Let's see if we can find out what happened to Dan, then we'll visit a criminal lawyer and understand our options."

"I don't know."

"And we need to tell Susan what really happened to you and not shield her from it anymore. She's not a bad kid; she's just fifteen. I had thought it was best for her not to know, but now I think we've got to tell her. I don't think she heard us last night, at least not what you said in the bedroom. But we should be certain."

I ponder what Kelly has said and finally nod in agreement. In the back of my mind, I plan on developing an escape plan in case anything goes awry.

I listen to Kelly as she calls John and does as we discussed. He talks for a long time, no doubt trying to convince her otherwise. In the end, she hangs up confirming he'll do as she asked.

Next Kelly looks through the phone book under detective agency for a private investigator. Dialing the number, she makes an appointment for that afternoon. She spends the next hour on the phone with tutors telling me that we don't have time to waste with my education. I sit there helpless not knowing what to do as I watch Kelly describe what she wants for me in a tutor. After lining up two tutor interviews for tomorrow, she makes lunch for all of us. Around one, I'm left alone to watch the boys as Kelly goes out to meet the P.I.

Kelly returns around three in the afternoon. She recounts her meeting, describing the P.I. as an older guy who had been an ex insurance investigator. She tells me not to worry. I nod and don't mention to her that as soon as the boys fell asleep for their afternoon nap, I devised an escape plan. I packed up a change of clothes in two separate bags and placed five hundred dollars in each. I hid one in the coat closet by the front door and the other in the backyard inside Justin's plastic playhouse. I placed a trash bag inside my closet for my third option and practiced how fast I could stuff it full of my remaining clothes and cash. I resolved to keep as much cash as possible with me at all times, even though the large wad of twenties and tens made it difficult. I found a rope in the garage and tested the length from my bedroom window rationalizing that in a pinch, I could make it out of the second story to freedom if necessary.

Susan saunters in around three thirty and slams the door, which successfully awakens Justin and Jason. She immediately goes into the kitchen for a snack as Kelly gives her a look.

"Get your homework done before dinner. We're going to have a long talk tonight," Kelly says to Susan as she rolls her eyes. Grabbing a soda and a handful of cookies, she heads to the stairs passing by me on the couch. Making sure Kelly's head is turned, she smiles sarcastically before climbing the stairs.

Susan pushes her food around her plate taking only a few bites of the vegetables and chicken breast that Kelly has cooked. I look at her astonished Kelly is allowing this. Sure, I'm craving a Big Mac instead of the steamed plain carrots in front of me, but this is hardly the worst food I've ever eaten. I stand, ready to clear the plates, when Kelly orders Susan to do the dishes. With a huff and a lot of heavy exhaling, she completes the task.

A few minutes after the boys have been put down, Kelly picks up the remote and turns off the TV ignoring Susan's protests. I motion to Kelly if she wants me to go upstairs but she shakes her head. Sitting down next to Susan, Kelly tells her my story, albeit with a few areas omitted. Her version focuses on Mom dying and Dan being a bad uncle who drank, smoked, and abused me. She glosses over any

Piggy

hospital 'visits' and paints Dan as evil and the person who torched the house. Susan is taking it in and seems moved. Next, Kelly turns to me so that I can tell the story after I left the neighborhood.

Taking my queue from Kelly, I hit the highlights. "We bounced from town to town. The longest we stayed anywhere was a little over a year, but mostly, it was three to five months at a time. Each time, we lived in the car for a few days, or a dirty motel, until we found a place to live. And each time, I was enrolled in a new school. Dan left me alone a lot. Sometimes for days and I was expected to never talk to anyone or tell anyone where he was. Sometimes, he would hit me; but mostly, he treated me like crap." I paused before continuing.

"Until last week, I had never owned a new piece of clothing. Dan made me shop at Goodwill."

Susan gasped. Apparently, Goodwill is the epitome of evil, and being abused pales in comparison.

"For the last several years, we lived in a van in the middle of a junkyard. I wasn't allowed to go to school. I wasn't allowed to leave. We took showers at a church once a week."

Susan now seems to understand the situation making the appropriate facial expressions.

"Remember the doll I used to have? Betty?" I wait for Susan to acknowledge some memory of her. "The day I ran from the junkyard, I found one. It must have been thrown out by some family and it came in the truckload of junk Dan would buy. It wasn't Betty, but it was enough like her. Betty was my only friend when we first left. I guess she was my only friend since you. I wasn't allowed to talk to anyone when we were moving from place to place; Dan prevented me from becoming friends with anyone. He was afraid I'd say too much. When I found Betty, or the doll that looked like her, it brought back memories of you, home, and how much I missed Mom and my old life. I had lost Betty, my real doll, years before when Dan and I had to leave a town in Wyoming fast. She got left behind and Dan wouldn't let me go back to get her." I pause for a moment. "Dan threw the Betty doll I found into the fire."

Piggy

Susan gasps. I sit there looking down with the images flooding back to me. How quickly he snatched her and how fast she went up in flames. I wasn't mad anymore, only sad. Sad at what I lost.

"What happened?" Susan asks with her voice cracking.

"I ran. I've been running ever since."

"Susan, Heather and I are telling you this so that you'll understand her situation and to keep the details of where she came from and who she is a secret until we decide how to handle it."

"I will mom," Susan says. Turning to me, "I promise. I won't tell anyone."

"Susan," Kelly says, "I know when you were younger, we had it rough, but things are good now. And in the scheme of it all, you've had a really good life. Heather hasn't. You need to understand that when I buy her clothes or take her out, it's no different than what I've done for you for years. It may seem like more right now. But you're my only daughter and nothing is going to take that away. Understand?"

Susan nods as Kelly wraps her arms around her. For the first time, I see a glimmer of the girl that had been my best friend.

Chapter 43

The next morning, Kelly wakes me up early.

"I'm taking you to school today" she instructs. I walk to the bathroom as Susan is exiting wrapped in a towel.

"It's all yours," she says with a smile.

I take a shower and do my hair the way I've been taught. Popping downstairs, I'm able to finish a bowl of cereal before we get into the car.

"I thought the tutors were coming here," I ask Kelly.

"They are, this afternoon, this is for something else," she replies.

Once she drops off Susan, I get into the front seat. Kelly pulls into a parking spot and I turn unsure what she's doing. Her hand goes into her purse and pulls out the blue Monarch paperweight and I know this is the something else.

"I'm taking you back to Mrs. Adams and you're going to return this."

"Why?"

"Because you stole it and that isn't right."

"Her office is so cluttered, I bet she hasn't even missed it. Probably doesn't even know she had it."

"That's not the point. The point is stealing is wrong. It's against the law and you can't live with me if you continue to do it."

"It's worth nothing. It isn't even made of glass, just some cheap plastic."

"Heather, I get you've had it hard and I wish I could change it, but I can't. Dan taught you bad things. I know you were surviving. But now I can do something to help you and it starts here. Stealing is wrong. Stealing from anyone is wrong."

I look at her. I know she's right but for this thing?

"You're going to go in there and apologize for taking it."

"She'll have me arrested."

"She won't."

"How do you know?"

"I know."

I look at her for a long time. I know stealing is wrong. I've only done it when I've needed to. I ponder raising this as an argument, and then realize no one needs a paperweight.

"You're coming with me?"

"Yes," she says as she begins the unloading procedure.

We walk together down the hallways that are bustling with kids and arrive at Mrs. Adams's door. She's on the phone so I'm given a momentary reprieve. Hanging up, she stands up as Kelly nudges me in the back to walk inside.

"Mrs. Adams, hello, Heather has something to say to you," Kelly starts off.

I look down. The butterfly is clutched in my right hand and is small enough that you can't see it. While the hallway was loud with kids screaming and shouting, in here, it's quiet. I stand thinking for a long time. Kelly nudges me again.

"Mrs. Adams," I say sucking in my breath. "I.. I.. I took this from you yesterday," I finally say holding out my hand so she can see. Her expression turns from a polite greeting to judgmentally raised eyebrows. "I'm sorry, I know it's wrong. I saw it and I took it."

Piggy

"Thank you for returning it. It is wrong to steal and when you are enrolled this fall, I expect you not to exhibit this behavior again."

"I won't. I'm sorry. I shouldn't have taken it but I did."

"Let this be the last time," she says placing the butterfly on her desk.

Tears well up in my eyes. I'm not sure why I'm crying. Maybe it's because this is the first time anyone cared about what I did; cared about me.

"That wasn't so bad," Kelly says as we return to the car. "Stealing is wrong. You can't do it. Next time, it will be much worse than an apology."

"I know."

"I understand that it probably reminded you of your mom, but that still isn't a good excuse," she says pulling out of the parking lot and heading back home.

That afternoon, two different tutors come by and outline their plan to get me back on my educational track. Both Kelly and I like the second one better, despite his heavy accent. Before Mr. Akmed, a tiny older Indian fellow, leaves, Kelly arranges for him to come every morning from nine until noon.

Shutting the door, Kelly sits me down and explains my new life.

"This isn't a vacation. You have to treat this like a full-time school. Tutoring in the morning, then you'll either watch the boys in the afternoon or do homework. Nights are for more studying with no more than two hours of TV."

I nod.

Chapter 44

I take to heart what Kelly says about studying. She has to pull me away from my homework exercises just to eat dinner. Before Mr. Akmed left, he handed me several exercises that he said would help him assess where to start me off. He told me to get through as many as I could.

I stay up late and complete all the exercises and mini tests he provided. Cheerfully handing him my work the next day, he looks surprised at what I accomplished in one day.

I examine him as he grades my reading exercises first. He's really tan, but Kelly says that he isn't tan, he's from India. His thinning hair is slicked back across his tan scalp. He wears a three piece tweed suit that has some sort of muted black, brown, and off white color pattern in it. His tie is plain green polyester, the kind I've seen at Goodwill. Deep grooves cross his forehead and the sides of his cheeks, a testament to his age. His hands have an interesting pattern of excess skin around the knuckles then taut everywhere else including his long narrow fingers that extend into his yellowing thick nails.

A few grunts and he digs into his briefcase for the appropriate workbooks for English and reading comprehension -- level three for grammar and level four for reading. He instructs me to read chapter one while he grades my math and science tests.

Mr. Akmed tells Kelly that tomorrow he'll have a full schedule outlining what will be covered each of the next four weeks in all three subjects. He also hands her a list of books to buy. He leaves me with new workbooks for math and says he'll start actually teaching tomorrow.

The rest of the week, I soak up whatever Mr. Akmed says. It takes me the first day to get used to his accent, but he often repeats what he says using different words so it isn't too hard for me to understand. Reading is by far my favorite with math a close second. Science isn't so good. Mr. Akmed says we'll cover biology next week choosing to focus on developing my reading and math skills first.

At one point, I overhear him tell Kelly that it is best to work on my strengths to keep my enthusiasm strong. Then after some wins, he'll tackle my less developed areas. I'm not sure if that sounds good

Piggy

or bad, but I don't care. I've been starved for learning all these years. I don't remember if I loved school before Mom died or not, but it seems to be the one area I get. Hanging out with Susan at night and watching her do her homework still leaves me feeling inept. I never know what to say to her, that won't result in a quizzical look and laugh. I'm out of her league because I don't know who The Red Hot Chili Peppers are or how many times some celebrity has been married.

Friday comes and Susan is excited because her real dad is coming to pick her up after school. She packs an overnight bag to shove in her locker until the end of classes. Kelly leaves to drive her to school. I clean up the kitchen and watch the boys until Mr. Akmed arrives. We have taken over the dining room table for my tutoring, leaving the family to eat around the kitchen counter this week.

Mr. Akmed says some pleasantries as he enters and takes his place at the head of the table. He is a man of few words, although when it comes to answering my questions he is animated and long winded.

The phone rings in the middle of my reading lesson. Kelly answers it and immediately turns her back to me. A few minutes pass and I strain to eavesdrop but her voice is too muffled. Mr. Akmed taps his pencil loudly to get my attention. I am too distracted by who has called, to pay attention to Mr. Akmed. From the look on Kelly's face, I know it's either John or the P.I. she hired.

The morning drags on until Mr. Akmed leaves and I rush directly to Kelly after shutting the door to ask her what was up.

"That was the detective I hired," she says.

"And?"

"He contacted a guy he knew in Wisconsin to help him search but nothing directly came up in the records. No death certificates and no activity under Dan's name, but there were a few deaths of unidentified men matching Dan's age range since October. He's got photos of those men. Based on what I told him, he doesn't think Dan's one of them, but he thinks I should review to be sure."

"Could he be wrong?"

"I didn't give him that much to go on. Only Dan's name and the name of the town that you lived near. I told him we had heard through an unreliable source that Dan had died in October and to look for any records that confirmed it. I couldn't tell him how Dan died because then I'd be telling him more than I wanted. I kept my request vague."

I nod. "Now what?"

"He has copies of the photos that I can pick up. You stay here and study and I'll go get them. Then that may be the end of it."

"End of what?"

"If we can't find him, neither can John or anyone else."

"What are you saying?"

"I think we should have John file a challenge to the guardianship and do what he recommended."

"What if the detective you hired is worthless and John finds something else out?"

"The biggest thing you're concerned about is a dead body and there isn't one, at least not yet. Either no one has found him, that guy Warren buried him, or he's been misidentified. This is good news."

"I don't know. What if John's investigator is better or his questions raise new information and they find out what happened to Dan?"

"There's always going to be unknowns. To me, this is good news."

"I... I got to think about it."

"Let me go see what this guy has and make sure Dan isn't among them. Then we can talk to John,"

After lunch, Kelly put the boys down for their naps and I open up the homework Mr. Akmed has assigned to me. Kelly leaves around one thirty to go see the detective.

Piggy

There's a soft knock at the door. Kelly must have forgotten something, I think. I open the door and Dan is standing in front of me.

Chapter 45

His face is taut and pale. A thin scar runs from below his left ear across his neck and I recognize it as my handiwork. His bulky black jean jacket is pulled over a red plaid flannel shirt. "Hey, Piggy," he says before his right arm thrusts to me and I am jolted with electricity before blacking out.

I come to and focus my eyes. The taste of blood is in my mouth but I can't move my lips because a piece of duct tape has my mouth sealed. I lift my head but get dizzy and drop it back down. A shooting pain in the back of my head causes me to silently scream into the tape. I squeeze my eyes shut and wait for the pain to subside. Gently rolling my head from side to side, I can feel the goose egg that is on the back of my head. I lift up my hands which are also bound by duct tape.

A clanking on the stairs makes me turn and see Dan coming down. He's got a trash bag half full in his right hand. His left arm is hanging unnaturally to the side. My thoughts turn to Justin and Jason. What has he done? They were both upstairs in their room. I strain to listen for any sound that will let me know they're okay. I close my eyes to buy myself time before Dan knows I'm conscious. I can't see the kitchen but hear drawers opening as I open my eyes wide to figure out where I am. I'm still near the front door, about six feet into the landing. The living room is torn up with cushions haphazardly thrown on the floor and all the TV cabinet doors open. A halfhearted kick to the top of my head sends shooting arrows through my skull.

"Good you're up. I ain't dragging your ass."

I tip my head upwards to see Dan looking down on me.

"I found your stash. You haven't learned anything about hiding stuff have you?" he says. "You got any more?"

I hum a muffled no.

"What about Kelly? Does she have a stash anywhere?"

I repeat my mumble.

"Where'd you get so much cash? You rob her or something?"

I look at him. What's wrong with how he looks?

"Get up," he commands.

I roll to one side and pull my knees up to my chest. Dan yanks on one of my shoulders which helps me get to my knees. I stand up looking down to avoid facing him.

"What about jewelry? She got any? I found some junky stuff; does she have any good stuff?"

I shake my head.

"Let's go," he says while turning to his right to give the living room one last look. His jean jacket falls open a bit. I follow the left sleeve down and see his hand hanging listlessly at his side. Dan whips around and takes a look at me.

"Yeah, bitch, I nearly lost my arm because of you. But don't you worry, I've got plans to take care of you," he says leaning in so I can smell the stale cigarettes on his breath.

Looking me up and down, he opens the coat closet behind me and finds a scarf which he wraps around my neck and face. Then he takes out what must be one of Bryan's coats and drapes it over my shoulders and buttons it closed. He nudges me to the door. Apparently, my duct tape is concealed enough to emerge from the house. He opens the door and pushes me through. I stop to say something, but he keeps pushing me out to the driveway. I still haven't heard a peep out of the boys. Maybe he didn't hurt them. Maybe they slept through it all.

A dark green van with only a few rust spots around the bottom sits in the driveway. On the upper back half is a medium size white and yellow sign advertising 'Rick's Plumbing Services'. Dan must have gotten a new van or stolen this one because it's in better shape than the one we lived in. He opens the side door and shoves me inside behind the driver's seat. The first row of back seats remain but Dan pushes me down on the floor and picks up a blanket to cover me. The door slams shut and a moment later, a cool breeze hits the top of my head as Dan opens the driver's door. I'm not sure how long I blacked out for so I'm not sure if Kelly is on her way home or not. Either way, she shouldn't be gone for more than an hour. I can only hope the boys will be okay when she gets back. Dan backs out of the driveway and aggressively drives through the neighborhood. After a few turns, he slows down and hits me on my side with his right hand.

"Don't say a fucking word."

He slows and rolls down the window. "Thank you," he says presumably to the guardhouse at the gate which has no guard. Maybe he thinks he's on camera.

Closing the window, he speeds up and doesn't hesitate taking corners at full speed, tossing me from side to side. I shout into my tape in hopes my pleading will get him to slow down but he ignores me.

"You little bitch, running away like that. Who do you think you are? After all I've done for you."

Under the blanket, I roll my eyes thinking about what he's done for me. I squeeze my legs together as I fight off a sudden urge to pee.

"And what do you do? You try to cut my throat and stab me." His hand surprises me as he slugs my upper arm. I wince. Unsatisfied, he grabs me and pinches as hard as he can through a blanket and heavy coat. I scream in pain with sweat beginning to run down my forehead.

"Took me a long time to heal. They almost had to amputate my arm but I was lucky, at least that's what they said. And Warren, that idiot, he poured whiskey on it. Burned like hell. But I survived. I bet you didn't think I would. Yeah, bitch, its payback time for you. I still haven't decided yet what I'm gonna do to you."

The car slows and takes more turns. A parking lot I think. Coming to a stop, Dan pulls the blanket off.

"Here's what's gonna happen," he says grabbing the scarf around my neck and pulling up. "You're going to quietly walk next to me. You're not going to look up and you're not going to try to scream or run. You do, and you'll be sorry."

I nod.

Piggy

He walks around and opens the side door. Tugging at my arm, I sit up and scoot down to the edge of the open door. Standing up, we're in a motel parking lot. Dan does a quick scan and points to an open room door. I walk briskly into the room. The van door slams shut and Dan is behind me a moment later shutting the door with a bang.

"Get on the bed."

I do as he says and put my feet up so that I can lean against the headboard. My hands come from under Bryan's coat and work on undoing the buttons in an effort to cool down. Dan walks over and finishes taking off the coat and unwraps the scarf. He pauses at the duct tape across my mouth but resigns to leave it on. Walking over to the small round table near the window, he peeks out.

"We're leaving here tonight, but first I'm meeting someone. We got time to kill," he says.

"I bet you thought I was dead. You should have seen the look on your face. It was like you'd seen a ghost," he chuckles.

I mumble the word bathroom but it is inaudible even to me. He walks to me and places his hand on the tape.

"You make any noise and I will hurt you so bad."

I nod and in one fast motion, he rips the tape from my mouth. It feels like my lips have come off and I gasp for breath. Rubbing my face on my shoulder, I'm finally able to say bathroom in a whisper.

"Shit," he says undoing my wrists. Taking a step back he points to the door. I enter and turn to get out of the way of the door.

"Leave it open," he orders.

I do my business relieved he doesn't make me pee my pants. I walk back to my place on the bed hoping he'll leave me free of duct tape.

"You actually look good," he says. "Your hair's different."

"Kelly took me to get my haircut."

"She buy you new clothes too?"

I nod.

"You getting soft living with her?"

"I like it there."

"Well, you ain't ever going back."

I remain silent and let him decide where the conversation will go. Remarkably he looks different to me, yet the only difference I can spot is his lame arm. I can't believe it has only been three months since I ran. He lights up a cigarette and leans back in his chair.

"How'd you find me?" I finally ask scared the silence is going to lead to nowhere good.

"You didn't even make it difficult for me. Didn't I teach you anything? I expected you'd come crying home and the only person you know is Kelly. How hard do you think that was?" He leans forward and rests his right arm on the table. "Once I found out she moved, I figured at some point you'd be going to see that lawyer so I camped out at his office until you showed up. Took all of two days."

"When did you get here?"

"Let's see. You ran in October right after slitting my throat and stabbing me through my shoulder. So excuse me if it took some time to recuperate. Then, I had to get here and Warren took off with my van before I got out of the hospital."

His face reddens and I can see his anger building. I hope it is aimed at Warren, but then he did lose the functionality of his arm to me. He lunges without warning onto the bed and straddles me before I can react. Once I'm secured by his weight, he takes a long puff on his cigarette and then puts it out right between my eyes. The pain is intense and his hand dips down to cover my mouth as he takes the cigarette between his teeth and holds it down. Our faces are inches away and I stare into his bloodshot eyes. I cry out but he only presses harder. When no smoke is visible, he releases me. Ashes are in the crevices of my eyes as I roll to my side and brush them away. Feeling my way to the sink outside the bathroom, I turn on the cold water and

Piggy

splash it repeatedly onto my face. Dan is laughing behind me as I hear the familiar flick of a lighter for another cigarette.

Opening my eyes, the red mark is blistering and hurts like hell. I know from experience not to cry. It will only provoke him. Instead, I bite my inner lip and get back on the bed. This time, I keep my right leg close to the edge so I can stand up quick if necessary.

"I guess I deserved that," I say.

"Damn right you did."

"I went to see John on Monday, why not come get me before now?"

"Well, well, well, guess Kelly isn't so trusting. She went to see him on Wednesday. Looks like she's pulling a scam on you."

He's right. Kelly and I went to see John on Monday. I stood by her as she called him on Tuesday and told him to sit tight. What was she doing seeing him without me on Wednesday?

"It's still been two days, why wait?"

"Had to see what I was up against. Didn't know if Kelly had a guy and didn't want any part of her anyway. And thanks to you, I don't get around like I used to," he say leaning forward. I brace myself for another attack but it doesn't come.

Looking at his watch, he shakes his head. He walks to the bathroom sink and my eyes flick to the door. I look around for anything I can hit him with but then pause, I'm not watching him. I see it this time -- a small black box with a large button on the front and two small metal rods sticking out of the top from either side. Pressing it against my upper arm, Dan leans in and my body shudders with electricity.

I have no idea how much time passes when I wake up with tape across my mouth. My hands and legs are taped spread eagle to each corner of the bed. I can't move and my arms are falling asleep. The spot between my eyes is throbbing in pain. I wiggle my limbs but each are tightly wrapped and affixed to the bed. Next I bounce my butt up and down but only succeed in hurting my ankles in the process. I lay motionless for what seems like hours before the door opens with

Piggy

Dan carrying a brown paper bag. It's dark outside and the motel sign is on.

Dan looks to see my eyes are open. "I think I like this thing," he says pulling the black box out of his pocket. "They use this on cattle. Picked it up in Wyoming on the way here. It sure worth its weight in gold."

I watch him as he unpacks a name brand six pack and opens a bottle. He normally got the cheapest beer he could find, but my cash has funded his high rolling lifestyle for the night. Slamming down half the bottle, I can tell by the way he's sitting and his expression, he's already had a few. Good, that may give me an opportunity.

I make a long pleading sound and he takes another swig of his beer before sitting on the bed next to me. Without any pause, he rips off the tape again. This time I can feel the skin at the corner of my mouth come off and I yelp in pain. Running my tongue to the side, I feel a burning sensation and taste blood.

"I have to go to the bathroom again," I say.

"Nope, you gotta go, pee right there. I ain't tying you up again. We got another hour to wait before meeting Jay. Then you can go."

"Can I have some water?"

He walks to the sink and takes a bit too long taking off the plastic wrap from the cup. Filling it he tries to hold it to my mouth, but only a few drops enter my throat; the rest runs down my neck. Laughing, he walks over to the table and returns with his bottle.

"Open wide." Pouring a mouthful of beer into me, I shut my lips and swallow hard. He pours a few seconds after I close my mouth and now the smell of beer is spread across my face. I say nothing. Once he opens his second beer, I turn to face him.

"What are you going to do with me?"

"I haven't decided yet."

"If you're going to kill me, get it over with."

Piggy

"Why would I kill you?"

I'm taken aback by his response. Why else would he come back?

"Why would I kill my meal ticket?"

I look at him with my eyebrows furrowed. "When Kelly and I met with John, he said you hadn't taken any money out of the trust since we left."

"True. I can't neither. But you can."

"He told me I couldn't."

"Not until you're eighteen."

"You're going to keep me for two years?"

"Two years, five months, but who's counting."

"But once I'm eighteen, you aren't my guardian anymore."

"True, but you're going to give me the money anyway."

I consider this for a moment and change tactics. "If you wanted the money, why didn't we stay?"

"Things started falling apart."

I wait for him to continue. He opens his third beer and stares at the wall. I remain quiet and uninterested knowing that if he knows I want something, he'll never give it to me.

"That bitch, Kelly, turned me into social services. I was able to skirt by her alleged complaint when some fucking audit comes out of nowhere. No doubt that lawyer tipped them off. I knew I couldn't pass the audit. I'd spent all the discretionary money I could and all that was left was the monthly payments. And then they were threatening to take that away. Plus I had Stu breathing down my neck. I had to change the situation. I set the house on fire and got my own lawyer. Once we were on the road, the checks kept coming until my lawyer told me they determined the fire was arson. Well, no shit. I tried to blame it on Stu, but the lawyer said I'd have to bring that up during the hearing. I knew that wasn't gonna go my way, so I skipped out."

Draining his third beer, he burped loud and went into bathroom. Zipping up as he walked out, he comes to sit on the bed next to me.

"I knew how the trust worked and I figured I'd wait 'til you turned eighteen. Besides, you were a big help at the hospitals. Then it was just useful having you around."

Is he seriously telling me he liked having me around?

"And I know about the college fund. I figure, you turn eighteen and you fork over the money to me and then we're even for my arm."

"Once I'm eighteen, you can't make me do anything," I say before thinking through how he would react.

"Oh, you'll give it to me," he says leaning in so his face is close to mine. "Or I'll come back and take out those two little boys you like so much and Kelly, too."

My eyes open wide showing my fear. So he did see them.

Leaning back he laughs and goes back to the table for another beer. A ringing sound pierces the air. Dan pats his hand on each of his pockets before retrieving a pager. Checking it, he reaches for the phone.

"Hey, you got my message, great." He sounds nearly joyful.

"My plans came together a bit faster than I thought so I'm headed out tonight. Can we move up our little meeting?"

"Yeah, I know the place over on State Street."

"See you in an hour."

Hanging up he slaps the phone down on the table.

"We're gonna get out of here."

"Who was that?"

"You remember Jay, don't you?"

"What are you doing with him?"

"I looked him up last night and we had a few. Then he gives me a call while I'm waiting for that bitch to leave the house and tells me he has the money he owes me. We're gonna pick it up and then we'll be on our way."

"Where to?"

"Don't know yet. I'll see where the road takes me." Walking to the edge of the bed, he pulls out a knife and cuts off the duct tape from each of my ankles.

"Why don't you leave me here? Come back when I'm eighteen to get the money?"

He tilts his head. "Jeez, you'd just give it over to me?" I nod. "Do you even hear how stupid that sounds?"

"You already threatened the boys. They'll always be in danger so I'll be happy to give you the money to save them."

"And like, you won't run away and hide from me? Or convince Kelly's little family to hide with you?" He cuts the tape on my left wrist. "Not a chance. You're coming with me."

My right hand is still taped to the bed as Dan pulls my left hand over to it and wraps a new piece of duct tape around my two wrists. Then he wraps a piece of duct tape around one ankle, yanks a long strip free and then wraps the other ankle; forming makeshift shackles. At last he cuts my right wrist free from the bed post. He drapes the coat over my shoulders, wraps the scarf around my neck, and places a big piece of tape over my mouth. A tear runs down my cheek at the thought of the next time he yanks off the tape. Dan opens the door looking both ways to make sure no one is watching. He puts me in the same spot in the van, but takes the coat off so that I don't sweat again. Slamming the door, he arranges the blanket over me once he gets into the driver's seat.

Piggy

  We drive for a little while before he stops to get gas. His familiar warning about staying quiet is made along with a little rub on the burn between my eyes. I resign myself to submit to whatever he wants and wait for a good opening before making any move. Ten minutes after stopping, Dan is back in the driver seat putting a sack of snacks on the seat next to him. Likely more beer and cigarettes for our drive to who knows where.

  I roll onto my back to prevent myself from rolling around when Dan turns the corner. He's always been somewhat of a reckless driver and a thought flashes in my head. What if I get him pulled over? Like a traffic stop? He couldn't out run a cop and then I could scream which even muffled would likely be heard. I think of ways to cause a traffic stop when we turn left onto a poorly paved road. I'm jostled a bit before Dan stops. He lights a cigarette and doesn't say a word.

  Fifteen minutes pass until I hear a car pull in near us. Dan rolls down the window as I hear a car door open.

  "Hey Jay, thanks for meeting me earlier," Dan says.

  "No problem," Jay says from a distance. I hear footsteps in what must be gravel.

  "You could have pulled in next to me like the cops do," Dan says.

  A second set of footprints is coming up from the side of the van. I can hear them but they're further away than the ones I detected to be Jay's.

  "What's going on?"

  "Sorry, Dan," Jay says.

  I hear a click of a handgun right above my head.

  "Wait a minute," Dan pleads.

  "This is from Stu," a voice says as the shot rings out like an explosion. I clutch myself together and for the first time, I'm glad I have the duct tape over my mouth.

"Jesus!" Jay screams. "I thought you weren't going to do it here."

"It's easier this way," the voice says.

"Fine, so I'm square now?" Jay asks.

"Yeah, you're square with Stu now," the voice says and another shot rings out. I hear what I assume is Jay's body fall onto the gravel. I suck in any breath I have and don't move an inch. There is some rustling in the driver's seat. The gun man is rummaging through Dan's pockets. Two minutes later, his footsteps retreat and a car door shuts. The car drives off and I continue to hold my breath.

Chapter 46

The sun is already sweltering as I park my car in the student lot and grab my backpack. Slinging it over my shoulder, I jog to class. The Davis campus is huge so I have to move quickly or I'll be yelled at by Professor Sorenson. I don't know why I can't get out of bed when my alarm first goes off.

Walking through the double doors, I slide my backpack off my shoulder and freeze. Something's caught on my chain again. I gingerly grasp my diamond and sapphire butterfly pendant and then thread my fingers along the chain until I find the spot that is caught. Freeing my necklace, I drop the backpack to the ground and rummage for a pen and my notebook so I'm ready when I enter the classroom. Zipping up, I touch my pendant again to ensure its safety. It was a high school graduation gift from Kelly. I had been able to catch up grades and graduate just a year after Susan. The necklace was meant to be a reminder of where I came from, where I could go, and of course, of Mom.

I think how lucky I am to be at college. How lucky I am I didn't make a sound the day Dan got shot. I had been found hours after and smartly feigned a concussion. While I felt sorry about Jay, Dan got what he deserved and there was no way I was going to help find or convict whoever shot him. Kelly and Bryan became my guardians and my life finally approached a level of normal.

Clutching the knob, I crack the door open and squeeze through.

"Ms. Jenkins! You're late again. See me after class," Professor Sorenson barks.

About the Author

Jill Keiderling was born in Nebraska and has lived the majority of her life in southern California with her husband, Sean, and her dachshund, Tim. Taking a sabbatical from a corporate America job, she explored writing among other hobbies. The idea for this book came out of a writing exercise in November 2011. After circulating a short story among friends, she made the commitment to write the book and completed the first draft in six weeks. Almost a year of editing ensued before publishing. This is her first novel.

Self published by Jill Keiderling
Via Createspace.com

Copyright © 2012

All rights reserved.
No part of this book may be reproduced, scanned, or distributed in any printed or electronic form without permission. Please do not participate in or encourage piracy of copyrighted materials in violation of the author's rights. Purchase only authorized editions.

Comments welcome
www.facebook.com/Piggythebookbyjill
piggythebook.com

Made in the USA
San Bernardino, CA
19 December 2012